PRAISE FOR CATALYST

"A fast-paced, action-packed story."

~TEEN READS

"An amazing young adult thriller! Full of intrigue, high stakes, and danger, this read will keep your heart racing and your mind turning deep into the night."

~KIMBERLEY GRIFFITHS LITTLE, AWARD-WINNING AUTHOR OF THE FORBIDDEN TRILOGY (HARPERCOLLINS)

"An action-packed sci-fi thriller filled with romance, danger, and twists you won't see coming, Catalyst provides a glimpse into an eery future depicting what can go wrong when those in power attempt to make things right."

~ILIMA TODD, AUTHOR OF REMAKE

"Compelling. Intriguing. Fantastic! Catalyst gives us a view into a different world, but with relatable characters that everyone can understand. The novel's exhilarating pace only gets better as the story reaches its heart-pounding climax. A YA read reminiscent of the best that the genre has to offer. Hunger Games and Divergent, eat your heart out."

~MARK NOCE, AUTHOR OF BETWEEN TWO FIRES

Forgotten

By: Kristin Smith

Forgotten

clean
teen
PUBLISHING

ISBN 978-1-63422-237-2
Cover Design by: Marya Heiman
Typography by: Courtney Knight
Editing by: Cynthia Shepp

For Adam
Even if the moon turned to dust and all
the stars in the sky collapsed, your love
is one I could never forget.

For more information about our content disclosure, please utilize the QR code above with your smart phone or visit us at www.CleanTeenPublishing.com

If you love something, let it go,
If it comes back to you, it's yours,
If it doesn't, it never was,
and it's not meant to be.

~Albert Einstein

1

Sienna

I t already feels like a lifetime.

Although it's only been a week.

This is what I know about amnesia from doing a quick search on Zane's comscreen. Amnesia is most often defined as the loss of memory, including information, facts, and experiences. It typically does not affect self-identity. And there is no specific treatment.

Problem is, Trey doesn't have amnesia. According to the doctors inhabiting Zane's home at all hours of the day and night, Trey doesn't have memory loss—his memory has been altered completely. Erased.

"How are you holding up?" Zane asks, taking a seat next to me on the wooden bench.

I find myself drawn to his garden lately, amazed that his gardeners are able to grow beautiful white lilies and creeping purple coneflowers, plump peonies and blood-red roses, despite the desert heat.

I give him a wry smile.

"I think I know a good distraction," he says. "How about the pool? Emily's been begging to go swimming all morning."

Thinking of swimming puts a vivid mental image in my mind. An image of Trey and me in the lagoon, laughing, his hands at my waist, my arms around his neck.

I shake my head quickly to get rid of the images.

"I don't think so," I say. "But thanks."

I keep my eyes focused on the tiny blue flowers in front of me that wave and dance in the breeze like they have their own orchestra playing for them.

"Forget-me-nots," Zane says.

"Huh?" I turn to look at him.

"Those flowers. They're called forget-me-nots." He kneels and plucks one from its stem. Laying the delicate flower on my lap, he says, "There's an old story that goes with it. Are you familiar?"

I shake my head and pick up the flower, studying it. Five petals mirror the blue of the sky with a butter-yellow center. The petals are small, delicate, and clumped together on one stem as if they can't bear to be separated.

"Legend has it that when the Creator finished naming all the plants, there was one flower that didn't receive one. A tiny voice was heard crying out through the sky, 'Forget me not, Oh Lord!' To which the Creator replied, 'That shall be your name.'"

I smile. "Cute story. Too bad the flower doesn't have healing properties to help people remember."

"I think it helps gunky eyes." Zane's mouth tweaks at the edges before he glances down at his feet. "I know this is hard, Sienna. But just know that I'm here for you." His eyes sweep to mine. "Always."

I swallow back the lump clawing up my throat. "I know. And I appreciate that. I really do."

Leaning over, he gives me a light kiss on the cheek, his lips lingering next to my ear, his warm breath tickling my skin. "This is one guy who will never forget you."

Before I can say anything, he's gone.

With a fistful of tiny blue forget-me-nots, I stand outside Trey's door, my palm lightly pressed against the cool wood. All I have to do is push and the door will swing open. But I hesitate. *Will he recognize me today? Will his memory return?*

Closing my eyes, I breathe in slowly, filling my lungs to their fullest capacity. Like a balloon, I'm full of so much hot air that I should float to the sky, but the heavy weight of sadness keeps me grounded.

I picture him. I picture us. Stealing kisses in the hallways, our trip to the lagoon, our last night together in the Compound. I blush just thinking of lying next to him in his bed. But he remembers none of that. To him, I'm just a stranger who has taken a keen interest in his recovery. What he doesn't realize is that I'm far from a stranger. I know so much about him, and yet, not enough.

Sighing heavily, I push the door open. Trey sits up in his bed, looking better than he has in days. The color has returned to his cheeks, and his lips now have a rosy hue. Much better than the pallid boy I held in my arms as the Satellite Government Facility crumbled around us.

But he doesn't remember that either.

He smiles when he sees me, and my heart does flip-flops. I try to tell myself he's only happy to see someone he recognizes after the ordeal he's been through. That his smiles aren't really reserved for *me*.

"Hey," he says.

"Hey."

"What do you have there?" He eyes the flowers clutched in my hand.

"Forget-me-nots. I thought—" I glance around. "I thought you could use some color to brighten the room."

He motions for me to come in.

A small, decorative vase already sits on the nightstand, so I drop the flowers in and take it to the bathroom to fill with water.

"Guess what?" he calls out, his voice slightly muffled through the walls separating us. Even from a distance, I can hear the excitement in his voice. As I re-enter the room with the vase of flowers, he says, "I had a breakthrough this morning."

I swallow hard. "You did?"

"Yeah. I was just about to call Dr. Hammond to tell him." As he reaches for the button on the monitor beside him, his eyes flicker to me. "Do you mind?"

So many emotions are bouncing through my body, but I shake my head and settle into the chair beside him. He dials Dr. Hammond, the wiry man's thin face popping up on the screen. Once Dr. Hammond promises he'll come by in a few minutes, Trey eases back against the pillows. As he lays there, he's quiet, and I don't pressure him to speak. According to Dr. Hammond, it's best if we let Trey take control of the conversation, so if he does have a memory, it will come from him and not be implanted by something we inadvertently say.

"I remember," he says softly.

I lean forward, wanting to be close when he says he remembers us.

"I remember who I am."

"You do?" Trying to contain my excitement, I squeeze my hands in my lap so they don't flap wildly and scare him to death.

The door to his room swings open and in strides Dr. Hammond, followed by an entourage of nurses. The three doe-eyed nurses cluster around one side of the bed while I scoot out of the way to allow Dr. Hammond to examine Trey on the other. After shining a light in Trey's eyes and checking his heart rate, Dr. Hammond draws up a chair beside me and takes a seat. The nurses still hover, their eyes never leaving Trey's face. I roll my eyes because clearly, they're not here to help Trey, but to look at him. And Trey is completely oblivious to the three drooling nurses.

"So, you've had a development, you say?" Dr. Hammond questions.

"Yes, I have." Trey licks his lips. His eyes flit from the doctor, back to me, and then to the doctor, almost as if he's unsure whom he should inform.

"Well?" Dr. Hammond presses.

"I remember." He pauses for a moment. "I remember everything. The explosion—"

My ears perk at his mention of the explosion. As I lean forward, the words rush out, "You remember the explosion?"

He closes his eyes, as if he's concentrating on some distant memory. "I was having lunch at a cafe in the Capital. There was an explosion. Caused by some crazed Fringe member." His eyes open. "Then I woke up here."

I stare at him, trying to wrap my mind around what he's saying. "Wait. What? The Capital?" The doctor shoots me a look.

"I was eating lunch in Rubex—"

"You think you were in the Capital? Why?" I demand.

"Because that's where I work. And live." His next words are pointed right at me. "With my *fiancée*." He enunciates each syllable like I'm a child learning a new word.

He isn't joking. There is no mirth in his eyes. No humor. Only lucidity. Like he finally remembers and wants us to know that he is of sound mind and understanding. I don't know what they've done to him, but it hurts. More than anything else.

Shaking my head, I lay my hand over Trey's. "You don't have a fiancée. And you don't live in the Capital." Dr. Hammond gives me a warning look, but I choose to ignore him. "Trey, don't you remember? You *are* a member of the Fringe. You're the *leader* of the Fringe."

Trey laughs, a deep, husky sound that I know so well. And I've missed too much. He slides his hand out from under mine,

and I feel the sting of his rejection.

"I know you want to believe I'm someone I'm not. Someone you lost. But the truth is that I *have* a life. Somewhere else." He swings his legs over the side of the bed. "Now if I can just get back to it."

I bite my lip to keep from crying out in anger and frustration. I can't stay here. Not while he's looking at me with so much pity that it makes my heart ache.

Standing quickly, I say to the doctor, "Can I speak with you for a moment?" I glance back at Trey. "In private?"

Dr. Hammond nods and follows me out the door. Once the door is closed behind us, I pounce on him. "What's wrong with him? Why does he think he lives in the Capital?"

The doctor exhales slowly. "My best guess is he was given a memory-altering drug."

"Is it permanent?"

"Without doing more tests and scans of the brain, I really don't know."

"Tests? More?"

"Well, yes. Before, we were looking for trauma to the brain, but now—" He pauses and licks his lips, a hint of excitement in his eyes. "But now, this is all new territory."

I focus on breathing. And not on the gleam in the doctor's eye. I understand he's excited to work with a new case. To delve into the science behind Trey's memory alteration, but the cause of his excitement is the anchor of my heartache.

Because only steps away is the boy I love, and yet, he doesn't even know me. Is there any pain greater than that?

2
Zane

My personal gym is a mustier, sweatier version of the person using it. The mirrored walls are lined with dumbbells and bar weights, the inner part filled with machines and equipment. I have the heat cranked up, because that's the way I like it, so I'm a sweaty mess as I stand in front of the mirror with a dumbbell raised over my head. My muscles are straining, every inch of my body tensed with the effort, when Sienna bursts into the room. The first thing she does is wrinkle her nose.

The bar and weights come down with a thud, bouncing against the black rubber floor. As I straighten up, I notice the way her eyes widen as they flit over my upper body. It's too hot to wear a shirt in here, so I don't.

After I wipe the sweat off my face with a towel, I pull a shirt on. "How's Trey doing—" I stop when tears build in her eyes. Her beautiful bright green eyes. "What happened?" I ask.

A small sob bursts from her throat and tears at my heart. I throw the towel down and stride over, pulling her into my arms. Her face is pressed against my chest, her hair tickling my chin. Her small shoulders shake as I stroke her hair, whispering soothing words that I doubt she can hear. When she pulls away, she dries her cheeks with her palms and sniffles.

"It's worse than we thought," she says, her eyes still glistening with leftover tears. "It's not trauma. They did something to him. Altered his memories or something. He thinks he lives in the Capital and that he's engaged. Engaged! Can you believe that?" She sounds so completely broken that it takes all my willpower not to pull her in again.

"You think they brainwashed him like they did your mom?"

"I don't know. Obviously not the same thing because he wasn't hooked up to that rotating machine—" She stops and purses her lips together like she's remembering something.

"What is it?"

"Well…" She hesitates. "When we rescued Trey from the government facility, there was a machine I'd never seen before."

"You think it might have something to do with his memory alteration?"

Her small shoulders rise and fall as she shrugs. "I don't know. Maybe?"

"But why? Why would Radcliffe or anyone want to alter Trey's memories? Wasn't it enough that they captured him?"

Her eyes are sad when she responds, "For the government, is anything ever enough?"

Before I can answer, the door to the gym bangs open for a second time and Emily runs in, followed by her huffing mother.

"There you are," Emily squeals when she sees Sienna and me.

Sienna and her mother are now fully recovered, but I know Sienna doesn't want to leave Trey, and Vivian doesn't want to leave Sienna. So I've offered to let them stay here as long as they like. It kills me to see Sienna hanging over Trey's bed constantly, but I only want to do what's best for her.

Thankfully, my father has stayed out of the way, for the most part. And what little I've seen of him has been met with his persistent denial of knowing anything about Trey. How could my father not know I had another brother? How could he not know my mother carried two babies in her womb? Here is my father, a genetic genius, and yet he let something like this slip past him? It doesn't seem probable or likely. Which makes me wonder what he's hiding.

And then, there's Trey. He's my twin by all meanings of the definition, and yet, we couldn't be more different. He is a desert rogue, and I, the heir of a great empire. We may share the same blood, but we'll never be brothers. At least, not in the truest sense of the word.

"Do you wanna go swimming with us?" Emily begs. "Puhlease, Si-Si? Puh-lease?"

I can't help but smile at Emily's persuasive skills. She's a force to be reckoned with, just like her sister. "Told you," I whisper to Sienna. "She's relentless."

"I'm sorry, Em," Sienna says. "Not right now. Maybe later?"

Emily turns her blue eyes to me. "Zane? Do you?"

Before I can respond that *yes, I would love to go swimming with you just as soon as I finish talking with your sister,* Sienna sighs and says, "Just give it a rest, Emily. Zane doesn't want to go either."

A frown crosses Emily's little face, but before she can cry, I bend down and gather her pudgy hands in my own. "I'll swim with you in just a bit. Sound good?"

Her frown is immediately replaced with a tentative smile.

Vivian wraps an arm around Emily's shoulders. "Is everything okay?" she asks her older daughter.

I straighten up and stand to the side, listening, as Sienna fills her mother in on the latest development with Trey. I'm not sure how much Sienna has told her mother, but I do know that Vivian has been in to see Trey a few times.

When Sienna finishes speaking and takes a deep breath to calm her quivering voice, her mother replies, her face full of sympathy, "I'm sorry, sweetie." Vivian opens her mouth like she's about to say something else, but Emily tugs on her arm.

"Come on, Mommy, I want to go swimming."

Vivian throws us an apologetic smile. "Zane, perhaps Sienna needs a little distraction? Hmm?" Her eyes rest on me, conveying the meaning behind her words.

There's nothing I'd like more than to make Sienna forget about Trey. Forget she ever loved him—my long-lost, delinquent brother. With effort, I keep my jaw from clenching. "Of course. I'll see what I can come up with."

When they exit the weight room, the door clanging closed behind them, Sienna turns to me with fire in her eyes.

"What was that?"

"What?" I ask innocently.

"You? My mother? Are you two *conspiring* against me?"

I scoff. "Not against, only for."

She props a hand on one hip and narrows her eyes. "What kind of distraction?"

I think fast, trying to come up with something that would appeal to her. "Maybe we should go somewhere to get your mind off everything. The dam?"

She shakes her head quickly.

"I would suggest the Megasphere, but that's out." As soon as those words exit my mouth, I want to put them back in as her cheeks redden.

"Please don't start," she warns.

My hands fly up in surrender. "Sorry."

There *is* one place she's probably never been. "I know the perfect place."

The Gateway feels like the dead part of the city with its broken buildings and crumbling structures. So when we pull up to one forgotten building in particular, a square brick structure, it's no wonder that Sienna shivers beside me. All the life has been sucked from this part of town, and all that's left is death and rot.

As we climb out of my car, Sienna's eyes never leave the building. When she turns to me, the question is written on her face. "What is this place?"

The half a dozen marquees that once lined the walls are now crumbling and missing their corners. A layer of dirt and grime covers them so completely that if they once displayed what was playing here, it is now completely unreadable.

I swipe my fist across the dirt on one of the marquees, and the pretty face of a dark-haired actress shows through. Not someone I recognize though. An actress from a different era, a different time.

"A movie theater," I finally say.

"Really?" Her face lights up. "I've always wanted to see one."

"And now's your chance."

I stride to the car and place my hand on the trunk. Once it senses the heat from my hand and has read its print, it pops open. Nestled inside is a crowbar, which I pull out, along with a duffle bag.

"We're breaking in?" she asks, her excitement deepening.

"I wouldn't call it breaking in." Shouldering the bag, I insert the crowbar in the space between the old wooden frame and the door. "My father owns this place. Well, actually, his family did. He just inherited it. Along with half the other crumbling buildings along the Gateway."

The crowbar finds a good foothold. Using my muscles, I work at it until I'm able to pry the door open. We're greeted with blackness and a mildewy smell that clings to us.

"Why doesn't your dad tear down places like this? Or those other old casinos? He could build something better. Something useful," she says as we step inside.

I've wondered the same thing, even begged my father to do something to make this part of the city look better. But according to him, his hands are tied.

"He can't." I pull out my Lynk and shine it around the dark corners of the room. "The government forbids it."

Sienna's voice is heated when she responds. "But it's his property. They can't tell him what to do with it."

"Sadly, they can. They give him a monthly stipend for leaving them as is, but threaten to fine him if he removes them."

"Why? Why do they care so much about Legas or this part of the city? Why do they want it to be so hideous?"

I try to keep the bitter tone from my voice, but it's hard. "They want it to be a reminder. A reminder of who is in control. And what we've lost."

The Upheaval wasn't that long ago, yet it was before my father's lifetime. It's said that a great nation once existed, one with power, military, and money. But that power is also what led to its downfall. And its own civil war.

"I hate them," Sienna says fiercely. "I hate them all."

The fire in her voice, and I'm sure in her eyes as well if I could see them, makes me chuckle.

I shine the light on the dusty ticket collector's box. The see-through glass is smudged with dirt and age. "This is where they collected tickets." We walk a little further, and I'm vividly aware of Sienna's arm brushing against mine. "And that," I say, pointing to the long counter, "is where they sold candy and popcorn."

We turn and make our way down the wide hallway of doors, each one leading to a different theater. If you count them, there are twelve in all. I pick one at random and hold the door open for Sienna to enter. Shining the light in front of her feet, I follow her into the pitch-dark space. Once we reach the apex of a small incline, we are greeted with dozens of rows of seats, all angled toward the three-story movie screen in front.

Sienna's breath catches beside me. "Oh wow. It's bigger than I imagined."

My hand finds her elbow, and I gently lead her up a few

stairs to a middle row, and then into the very center. The seats are coated with dust, but Sienna doesn't seem to mind as she sinks down into one.

"I think I'll just sit here and pretend, if that's okay," she says.

"I can do you one better than that," I say. "Do you have your Lynk light?"

She nods, pulling her Lynk from her back pocket and clicking it on. The light illuminates the dirty seat in front of her.

"Stay here. I'll be right back."

With the duffle bag on my shoulder and my Lynk in my hand, I exit the theater and search for the Digital Command Center. It's a small room filled with old computers and equipment. I dump my bag on a table and unzip it, searching for the handheld generator tucked inside. The metal is cool against my fingers as I pull it out and look for an outlet, using the light from my Lynk. Once I find one, I insert the generator and wait a few seconds for it to kick in. The lights turn on with a hum and a groan like they're protesting their usage.

Glancing around the room, I eye what I have to work with. Obviously, I've never used a digital projector before, but honestly, how hard can it be?

I remember my father saying once that all the projectors were controlled from here. If I can hack into the system, I may be able to gain access to one.

I pull my comscreen from my duffle bag and set it up on the table, bypassing a few access codes that are elementary in comparison to what we have nowadays. And then I'm in. I search for a movie that might sound familiar, but there aren't any. They are all too old. So I do the next best thing—I scroll through until a title stands out.

Unmatched Circuits.

I click on it and wait for it to pull up, then I select a screen and hit play. As I exit the room, closing the door behind me, I'm not sure if it worked. However, when I enter the theater where I left Sienna, there's crackly music playing and the three-story screen is lit up with credits.

Sienna smiles when she sees me. "I'm not sure how you did it, but this is awesome."

I settle into the seat next to her and pop open the recliner. "How'd you—?"

Reaching over her, I press the button on the side of her seat. She immediately goes back, her feet flying into the air. She laughs so hard that when she stops, she's breathless.

"Thanks," she says. She turns to watch the screen, and I have a perfect view of her profile. Even in the dark, she's beautiful.

She must feel my eyes on her because she turns to me. "What?"

I look away. "Nothing."

Her gaze stays on me for several seconds before she turns back to the screen. The movie crackles and cracks at times, but at least it's working. It's about a robot girl who has feelings and falls in love with a human boy. I have a hard time concentrating on the movie with Sienna so close. When she moves, I catch the berries-and-vanilla scent of her hair. When she places her arm on the rest beside mine, it takes all my willpower not to slide my fingers through hers.

"What do you think it was like?" Sienna whispers during one particularly boring part of the movie.

I look at her, not sure what she's referring to.

"Back then. What do you think it was like? When there were casinos and movie theaters and… fun."

"You mean before Pacifica and the other Provinces?"

She nods, tapping a finger against her lips. "I mean, I imagine it was nice. But I wonder if people still thought the same things. Still acted the same way. Still hoped for more."

"I'm sure they did. People have always wanted more. Since the beginning of time. That's what helps our society grow and change, progress and advance."

"Spoken like a true Chromo 120 poster child," she says, her tone wry.

I believe she views herself differently because she isn't genetically modified, but I hope she knows I don't care about that. I've never met anyone like her, genetically modified or not.

Because it's too tempting and because I'm tired of denying myself, I take her hand in mine, the warmth of it running through me.

"Listen, genetic modification is something I have. It isn't who I am." I turn her arm over and inspect the brown spots on her arm, the same ones that are sprinkled over her nose and along her cheeks. "Take these brown spots for example."

She wrinkles her nose. "My freckles?"

"Yes, your freckles." I've heard the term, of course, but haven't been around many people who have them. Just one more thing I adore about Sienna—one more thing that makes her different. I rub my finger over her arm, the movie in the background creating dancing shadows. "These freckles are something you have, but they don't define who you are."

She tries to pull her arm away, but I won't let her. "I hate my freckles," she says. "They're ugly."

To prove a point, I lift up her arm and kiss one freckle and then another. "I like them. They're unique. They're beautiful." I look at her then, the lights from the movie highlighting her cheekbones and pursed lips. "Just like you."

Not even the shadows can hide the deep blush that spreads up her neck to her cheeks. And this time, when she pulls away, I let her.

We're both silent for the rest of the movie, and I'm internally kicking myself for making her uncomfortable. She's made it clear she loves Trey, so I should keep my distance. But when it comes to Sienna, it's hard to stay away.

And then there's Arian. I know it's wrong, but when I'm with Sienna, I try to forget I'm betrothed to someone else, someone who is a perfect match for me. A girl who is flawless and beautiful and my equal by all accounts. And yet, despite her perfection, she doesn't hold the same appeal that Sienna does. I don't know what it is about Sienna that gets under my skin. She's like an itch that can never be reached—a prize that can never be won. And it makes me want her even more.

Once the movie is over and we've gathered everything from the Digital Command Center, we walk to my car. Sienna places her hand on my arm.

"Thanks," she says. "I needed that."

Her hand is burning a hole through my skin. "Good distraction?"

She smiles. "Very good."

I lift open her car door and wait as she climbs inside. "The day isn't over yet."

"You have something else planned?"

I close her door and cross to the other side of the vehicle, sliding inside. "Perhaps."

With a flick of the button, the top comes down off the Aria, turning it into a sporty convertible.

"You like to go fast, don't you?" I ask with a grin.

She rolls her eyes. "I own a motorcycle. What do you think?"

I look pointedly at her seat belt. "Then you'd better buckle up."

Once her belt is snapped into place, I put the car in gear and take off down the Gateway. It's such a long, straight strip of road that it's perfect for gaining high speeds. Sienna squeals and throws her head back, and for a second, I get a glimpse of the carefree girl she probably once was. Before her father died, before all that crap went down with Radcliffe, before she met Trey.

I'm not too worried about Enforcers, mostly because they don't come around the Gateway until their nightly round up. We have the entire street to ourselves. We speed past towering casinos and tiny chapels. The faster I drive, the wind whipping through Sienna's short hair, the deeper her smile, and the lighter her laugh.

It's only the two of us. And a car fast enough to make her forget. As I drive, my only hope is that if she wants to remember, she'll try to remember this. Me. Us.

When we get to the end of the Gateway, she turns to me and says with a wide smile, "Let's do it again."

So we do.

3
Sienna

nce we've driven down the Gateway several times, and I've paused to catch my breath from laughing so hard, I know where I want to go next. To see the one person who can keep this happiness and lightheartedness going—Chaz.

Zane readily agrees to take me to Chaz's apartment, a building close to this darker side of town. Regrettably, it's been weeks since I've seen my best friend in person, and I've missed his teasing smile and quick wit terribly.

When we pull up to Chaz's apartment, I hesitate. The polite thing would be to invite Zane in to meet Chaz, but I'm feeling selfish. I want Chaz all to myself.

Zane must sense my hesitation because he immediately pipes up. "I'll drop you off, if that's okay. I need to run over to the Match 360 Legas facility."

In an attempt to make him feel less unwanted, I say vaguely, "Sure you don't want to come in?"

"Normally, I'd love to. Truth is, I think you could use some time away from me, my house, Trey… everything."

I smile at him because he's right.

"Pick you up in a couple of hours?"

"Sure." I step out of the car and watch as the Aria speeds away.

As I walk up the crumbling brick steps to Chaz's apartment, it does feel as though I'm leaving everything else behind. Maybe for a little while I can pretend that I'm back in GIGA—the Genetically and Intellectually Gifted Academy where Chaz and I met years ago. Maybe for a few minutes, I can have a simpler life, one where I'm not running from guns and bombs and boys who don't remember me.

When Chaz opens the door, I fling my arms around him. His body is soft, warm, and familiar. He takes a step back in surprise.

"What's that for?" he asks.

"I missed you," I reply. "Do I need a reason other than that?"

When Chaz smiles, his eyes get lost in his plum-like cheeks. "I suppose not." Just as quickly as it appeared, his smile fades. "Wait, do you *need* something from me?"

I laugh and take his arm, guiding him to the worn couch in his living room. There are several snack cake wrappers and chip bags scattered across the coffee table, along with a pile of dirty plates. "No, Chaz. There's no hidden agenda. Not this time."

"You know I'm teasing, right?"

"Of course. I'm the one who keeps your life interesting. Without me, you would be *so* bored."

Chaz chuckles, picking at the knotted fabric of the couch. "How's Trey doing?"

My chest tightens in response to hearing Trey's name. I proceed to tell Chaz everything—about how Trey believes he works in the Capital and has a fiancée.

Chaz watches me with round eyes. When I'm finished, he says, "Wow, they're good."

"Who?"

"Whoever was behind this. While Trey is off in la-la land thinking he's some business executive in Rubex with a swanky car and fat wallet, the Fringe doesn't have a leader. They've managed to cripple the Fringe with the intent of gaining access to everything Trey knows."

"Radcliffe's dead," I remind him.

"Then you should have nothing to worry about. A puppet can't operate without its puppet master."

I turn Chaz's words over in my mind. He's right. With Radcliffe dead, there's no one left to pull the strings.

Then why do I feel like this is far from over.

Sinking back against the couch, Chaz props his feet on the coffee table. "You wanna watch a show?"

We used to do this all the time when we went to GIGA. We'd come here after school, Chaz would help me with my homework, and then we'd watch a show together. Those simple days seem so far away after everything I've experienced. That Sienna was naive and innocent. She'd never shot a man and left him for dead. Nor was she responsible for the deaths of hundreds. I wonder if that innocent girl is still somewhere inside of me. Or if she's gone forever.

I sink back next to Chaz on the couch and place my head on his wide shoulder. "Definitely."

Chaz's two favorite shows are Return to Space—we've watched every season several times—and False Prophecy. I'm almost relieved when the background music for False Prophecy begins to play. I'm too distracted to truly enjoy the show, but one thing's for sure—for exactly one hour, I shed my guilt, I forget my pain, and I become the old Sienna.

4

Sienna

It's the same dream. It's always the same. Smoke filling the room, making it impossible to breathe, screams echoing down a long hallway, and blood. So much blood. There's a body half-hidden beneath concrete and debris. And a frantic urge to clear the debris and save the person trapped. When the last piece of concrete has been removed, the only thing underneath is a skeleton, its bones cracked and twisted at odd angles.

I bolt up in bed, the scream dying on my lips, my heart thundering, my nightshirt soaked with sweat. Footsteps pound down the hall and the door flings open. Zane stands there, shirtless, his hair disheveled, his eyes wild and sweeping the room.

"Are you okay?"

When I nod, he exhales slowly. "Another bad dream?"

With the back of my hand, I wipe the beads of sweat from my brow and nod again.

Zane rests his hands on the doorframe above his head. "Same one?"

"Yeah." I finally speak, but it comes out hoarse. "Always."

His eyes sweep the room again and settle on the chair in the corner. "Want me to stay?"

When I nod, he grabs a blanket from the end of the bed

and settles into the chair, as he's done almost every night since I've been here.

"Go back to sleep," he murmurs, sinking deeper into the chair and closing his eyes. "I'm right here."

As my heart rate gradually slows, I lie back against the pillows and pull the covers up to my chin. I stare at the shadow-covered ceiling as images of the dream replay through my mind. The memories of that night in the Compound are still so strong that, without even trying, I can re-experience the horror of it all, including the terrifying sounds of screams, the sight of Trey with a rebar protruding from his chest, and the taste of sweat and smoke.

"Zane?"

"Mmm?"

"Why do you think I keep having the same dream?" I ask.

There's a pause. For a moment, I think he's already fallen asleep. "It's probably your subconscious reliving that night," he finally says, his voice slightly muffled.

"But bones? Why bones?"

"Bones are the epitome of death. And isn't that what you're most afraid of? Trey dying?"

I'm more afraid of something bad happening to Mom or Emily, but I don't correct him. Yes, I've seen Trey "dead," and it's something I'd rather not experience again with anyone I love.

"I guess you're right," I say. I close my eyes, but an image of my father pops up behind my closed eyelids. I'm still no closer to knowing what he was involved in that made him change his name and eventually got him killed.

"I think I'll talk to your father tomorrow," I say, changing the subject and letting this new thought carry across the room. "Maybe he can shed some light on what happened twenty-one years ago. And who knows? Maybe it's connected with what's going on with Trey now."

"Good luck," Zane murmurs.

I roll over on my side. From here, I can see Zane, his head tilted against the back of the chair, his eyes closed. "And you're coming with me," I say.

I hear him snort, but he doesn't open his eyes. "Okay. But I've already warned you that he's like a steel trapdoor. Good luck getting information from him."

Tennis balls fly across the court behind the Ryder's massive home. Harlow Ryder is exactly where I was told he would be—hitting the balls ejected from the automatic machine.

Zane keeps step with me as we cross the court. It's so hot that even though I should probably be sweating, I'm dry as a bone. Thanks to the desert heat, the sweat dries quickly, leaving a salty film coating my skin. The heat shimmers like waves across the black tennis court.

I watch as Zane strides over to the machine and flips the switch. It groans and hisses like a dying snake before shutting down completely.

"Dad," Zane calls out, "may we have a word with you?"

Mr. Ryder twirls his tennis racquet a few times and pulls a towel from his back pocket, mopping the sweat off his face. He saunters over to the net where Zane and I join him. "What would you like to talk about, son?"

Zane looks at me and nods, indicating that it's my turn to speak.

Other than the initial meeting where Zane introduced his father to my mom, my sister, and me, I've managed to steer clear of Harlow Ryder.

I suck in a breath and straighten my shoulders. "Mr. Ryder, I have a few questions for you regarding my father."

Mr. Ryder squints at me, shielding his eyes from the sun.

"Who's your father?"

"Mitch Hoover," I say, using the name my father had when he was Harlow's lead geneticist.

"That's impossible," he scoffs. "Mitch died in a car accident almost twenty-two years ago. You're much younger than that."

"No," I say. "He faked his own death. And changed his name to Ben Preston."

Harlow studies me, as if he's trying to decide if he should believe me. "I don't know what kind of game you're playing, Miss Preston, but I don't—"

"I'm telling the truth! Just ask Zane."

Harlow's eyes swing from me to Zane. Out of the corner of my eye, I see Zane nod.

Harlow swallows, his Adam's apple bobbing. "Do you have a picture of your father?"

I pull my Lynk from my pocket and scroll through old photos. There's one of all four of us before Dad died. I think we were celebrating his birthday or something. I show Harlow the picture, and the color drains from his face. Ironically, he looks like he's seen a ghost.

"Incredible," Harlow mutters, shaking his head. "I can't believe it."

"Now will you talk to me?" I ask as I pocket my Lynk.

"There's nothing to discuss. As you can see, I was completely unaware that your father is alive—"

"*Was* alive," I correct him. "He died a year ago. Apparently poisoned by Radcliffe, although he led me to believe that *you* were the one who killed him."

Harlow's eyes narrow. "I don't understand how any of this has to do with me. Now if you'll excuse me—"

I'm not above begging. "Please, Mr. Ryder. I need answers, and you're the only one who might be able to give them to me."

Harlow rubs the back of his neck as he contemplates my request. I glance over at Zane but he shrugs, remaining neutral.

After a few awkward moments, Harlow gives me a curt nod. "Let me get cleaned up, and I'll meet you in my study in thirty." Without waiting for a response, he strides to the house, his towel slung over one shoulder and his tennis racket hanging loosely from his grip.

"Was he telling the truth?" I ask Zane as we follow Harlow to the house. "Your father seemed surprised that my dad faked his death. You think he didn't know?"

Zane tilts his head, his gaze fixed on the door his father went through. "He was definitely convincing."

"Yes, he was."

"And that went better than I thought," Zane adds.

"Yeah, no thanks to you. Where were you anyway? I could have sworn you were right beside me."

Zane grins. "I knew my father couldn't resist you. I wanted to give you plenty of space to be convincing."

I give him a disappointed frown. "You could have been a little more supportive."

His face is immediately remorseful. "Sorry."

After a pause, I say, "Well, that is my specialty."

"What?"

"Getting information that people don't want to give."

My fingers strum against the supple leather of the armchair as Zane and I sit and wait for Harlow to join us in his study. When he enters the room, his hair is slightly damp, and he smells of shower gel and aftershave.

Taking a seat in the upholstered chair across from us, Harlow fixes his gaze on me. He crosses his legs and clasps his hands at the knees.

"Now, what is it you want to know, Miss Preston?"

I lean forward. "What happened twenty-one years ago

when my father was working for you? I know he was involved in something."

For a moment, it looks like he's waging an internal war, his face trying to mask whatever it is he's feeling. But then he sighs as if the weight of the world is crushing down on his chest. "No one was ever supposed to know the truth," he says. "It was a mistake. An accident. I behaved poorly, and because of it, I've suffered more than I thought I could endure."

"What happened?" I ask, easing to the edge of my seat.

Harlow looks directly at Zane, measuring his words. "I suspected your mother was having an affair, but I didn't want to believe it." His gaze shifts to his feet for a moment. When he looks up, the lines around his eyes make him appear ten years older than he really is. "I had just mastered genetic modification and convinced your mother to carry the first genetically modified baby—"

I interrupt him then, because I can't bear to hear another lie spew from his mouth. "That's not entirely true though, is it? Zane isn't the very first GM, is he?"

Harlow leans forward in his chair and stares at me. "What do you mean, Miss Preston?"

"I mean," I say slowly, "that the Fringe have been harboring GMs from your first wave of genetic experimentations. Those who survived, that is." At Harlow's shocked look, I continue, "Yes, I know all about what you did to those innocent babies at the Match 360 Headquarters in Rubex. All in your quest to discover the perfect genome."

"Father, what is she talking about?" Zane asks, his voice even.

Harlow slumps against his seat, as if I've stolen every ounce of energy he has. "My sins."

"Is this true? Did you experiment on babies?" Zane's eyes are wide, incredulous.

"Yes, and it was… reprehensible. I know that now. Once

everything happened with your mother, I shut the program down."

"You shut it down?" I repeat, my mind reviewing what Trey told me in the Compound about the extraction from the AIG facility years ago that went terribly wrong, resulting in the death of many men and women, fathers and mothers. "Then that means you *gave* the government those children. For their own experiments."

Harlow frowns. "No. After Zane's mother died, I wanted to wipe my hands of it all. I told Steele—who was in University at the time and plenty old enough to manage part of the company—to take care of it."

"What happened to my mother?" Zane demands. "I want to know."

Harlow straightens a bit in his chair, ready to continue his story. "As I was saying, I convinced your mother to carry the first baby with the perfect genome. I'll admit, Penelope was a little too old to be the ideal candidate, but physically, she was strong and capable."

"But I thought—" Zane begins.

Harlow holds up a hand to stop him. "Please, son, let me finish." He pauses to gather his thoughts. "When I found out your mother was carrying twins, I didn't know what to think or how that was possible. On the one hand, the process for genetic modification doesn't really allow for duplicates, so my first assumption was that only one baby was genetically modified and the other was not. When she was in her third trimester, I ordered blood work done to check the development of the fetuses and to determine which was modified. My lead geneticist at the time..." His eyes flit to me. "Sienna's father took the sample, but when he gave me his report, I noticed parts of it were missing. Curious, I asked him about it, but he denied tampering with it."

My heartbeat pulses against my skin, making me keenly

aware of each beat. I might finally understand what happened with my dad so many years ago.

"Naturally," Harlow continues, "I did some investigating and discovered a shock beyond imagination. Both babies were genetically modified, which, per my theories, couldn't happen. But then I realized that while one of the babies was genetically mine, the other was not."

"How is that possible?" Zane asks, his voice rising in disbelief.

I reach over and place my hand on his knee, giving it a quick, reassuring squeeze before returning my hand to my lap. This does not go unnoticed by Mr. Ryder, who raises one eyebrow into a perfect arch. Zane ignores him, and Harlow continues.

"Apparently, my geneticist, Mitch Hoover, implanted two fertilized eggs, one from myself with all the qualities I had chosen for my son, and one Penelope, unbeknownst to me, had created with all the characteristics she wanted in a son. But it wasn't my DNA she used. Oh, no. She used the DNA of the man she'd been having an affair with—Bryant Winchester."

My eyes shift to Zane to see how he's handling this. His fists are clenched and a muscle in his jaw twitches.

"When I found out, I'll admit, I didn't handle it well. I confronted her, yelled a bit, made her cry—" He stops as his voice becomes choked with emotion. A good thirty seconds pass before he continues. "Then I did something I will forever regret. I don't know what I was thinking—" He shakes his head. "I went to Mitch and ordered him to take care of the baby who wasn't mine or else he would be fired. I suggested that maybe something could happen during delivery..." He stops, letting the thought hang like a poisonous gas filling the air.

My throat closes. An innocent baby. My thoughts turn to Trey, who I recently learned is not only genetically modified, but also Zane's brother. *Him.* Harlow wanted my father to kill *him*. The man I now love. Kind of ironic, really.

Zane shifts in his seat, and I look at him to gauge his reaction. His head rests in his hands.

"I'm not proud of what I did," Harlow continues. "I drove your mother away. She ran off to be with Bryant Winchester and give birth to her sons. When I realized where she'd gone, I tried to find her. At the time, the Fringe was barely getting off the ground, but I'd heard they were hunkered down in some abandoned building until they finished their Compound. An old friend of mine, George Radcliffe, offered to help. He had military training and said he could find them."

Harlow pauses, filling his lungs with a deep breath, before exhaling it slowly. "And find them, he did. I guess I didn't think for a minute what the repercussions of showing up at the Fringe site with a government official and a few soldiers would be." His face takes on a pained expression. "Your mother had just given birth to the two of you only hours earlier. She was still recovering... When Radcliffe and his men stormed the Fringe site, she was caught in the crossfire. She was killed along with several other Fringe men and women." Harlow swallows hard, his eyes watery. "In all the confusion, Bryant grabbed one of the babies, and Radcliffe grabbed the other, not knowing if the baby they held was the one with the *right* DNA."

Finally, it all makes sense. My father's role in this. The guilt he must have felt knowing he was the one who helped Penelope fool her husband, which in the end resulted in her death. And perhaps after Penelope's death, he *did* fear for his life. Harlow's wrath.

"At first, I didn't want to know." Harlow's eyes are brimming with tears. "I didn't want to know if the baby Radcliffe brought to me was mine genetically or not. But then, I had to. It was like a disease spreading through me. I'd lie awake at night. Wondering." He glances at Zane, who is sitting straight as a board, hardly breathing.

"After I did the testing, I decided it didn't matter—"

"Wait," Zane interrupts. "Why wouldn't it matter?"

"Because I decided that, no matter what, you were my son."

"Which means…" Zane says slowly.

Harlow heaves a huge sigh. "Which means that, genetically, Trey Winchester is my son."

5

Sienna

The room is deathly quiet until Zane bursts to his feet and roars, "How could you keep this from me? All these years? How could you?"

Harlow's face goes pale. "I'm sorry, Zane. I didn't want you to think less of me—"

"You mean you didn't want me to know the truth. About how you killed my mother," he snaps. His forehead is scrunched and a muscle in his jaw twitches uncontrollably. I've never seen him look so angry, like he could smash through a wall with one swipe of his fist.

Zane closes his eyes and lets out a rush of air, before opening them and fixing Harlow with his steely gaze. "I can't do this." He strides out of the room.

I'm about to go after him, but Harlow's voice stops me.

"Sienna—" he starts.

I turn and glare at him. "You're such a coward. Did you honestly think he wouldn't find out?" Without waiting for a response, I hurry out of the room after Zane.

I don't catch up to him until I reach the driveway. He's already sliding into his silver Aria. He probably wants to be left alone, but I don't care. Hopping into the passenger seat, I say, "Where are we going?"

"Anywhere," he growls, throwing the car in reverse.

He drives fast, almost reckless, as if the anger and adrenaline are flooding his system—and his brain. He drove fast yesterday on the Gateway but that was different. It was controlled and fun, whereas this feels like he's taunting death.

After what seems like an eternity, I dare to speak. "Are you okay?"

"I'm fine," he snaps.

I wait a few more seconds. "Um… you don't sound fine."

"My entire life has been a lie!" He slams his fist on the steering wheel.

"I'm sorry," I say, my voice small. "I know this must be really hard for you—"

"You have no idea how I feel right now," he seethes. The car swerves a little.

"Zane, pull over. Let's talk about it. You're hurting. And I want to help."

"Like you let me help you? All this time you've been hurting. Mourning Trey like he's dead or something. Why can't you just be glad he's alive?"

His words are like a smack to the face. Stunned, I say, "How dare you bring him into this?"

"Why shouldn't I? He's my *brother*. Which is more than he is to you right now."

I want to punch him so bad—want to make his nose bleed and his jaw ache. I clench my fists, but then the calm, more rational part of me decides it might not be a good idea to attack the man who's driving one hundred miles per hour on this winding road to the dam.

The dam. I didn't realize that's where we are headed.

Instead, I cross my arms over my chest and turn to face the window. When we reach the top of a large hill, I can see the turquoise waters of the lake below. The sun glints off the crystal water, creating an almost blinding effect.

Zane breathes deeply beside me. "Listen, Sienna, I'm really

sorry. I don't know what came over me—"

"It's called anger, Zane," I say sarcastically. "Not even you can be perfect all the time."

His voice comes out quiet. "I'm sorry. I should have thanked you for caring, but instead—" He stops himself. "I'm an idiot."

I soften at his words. "It's okay. I understand you're just lashing out. But don't *shut* me out."

Zane's mouth tweaks at the corner. "Same goes for you."

"Deal."

Zane parks his Aria on the lake side of the dam, and we both climb out.

"Bring back memories?" Zane asks with a wry grin.

"How you thought I was trying to kill myself? Again?" I laugh. "I don't know why you thought I was so suicidal."

Zane shrugs. "Maybe I didn't. Maybe I just wanted an excuse to rescue you."

My heart trips over itself. "Zane," I say softly, "you can't keep saying things like that."

He moves around the side of the car. "Why not?" When he takes my hand in his, the warmth of his fingers heats up my whole body.

"This isn't a good idea," I mutter, but I make no move to extract my hand from his.

He looks down at me, then at our entwined fingers. "But what if it is? What if it's the best idea in the whole damn world?"

"Because—because you're engaged. To someone else."

"But I don't want to be," he says, his voice low. He takes a step closer until he's so close that I could wrap my arm around his back if I wanted to.

"Zane," I warn, but the warning gets caught in my throat. He's giving me that look. The same one he gave me before he kissed me that first time on the couch in his house.

"What?" he whispers.

"Please, don't—" But he's already leaning down, his eyes focused on my mouth. My breath comes out shaky as his fingers slip from mine and his hands touch my waist, gently bringing me closer. Before I can stop myself, our lips meet, and a thousand nerve endings converge to a single spot. His lips are fire and warmth and need. And that single spark ignites an already-smoldering flame.

An image of Trey flashes in my mind, his broad shoulders, his wide grin. I push Zane away. "Zane, please—"

Zane takes a step back and scrubs a hand over his face. "He doesn't even remember you."

"That's not the point. What about Arian?"

"I don't care about Arian! Trey's been living my life." He throws his hands up. "Who knows? Maybe you and I would have ended up together if Trey and I weren't switched at birth."

"And then you would be the one laying in that hospital bed with no recollection of who I am. Is that what you want?"

"No, of course not. It's just that—" He runs a hand through his hair. "My whole life has been a lie. But this—" he motions to the two of us "—this feels real."

"It's not, Zane. It's not. You're—you're hurt. Confused. That's all."

His face softens. "I'm not confused, Sienna. I'm in love. With you."

I rub my temples, as if I can scrub all the confusion away. "I can't think about that right now."

"And I can't *stop* thinking about it."

Zane turns away and walks toward the water. When he's at the edge, he stands there, hands in his pockets, staring across to the other side of the lake.

After what seems like an eternity, I hesitantly step beside him. I gaze across the lake at the rocky slope and the way the waterline divides the light rock from the darker, redder rock. "Why did you want to come here?"

"I would have gone to the Megasphere, but someone blew that up," he says tersely.

"I'm sorry—"

"Look, Sienna, you can stop apologizing. I know you're sorry for all that happened the past few weeks, but compared to the lies my father's told me the past twenty-one years, yours is a minor blip." He heaves a deep sigh, and I'm not sure what I can say or do to make him feel better.

I take a seat at the water's edge, remove my shoes and socks, and dip my toes in. It's at least one hundred and fifteen degrees outside, and yet, the water still feels cool.

The water level is lower than the last time I was here. It would be really stupid to cliff jump now, even though I suddenly have an insane desire to do it anyway.

Zane settles next to me and leans back on his hands. "I think I'm gonna tell Arian it's over between us."

"What? Zane, you can't do that. What about your future?"

"Technically," he says, "it's Trey's future."

I turn and face him. "You listen to me, Zane Ryder. You were the one raised by Harlow; you were the one bred for this. You know the lab; you even created your own miracle healing serum. You *are* Harlow's son. Who cares what your genes say?"

"Yes, but Trey is the poster child my father created." He makes a face. "I'm just—a product of my mother's affair."

I shake my head. "Don't talk like that. You sound ridiculous."

That comment provokes a smile from Zane. "I really want to kiss you again."

Internally, I'm struggling. A part of me wants to kiss Zane. Maybe it would help to forget about the hurt I feel at Trey not remembering me, claiming he has a fiancée. But I still love Trey. Wouldn't it be wrong to kiss one guy while I'm still in love with another?

"But we can't," I say firmly, not sure if I'm trying to convince him or myself.

"You're right," he agrees. "Not while I'm still engaged to Arian." He hops to his feet and strides to his car.

It takes me a little longer to join him as I have to put my shoes and socks on wet feet. When I slide onto the leather seat next to him, I say, "Can you take me someplace?"

I need to see it. I need to see for myself what it looks like now that the dust has settled and the guilt has thickened. Will there be anything left?

"Sure. Where do you want to go?"

"The Compound."

6

Zane

I drive along the abandoned railroad tracks until we reach a tunnel that Sienna claims is the entrance to the Compound. However, the entrance is caved in, with a few spots that might allow a person to squeeze through. According to Sienna, half of the Fringe members who survived are camped out at someone's farm, staying in the barn or something.

I'm still trying to come to grips with all that was revealed today. I'm *not* the first genetically modified human as I was led to believe my entire life. There are others in hiding, being protected by the Fringe. When I think of my father experimenting on innocent children... the very thought leaves me queasy. How could anyone do that, let alone the man I've admired and looked up to since I was a small boy? And now that I know Trey is my father's son, making him the poster child of Chromo 120 and the rightful heir to Harlow Ryder's company, where does that leave me?

We park and get out. "Are you sure you want to do this?" I ask her.

She hesitates, but then nods. "It's because of me that this happened. All of these people—dead—because of me. I led Radcliffe right to Trey and the Fringe Compound, and I can never forgive myself for that."

"Sienna—" My voice is a warning because there's no need

for her to carry the blame.

"No, Zane, it's true."

Before I can protest, she slides through one of the narrow openings, her leg scraping against a pointy rock.

"Careful," I call after her. "We don't know how safe this is."

Sienna switches on her Lynk light, illuminating the cavernous space. Piles of rocks block the way a few feet ahead of us, but once again, there are spaces like someone already came through here, digging a way in—or out.

We squeeze through the next space, and the tunnel opens up.

"This was the supply entrance," Sienna explains. When her light shines on the mangled metal of a couple of semi-trucks, she gasps. There's a black vehicle—a truck maybe?—that's now flattened like sheetrock, several large boulders sitting atop.

"That was Trey's truck," she whispers. Her eyes are wild as she moves closer to the wreckage. I'm about to tell her to be careful when I catch sight of her Harley at the exact moment that she does. Her bike is sandwiched between the two semi-trucks. It's beaten and a little bruised, but miraculously enough, the semis have somehow managed to take the blow, sheltering her motorcycle from the falling rocks and debris.

Sienna lets out a cry and moves toward her bike, climbing over the boulders that separate us from the wreckage. When she reaches it, she runs a hand over its handlebars and leather seat, assessing the damage.

"Need help?" I call out.

"It's my Harley! She's okay, I think. But she's wedged in good."

I climb over the boulders and jump down, my feet kicking up a cloud of dust and dirt. "Let me take a look." I lift the back end, testing the weight of the bike. "I think I can lift it out."

She stares at me incredulously. "Are you crazy? She weighs five hundred pounds at least."

I shrug. "So it's a little more than I normally bench press. I've got this."

"You have nice muscles and all, but five hundred pounds, seriously?"

My ego takes a bit of a hit with that comment, and now I'm more determined than ever to prove myself to her. So instead of responding, I brace myself and lift, the muscles in my neck straining. Sienna stands still, watching in awe.

"Go clear a way through," I say through clenched teeth.

She moves quickly, scrambling over the piles of concrete to the wall of rocks. As she chucks hand-sized rocks out of the way, I take a deep breath and move up the mountain of rocks, carrying the bike in my arms. Every muscle quivers from exertion, and my heart beats against my chest, pumping adrenaline through my veins. I focus on the bike-sized hole Sienna is creating and her own muscles that strain from the effort. A groan escapes as the bike starts to slip from my fingers. Sienna stops and turns, staring at me with her mouth slightly parted.

"Hurry!" I hiss.

"Right. Sorry," she says.

I find my footing on the ground past the rock mountain, and the bike comes down with a crash.

"I think we can push it the rest of the way," I say, leaning over to catch my breath, one hand still holding her Harley upright.

"I almost have this cleared," Sienna says, puffing from the exertion.

Once my heart rate has slowed, I grab the handlebars and begin to push. It moves slowly, like it's resisting my efforts, but at least I don't have to carry it.

I push her Harley through the first opening, and then we're met with the next wall of fallen concrete. Sienna holds the bike while I work to pull out the rocks, tossing them to the side. But I guess I'm not careful enough. When I seize a large boulder with both hands, there's a low rumble, and an avalanche of rocks almost topples me.

"Watch out!" Sienna screams, grabbing my arm and pulling me backward. I lose my footing and stumble, falling back on my rear. My hands are coated with dirt and grease from touching one of the bike's sensitive areas, and my clothes are smeared with brown clay. A cloud of dust kicks up, settling in my chest. I cough, trying to find some clean air to breathe.

"We need to get out of here," Sienna says.

I jump to my feet, waving my hands in front of me as if I can clear the air around us by doing so. "Everything's hazy now, isn't it?"

"Imagine," she says, "that you're trapped underneath this mountain while bombs rain down and fire and smoke consumes everything."

This is the most she's said about that night. Other than the nightmares that wake her, she doesn't talk about it.

"It wasn't your fault, Sienna."

She laughs, her tone bitter. "Tell that to the hundred dead people on the other side of these walls." Tears fill her eyes, but she looks away, always trying to be the strong one. I wish she didn't feel like she has to be strong for me. I wish she could let me in, show me her weaknesses. I'd still love her for them.

"I'm sorry, Sienna," I say. "I'm sorry you had to experience that. And even more so that I left you at the Satellite Government Facility that day. Everything that man said—"

"It's over now," she cuts me off. "And we've moved on, right? We're good."

I wish she understood how much I regret leaving her at the SGF, how if maybe I'd stayed, things might have turned out differently. What if I hadn't left? She might have come home with me, stayed at my house, and spent time with her sister. She wouldn't have been in the Compound at all. She wouldn't have led Radcliffe back to their hideout, and therefore wouldn't be plagued with these endless nightmares of guilt and blame.

"Yes, we're good," I confirm. I push the bike through the opening my little avalanche created. Sienna walks alongside me as we follow the railroad track out of the tunnel. The sun is bright when we exit, and I blink a few times to allow my eyes to adjust.

Once we reach my car, I prop the bike on its kickstand. "Now what?" I ask.

Sienna fiddles with the key in the ignition, and I already know what she's thinking. "You want to go for a ride, don't you?"

"I just want to make sure she still works okay." She bends down, checking the bike over. "T-CLOCS," she mutters.

"T-what?"

"Sorry." She gives me a sheepish look. "I was talking to myself. T-CLOCS. It's a little checklist to make sure my motorcycle is safe to ride. It stands for Tires, Controls, Lights, Oil, Chassis, and Sidestand."

My eyebrows rise. "Impressive. How do you know so much about motorcycles? Did your dad ride?"

She laughs outright at my question. "My dad on a motorcycle? No way. Dad was a mixture of leather, coffee, and books. Not oil, sweat, and grease."

After lying down on her back, she scoots up next to the bike, checking the rims and spokes to make sure there's no damage. "It kind of became a hobby of mine after my dad died. Do you know the junkyard off Chantilly? Never mind, of course you don't. Anyway, I found Harley there when I was looking for some old furniture to decorate our trailer with." She looks up at me. "We didn't always live in a trailer, you know."

I try to hide my surprise. I assumed the opposite. "What happened?"

Forgotten

"After Dad died, Mom became sick. We couldn't afford to live in our house in the suburbs anymore, so we sold it and everything in it, and found the trailer on the outskirts of town. That's when I dropped out of school and started taking on odd jobs."

She says it all with such a matter-of-fact tone, but I sense the truth. It was hard for her. It was more than any teenage girl should have to deal with. But she's too strong to admit it.

"I don't know how you did it," I say.

She sits up, wiping her hands on her shorts. Unconsciously, I find my eyes shifting to her bare legs.

"I didn't have a choice," she says. She rises to her feet, straddles the bike, and bounces up and down a little. I can only assume she's checking the chassis to make sure everything is working properly.

"Anyway," she says. "When I found Harley, I took her home, researched antique motorcycles, and fixed her up. There's a shop near the Hollow that sells parts, so that's where I headed after I got my first paycheck." She pats her bike fondly. "Never regretted it."

When she turns the key, the engine roars to life, bringing a brilliant smile to her face. I want to tell her all the ways I think she's amazing, how she's unlike any girl I've ever met, how I find her beautiful, resourceful, intelligent, and intriguing, but she doesn't want to hear those things. Not from me anyway.

So instead, I take a step toward her and the bike. "Can I ride too?"

She gives me a coy smile, and my normally strong heart falters a bit. "As long as you don't mind a girl being in control."

Enjoying her playfulness, I lift my hands in surrender. "I don't mind at all. In fact, I *welcome* it."

"Climb on, then," she says, jerking her thumb behind her.

As I climb on and wrap my hands around her waist, her body stiffens.

"Was this a ploy to get close to me?" she murmurs over the engine.

I lean in close, my lips barely brushing her ear. "Of course."

7

Sienna

When we arrive at Zane's house hours later with me on my motorcycle and him following in his car, there's a bit of a commotion.

Dr. Hammond rushes up to us when we enter the area of the house that's been deemed the "hospital wing."

"Against my better judgement, Mr. Winchester has decided to leave. I've advised him to stay longer so I can do more tests, or at least admit him to the hospital, but he refuses. Something about getting back to the Capital where he has important business to attend to."

Zane and I exchange a look. *This is bad. Really bad.*

"Physically, though, is he in any condition to be traveling?" Zane asks.

"Physically, he's fine. Healthy as a horse thanks to your ReOGene serum, but it's the mental aspect I'm worried about."

"I guess we can't chain him to the bed, can we?" I say, only half-joking.

Neither of them seems to think that's funny.

"Maybe Sienna and I should talk to him. Try to reason with him," Zane suggests.

Dr. Hammond looks doubtful. "You're welcome to try, but I don't think it will do much good."

As the doctor walks off, I take a deep breath and look at

Zane. His brows are furrowed in concern. "We have to at least try, right?" he asks.

"Of course. I'm not letting Trey just walk out of here. Not when I worked so hard to get him back."

When we reach the door to Trey's room, I knock softly before pushing it open. Trey is dressed and staring out the window, his hands tucked into the pockets of jeans I can only assume are Zane's. He still doesn't know that he and Zane are brothers. Everyone—myself, Zane, even the doctors—figured it would be best not to add to his confusion right now.

He turns to the door as we walk in. "Ah, there are the lovebirds," he croons.

I frown at Zane before focusing on Trey. "Zane and I are only friends."

Trey gives a low chuckle. "Not according to him." He nods in Zane's direction.

I turn and glare at Zane. "What did you tell him?" I hiss.

He shrugs. "The truth. That I'm in love with you."

"You shouldn't have done that—"

"He asked. What did you want me to do? Lie?"

He asked? Why would he ask? Unless… unless he cares.

When I look at Trey, he's staring at the two of us, an amused expression on his face. "I can hear you, you know."

I move toward him. "Listen, Trey, you can't leave. Your home is here." I glance around. "Okay, not here, exactly. But you have lots of friends. Friends who need you. And you have me." I hurry on before he can say something. "I know you don't understand what that means, but I'm someone who will be devastated if you leave. Please, Trey," I plead. "Stay a little longer until we can figure this out."

"There's nothing to figure out," he says. He looks out the window again. "Rayne will be here at any moment."

My throat closes. "Rayne? Rayne who?"

"Rayne Williams," he says. "*My fiancée.*"

Images of Rayne flash through my mind. Rayne and her entourage of perfect friends striding past me when we went to school together at GIGA. Her gorgeous smile, long legs, and silky blonde hair. My stomach churns.

I can feel myself quickly losing control. "You don't have a *fiancée!*" I shout. "And it sure as hell isn't Rayne!"

Trey takes a step back, stunned, as Zane's hand latches onto my arm. "Sienna, this isn't the way," Zane says, his voice low.

But I'm too angry to care what damage my words might do. Too upset to calm my feelings and curb my words. Trey has to stop living in this delusion. He has to be fixed before he loses everything and everyone he's ever cared about.

And Rayne? Of all the people to think he's engaged to, it has to be Rayne Williams? Seriously? How does he even *know* her?

Moving across the room until there are only inches between us, I grab his face in my hands. His skin is familiar, the stubble from his last shave pricking my fingers and reminding me of our last time together, in his room in the Compound.

It can't be over, can it?

I feel a desperation growing inside of me like a seed that's sprouted and needs room to spread out. *He has to know.*

"Look at me, Trey." My voice softens. "The truth is, I love you. I've been waiting for the right moment—"

I stop when Trey's uncomfortable gaze shifts out the window. "She's here," he announces.

My hands drop at the same time my heart does, and I bite my lip to keep tears from welling in my eyes. Why should he care that I'm pouring my heart out to him? He doesn't remember me. I'm nothing to him.

I turn and peer out the window. Sure enough, a sleek white convertible squeals into Zane's driveway, and the familiar figure of a tall, perfectly proportioned blonde steps out of the car.

"You've got to be kidding me," I mutter.

Zane joins us at the window. "Wow."

I glare at him, and he gives me an apologetic smile. "She has nothing on you," he whispers in my ear.

"Shut up," I say. I turn my attention to Trey. "You can't honestly think that Rayne Williams is your fiancée. Where did you meet her? How long have you two been together? When are you getting married?"

When Trey looks at me, I hope to see confusion, but instead, I only see pity. *Does he pity me?*

Careful not to touch me, he slips past and starts toward the door. He's halfway there before he turns and says, "Trust me, Sienna, I'm not the guy for you." He looks at Zane. "But the one who is may be closer than you think."

And then, he's gone.

No. No, no, no, no, no. Clenching my fists, I stare out the window. I didn't work this hard to get him back only to lose him to a fake fiancée. Radcliffe may be dead, but apparently, his agenda lives on.

I sprint out the door and bound down the curved staircase, flinging the heavy front door open. Henry, the Ryder's butler, stands in the foyer, looking confused.

"Everything all right, Miss Sienna?"

Ignoring him, I run out the door, immediately hit with the dry, stifling heat. Trey is already climbing into Rayne's car, but she's crossing to her side of the convertible when I burst outside. She looks at me with narrowed eyes, and then leans in the window to say something to Trey.

As I get closer to her, she extends a delicate hand. "Thank you for taking such good care of my fiancé," she says, her voice honey sweet and coated with fake sugar. "I don't know how I can ever repay you."

I slap her hand away. "What do you think you're doing,

Rayne?"

Rayne smiles and crosses her arms over her chest. "Nice to see you too, Sienna."

I match her stance. "Why are you pretending to be Trey Winchester's fiancée? Who hired you? How much did they pay?"

Her eyes widen, and she puts a hand over her chest. "Why, Sienna, I'm hurt. How could you accuse me of such a thing?" She leans forward. "Truth is, I've known Trey for years. Way before you ever met him." She shrugs. "We're in love."

By now, Zane is standing beside me, and Trey is climbing out of the car.

"You do realize," I threaten in a low voice, "that Trey is the leader of the Fringe, and when we figure out what you've done to him, we will find you, and we will end this."

Rayne smiles and flicks her long hair over her shoulder. "I don't know what you're talking about," she says, her voice dripping with sweetness.

When Trey reaches Rayne, he places his hands on her shoulders and steers her away.

As Trey opens her door, I call out to her, "Who are you working for?"

She stops and spins as if she's in slow motion, her perfectly tan legs on display in her little red leather skirt. "This isn't a game, Sienna. It's the truth." Rayne smiles up at Trey. "I can prove it to you."

The next thing I know, her lips are on his, and she's kissing him. No, they're kissing, because the way his hands wrap around her waist and pull her toward him are proof.

My heart feels like a dozen arrows have been shot through it. I can't watch. I can't watch the man I love kiss another woman. I look away. I feel Zane's hand rest on the space between my shoulder blades, anchoring me, providing me comfort.

When I turn back, Rayne is seated in the driver's seat and Trey is closing her door. Before crossing to his side of the car,

Trey looks directly at me and says, "Just let it go, Sienna. Please."

My heart is ripped wide open as I watch Rayne start the car and back out of the driveway. I stare after her and Trey until they've turned the street corner, but sadly, he never looks back.

The ice cream Greta supplies me with doesn't help. The swim in the pool with Zane, Emily, and my mother doesn't help. And a walk through the gardens in which I see the array of forget-me-nots waving in the breeze, like they're taunting me, doesn't help.

Nothing helps.

That night, I'm sitting on the bed in the room that's been designated as mine in Zane's house, trying to figure out how to break the news to Emily that it's time to go back home to our trailer—after all, Trey's gone now, so there's no reason to stay—when there's a soft knock on the door.

"Come in."

Zane pokes his head in, his face grim.

I sit up straight, my back rigid. "What is it?"

"Sienna," Zane begins, coming into the room.

I clutch the comforter in my fist and wait for him to continue. *Something happened. Something really bad.*

"This probably isn't a good time—"

"Just tell me," I say, a bit too impatiently.

He holds up a comscreen. "There's something you need to see. It aired a few days ago."

A pretty brunette with shoulder-length hair fills the screen, and her no-nonsense voice wafts out of the speakers. "Days ago, Colonel George Radcliffe was pulled from the rubble of the Satellite Government Facility. He is now resting comfortably in St. Christopher's, the government hospital located in Rubex. Despite losing both legs, doctors believe he will make a full recovery. We spoke to Assistant President Neiman, who was seen exiting the hospital earlier today."

The camera shifts to a severe-looking blonde woman with tight lips and a pointy nose. When she tries to smile, it looks more like a grimace.

"Assistant President Neiman, how is Colonel Radcliffe doing?"

"The colonel is doing as well as can be expected. He has a long road to recovery, but his doctors are optimistic." She smiles, or rather grimaces, at the camera. "If you'll excuse me." The camera follows her blonde bob—and her entourage of security guards—as she strides away and slides into a sleek black car with Pacifica's flag attached to the antenna. As the car pulls away from the curb, several other black cars flank it. The camera returns to the face of the pretty brunette.

"Our news correspondent Sinclair Jones was able to visit with Colonel Radcliffe for a few minutes this morning. The colonel had this to say about the Fringe attack on the Satellite Government Facility."

The image shifts to a hospital bed with a man who is unmistakably George Radcliffe. There are a few cuts on his face, and his arm is bandaged, but it's his voice that makes my blood run cold.

"The Fringe will pay for what they did to the SGF and all the innocent men and women who died that day. I have a particular score to settle with the young woman who shot me and left me for dead." His eyes narrow. For a brief second, it's as though he can see me through the screen. "When I find all of you, I will crush you. Again. And again. Until there is nothing left."

I inhale sharply as Zane's finger moves over the screen, turning the device off. The room spins a little, and I close my eyes, blocking out the tick-tock sound of the antique hall clock that keeps me up at night, and the small whoosh of air from the overhead vents. Everything is fuzzy, muffled. I feel the pressure of Zane's hand on my back, and I think he's saying something, but I can't make out the words. All I can think about is Radcliffe. Alive. And he's coming after me. This time, there will be no mercy. This time, it won't matter who tries to stop him.

He will find me. He will break me.

8

Sienna

"Wait, where are you going?" Zane says as I stride past him. He grabs my arm, forcing me to face him, our lips only inches apart.

"Don't you get it, Zane? This is Radcliffe. This is all his doing. Even after all that's happened, he's still controlling me. Now he has Trey and who knows what he'll do to him—" I swallow hard, remembering what Chaz said. *They want to gain access to everything Trey knows.* "I have to inform the Fringe."

"Tonight?" Zane asks, staring at me incredulously. "Can't it wait until morning?"

I shake my head. Every minute Radcliffe has Trey means he's one step closer to crushing the Fringe and all they stand for.

"I should have never let Rayne take him," I mutter.

"What could you have done, short of tying him up?"

"Hey, I suggested that, and you and Dr. Hammond looked at me like I was crazy," I remind him.

"Because it was, and still is, crazy. Do you hear yourself?" He gestures with his arms. "Trey chose to leave. There's nothing you or I or Dr. Hammond could have done to stop him."

I heave a deep sigh and step away until my back hits the wall. "I'm tired, Zane. I'm really tired. I'm tired of running. Tired of fighting. But it's not over. It never will be, not with Radcliffe alive." A new worry hits me. "And what about Mom and Emily? They aren't safe now either."

Zane steps close and rests one hand on the wall beside me. "They will be. There's a safe house a few hours from here. We have it for emergencies like this. They can stay there until we work everything out."

We?

"And," he continues, "you aren't fighting this guy by yourself this time." A muscle in his jaw clenches. "I left you alone once before, and it was the worst decision I've ever made. It won't happen again. I promise."

My breath catches. He's so close I can see the little yellow flecks like melting butter in the brown of his eyes. I avert my gaze. "I'd better go," I say.

"I'll drive," he says, moving back a few steps.

"No—" I start to say before he stops me.

"I'm driving. End of discussion." He motions for me to leave the room first.

There's no use trying to argue with him, so I relent. On our way down the hall, I pop my head in Mom's room and let her know that Zane and I are going out for a while, so she doesn't worry. Emily is already curled up next to her in bed, asleep.

Mom's eyes scrunch in concern as she looks between Zane and me. "Where are you going? Isn't it late?"

Thankfully, Zane covers for me so I don't have to lie to her. "It was my idea, Mrs. Preston. I promise I'll take good care of her." He smiles and my mom is suckered in, her worry lines disappearing.

"Of course you will, Zane. I trust you completely," she says.

This response isn't surprising in the least. Even though I know she would never admit it, Zane is her favorite. I can tell by the way she gets a little flustered when he asks her a direct question. I guess even for a grown woman, Zane's gaze is unnerving.

"Good night, Mom."

I'm about to leave when she stops me. "Sienna." I turn around. "I'm sorry about Trey." Her eyes shift to Zane beside me. "But maybe it's for the best?"

Biting the inside of my cheek, I turn away so I don't say something I'll regret. Why does no one understand? I didn't only lose the guy I love, but the Fringe also lost their leader. And it's all because of Radcliffe and his stupid lies and brainwashing. Not for the first time do I wish that I'd aimed the gun at his chest instead of his kneecaps in the SGF.

Zane and I have almost made it out the front door when we're stopped by Harlow, who's sitting in the living room off to the right of the foyer. It's the room with the black grand piano that I admire every time I pass. I haven't dared to touch it yet, though.

"Zane," Harlow says, rising to his feet. He walks over to us. "There's much that needs to be said. I'm afraid I handled things poorly, not only for the past twenty-one years, but also this morning as well." He pauses. "You're still my son, no matter what a genetic test says. I don't want you to ever feel differently. You're the one who will inherit my company."

"And what if I don't want it?" Zane replies, his voice cold.

Harlow's eyes flit to me. "This really is a family matter," he says.

"Of course," I say. "I'll go wait in the car."

"No," Zane says. "We're done talking."

"Zane, listen," Harlow begins.

"Why should I listen to you when all you've done is lie to me for the past two decades? I can't trust anything you say."

"Perhaps we could sit down for coffee tomorrow morning and hash this all out. Surely we can find—"

"I don't think so," Zane cuts him off. Jerking the mahogany door open, he gives me a sideways glance. "Coming?" Without waiting for an answer, he stalks out the door.

Harlow turns to me, his eyes pleading. "Surely you

understand where I'm coming from? Can you try to talk to him for me?"

I'm about to respond that it's none of my business, but then I think of my father. He lied to me, to us, for years. Why? To protect us? Is Harlow Ryder any worse for wanting to protect his son?

"I might be willing to do that," I reason, "if you would be willing to stop doing research on juvenile inmates." I'm referring to what I discovered when I joined the Fringe. That juvenile inmates are being transported to the Chromo 120 labs for experimentation and DNA alteration.

Harlow tilts his head and stares at me, confusion lining his eyes and making them crinkle. "What are you talking about?"

"Oh, come on, Mr. Ryder. Don't play dumb. The inmates you've been experimenting on? Trying to change their DNA so they won't be a scourge to society anymore?" I lean forward. "Zane found your little hideout in the basement of the Match 360 Legas facility. I imagine pretty soon he'll start asking you questions about it." I frown and pretend to be concerned. "Too bad he'll discover more of your lies."

Harlow slowly shakes his head. "I don't know what you're talking about, Miss Preston. After the traumatic incident with Zane's mother, I washed my hands of genetic experimentation and moved my son away from Rubex." His mouth forms a hard line. "Perhaps you should reconsider before accusing a man, in his own home, mind you, of doing something so heinous." He strides away down the hall.

Surprised by his blatant denial, I stare after him until he enters his office. When the door clicks closed, I hurry outside and down the steps to where Zane waits in his car. I slide onto the seat beside him.

"Did my father say something to you?" Zane demands.

"Well, yes—no." I shake my head to clear my thoughts. "He wants me to talk to you, reason with you, I guess."

Fists clenched, Zane bangs the steering wheel so hard that the horn begins to blow, stuck on the annoying sound. I laugh when I see the look on Zane's face. A mixture of surprise, anger, and annoyance.

"How do I turn this thing off?" he asks over the blaring noise.

"Hit it again!"

He does, and it somehow manages to dislodge the horn. It goes quiet. When he looks at me, I struggle to hold in the laughter, pinching my lips together to keep it from spilling out.

"Go ahead," he grumbles.

"What?" I ask innocently.

"Go ahead and laugh."

That's all it takes. I laugh so hard that my belly hurts. "I'm sorry," I gasp, tears filling my eyes. I wipe them away and try to compose myself, but another fit of giggles invades me. Before I know it, Zane is chuckling too.

"It's nice to see that even though you have perfect genes, you're still human," I say as the giggles subside.

"You like that, don't you?" He starts the car and backs out of the driveway.

As we're driving, I tell him about his father's denial of experimenting on juvenile inmates. "I don't understand why no one has heard of it when I saw, with my own eyes, Trey bring in a girl who was being experimented on."

Zane gives me a sidelong glance. "Are you sure Trey was telling the truth?"

"Of course," I say in indignation. "Why would he lie about something like that? Besides, there were dozens of people he and the other Fringe had rescued throughout the years. It's not like Kaylee was the only one." Saying her name brings a stab of pain to my chest. I might not have known Kaylee well, but the girl with the blonde ponytail will always stick in my mind.

I couldn't save her. I couldn't save anyone.

At Zane's confused look, I clarify. "Kaylee was one of the inmates brought to the Compound."

He nods. "I'll have a talk with my father—I mean, Harlow."

"Zane," I say. "He's still your father."

His hands clench the steering wheel. "Yeah, I know. I just need time to process everything."

Harlow's words ring in my ears. "I think you should give him a chance to explain himself. What he did was awful, but it was years ago. I'm sure he's been punishing himself ever since."

Zane glances at me with narrowed eyes. "Since when did you become an advocate of my father?"

"I think," I say slowly, "that sometimes our parents do what they think is best for us, without ever really thinking of the consequences of what might happen when we find out the truth."

"You're thinking about your father?"

Biting my lip, I nod.

"I'm sure your father was only trying to protect you," he says.

"So was yours."

Zane is quiet for a few minutes, the purr of the engine the only sound in the dark car.

"I guess it wouldn't hurt to hear him out," he finally says.

Satisfied with his response, I send a message to Trina on my Lynk to let her know we're coming. Shortly after the bombing, the Fringe survivors split up. Half are hiding out at Jones' farm, trying to stay off the grid. Trina sends me the coordinates for the farm, and then I share them with Zane.

When we arrive at Jones' farm, there is no sign that anyone else is here. No sign of anything out of the ordinary. The only light comes from the front room of Jones' farmhouse, but the giant red barn and the yard are dark.

"If they're here, they're doing a good job of hiding," I whisper as we walk to the front door.

"These people are nice, you say?"

That's right. Up until a few days ago, Zane believed that the Fringe were the ones trying to kill him and his family. He, along with the rest of Pacifica, believed the Fringe to be unfeeling monsters. No wonder he looks nervous.

"You'll be fine. Just don't tell them who you really are. Around here, the name Harlow Ryder is akin to a very bad curse word."

"Good thing he's not my real father," Zane mutters.

It takes Jones a minute to shuffle to the door when I knock. His weathered face from years in the sun registers his surprise at seeing me. He takes a step back and invites us in.

The inside of his home is decorated with country decor—handmade patchwork quilts draped over the worn couch, pictures of chickens and old red barns decorating the walls, and thick-planked wooden floorboards underneath hand-tied rugs. It has a woman's touch—especially the milk-glass chickens lining the shelf on the opposite wall—which makes me fairly certain that, at one time, there was a Mrs. Jones.

"What brings you out to the farm?" Jones asks as he settles into a navy-blue recliner. He's traded his overalls from the last time I saw him for some flannel pajama pants and a button-down sleep shirt. Zane and I settle on the edge of the couch, facing him.

"I guess you heard about Trey," I say. "That he's still alive?"

Jones nods, rocking back and forth in the oversized chair. "Surely did. Best news ever. I got to tell ya, I did a happy dance when I heard."

I hesitate, not wanting to be the bearer of bad news. "Unfortunately, his memory's been altered. Doesn't remember who he is or any of us."

Jones' mouth drops open. "Nah. Surely they can give him a shot of something—and I don't mean the liquor kind."

If only it were that easy. I decide not to tell him about

Trey's little escapade to the Capital. News like that would hurt this poor man, even more than knowledge of Trey's death.

"I heard from Trina that Fringe members are hiding out here. Is that true? They're doing a great job of being discreet."

Jones grins. That's when I notice for the first time the top tooth he's missing, third from the front. "They're in the barn. But I told 'em lights out at dark. I can't 'ford to have Enforcers sniffin' 'round here."

"Do you mind if we go out there?" I ask. "I really need to speak with Trina."

"Sure thang. Just watch yer step on the way. There's a snake that's been lurking 'round here lately. Though he's prolly asleep now."

My skin crawls. I hate snakes.

Zane clears his throat. "A snake?" he asks.

Jones waves his hand. "Oh, it's just a little rattler." Jones pushes himself out of the recliner. "I'm sure you'd much rather visit your friend than talk to this old man."

Zane and I follow Jones' to the back door. When he opens it, I see the barn a short distance away, only about twenty yards or so.

"Don't be a stranger, ya hear?"

"Of course," I say.

Jones closes the door, and Zane and I both hesitate on the top step. He looks at me, and I look at him.

"A rattler?" he says.

Something about Zane being equally afraid gives me a surge of confidence to cross the long grass that leads to the barn. I make my way down the stairs and start across the yard with Zane right behind me.

"Maybe with your super strength, you can kill it with your bare hands," I tease.

Zane gives me a look. "I'm not superman, you know."

"Such a shame. I think you'd look good in tights."

"Are you—? Are you flirting with me?" Zane asks.

I raise a finger to my lips. "Shh, you hear that?"

Zane stops moving. "What?"

"That—that rattling sound." There isn't a rattling sound, but I sure am enjoying finding Zane's weakness. Even if it might be the only one he has.

"That's not funny," he says.

I laugh and keep moving toward the barn.

Zane picks up the pace, bringing his knees high as he walks, like that will somehow keep him from getting bit. He passes me. When he reaches the barn, he grasps the handle and pulls hard.

"Zane, wait—"

My words are cut short by the sound of at least a dozen guns cocking bullets into place.

"Trina," I call out. "It's me. Sienna." It's too dark to see inside the barn, but the colorful scenery tattoos of the Fringe members glow around the room. Yellow flowers, green vines, orange birds. Of course, Trey's tree tattoo isn't here. And for some reason, that hits me harder than it should.

When I glance to my right, Zane is standing statue-still, his hands raised in surrender.

"Guys, it's okay," Trina calls out. "They're friends."

An audible whoosh of air can be heard through the thick darkness as several people breathe out at the same time, and safeties are clicked back into place. Looks like they're as glad to avoid a blood bath as I am.

Thin arms encircle me, and I'm pulled into a cushiony pillow of a chest. After a moment, Trina releases me and says, "It's so good to see you, Sienna." In the next beat, she asks, "How's Trey?"

A few propane lanterns click on, and now I can see everyone. Huddled around hay bales, lying on the ground in sleeping bags, standing off to the side, all eyeing us. The air is thick with the musty smell of dirt, dust, and unwashed bodies.

Trina, despite her circumstances and lack of ability to shower, looks as beautiful as ever. Who knew the grunge look would become her? Truthfully, I think any look would.

"Not good," I say.

Her eyes widen.

"No, I mean, physically he's fine, but mentally…" I trail off as Nash comes to stand beside Trina.

"Mentally, he's what?" Nash demands.

I watch as Curly walks over and stands on the edge of the circle like he wants to hear, but isn't sure if he's invited. I give him a nod, remembering all he did to help me escape the Compound that night. If it wasn't for him, neither Trey nor I would be alive.

Zane steps in. "Trey doesn't remember anything. He thinks he works in the Capital—"

"And that he's engaged to this girl I know from GIGA named Rayne," I add.

Trina's hand flies to her mouth as Nash's gaze narrows. "What did your doctors do to him?" he accuses Zane.

"They didn't *do* anything," I say, anger flaring inside me. "You can thank Radcliffe. He's the one who brainwashed him, I'm sure."

"Radcliffe's dead," Nash says coldly.

"No," I say. "He's still alive."

"Unbelievable," Nash mutters, staring down at the ground. His eyes lift to mine. "Maybe I should talk to Trey—"

"You can't," I say.

"Why?"

I bite my lip and glance at Trina before responding. "He's gone. He left tonight with Rayne. Said he needed to get back to the Capital."

"So, they're controlling him?" Curly asks, his face incredulous.

I nod. "Probably something similar to what they did to my mom. But I have a feeling that whatever they did to Trey is an advanced version of my mother's brainwashing. They wouldn't have had time to do the same thing. He was only in their grasp for a few hours."

"So, what do we do?" Trina asks, her voice shaking. "How do we get Trey back?"

Before I can answer, Nash scowls at me. "You don't waste any time," he sneers, giving Zane a contemptuous look.

Hands on my hips, I turn to face him. "What's that supposed to mean?"

Nash stares me down, and I feel like we're right back where we were the very first day I showed up at the Compound and asked to join the Fringe.

Instead of responding, he turns on his heel and stalks away.

Trina throws me an apologetic look. "You know how he is when it comes to Trey. He's like the protective older brother."

"Yeah," Zane mutters. "I have one of those too." A pause. "Or had."

Frustration builds in the back of my throat, making it difficult to swallow. "Yeah, but by now, he should know how much Trey means to me." I shake my head and rest my backside against the nearest hay bale.

"He does," Trina assures me. "He just has a hard time controlling his emotions."

"And anger just happens to be at the forefront most of the time," I mutter.

Trina laughs. "Pretty much." She glances over at Zane and sticks out her hand. "I'm Trina, by the way. Sienna has told me a lot about you."

Zane raises an eyebrow at me before taking Trina's hand in his. "Nice to meet you, Trina."

I motion to Curly, who is still standing to the left of Trina. "And that's Jeb, but I like to call him Curly." Looking at Curly,

I say, "You don't mind, though, right?"

Curly chuckles. "Nah. You can call me whatever you want. After all, you did let me ride your motorcycle once."

"I don't really think I had a choice," I say. "But since you saved my life, you can ride my Harley whenever you want."

Curly was in the midst of holding out his hand to Zane, but when I say this, he stops, frozen. "She's okay?" he whispers.

I nod, a smile breaking out on my face. "Zane helped me get her out of the rubble. A few dents and scratches, but she still drives."

Curly grins. "Good to hear." With his hand held out to Zane, he says, "Thanks for helping get my buddy Trey out of that building. If you hadn't been there—" He stops. "Thank you."

With a nod, Zane firmly grasps Curly's hand.

Trina turns her attention back to me. "So, what's your plan? I know you must have one, 'cause there's no way you'd let Trey leave with that slut without one. Right?"

"Yeah, I have a plan."

Trina's eyebrows rise as Curly and Zane look at me, all three waiting expectantly. "Well?"

Taking a deep breath, I say, "I'm going to the Capital."

9

Sienna

"When were you planning to tell me?" Zane asks under his breath. His brown eyes stare at me, concerned.

"You're going to the Capital by yourself?" Trina says, her face doubtful.

"No," Zane says, firmly, like he just made up his mind. "She'll be with me."

I turn to look at him. "What are you talking about? You have to stay here. What about Arian?"

Zane's gaze cuts into me. "I'll figure that out. Besides, Trey is my brother. If anyone should help, it should be me."

Both Trina and Curly look like they've been slapped. "Did you just say you're Trey's *brother*?" Trina sputters, looking at me for confirmation.

Even though we've talked a few times over the Lynk since this whole ordeal happened, I never told Trina the truth, mostly because I felt like Trey should know before it was broadcast to everyone else. Now, I'm regretting that decision.

Biting my lip, I say, "Yeah, but we just found out when the doctors did blood work at Zane's house." I don't attempt to explain the Harlow and Bryant baby switcheroo. No one else needs to know about that right now. Besides, that's Zane's story to tell.

"How is that possible? You look nothing alike," Curly says, taking a few steps closer to form an intimate huddle of the four of us.

"My dad," I say. "He implanted two different embryos into Penelope Ryder's womb. Two genetically modified embryos," I clarify.

"Trey's a GM?" Trina whispers, but then glances behind her to make sure no one else heard.

"Yes, but please keep this between the two of you," I say to Curly and Trina. "Trey doesn't know any of this yet. The doctors thought it would be too much for him to handle, especially with this false reality already in his head."

Trina nods. "Of course. We won't breathe a word."

"Not even to Nash?"

"Not even to Nash," Curly confirms.

My eyes sweep the room. Nash is now standing off to the side where the behemoth aerodyne used to be. "What happened to the aerodyne?" I'm asking Curly because he's the one who was with me when we came to get the guns and ammo after the Compound was blown up.

"Jones had us move it behind the barn for now." Curly shrugs. "There wasn't much space for us to hide out with it in here."

"Jones has an aerodyne?" Zane asks.

"An antique crop duster," I tell him.

His eyes light up. "Cool."

"It is pretty sweet," Curly chimes in.

While the two of them debate whether or not flying the aerodyne would be similar to a virtual flight simulator, I lean toward Trina, keeping my voice low. "Do you think it would be possible to get some… guns?"

Trina looks over her shoulder at Nash before giving me a quick nod. "How many do you need?"

"Probably two. One to use and one for backup."

"We have a stash in the corner over there. I'll meet you outside in a few minutes."

Straightening up, I raise my voice. "Well, we better get back." Several people are already slipping into their sleeping bags. "It's getting late."

Trina pulls me in for a rib-cracking hug. "Take care of yourself in the Capital. And call if you need help. I wouldn't mind a little road trip." She grins.

"What are you guys gonna do? Just hang out here?" Honestly, how long can they do that? In the very least, they need indoor plumbing. The smell of unwashed bodies is already getting to me.

"Nash says there's a community of people, not too far from here, who call themselves Zenith," Trina responds. "He thinks we may be able to join forces with them, at least until we sort everything out."

"All right, everyone, lights out," Nash calls. A few of the lanterns flicker off. It's time for us to go.

I embrace Curly, his dark curls tickling my nose as he leans down to hug me. "Be careful," he says. "I won't be there to have your back this time."

He releases me, and I smile at him. "I know."

Trina grips my arms. "Bring Trey home. Please."

"I will. Promise."

As Zane and I leave, Nash watches us from afar. I'm about to turn away when he gives me a slight nod. If I'd blinked, I would have missed it. Not that I'd ever hope for much more than that from him, but finally, he's giving me something. And strangely enough, it means everything.

Zane and I are both silent on the drive home, the only sound the whoosh of cool air from the air conditioning unit. I stare out the window at the passing city lights. Even though I don't want to go there, my mind churns with pictures of Trey and Rayne and that long, lingering, bodies-pressed-together kiss. The mental image is torturous.

Groaning inwardly, I bite my lip. As strong as I've tried to be through this whole ordeal, this hurts the most. It's one thing for Trey not to remember me; it's another for him to think he's with someone else. A perfect GM specimen. How can I ever compete with that?

This takes me right back to my days at GIGA. I could never keep pace with girls like Rayne Williams. Therefore, I didn't try to. But now... now I have to. If I ever want Trey's memories restored—if I ever want to get him back—I have to. Not only do I have to compete with Rayne, but I also have to beat her. No pressure, of course. I only have all the Fringe members counting on me.

Yeah, I think sarcastically, *no pressure.*

"You doing okay over there?" Zane asks, breaking the silence. I feel his gaze land on me, but I don't turn.

"Just thinking."

More silence until Zane clears his throat. "So the Capital, huh?"

"You're not coming with me."

"Of course I'm coming," he says, his tone firm.

Now I do turn to look at him. "You can't. I need you to help protect my mom and sister. I need you here."

"I'm not letting you go by yourself."

"It's not up to you, is it?" I cross my arms over my chest.

Zane sighs, his fingers tightening on the steering wheel. "I don't know why you have to be so stubborn. Especially when someone is offering you help."

"This is something I need to do on my own," I say.

"Why? Give me one good reason."

I falter. "Because—because it just is."

Zane chuckles. "Not very convincing."

I turn away. Zane would never understand that I don't want him to come because I'm trying to protect him. People close to me are collateral damage, and I can't afford for anyone else I care about to be hurt.

If there's one thing these past few weeks have taught me, it's that I will fight for the ones I love.

10

Zane

The ivory keys are familiar beneath my fingertips as I sit at the Stetson piano in the study. It's been too long since I've played, and yet, my fingers know the song and move on their own accord.

It's a beautiful melody, one I wrote a few years ago. Back then, when I spent hours playing and perfecting the song, I anticipated playing it for Arian on our wedding day. But now—

So much has changed.

How can I conceive of marrying a woman I don't love? How can I plan a life and a future with someone when all the while I'm wishing it were someone else? It doesn't seem fair to Arian or me.

I'm fiddling around on the piano when a new melody pops in my head. It starts off wistful and light with lilting chords and soft passages. Ironically, it mirrors my feelings for Sienna. This new song seems to flow from my fingertips, and it's probably the most beautiful thing I've ever played or composed.

As I pour the song from my heart to my hands, I picture Sienna's green eyes, her freckled cheeks, her blazing hair. She's strong and fiery and unlike any girl I've ever met. But she can never be mine. The song moves to a heavier undertone, like it senses the weight of my heart. My fingers pick up the pace, moving quickly up and down the keys.

Forgotten

I wish Sienna would allow me to go with her to Rubex, but no matter how much I demand, how much I plead, she refuses. She has her reasons, and I'm willing to respect her decision. For now. But as soon as her mother and sister are secure in the safe house, I'll find an excuse to go to the Capital. Because I meant it when I said she isn't fighting Radcliffe alone. I left her alone once before, and I don't intend to do it again.

I don't realize how enraptured I am in the song until I play the last note and heavy hands clap from behind me. With the last note still ringing through the air, I turn on the bench to find my father leaning in the doorway of the study.

"Your mother would be proud. She always wanted a son who could play the piano." He comes in and takes a seat on an armchair across from me. "She used to play. Did you know?"

I shake my head. My dad has never said much about my mother. All that I've learned about her I've gleaned from talking with Greta.

"She was an amazing woman," Harlow says with a glazed look in his eyes. "I loved her so much. But I guess it wasn't enough."

When I don't say anything, he clasps his hands together, his expression earnest. "Listen, son—"

"Please don't—don't call me that," I say through clenched teeth.

"You are still my son. Please, Zane, try to understand. I didn't want to hurt you."

I rise quickly from the piano bench. "I don't know who you are anymore. A man who experiments on children? Who orders his geneticist to kill an innocent baby? Who gets his wife killed?"

"Zane, please—"

"No, you listen, Father. The damage has been done. I don't know if this—" I gesture to the two of us. "Can ever be repaired."

Harlow rises from his chair and takes a few steps toward me. "Tread carefully, son. This is your future we're talking about. Don't go throwing it away over my stupid mistakes."

"They're more than mistakes, Father. What you did was horrible. Unforgivable." Shaking my head, I back away from him. "I don't know if I can ever forgive you."

My father's eyes plead with me. "Please, Zane, don't say that. I still want you to take over the company someday, and I still need you to marry Arian."

"Perhaps you should get your real son to do that."

"Now, Zane—"

I hold up my hand to stop him from speaking. "Please, don't. I've heard enough."

As I stride out of the room, Harlow calls after me. "If you turn your back on me, you'll regret it. I can promise you that."

He may be right, but at this moment, it's the only defense I have. Without looking back, I leave the room, and my father, behind.

11

Sienna

The goodbye is a bittersweet one. I'm anxious to get to Rubex and figure out what is going on with Trey, but who knows how long it will be before I see Mom and Emily again.

We're standing on the platform, waiting for the bullet train that will take me to Rubex while a black vehicle waits only a few feet away, ready to take Mom and Emily to the safe house. Zane and the one security guard he's hired are standing off to the side, giving us some privacy.

Squeezing Emily tight, I whisper in her ear to be good for Mom. She's so young that all the changes don't seem to affect her much. But it's my mother I'm worried about. Her eyes are red and swollen and have been leaking tears ever since I told her I'm going to the Capital, and she and Emily to a safe house.

Mom pulls me in for a lingering hug. "Please be careful, Sienna."

My arms tighten around her back. "I will."

When she releases me, she gives me a sad smile before taking Emily by the hand and moving toward the vehicle. The guard named Ruben hurries forward and opens the back door for them. As they climb into the backseat, Zane grips my elbow and leads me a few feet away.

"I'll stay a couple of days until they're settled," he says, speaking low. "And Ruben won't leave their side."

"Can he be trusted?"

"Absolutely. I trust him with my own life." He hands me a micro card and something that looks like a key chip. "When you get to Rubex, go directly to my condo there. The door has an electronic lock, but the key should get you in."

"Should?"

"Sorry. It *will* get you in." His eyes find mine. "Please be careful."

"Okay."

"The condo will be stocked with food, but the micro card can be used for any purchases you need to make."

"Zane—" I start to protest. This is too much. I'm not sure how I'll ever repay him for all he's done for my family and me.

"Just use it," he says. He then pulls a small box from his pocket. "Lastly, this is for you." He gives me a tentative smile as he hands it to me.

Surprised, I take the box and carefully lift the lid. A soft gasp escapes when I catch a glimpse of what rests inside on the soft velvet. An oval-shaped locket with the imprint of a butterfly etched on the golden surface.

"It's beautiful," I say. "But you shouldn't have—"

"Your Fringe tattoo connects you to Trey. I wanted you to have something that connects you to me." He nods at the locket. "May I?"

Taking the necklace, he moves behind me, sweeping my hair to one side, and clasps the jewelry around my neck. His warm fingers brush against my skin, raising the hair at the nape of my neck. Once it's in place, the locket rests in the crevice between my breasts, only a few inches from my heart, and I think how symbolic it is.

"I know how much you like butterflies," he says as I turn around to face him.

My fingers brush against the cool metal, tracing the

intricate outline of the butterfly. "I love it. Thank you."

His eyes linger on me, searching my face, before he leans in and gives me a quick kiss on my cheek. "Be careful," he whispers in my ear.

I watch as he climbs into the SUV, and he, Ruben, Mom, and Emily pull away, my sister waving frantically from the back window. My throat constricts a little watching them go, but I know it's necessary to protect them. As long as Radcliffe is out there, they'll never be safe. *I'll* never be safe. And the sooner I can get to the Capital, the sooner I can finish this.

Once they're out of sight, I take a seat on a bench under one of the white mushroom-shaped covered platforms and wait for the bullet train. When I catch a chestnut-haired guy seated under one of the other platforms staring at me, I look away.

The sleek silver train enters the station with a whoosh of air. Along with all the other passengers, I move to the sets of doors that open automatically. I'm jostled a bit, but once inside, I scan the micro card Zane gave me and find a seat near the back of the car. I scoot over until I'm closest to the window. The seats are firm and upright, but thankfully, with the bullet train traveling at over six hundred kilometers per hour, this trip shouldn't take long.

As the train begins to move, I feel a body slide into the seat next to mine, and I turn, surprised. It's the guy who was staring at me on the platform.

Clearing my throat, I say, "This seat's taken."

His face twists in confusion. "It is? I'm sorry. It looked like you were all alone."

My hand unconsciously moves to the necklace at my throat. I swallow hard, all of a sudden wishing Zane were with me. "Well, I'm not." I glance behind me down the long aisle. "My boyfriend's in the bathroom. He'll be out in a minute."

The guy rises from the seat. "I'll get out of the way then."

He moves a few feet away to an aisle seat only one up and

diagonal from the one before. If he turns his head, he has a perfect view of the empty seat beside me, and as the minutes tick by and my imaginary boyfriend has yet to show, I start to sweat. The only good thing is that he's immersed in the comscreen in his hands.

Trying to be as discreet as possible, I shoulder my bag that contains the few clothes I had a chance to grab from my house, and move down the aisle, away from the chestnut-haired guy and his downturned head. When I reach the end of the car, the doors open with a whoosh. I step across the metal platform and enter the other car where there are considerably more people. Heaving a sigh of relief, I find an aisle seat next to a smartly dressed woman who's so busy talking on her Lynk that she barely notices me.

The closer we get to the Capital, the tighter the knots in my stomach become. Then, when we're only a few miles out, and there's an abundance of green and trees—so much different from our desert landscape—I think I'm going to vomit. I've only been to the Capital a couple of times in my life, and both times were with my parents, when I was much younger. It was back when the towering buildings held interest and intrigue, not danger and deception.

As the first mega skyscrapers appear, I am in awe. They are so much bigger than any of our buildings back home. From here, I can see the Bulletins, the giant netscreens displayed all over the city, each one flashing a different celebrity picture, product ad, or insta-news report. The screens are attached to the skyscrapers and tower over much of the city. I remember my dad used to remark that the Bulletins always reminded him of giant eyes watching our every move. I guess in a way, they do feel like that, but still, I like all the lights and flashing pictures. It makes me wonder if this is what Legas looked like years ago.

Craning my neck, I try to see past the woman beside me who is still doing business on her Lynk. There's one thing I'm more interested in seeing than anything else, one thing that was the highlight of our trips when I was a kid, and the one thing I've always wanted to see again.

As we enter the city, the towering glass buildings dwarfing us and casting us in shadows, I catch a glimpse of it in the distance, the blue water sparkling in the sunlight. Pacifica's ocean.

And then, it's gone. Now that I'm surrounded on all sides by buildings, the ocean is hidden from view.

The bullet train begins its speed decrease, and I can feel it in my belly, like one part of me is still half a mile back there on the tracks. Once we've pulled into the station, I gather my bag and follow the crowd of people to the doors. There are so many languages being spoken that I don't understand what anyone is saying. Not until I hear a voice behind me as I'm walking down the platform away from the train.

"You didn't have to lie, you know."

I turn to see the guy from earlier. He's only a few steps behind, clearly moving in the same direction. *Is he following me?* Fear makes my fists clench.

"I don't know what you're talking about," I say, my tone defiant.

He takes a step closer. All of a sudden, we are an island in a sea of people who are trying to navigate around us. I try to step back, but there are too many people.

"Your boyfriend? Is he still in the bathroom?" It's hard to tell if he's angry or being playful, because he's pulled on sunshades and I can't see his eyes.

"That's none of your business," I snap. Turning on my heel, I stride away, telling myself not to look to see if he's following me until I'm a good distance away. It's only as I exit the station that I dare a glance back. Thankfully, he's nowhere in sight.

Zane's condo is a high-rise building on the water. As I step into the elevator and push the seventy-eighth floor, I have to press my lips together to keep a goofy grin from spreading across my face. I'm the only one in the elevator, so when it starts to move and my stomach literally drops to my knees, I'm not too embarrassed to wrap my arms around myself and hold tight. Pressure builds in my ears and I yawn, so grateful for the pop and sweet release that follows.

As I exit the elevator on the seventy-eighth floor, I gather from the giant R etched in the glass wall that this is the Ryders' own private floor. I try to prepare myself for what his penthouse might look like, but when I use the key chip to open the door, there aren't words to describe what I see.

I inch my way over to the floor-to-ceiling windows. They look out over the ocean and make me feel like I'm not only looking out over the water, but also the whole world. From here, I see the endless blue of the sea, not the churning, frothy tides or the undulating waves. Just an eternal blue, with no beginning and no end. I've never seen anything so beautiful.

The people and cars below look like miniature versions of themselves, so tiny that they are like an entire community of shrunken people. Tiny people who hurry to work, drive tiny cars, and stop for tiny lights. The only large thing about the view, other than the ocean, are the giant Bulletins, displayed all throughout the city. I'm so high up that I now look down on the screens and can barely see what is advertised.

Once I tear my gaze from the window, I take in the inside of the condo. According to Zane, the Ryders only come here a few times a year, and yet, the place is immaculate. It's decorated in neutral creams and grays that instill a calm, soothing effect. A pewter vase filled with a bouquet of flowers in all colors of the rainbow rests on the glass coffee table, almost like someone was expecting my arrival.

I set my bag on the couch that looks like it would be incredibly uncomfortable to sit on, and I look around. There's a huge bedroom off to the left, with a walk-in closet the size of my room back home, and a bathroom with a tub so big two people could go swimming in it. I'm tempted to jump on the king-sized bed.

The rest of the condo reveals three more bedrooms and at least four more bathrooms, a game room, an office, and a small library. Even though I'd like to revel in the moment of being in a place like *this*, it's time to get to work.

Taking a seat on the couch, which turns out to be more comfortable than it looks, I pull my bag onto my lap. My overnight bag only contains a few clothes because the rest of the space is filled with equipment. Pulling out my transcriber, the handheld comscreen Zane let me borrow, my Lynk, and the two guns Trina gave me, I place them all on the glass-topped table.

I dial Chaz.

He already knows everything about this trip to Rubex, thanks to our conversation yesterday, so I'm not surprised when he answers immediately.

"I'm here," I say when I see him.

"How was the bullet train?" he asks, his grin taking up most of the screen. "I hear it's even faster now than it used to be?"

"Fast," I say. "You would love it."

"I still think you should have let me come with you," he says. "I could have provided much-needed entertainment when you get lonely."

I return his smile. "You know why you can't be here, Chaz. It's too dangerous, for anyone who's close to me." I clear my throat, ready to get down to business. "Now, here are the coordinates of where I'm staying. Have you been able to get a hit on Trey yet?" Chaz was supposed to be checking traffic cams to see if Trey's facial image would ping.

"I did. Twice. For the past two days, at exactly one o'clock, his image pinged near the fountain at Gable Street. There's a park there. And guess what's directly across the street from the park?"

Chaz doesn't wait for me to guess.

"The launch for the AIG facility," he says.

"The launch?"

"Yeah, this facility is actually built over the water, not too far from shore. Those who are allowed access use the launch—an underwater tube—to get there."

Deep down, I knew this was where Radcliffe would want Trey—the AIG facility. But whether it's to study him or use him to gain information, I have no idea.

"Can you send me the coordinates for this park?"

"Sure thing." A few clicks of the keys, and then he says, "Done."

"Thanks, Chaz." I contemplate telling Chaz about the guy on the train, but then think better of it. It was probably nothing, just someone I should forget about.

When we hang up, I grab something to eat from the pantry that's already stocked with pre-packaged food. All I have to do is zap it in the micro-heater and a perfectly delicious steak and potatoes emerges. It may be a little much for a late-morning snack, but I'm not complaining. It's better than Meat Crap Delite, any day.

I could get used to this lifestyle.

Once I'm finished and my serving container has practically been licked clean, I pocket the micro card Zane gave me, just in case I need to use it, and leave the penthouse. As I exit the building, I'm almost giddy with excitement. I'm finally doing something to get Trey back.

The air is cooler here, probably a result of the breeze that comes in off the ocean, and the shadows the large buildings create. Using the coordinates Chaz gave me as a guide, I maneuver past the dozens of Citizens on the streets. The park Chaz told me about is only a few blocks from Zane's high-rise condo. Sure enough, I can see the distinct silver horseshoe-shaped building set over the water a few hundred yards from shore. The supposed "launch" at the shore's edge is heavily guarded by men with guns.

I take a seat on a park bench, giving me a perfect view of the launch. Surrounded by the gray, steel, and glass of the nearby buildings, the bright green of the grass and outlying trees is a nice contrast, as is the blue of the ocean that I can see clearly from here. Water pours over the rotating silver orb of the fountain to my left, some of the spray landing only inches from my feet. Pulling on a pair of sunglasses, I commence my "stakeout."

Women walk by wearing holographic business suits with miniskirts. One woman in particular, her hair twisted up into an elaborate updo that fans around her head like a peacock, is wearing a tight dress covered in tiny scales that shimmer in the sun. I glance down at my own outfit—pants and a black tank top. I look ridiculously out of place here.

After about half an hour of people watching, I see him, and my throat closes. He looks so different that I almost don't recognize him. Dressed in a business suit, he's making his way past the guards at the launch, a brown briefcase in hand. I'm used to seeing him in T-shirts, with muscles peeking beneath the sleeves, so to see him dressed so formally looks wrong.

A part of me wants to run to him, the part that, deep down, still believes he loves me. But the rational side forces me to remain in my spot on the park bench and watch him. Strangely, when he's halfway between the launch and me, he stops and glances around. I duck my head, pretending to be immersed in my Lynk, but occasionally peeking up at him.

His mouth turns down into a frown as he stares at a cafe

across from the park. I'm not sure how long he stands there, staring, thinking, before he shakes his head and continues.

If I turn slightly in my seat and rest my arm over the back of the park bench, I can watch Trey walk the path through the park until he reaches another bench where a blonde girl is waiting for him. My stomach recoils.

Rayne.

Trey takes a seat next to her, and then leans over, giving her a quick kiss on the cheek. I want to scream when, as he pulls away, Rayne wraps her arms around his neck and draws him back in, kissing him deeply on the mouth. I have to turn away, my stomach dipping and churning.

When I think it's safe, I venture another glance. Rayne is pulling wrapped food from her bag, which she hands to Trey. Trey unwraps a sandwich and takes a big, messy bite, an action that produces a memory of us in the Compound cafeteria. Table manners were never his strong suit. For a moment, I see him as the guy under the suit, the one who rescued me from the SGF when Radcliffe and his cronies were water torturing me, the guy who led rescue missions for juvenile inmates, and the one who is the leader of the Fringe.

But as I watch him and Rayne, eating, conversing easily, it all seems so real that I start to second-guess myself. What if *this* is real and what we had in the Compound was pretend?

When they finish eating, Rayne takes all the trash and deposits it into one of the compact incinerators that can be found every fifty feet or so around the park. Even though I don't want to, I watch as Trey rises from the bench. I can't tear my eyes away. He and Rayne embrace, a long, lingering hug that turns into an even longer kiss.

I inhale deeply, trying to work past the knot in my throat. This was a mistake. I should have let Zane come with me. His soothing words and strong arms would be reassuring right about now.

Positive I've seen enough, I get up from the park bench, and with my head down, start back to the high-rise.

I'm no closer to figuring out how to help Trey, and yet, I now have all these doubts swimming through my head. Trey's mind may have been altered, but those are his own emotions. And he sure as hell didn't look like he was being forced to kiss Rayne, not today nor the other day at Zane's house. Which leaves me to wonder...

What if he doesn't want to remember? What if he doesn't want to be fixed?

12
Zane

Once Vivian and Emily Preston are settled at the safe house in the mountains, with Ruben acting as their security guard, I return to Legas. As soon as I pull into the driveway of my home, my heart sinks. There, parked in the driveway, is Arian's red convertible. I haven't seen or spoken to her in days, and I'm dreading this confrontation.

I find her in the kitchen, sitting on a barstool, talking with Greta. When I enter the room, Greta gives me a knowing look and excuses herself, muttering something about the laundry. Arian's eyes flash when she turns to me.

"Where have you been? I've been trying to call you—"

"I had my Lynk turned off," I explain. I didn't want anyone to be able to track my whereabouts and therefore the location of the safe house, so I'd turned my Lynk off to be cautious.

Arian frowns. "But where were you?"

"I had to go away for a few days." I'm not prepared for this. I haven't come up with a good story to tell her yet.

Her forehead creases as her frown deepens. "But you didn't tell me you were leaving. I—I was worried about you."

I soften at her words. "I'm sorry. I didn't mean to worry you. It was a last-minute trip."

She slides off the barstool and moves closer. "Please don't do that again. Leave without saying anything."

"I won't. I promise." Even as I say it, I'm not sure it's a promise I can keep. And it kills me to lie to her.

"We're going to be married soon," she continues, placing her hand on my chest. "We should tell each other everything." Her eyes peer into mine, her blue eyes framed by long lashes. She's gorgeous. Any man would be lucky to have her. And yet, I feel a pull to someone else. Does that make me crazy? Or just plain stupid?

"I agree," I murmur as she moves closer.

"I miss you when I don't see you," she adds.

How can I tell her that I don't feel the same? That when I'm with her, I'm thinking of someone else. That when I'm not with her, I'm still thinking of someone else.

"I'm here now," I say.

"Yes, you are," she whispers before her lips settle on mine. I can't very well push her away. She is, after all, my fiancée. But kissing Arian is so completely different from kissing Sienna. Sienna's kisses are lightning, passion, and fire whereas Arian's are sugar, softness, and honeysuckles.

She even tastes like honeysuckles.

"What was that for?" I ask when she pulls away.

She shrugs. "Like I said, I missed you." She takes a seat on the barstool again. "And I'll miss you when I leave for the Capital tomorrow."

I stiffen. "The Capital? You're going to Rubex?"

"Yes. They're having a wedding expo in Rubex the next few days, and I thought it would be fun." She gives me a coy smile. "Care to join me?"

That's one way to get to Rubex and check on Sienna.

I smile at her. "I would love to. Where were you planning to stay?"

"My father's beach house."

"That's perfect. I'll stay in the condo, you can stay in the beach house, and then we can meet up."

Arian tilts her head to the side. "I'd prefer to stay in the condo with you. It's so close to everything since it's right there in the heart of the city. It takes almost an hour to drive from Father's beach house."

I hesitate. "Well, Sienna's there now. You remember my cousin Sienna, don't you?"

She nods. "And I also remember that the Ryder condo has several bedrooms. Am I correct?"

"Well, yes——"

"Perfect!" She beams. "This will give me a chance to get to know Sienna. I know how close the two of you are."

My brain moves quickly through the scenario. Arian, Sienna, and I in the same condo. It would be crazy. Ludicrous, actually. But how am I supposed to get out of this?

The muscles in my neck tighten, but I manage to force a smile. "What a great idea. Sienna will be so surprised." *That's an understatement.*

"Oh good!" Arian laughs. "This is so exciting." She hops off the barstool. "I'll hurry home and start packing then." Leaning in, she gives me a light peck on the cheek. "See you in the morning."

I watch her until she's left the room, and then I sink down on the barstool she was just occupying.

Oh, crap. What have I done?

13

Sienna

For two days, I do this—go to the park around noon and wait for Trey to come out of the launch, kiss Rayne, and unwrap a sandwich. Their routine is simple, predictable, the only things changing are the outfits Rayne wears and the color of Trey's tie. And each day, Trey stops just after exiting the launch and stares off at that little cafe across from the park. If he wants to go there so badly, I don't know why he and Rayne don't just eat there instead.

But after two days, I know I need to do something. I feel this itch under my skin to find information. To get the answers I came here for.

I've just entered the condo after my daily outing when I'm immediately put on high alert. Suitcases are stacked in the entryway—enough for a couple of months stay—and there's a sweet smell in the air, like ambrosia mixed with honeysuckle. The tinkling of laughter can be heard coming from the kitchen.

Blood pulses against my temple, and I press my body against the wall. Zane didn't mention anyone else coming to stay. I grab a heavy decorative candlestick off the credenza in the foyer, and with quiet footsteps, I make my way past the living room to the kitchen, only to be shocked by the sight of Zane and Arian.

Arian is the first to see me standing there, the candlestick raised in my fist. Her mouth drops open in shock as Zane turns and sees me. He hurries over and grabs the candlestick from my hand.

"No need for that," he murmurs.

"What are you doing here?" I demand. "I told you not to come."

"Need I remind you that this is my condo?" Zane replies through clenched teeth. "I can visit if I like."

A heated flush spreads over my body, and I immediately feel stupid. Of course this is his place, and it's his right to put me in mine.

Arian rushes forward. "Hello, Sienna, it's so good to see you," she says, pulling me into a delicate embrace. I can feel the lean muscles of her back through her shirt. "And please don't be angry with Zane. It was my idea to surprise you."

"I'm definitely surprised," I say.

Arian smiles, showing off her perfect white teeth. "Oh good! I absolutely love surprises. I knew you'd love this one."

I force a smile. "I do." Then turning my attention to Zane, I say, "Zane, can I speak to you in the other room for a minute?"

Zane's eyes flit from me to Arian before he nods. Grabbing his arm, I pull him into the living room, flashing Arian a reassuring smile as I do.

Once we're out of earshot, I hiss, "What are you doing here? And why did she come?"

"I'm sorry," he says. "She was already planning a trip to Rubex and I wanted to check on you, so it seemed like a good idea at the time. Maybe not such a great idea now."

"I told you not to come. Do you know how much harder it will be now? With her here? This totally screws up everything!"

"I know, and I'm really sorry." He pauses. "But the good news is that she'll be busy doing her own thing in the city. There's a wedding expo this week with hundreds of different vendors that she's really excited about."

I shake my head, too angry to speak. This isn't a freaking holiday. We aren't here to have fun or look at wedding dresses. I have two things I need to do. One—eliminate Radcliffe. And two—get Trey back.

"Don't worry about me," I snap. "I'll take care of everything while you go off gallivanting with Arian and planning your future wedding celebration. I'd hate to get in the way of that." I start to stride away, but Zane's hand latches onto my arm.

"Sienna, wait, it's not like that and you know it."

Shaking him off, I stride down the hall.

"Wait, Sienna, where are you going?"

"Out. I need some air."

"But we're not finished talking," he protests.

I hear Arian call for Zane from the kitchen. I walk out the front door and jab the elevator button. Zane follows me.

"Yes," I say. "We are." The door dings open.

"Just give me a minute—"

I step in, and the doors begin to close. Zane reaches out his hand to stop them, but then slowly removes it as if he's resigned himself to letting me go. His mouth is set in a hard line, his eyes a mixture of anger and disappointment. I look down at my feet until the elevator closes completely.

I stand in the elevator with my back pressed against the wall, breathing hard, my heart strumming a rhythm against my rib cage, my hands trembling. I'm already regretting my decision to walk out, and I'm half-tempted to go back in and apologize. But when I think of Arian, who Zane *allowed* to come, the anger flares back up like a glowing furnace.

He could have come up with an excuse for her not to come. Or at least not to stay in his condo. Which means that deep down, he wanted her here. And, yeah, that stings a little.

I need to cool off. Maybe a walk will help.

I punch the ground-level button and wait. The trip down is filled with stomach-dropping quickness, ear-popping pressure, and time to think.

I need a plan. There's no way I'll be able to get close to Trey until Radcliffe is out of the picture. Yet, Radcliffe is bound to be heavily guarded, and he's on the lookout for anyone associated with the Fringe, which could make it difficult to gain access to him.

When I exit the building, I stop, deciding which way to go. I know the park is a few blocks to the left, but I've yet to explore this other part of the city. I head down the sidewalk, away from the high-rise condo. Once again, I stand out in my dark pants and shirt while everyone else is dressed in the latest fashions—shimmery skirts, faux-metal corsets, and spiked heels.

I pass hotels, other condos equally as impressive as Zane's, and business buildings. Every so often, when the block ends, I catch a glimpse of the bay. Longing to be closer to it, I turn down a side street. Once I cross the street again, the only thing separating me from the blue waters is the metal railing. Leaning over, I inhale deeply, the salty air filling my nose.

I close my eyes and tilt my head back, the sun warming my face, the ocean breeze cooling my skin. I'm thinking how peaceful it is here by the ocean, despite the occasional air horn that blares in the distance, when someone grabs me from behind. I open my mouth to scream, but the sound is stifled by a hand clamping over my mouth.

"Well, well, Miss Preston," a voice I know all too well says. "It's good to see you again."

Before I can fight back, I feel a pinch in my neck, the ocean spins, and everything goes black.

14
Sienna

My body is a leaden, dead weight. I can't move anything, not my legs, not my arms, not even my eyelids. My eyes refuse to open. Only my other senses remain intact. Muffled voices move in and out of hearing range. The smell of disinfectant hangs thick in the air. My mouth is dry and cottony and feels like it's stuffed with a thousand paper towels. When I try to move my hand, my fingers twitch, causing a slight rustle of medical bed paper.

My right eyelid is forced open, and then I'm staring at a bright red light. The light has several rings around it, like a bullseye. The fingers holding my eyelid let go, and then move to the left. There's no pain, no pressure, only a feeling of numbness from my head to my toes.

I focus on the voices around me. One is male, deep, and oddly enough, sounds very familiar. It's not Radcliffe's voice, I'm sure of that, but I can't place it. Or recall how I recognize it.

"She volunteered to have her DNA altered, you say?" the one voice speaks.

Another voice I don't recognize. "Yeah. Just walked right up and turned herself over to Radcliffe. Something about being an orphan and knowing there's mental illness in her family. Didn't want to risk getting the same disease or something."

Me. They're talking about me. I try to force my eyes open, concentrating every last bit of energy on my eyelids. They open a tiny sliver, and bright white light forces its way in. Wincing, I squeeze them shut before trying again.

The room is blurry, fuzzy. White pendant lights hang from the ceiling and warm my body like an artificial sun. Everything is white—and sterile.

A figure moves into view, and even though it's blurry, I try to focus on the person's face. It's a man, an older gentleman dressed in a white lab coat with salt-and-pepper hair. He leans closer when he sees my eyes open, and my throat goes even drier, if that's possible.

I blink a few times, my eyelids so heavy they feel like they're coated in honey. I expect the face to change, to look different, but it's the same. The same brown eyes, the same graying hair, the same lines around his mouth.

No. This can't be real. I must be hallucinating.

I try to open my mouth to ask them what drug they gave me. To tell them I'm seeing things. But nothing works. Not my mouth or my tongue. My mind floats just beyond reach, past the point of making sense.

My father is dead. I saw him right after he died. I watched them bury his body.

And yet, this man—this man who moves around me and studies me with the clinical eye of a doctor—looks exactly like my father, right down to the tiny scar on his chin.

I can't breathe. I can't breathe. And I will suffocate right here.

I try to inhale, but it's as if a ton of bricks are pressing down on my chest. My mouth works like a fish, but no words come out. No words and no air.

"Elevated heart rate. She's showing signs of distress."

And of course I recognize the voice now. The voice of the man who soothed me when I had bad dreams as a child; the man who taught me how to find Ursa Major by studying the stars; the man who undoubtedly is my father.

My eyes roll back into my head, and blackness consumes me.

I'm floating above my body, looking down, looking down on the pale body of a red-haired girl who's lying on a paper-lined bed. A girl with a small locket hanging from her neck. The dark-haired doctor is checking vitals while the two women in lab coats write things down on a clipboard. The room is white, sterile, and uninviting.

When the man pricks me with a needle, inserting an IV, I don't feel a thing. The body on the table jerks in response, but it's not me. That girl isn't me because I'm right here. How can I possibly be two places at once?

For a moment, I feel a sense of escape, yet I'm not sure what I've escaped from. All I know is that I feel a freedom I can't explain. But as the man turns, and with fear in his eyes, pleads with the girl on the table to breathe, it all comes rushing back, like an ocean wave crashing over me, drowning me with the truth.

I haven't escaped anything. The knowledge is right there, teasing me, tormenting me.

My father is alive.

In an instant, I feel as though I've been kicked in the chest, and all the air leaves my lungs. When I look down, I see that the man, my dad, is giving me CPR.

Every inch of skin from my fingers to my toes tightens until I feel like I might rip through my skin. My chest squeezes like it's being gripped with an iron fist. I press my eyes closed and try to scream, but no sound escapes. There's a final tightening, a slight whoosh of air, and then my body feels heavy again as I inhale a long, raspy breath.

"Thatta girl. Breathe in. Nice and slow," the man says.

When I open my eyes, I find him staring at me, a small smile tweaking the corner of his mouth. That smile is so familiar it brings tears to my eyes. I've longed to see my dad smile, ached for his touch. And now, here he is, only inches away, and the most I can do is cry.

I try to speak instead. "Daddy," I whisper, but it's too soft. He can't hear that. Wetting my lips with my tongue, I try again. "Daddy?"

He tilts his head and gives me a sympathetic smile before looking across the room. "You told me this girl is an orphan. That she has no parents to speak of."

"That's right. She's a nobody." Wait. I recognize that voice. The voice of the man I hate more than anything or anyone who's ever walked the face of this earth. The man who ruined my life.

"Then why is she asking for her father?" My dad's face is slightly skeptical.

"She's probably just disoriented. She had a pretty big dose of Anamarin when we brought her in."

I try to turn my head to see him, this man I hate, but my neck is too stiff to move.

"Why did you give her Anamarin?" Dad asks.

"She was nervous. We thought it would help calm her down."

Liar.

"And you say that she volunteered?" Dad checks my vitals once more. His fingers are warm against my wrist.

"That's correct. Said she wanted to help improve our society."

A light flashes in my eyes, blocking my vision and causing black spots. "You gave us quite a scare," my dad murmurs, and I know he's talking to me. But what I don't understand is why he's not happy to see me? Why hasn't he pulled me into his arms and whispered that everything is going to be okay? Why is he pretending not to know me?

"Please keep me abreast of her progress over the next few days," Radcliffe says, his voice drawing closer. As he leans over the bed, I try to look away, but he's there, only inches from my face, and I can't move. "When we're through with you…" he whispers, his mouth mere inches from my ear. "You'll barely remember your name, much less that you ever had a thing for Trey Winchester."

Fear grips my chest and claws its way up my throat. I try to spit at him, but my mouth isn't working properly, so the only thing I manage to do is drool on myself.

Radcliffe laughs as he leans back. "I see you haven't lost your spunk." He winks at me. "It's only a matter of time."

I watch as he hobbles to the door, his titanium legs peeking out from the hem of his pants. The door closes behind him and I turn expectantly to look at my dad, sure he'll drop the act now that Radcliffe is gone. But he's too busy sitting on a stool in front of a computer screen, analyzing the lines and data that are pictured there.

"Dad," I whisper, trying to get his attention. He doesn't hear me, so I try again, louder. "Dad."

This time, he looks up, startled. Almost in a daze, he slides off the stool and walks over to the bedside.

"Dad, please," I whisper hoarsely. "It's me, Sienna."

"Just relax, Sienna. As soon as I'm done studying your body scan and DNA, we'll begin the procedure."

My eyes widen. Procedure? What procedure?

I give a low whimper. "Help me, please."

I feel his hand rest on mine. "It's okay. There's no need to be afraid. I promise you won't feel any pain. We'll keep you heavily sedated the next few days until all phases of the procedure are complete."

Tears fill my eyes. Why is he talking like this? Why does he refuse to acknowledge me?

Kristin Smith

"Dad," I whisper, trying one more time. "I want to go home."

He gets a sad look in his eyes before he says, "But, sweetie, you ran away from your home. Remember?"

And that's when it all comes crashing down. The truth I was denying. The reality I refused to believe.

My dad is alive. But he doesn't know me.

15
Zane

When Sienna hasn't returned by nine o'clock that night, I'm angry. By ten, I'm wary. And by midnight, I'm panicked.

Arian has long since gone to bed, and now I pace the living room floor, waiting for the front door to open and Sienna to apologize for staying out so late, for making me worry.

But she never comes through the door.

By the next morning, when she still hasn't returned, and she won't answer her Lynk, I know what I have to do. I was saving it for an emergency, but now that she's missing, this qualifies as one.

On my Lynk, I access the tracker in her necklace. Sure, the butterfly locket is pretty, but it also keeps me connected to her, just like I told her at the train station. The map pulls up, and I lock onto her location. A red flashing light indicates that she's in the ocean, not far from shore.

What the hell?

I zoom in. There's a building in that exact spot, and a quick search reveals that it's the Agency for Intelligence and Genetics, or AIG.

Letting out a slow breath, I lean back in the chair. She must have snuck in last night and is gathering information on Trey. If I bust in there now, I could ruin everything for her.

I decide to wait.

16

Sienna

A thick fog settles around me, and I am like a boat bobbing in the ocean with no clear direction and no lighted path. The fog sweeps in and consumes my tiny vessel, drowning me in its thick haze, lending me no course. The occasional voice rouses me, but they are disembodied voices, only words without faces.

As I slip in and out of consciousness, I have no concept of time or place, only a lingering numbness and ache in my heart that must be associated with the constant needle pricks and DNA analyzation.

There are times I dream, of phoenixes and butterflies, but for the life of me, I don't know why it's always the two of them, like they're interconnected somehow. I also dream of blonde curls, rolling meadows, and laughter in the wind. Sometimes I wonder if they're dreams at all, or vivid memories. I wish I knew.

Most often, there's a guy in these dreams, a dark-haired boy with a dimpled grin who coaxes me to do dangerous things. At the edge of a cliff overlooking the ocean, he holds out his hand. "Come with me," he says. When I refuse, he hurls himself over the cliff anyway. And when I look over the edge, he's gone, his body swallowed up by the roaring ocean and surging tides.

Hours, days, maybe even years, pass like this; I really don't know how long I've been here or where here is really. There's only this nagging feeling like I should be somewhere else, *doing* something else. Is anyone looking for me? Does anyone care?

There's a loud noise, like a door banging open, or maybe it's not a door at all but a gunshot. Or a plate being thrown against the wall. I'm too tired to care. The numbness is thinning, leaving a residue of achiness—must be time for another dose.

There's shouting—angry voices, male voices. Tubes plucked from my veins, solid arms beneath me, lifting me, carrying me. Cool air hits my skin; goose bumps rise on my arms and legs. I want to tell the person to put me back in the bed because I'm cold now, so very cold, but my mouth won't open. Neither will my eyes.

The person holding me—a man, I think—says something. "Who gave you permission to do this?" His voice is angry, demanding. He shifts me in his arms, his grip tightening.

There's a muffled response.

"I should have known Radcliffe is the one responsible for this." The guy's voice becomes low, threatening. "You tell Radcliffe that this just became very personal. He may have people in his pocket, but so do I."

His angry strides jostle my body until my head flops onto his shoulder. It's too heavy to hold upright anyway, so this is a nice place to rest it.

More cold air blows across my skin, and then there's a brightness behind my closed lids like we're only inches from the sun. I think my skin is melting off, each layer peeling back slowly, exposing the muscle, cartilage, and then bone underneath. I imagine myself a heaping pile of bones and sinew. Then I realize the sun is bright and yes, it's really warm, but it's not melting me away. I'm okay.

"Hang on," the man's voice says in my ear. "I've got you."

Then we're rocking, tipsy like, the smell of the salty ocean so strong I know it's close. Seagulls caw like they're flying directly overhead. The guy says something, and then I hear the gunning sound of an engine. From a boat perhaps?

I'm settled onto a lap as the guy takes a seat and grips me tighter. My head flops against his shoulder, my nose pressed into the soft flesh of his neck, and hands, warm hands, run up and down my arm. Then we're moving, bobbing along, a slight misty spray hitting my skin. The rhythm of the boat, the undulation of the waves, is calming, and I find myself drifting back to sleep. After all, it *is* time for my next dose.

Hushed voices tiptoe around the room. My head feels clearer, less foggy, and my body less numb. When I try to open my eyes, they cooperate this time, and I see a room with gray silk curtains, cream walls, and sleek furniture. When I turn my head, I'm staring into the warm brown eyes of a guy I don't know.

"Sienna," he says. And that's all it takes for me to remember. His smooth, deep, melodic voice.

Zane.

"Say it again," I whisper. Why does it feel like it's been forever since I've seen him?

His lips turn up into a smile. "Sienna," he says, lingering on each syllable.

"Where have you been?" I ask, my voice hoarse.

He looks at me, confused. "What do you mean? I've been right here, waiting for you to wake up."

"Wake up?"

Leaning close, he studies my face, his eyes searching every part. "You don't remember?"

I give a little shake of my head, wincing as I do.

"You were in Radcliffe's lab. They… experimented on you."

The name Radcliffe vaguely rings a bell. But a lab? Why was I there?

I wet my lips with my tongue. "How long?" I manage to croak.

He clears his throat, clearly uncomfortable. "Two days."

I search the recesses of my mind for any memory of the two days I spent in some lab. But there's nothing. Just a fogginess I can't explain or erase. I focus on eliminating the fog, clearing the clouds from my brain. I stretch my mind, searching for something, anything that will help me remember. Then, like a lighthouse illuminating a dark night, there's an image of a man. Kind smile, brown crinkly eyes, salt-and-pepper hair.

I gasp, and Zane leans forward, watching me. I remember now—the lab, Radcliffe, the man who looked unmistakably like my dad… all of it.

"I remember," I whisper. I squeeze my eyes shut, wishing I didn't.

Zane's warm hand covers mine. "You okay?"

My eyes fling open. He's staring at me with this concerned look on his face. "I think… I think my dad's alive. He was in the lab."

The concern on his face deepens. "You may think you saw your father, but—" He shakes his head sadly. "He wasn't there. I can promise you that."

"But he looked just like him," I protest. "I even talked to him. He analyzed my DNA, convinced me it wouldn't hurt."

"Sienna, you were heavily drugged. It messes with your mind."

"No, Zane. He was there. I saw him."

"Sienna—" His fingers squeeze mine.

"It's the truth," I say, ripping my hand from his grasp. "I know what I saw."

I remember the way the man's eyes crinkled at the edges and how the lines around his mouth deepened when he smiled. He was so familiar. Even his voice sounded just like my father's. But is it possible I hallucinated it all? Is it possible I only saw him because that's what I *wanted* to see?

Zane's voice is gentle when he speaks again. "When I got there, you were so out of it. You couldn't have known anything. When I first saw you…" His voice hitches. "I thought you were dead."

I shake my head, as if by doing so I can force the truth from my mind. I don't want to believe it. I want to cling to the thought—to the hope—that my father may miraculously still be alive. But the idea is ridiculous. We buried my father over a year ago.

Like a swiftly moving river, the notion that my father's alive is quickly getting swept away.

Of course Zane is right. Most of my time in the lab is one big, foggy blur. Obviously, the doctor I thought was my dad only *looks* like my dad, and I imprinted on him all those other qualities that made him seem familiar, fatherly even. His voice, his smile, his eyes. Given the circumstances, that explanation makes the most logical sense. I suddenly feel embarrassed for thinking my father could possibly still be alive. Talk about wishful thinking.

I force a smile. "You're right, of course."

"I'm sorry. I wish it were true. I really do."

"Wait. How did you know I was there?"

Zane's gaze travels to my neck and his fingers lift the locket, brushing against my skin. "Like I said, I wanted you to have something that connects you to me."

I stare at him, surprised. "You mean this locket is a tracker?"

He ducks his head and gives me a sheepish grin. "What can I say? I worry about you." His shoulders straighten. "And apparently, rightly so."

"But how did you get in? Did you break in?"

"After I tracked your location, I called a friend of mine who works in the facility. He found you logged in the system and confirmed what I already knew. He told me to come by boat and left the back door open for me."

The door to the bedroom swings open and in walks a gorgeous girl with hair the color of mahogany. She gives me a broad smile when she sees me. In one swift movement, Zane is on his feet. He kisses the girl on the cheek, and something black and ugly licks my insides. Who is this girl?

I hear them talking in hushed whispers as the girl keeps glancing in my direction. Her voice is louder, so I'm able to clearly hear what she's saying.

"How is she?" she asks.

"Better," Zane answers, his eyes sliding to mine.

"I still think she should go to the hospital—"

"No," Zane says firmly. "No hospitals. She'll be fine."

They're talking about me as if I'm not here. And I don't like how the girl is resting her long, slender fingers on Zane's chest.

"Hi," I say, giving her a little wave. "I'm Sienna."

The girl looks at Zane before turning to me and smiling. "Hi, Sienna, I'm Arian. Zane's fiancée."

My mouth drops open. I look at Zane. "Your fiancée? You never told me you have a fiancée."

Zane's gaze travels from me, and then back to Arian, before finally resting on me. "You don't remember Arian?" He walks slowly toward me before sinking into the armchair beside the bed.

I look at Arian and study her delicate face—heart-shaped lips, perfectly arched eyebrows, slender figure, long, silky hair. I'm certain I've never seen her before. I shake my head, fear filling the back of my throat. What else don't I remember? Who else have I forgotten?

Thankfully, this Arian girl takes it as her cue to leave. "I'll be right out here if you need me," she says to Zane. The door closes softly behind her.

The first words out of my mouth are, "You're engaged?"

Kristin Smith

Zane nods, his eyes pained.

"Why? Why are you marrying her?"

"It's complicated," he says, his mouth tight.

"But—but what about us?" I ask hesitantly.

The sigh that escapes Zane's lips is barely audible. "You don't want an *us*."

"That can't be true—" I start to say, but Zane interrupts.

"Sienna, why are you here in the Capital?" He's studying me, his eyes searching every inch of my face like there's a detailed map there and he's trying to find the key to unlocking its secrets.

Hmm, that's a good question. I came to the Capital to… to…

I vaguely remember getting on the bullet train, but for the life of me, I can't remember why. I shake my head in frustration. "I can't remember."

Zane leans closer until his face is only inches from mine. He has the teeniest, tiniest scar on his eyebrow that I never noticed before. It's kind of cute.

"Does the name Trey Winchester ring a bell?"

Trey Winchester. Trey Winchester. I toss the name around my head a few times, but there's nothing.

"No. Should it?"

As I watch Zane's face for an indication of what I'm missing, I see the internal struggle he's having. Finally, he sighs and says, "We'll figure this out. Don't worry."

But when he stands and leans down to kiss my cheek, his lips lingering next to my ear, his breath warm on my skin, all I want to do is turn my head a few inches. Turn my head until my lips connect with his.

And as he walks out of the room, I suddenly have the feeling I've forgotten something. Something very important. But what?

17

Sienna

"Have you remembered anything more?" Zane asks me as we walk along the boardwalk closest to the ocean with drippy ice cream cones in our hands. The sun is bright and beats down on my back.

I lick my cookies-and-cream scoop before it can run down my hand. "Not really."

Zane leads me to a bench on the outskirts of a park that overlooks the water and the silver horseshoe that rises out of the ocean like a sentinel. We have a clear view of the launch that takes employees back and forth to the lab through an underwater tube. As we take a seat, Zane's leg brushes against mine. I watch as his eyes scan the area in front of us, almost as if he's looking for someone. I nudge him with my shoulder.

"Everything okay?"

"Of course." He smiles at me. "I'm just enjoying spending time with you."

I roll my eyes as I lick the other side of the cone to even it out. "Won't Arian be jealous or something? I mean, she is, after all, your *fiancée*."

Zane shrugs like it's no big deal, but I see the embarrassed flush that creeps to his cheeks. "She understands."

I tip my head to the side and stare at him. "Understands what?"

His head shakes slightly. "Can we talk about something else? I'd prefer not to talk about her while I'm with you."

"Okay," I say. I scoot a little closer and rest my head on his shoulder. My ice cream cone drips a little on his arm. "Sorry!" I sit up, laughing.

Zane chuckles and pulls a napkin from his pocket, wiping his arm. "It's okay."

As I lick all around the cone, I stare out at the ocean. The sun is now obscured by dark clouds that are moving in off the bay, like the beginnings of a foreboding storm. A chill runs up my back as the wind picks up.

"Looks like rain," Zane murmurs, but his eyes aren't focused on the clouds. Instead, they are on someone who's exiting the tube. A dark-haired guy with broad shoulders and a confident stride to his walk.

Zane turns to me. Following my gaze, he asks, "Does he look familiar?"

I shake my head.

Nodding at the man's retreating figure, Zane says, "His name is Trey Winchester."

By now, I've gotten to the cone part and I take a big bite of the sugary goodness. "Okay."

"And Trey Winchester..." Zane continues, watching me. "Well, he's the whole reason we're here."

I stop in mid-chew. "Huh?"

"Trey Winchester..." Zane repeats slowly, as if he's talking to a small child. "He is the reason you and I came to the Capital."

My hand lowers, ice cream forgotten. "I don't understand. Are you telling me that I know him?"

Zane nods. "Not only do you know him... you love him."

I feel as though the breath has been knocked out of me, like I've been kicked repeatedly in the stomach. When I lean over, my head touches my knees as I try to grasp what Zane is saying. *I love that person? How? I don't even know him.*

"Are you sure?" I whisper. I sit up, my eyes following this Trey guy as he takes a seat on a bench next to a very pretty girl with hair the color of honey butter, and then proceeds to kiss her. "Looks like he's taken."

"It's a long story," Zane says.

I turn and chuck the rest of my ice cream into one of the open incinerators a few yards away. It lands smoothly in the rounded barrel. Surprised, I look at Zane.

"Nice shot," he says, smiling.

I grow serious. "Tell me. Tell me everything."

Zane sighs. With his eyes fixed on the ocean, he replays the last few days—no, actually, he says some of this stuff happened a few weeks ago. Some of it I remember, like my mom being abducted by Radcliffe and Zane helping me rescue her from the SGF, but when he talks about the Fringe or Trey, I have no recollection. It's like he's talking about someone else. Someone who's not me.

"I was part of the Fringe? That extremist group?"

Zane nods. "You have no idea how much I wish I could lie to you and tell you that none of that ever happened—that you don't love Trey—that you didn't join the Fringe, but I can't. I can't lie to you. It wouldn't be right."

I stare across the park at Trey and the blonde as they eat their lunch together. "Does he not remember either?"

"His memories were altered, just like yours. He thinks he's engaged to that girl. Her name is Rayne Williams." He studies me. "You said you knew her?"

"No," I say, shaking my head. "I don't think so."

"You do. You just don't remember."

Biting the inside of my cheek, I say, "So, why are we here? In the Capital, I mean?"

"Right after the SGF bombing, when you and Trey were recovering in my house, I found out that Trey is my brother. Same mother, different father." Zane swallows. "We're here to help him. Help him remember. And bring him home."

"I don't think I'll be much use now," I say sadly.

"This was your idea," Zane says, his voice growing urgent. "You had a fire in you before. A desire for justice. Please tell me you didn't lose that too."

I concentrate for a moment on how I'm feeling. Mostly confused, a little irritated that I can't remember anything, but no fire, no passion.

I sigh in frustration. "I'm sorry," I whisper.

Zane's arms are immediately around me, pulling me to his chest. "Hey, it's okay. We'll figure it out." His voice is soothing, and when I look up into his eyes, into the yellow flecks embedded in the warm golden brown, I feel less confused. His gaze travels down to my mouth and then back up to my eyes, like he's searching for something. Inches, mere inches, separate our lips, and if I strain my neck just a little—

Thunder sounds overhead, and I feel the first raindrops hit my face. Drawing back, Zane grabs my hand and pulls me to my feet. "Let's find someplace to wait it out."

The rain pounds down in sheets as we duck our heads and run for the nearest building, which is a block away from the park. As we run, Zane pulls me along, my short legs trying to keep up with his long ones.

When we reach the building, it's locked. My chest heaves, trying to catch my breath.

"Business building," Zane says over the roar of the rain. I think he means a keycard or digital scan for entry is needed. So instead, Zane pulls me around the side of the building until we're protected by an overhang. The rain runs like a waterfall off the roofline, but the overhang protects us from getting wetter than we already are.

Zane's breathing is smooth and controlled, but mine is erratic, my chest rising and falling twice as fast as his.

"Great job keeping up with me," Zane teases, the water

droplets from his hair running down his neck and into his shirt.

"Hey, I tried," I protest, glancing down at my dripping legs. "With short legs like these, running has never been my forte."

A loud clap of thunder makes me jump, bringing me closer to Zane.

He grins, staring down at me. The air between is charged with electricity just like the stormy air all around us. His eyes fixate on my mouth, and I can feel the blood pulsing through my body. But to my disappointment, he looks away and sighs.

"What?" I ask.

He motions to the two of us. "This. Us."

"What about us?"

Zane's mouth moves into a firm, straight line. "You chose Trey. Every time. And now—now it's like everything's…"

"Different?" I finish for him.

"Yes, different." He looks away, past the wall of water. "I don't know how to feel about it."

"Does it matter how I felt before?" I say. "Does it matter who I chose before?" I touch the side of his face, using my fingers to guide his gaze back to mine.

"I want to say no; I really do. But I can't. It does matter. It always will."

"But I'm different now." I focus on his lips, his smooth, full lips that turn down when he's concerned. I wish I could kiss his concern away.

"I know," he says softly. "And that's what scares me, yet, thrills me at the same time."

"We'll figure it out," I say, using the same phrase he keeps trying to reassure me with.

His eyes focus on my mouth again, and his hands grip the front of my wet T-shirt in his fists, dragging me closer. "I'm sorry," he whispers before his lips touch mine.

I'm not sure why he's apologizing. It certainly can't be for the kiss because it is beyond amazing. One hand moves to my neck, sweeping aside the wet hair that clings to it, while the other fits perfectly around my waist. My arms encircle his neck, my fingers pulling through his rain-slicked hair and skimming his hairline. Zane shivers and kisses me deeper, his touch and kisses hitting me in the deepest part of my belly.

The rain is letting up around us, the thunder now a distant boom, but I focus on the feel of his lips on mine, the warmth of his hands through my damp shirt, and the smell of his skin. Sandalwood and spice. When we pull apart, my heart is hammering against my ribs like a bass drum, and my breathing is rapid.

Zane rests his forehead against mine and stares into my eyes. "I hope you don't hate me for doing that," he says.

Why would I hate him? It was the best kiss I've ever had. At least, I think it was...

"I don't hate you." I smile up at him. "All I'm thinking about is when we can do that again."

Zane chuckles, but I can see the worry in his eyes. "Not soon enough." He kisses me on the nose before releasing me. The rain has stopped completely now, and the sun is beginning to peek behind the clouds. The dark gray sky has moved past, and now only blue remains. Glancing up at the sky, Zane says, "Let's go home."

As we walk along the boardwalk, headed for the condo, I can't help but wonder why Zane looks so serious.

18
Zane

The condo is quiet when we get back; Arian must be out shopping, which I've come to realize she does quite a bit. I'm actually glad she isn't here to see Sienna and I enter the condo together, both drenched from the rain. I think the guilt would be written on my face, and she would quickly guess that there's more to Sienna than family relations. I'm almost surprised she hasn't already caught on. It's getting harder and harder to hide my feelings for Sienna.

When we enter, Sienna and I both go still. The place is trashed. It looks like someone came through and dumped out every drawer and tore apart every cabinet, leaving a wake of destruction. The cushions have been ripped from the couch and flung across the room. Lamps are overturned, the shades crushed, and books are strewn all over the floor.

Instinctively, I push Sienna behind me like I can protect her.

"What happened?" she asks, her voice small.

"Stay here," I whisper. I go room to room, and each one looks the same. Torn apart, emptied out, destroyed. They were clearly looking for something. Or someone.

"We have to get out of here," I say, hurrying back over to Sienna, who is still standing in the entryway. "How quickly can you change your clothes and pack a bag?"

"Um, pretty quick?" She bites her lower lip, and my eyes are drawn to her mouth.

I shake my head. *Focus, Zane. Now is not the time.*

"Meet me right here in five minutes," I say. "Okay?"

She nods, but I can see the fear in her eyes. With this memory loss, she's so different. She's a softer version of the Sienna I fell in love with, one I want to protect all the more.

I grab a duffle bag from my closet and fill it with clothes, toiletries, and a few books. After tugging off my wet clothes, I get dressed in pants and a shirt. When five minutes have passed, I return to the living room where I find Sienna gingerly stepping over a pile of books.

"Who would do this?" she asks, bending down to pick up one of the books. She stares at the cover, reading the title aloud. "Poetry Through the Ages." Her eyes focus on me. "Are you a fan of poetry?"

I shrug and grab the book from her hands. "We can take this if you want to read it." I shove it into my duffle bag and take her hand. "All set?"

She nods, scanning the place. "You're just going to leave it like this?"

"I'll have someone come in and clean. Once we're gone." I begin to pull her toward the door, but she hesitates.

"Where will we go?"

I haven't thought that far ahead, my only concern getting her to a safe place. "We'll figure it out."

Still, her feet remain firmly planted. "What about Arian? We can't just leave without telling her."

"I'll send her a message right now."

Satisfied with my answers, Sienna moves forward, following me out the door and to the elevator. On the ride to the ground floor, I send Arian a voice message so she won't come back to the condo and be shocked out of her mind.

"Arian, my father decided to have the floors in the condo

redone this week, so we can't stay there after all. Sienna and I will be at a hotel, but perhaps you'd be more comfortable staying with your friend Wendy for a few days? Once you let me know where you'll be, I'll have Geoff bring your bags over. Sorry for the inconvenience."

When I end the message, Sienna gives me a slight nod of approval.

Geoff, my chauffeur, has the car waiting by the curb when we exit the building. He lifts open the door for Sienna and me to climb into the back. When he asks where we're headed, I tell him the fanciest hotel that I can think of—the Windsor Hotel. I'm sure he's surprised I'm taking another girl to such an extravagant hotel, but he doesn't question me. Sienna, however, does.

"Why are we going *there*?" she whispers.

"You'll see," is all I say.

When Geoff pulls up to the ornate structure of a hotel that takes up an entire city block, I step out of the vehicle and ask Sienna to remain where she is.

"I'll be right back," I reassure her.

A portly man holds open the glass door to the building, and I stride over to the polished wood of the check-in counter. A smartly dressed female with a headset gives me a smile.

"Can I help you?"

"I'd like to book a room—the nicest one you have—for a few nights."

"Name, please?" She looks down at her computer, her fingers clicking against the keys.

"Zane Ryder." As soon as I say my name, not surprisingly, she looks back up.

"Mr. Ryder, I'm sorry—I, uh, didn't recognize you." She gives me an apologetic smile.

My name carries a weight with it that I'll probably never get used to. People may not know my face, because Harlow kept me sheltered for so long, but they definitely know my name. I sometimes wish I could go somewhere where no one has ever heard of me or the name Ryder. But that's a lot to ask in a place like Pacifica.

I return her smile. "There's no need to apologize."

She glances back at her screen. "Well, let me just get a room pulled up for you."

After a few moments, she hands me the key cards. When she asks if I need help with my bags, I graciously decline.

I can feel her eyes on my back as I leave the way I came and climb back into my waiting vehicle. Geoff tilts his head in my direction, waiting for instructions.

"Take us away from the city, toward Heathrow," I tell him.

Geoff nods, pulling away from the curb and into the flow of traffic.

"Zane, where are we going?" Sienna asks, her eyes wide.

Gripping her hand in mine, I say, "I'll explain everything once we get there."

Satisfied for now with my answer, she settles back against her seat.

"Do you ever get used to it?" she asks suddenly.

"To what?"

"To having people wait on you. People opening your car doors and bringing your dinner." She makes a face. "I don't think I'd like it very much."

I chuckle at her honesty. "I don't think about it actually. It's the way things have always been. Since I don't know any different, I have nothing to compare it to." I shrug. "But I don't mind."

"I can't begin to imagine what your life has been like," she mutters, her eyes trained out the window and the skyscrapers passing by.

I want to tell her that my life was boring and routine before I met her. That I didn't realize how much I was missing.

But instead, all I say is, "Nor I yours."

She gives me a small smile before turning back to the window.

The scenery quickly changes from magnificent skyscrapers to neglected buildings. Lights flicker outside one particularly rundown structure that advertises Booze and Babes, but because the letter B is out in Booze, it reads: *ooze and Babes*. Disgusted, I turn away, especially because the parking lot is full.

When it doesn't appear that our surroundings could possibly get any worse, I see what I'm looking for. A seedy motel that looks like it belongs in a horror flick. The sign barely hanging on out front indicates that it's the Restful 8 Motel.

"Geoff, pull in here, please," I instruct, ignoring the surprised look he gives me.

"Are you sure about this, Mr. Ryder?" he questions, his eyes flicking up and down the darkened street.

Sienna is doing her own survey of the surroundings. By the look on her face, I can tell she's not pleased.

"What are you doing, Zane?" she hisses.

I pat her knee reassuringly. "You can drop us off at the office, Geoff," I say. Once the car has stopped and the door lifts open, I slide out, waiting for Sienna to exit also.

Her eyes are fearful as she looks around, but she gingerly steps from the car. As Geoff gets out to retrieve our bags from the trunk, I stop him. "I'll take it from here. Thank you."

Sienna tries to grab her own bag, but I shoulder both of them.

"Do you need anything else, Mr. Ryder?" Goeff asks, his hands folded in front of him.

"No, Geoff. I'll call when I require your services again." I nod politely in his direction and lead Sienna to the door of the motel's reception area.

A stout man with a protruding belly and squashed nose, probably from one too many beer brawls, is manning the front desk. When he sees us, he scoffs. "You lost?"

"No, sir. We're looking for a motel for a few nights. Do you have any rooms available?"

The stunned man stares at us, his eyes swinging back and forth from me to Sienna and then back to me. "Look, buddy, I don't want no trouble. I try to earn an honest living—if you're shacking up with this girl and your wife finds out, I don't wanna be the one responsible—"

My teeth grind against each other. I take a deep breath before I speak. "I would actually like two rooms."

As soon as I say this, Sienna slips her arm through mine and tugs on it, forcing me down until my ear is level with her mouth. "I don't want to be alone. Can we get one room?"

My stomach tightens. "Of course." Straightening up, I say to the guy, "We'd like one room for a few nights. Do you have any available?"

The man grumbles under his breath. "I suppose. But if your wife shows up, you'll pay for the damages? Right?"

I give him a tight smile. "That shouldn't be a problem since I'm not married."

The sigh the man heaves is enough to rattle the papers on the reception desk. "Well, why didn't ya say so? Coulda saved me a lotta heartache, ya know?"

After he asks my name and I give him a fake one, the man hands me a brass key.

"What's this?" I ask.

"The key to your room. Duh." The man shakes his head, coming around the side of the counter. "Room sixteen is outside and down on the left. We used to have a comscreen in there, but it was stolen." He winks at me. "You might enjoy Booze and Babes down the road instead. It's half-price Tuesday."

The dirty look Sienna gives the man does not go unnoticed by me. "Um, thanks… for the information."

Sienna follows me outside and hurries to keep pace with

my long strides. "What are we doing here, Zane? This is crazy!"

"No one will ever think to look for us here. You'll be safe." The numbers to room sixteen are hanging so that the six looks like it toppled over. "Here we are," I say, inserting the key into the ancient lock. "I didn't know they made keys like this anymore."

"They probably don't," Sienna mutters. "I have a feeling this place was around during the Dark Ages."

The smell when we enter the room is overpowering. It's a mixture of stale air, old cigarette smoke, mildew, and sweaty feet.

Gagging, Sienna runs from the room, gulping huge breaths of outside air. I gingerly cross the room, looking for a good place to set our bags. The carpet is filthy and stained, and I try not to picture what might have made those stains. I finally decide to place our bags on the sagging wooden dresser. It might be the only thing it's good for.

When Sienna enters the room, with her nose plugged, her eyes immediately go to the double bed in the middle of the small room.

"Oh," she says, her hand dropping to her side.

"It's okay," I say. "I'll sleep on the floor." I cringe even as I say it.

She glances down at the disgusting floor and scoffs at the idea. "Of course not. You may contract a disease if you do."

"Then I'll sleep on the couch." I point to the dilapidated couch in the corner with the equally sad coffee table in front. I think only half my body would fit, but I'm not about to mention that.

"Don't be silly," she says. "You can't fit on that thing."

Chuckling, I make my way to the bathroom to check it out. "Okay, then. We'll place pillows between us."

Moldy upright shower, cracked pedestal sink, and one stained toilet—looks to be about what I expected.

Sienna gives me a teasing grin. "What are you worried about, Zane? That I may attack you in your sleep?"

I decide to ignore her comment. It would be wrong for me to encourage her when I know how she feels about Trey—if only she could remember.

As Sienna searches through her bag for something, I sink down on the edge of the bed. Now that Sienna is safe, I can focus on the next important thing—figuring out what they did to her in the AIG to alter her memories.

I watch as Sienna digs through her bag before triumphantly pulling out her toothbrush, the back of her hair still damp from the rain. "When we first walked into the room, I may have vomited in my mouth a little. Thought I'd—" She stops. "What?"

As I'm staring at the back of her head, I suddenly have a thought. It's so obvious that I'm almost shocked I hadn't thought of it before.

Standing, I walk over to her. "I think I figured it out," I say. "May I?"

Before she can respond, I sweep the hair away from the base of her neck and peer at the spot where her hairline ends.

"What are you doing?"

"I'm looking for—there!" I see it now. A tiny incision. Barely visible unless you're looking for it. "Just what I thought." I turn her around to face me.

"What is it?"

My fingers work their way under her hair and press lightly on the base of her skull.

"Ow," she says. "What did you do?"

"You have a tiny incision back here. And I think I know what it's from."

"Care to share?"

"I'd rather show you." I send Geoff a message, asking him to pick us up in a few minutes.

Sienna gives me a questioning look, but she heads to the bathroom to brush her teeth. I wait impatiently by the door, nervously tapping my fingers on the door handle. *I hope I'm right. I really do.*

As soon as she exits the bathroom, I pull open the door and motion for her to follow me outside.

"Where are we going?" she asks.

"The Match 360 Headquarters."

"Why?"

I make sure the door is locked behind us. "Because I think I figured out how your memories were altered and what we can do to get them back."

19

Sienna

The Match 360 Headquarters is an all-glass high-rise that looks like someone came through with a giant hand and twisted the structure, kind of like an oversized DNA helix. It's a unique building, with grass and trees growing out of various levels.

Zane has yet to tell me why we're here, but no matter; I'm just grateful to be away from that seedy motel room and its pungent smell of grossness.

Even in Rubex, Zane has a driver he uses, and as we exit the black vehicle, we thank Geoff, the portly gentleman who resembles a penguin in his chauffeur attire. Of course, I don't tell him that.

Zane nods to the guards at the front of the building, who hurry to open the doors for him.

"Good afternoon, Mr. Ryder. We weren't expecting you," one guard fumbles.

"It's okay, Solan," Zane says smoothly. "It was a last-minute visit."

Once we cross the threshold, I can't stop myself from looking up, into an endless expanse that keeps climbing until it reaches the very top of the twenty-story building, all the way to the glass roof and the blue sky beyond. On either side of this open expanse are floors upon floors of balconies.

Zane hardly even notices.

"Should I let your brother know you are here?" the guard named Solan asks.

"That won't be necessary," Zane says. "I just need to get something from my father's office, and then we'll be on our way."

Solan nods and takes a step back. "If you need anything while you're here, please don't hesitate to ask."

Zane thanks him before taking my elbow and leading me to a set of elevators. The doors are made completely of frosted glass, with the Match 360 symbol etched onto it, so it's easy to see the elevator coming and going. When it arrives, we take it to the twentieth floor, watching as the reception area drops below us.

Mr. Ryder's office is heavily protected with fingerprint-activation technology and retina scans, but Zane punches in a bunch of numbers and bypasses it all. He gives me a wry smile. "Perks of being the director's son."

"And the future owner of the company," I remind him.

He looks away. "Um, yeah, that too." I can sense hesitancy in his voice, but I'm not sure why it's there. He should be proud that he will someday inherit the company from his father.

The door opens with a click, and after fumbling around for a moment, Zane finds the switch. The room is immediately bathed in light. The walls are white, the floors are white, even the office furniture is white. Mr. Ryder's sleek white desk appears to be suspended in mid-air, but upon closer inspection, I realize it's hanging from the ceiling by invisible wires. Outside the floor-to-ceiling windows is a balcony with a small lap pool. The turquoise water shimmers in the sunlight.

As I look around the office, Zane goes right to a cabinet on the far wall and pulls open a drawer, then another one, and then another. "I could have sworn he kept it here," he mutters when the last drawer yields nothing.

"What are you looking for? I can help," I offer.

"It's a handheld x-ray device." He uses his hands to indicate how big it will be.

My mind spins. Why would he need a handheld x-ray device? Unless...

"You think they put something inside me?" I ask, my fingertips reaching for the back of my head, grazing the spot Zane pressed on earlier. I can feel the puckered skin there, and I can't believe I didn't notice it before.

Zane stops his search long enough to look up. "Yes, I do."

"You mean a tracker? You think they put a tracker in my head?" My throat closes at the thought.

"I'm not sure." Zane gives me an encouraging smile. "Let's find the x-ray device, and then we can figure everything out."

I nod and start my search with Mr. Ryder's desk, the movement making the desk swing a little on the cables. The end drawer is stuck so I give it a tug. The drawer comes tumbling out, its contents falling onto the ground with a clatter. A pen, a notepad, a keycard, as well as other items.

"Crap," I mutter, bending down to gather everything back into the drawer. But when I pick up the drawer and try to wedge it back into place, it won't go. Placing the drawer back on the ground, I peer into the empty space where the drawer should be.

Bingo. I see the problem. Something's sticking out in the back. A piece of paper, maybe?

I feel along the backside of the desk with my hands, trying to extract whatever it is, but I can't get a good grip. Then, something pops out of place, one of the slats. At first, I'm scared I just broke Mr. Ryder's desk, but as I'm feeling around, I realize it isn't a piece of paper at all, but something else.

I grab the item in my fist and slowly pull it out. It's a protective sleeve with several computer chips inside. My first thought is that it must have fallen through a crack and slipped behind the drawer. But then I think of breaking into the Match 360 Legas facility with the hidden safe behind the painting of a Trojan horse. There's only one reason why this sleeve of computer chips would be behind the drawer.

They were hidden.

Which means they contain something that Mr. Ryder doesn't want anyone to know about.

"Um, Zane," I say, rising slowly to my feet. "You might want to see this."

He abandons his search on the other side of the room and walks over. "What is it?"

I hold up the protective sleeve. "I found it behind one of the desk drawers."

Zane takes the sleeve and studies it. He dumps the chips into his hand. Tipping his head back, he holds one of them up to the light. "What the hell?" he mutters.

"What is it?"

"These come from the lab. They're the same kind we use for our DNA coding. See?" He points to the tiny symbol on the backside of the chip—an infinity sign made with side-lying triangles. The symbol for Match 360.

Zane takes a seat at the desk and inserts the chip in the backside of the computer. A screen pops up, denying access. "It's password encrypted," he says under his breath.

"Here, I can help with that." I dial Chaz on my Lynk, and his grinning face pops up on the screen.

"Sienna! How's the Capital? Does Trey remember you yet?"

My eyes narrow. How does Chaz know Trey? They must have met? I shake my head, frustrated I can't remember anything that concerns Trey. "Um, no. There's been a slight change in plans."

"Change? What kind of change?" Chaz's eyebrows pull together in confusion.

"Look, I'll explain later." I tilt the Lynk so Chaz can see

Zane too. "I'm with Zane in his dad's office, and we found something we need your help with." I hold up a couple of the computer chips. "We want to know what's on these."

Chaz stares at Zane for a moment. "I can totally see the resemblance," he says suddenly.

"Resemblance?" Zane repeats, glancing at me.

"You and Trey. You're brothers, right?" Chaz grins. "Sienna told me."

I did? Don't remember that either.

"You're the first person to say we look alike." Zane clears his throat. "About Trey and me, I mean."

"It's the cheekbones and the jaw," Chaz says.

"Can we get on with this?" I say impatiently.

Zane's eyes widen as he turns to look at me.

"What?" I say, defensiveness prickling through.

"For a moment there, you sounded like..." He pauses. "Well, like yourself."

I open my mouth to retort that I have no idea what he's talking about when Chaz says, "Just upload them on your Lynk and send me the files. They shouldn't be too hard to crack."

"Doing it now." I insert the first chip into the slot on the bottom of my Lynk. A gray bar pops up on the screen. *Download in Progress.*

When all three chips are loaded onto my Lynk, I send the file to Chaz. I hear him shuffling to his computer, and then a beep as he hooks his Lynk up to it. His face is tilted at a weird angle now, like I'm looking up at him from down below, which makes his nose look bigger than it really is.

"This might take a minute," he says before he starts whistling some indistinct tune. But then I realize it's not indistinct at all—it's the theme song for his favorite show, *Return to Space.* Which basically means I can remember things as insignificant as a theme song to a show I care next to nothing about, but I can't remember being in love with Trey. It doesn't make sense.

Why would someone want to erase my memories of Trey? Make me forget him?

"I think I've got something," Chaz calls out. "I accessed the data on the chips, and it looks like it houses a bunch of numbers. Zero-three, thirteen, twenty-one, twenty." He rattles off a few more.

"Chaz, can you send the file to me?" Zane asks.

"What's your account?"

"Zaneryder at Match360." Zane takes a seat again at the desk and maneuvers through the intra-pages until he's staring at the file that Chaz sent. Chaz is right; it's sequences after sequences of numbers.

Zane stares at the computer and mutters, "No, not numbers. Dates." Glancing up at me, he says, "These are dates. Zero three is March, thirteen is the day of the month, and twenty-one twenty is the year."

"He's right," Chaz says, the excitement evident in his voice. "Hang on. Let me see if I can cross reference these dates and see if something pings."

For a couple of minutes, we listen to the *clack, clack, clack* of Chaz's computer keys before he announces triumphantly. "I got it. All of these dates have one thing in common. A recorded bombing by the Fringe that occurred either a day or two after."

"Well, that's strange—" I start to say.

"Sienna, you know what this means, right?" Chaz continues, his voice rising a few octaves in his excitement. "This means that these chips contain the dates that juvenile inmates were transferred from Confinement to the Chromo 120 lab."

I turn my Lynk so I can see Chaz's face. "What are you talking about? How did you get that information from the Fringe bombings?"

Chaz stares at me. "Sienna, are you okay?"

Zane clears his throat and speaks. "Sienna had a little… accident. Some of her memories have been altered, but we're working on getting them back."

"Altered?" Chaz says, his voice at the top of the scale now. "Like what they did to Trey?" A whoosh of air. "Oh, Lord have mercy, we have stepped in it now."

"It'll be okay," Zane reassures him. "But, listen, I want to know more about this correlation between the Fringe bombings and the juvenile inmates. Sienna mentioned it to me before."

Chaz goes quiet. "How do I know we can trust you? For all I know, *you're* the one experimenting on those poor kids."

"You can trust him," I jump in. It's *Zane*. Of course he can trust Zane. Plus, I'm really curious about this correlation myself.

Chaz hesitates before sighing. "When the Fringe gets word that a juvenile inmate has been taken from Confinement to one of Mr. Ryder's labs, they plan a bombing in another part of the city. It's a distraction. They extract the inmate while the Enforcers are occupied somewhere else. Even if they trigger an alarm, it would take the Enforcers a while to reach them."

Zane lets out a low whistle. "That's a pretty elaborate plan."

I'm still trying to wrap my mind around what Chaz just said. If this is true, that would make the Fringe not a terrorist group at all, but a rescue group. And therefore, it would make Trey a hero, not a hoodlum. Can this be true? Is this why I fell for him the first time? Because of his desire to help others?

I suddenly have an image that sears into my brain. An image of flames, leaping up into the sky, the feeling of intense heat on my face, and hard pavement beneath my body. Almost like… I was there.

And strangely, even though it's as if I'm hearing all of this for the first time, deep down, I know I'm not. I can feel the truth, climbing up from the depths of me, bursting from my skin, trying to latch on to something, anything, that makes sense.

"Why are these dates hidden behind a drawer in your dad's

office?" I ask Zane.

"I don't know. Honestly, I don't." Zane goes quiet for a moment. "Remember when I asked my dad about the juvenile inmates and he denied everything?"

I shake my head. Unfortunately, I don't.

Zane groans. "Of course not. Well, maybe this is just more proof that he was lying then."

"You think he hid these dates in the back of the drawer?" I ask. "Why would he do that?"

"Maybe to get rid of proof that he was involved?" Zane says. He rises to his feet and swears. "I can't trust that man. Everything he says is a lie, and I'm sick of it."

I lay a hand on his arm and feel the muscles tensing beneath. "I know, and I'm sorry. But right now, we need to focus on why we're here. We still need to find that x-ray device."

"Sienna," Chaz calls out from where I left the Lynk on the desk. "If you're done with me, I'm gonna go finish watching the tenth season of Return to Space. Just buzz me if you need anything else." With a click, he's gone.

Zane draws a shaky breath and gives me a wry smile. "This isn't exactly what I expected to find when I decided to search my father's office," he says. "I wanted to believe him. I wanted to believe that he'd changed." He shakes his head. "My mistake."

"I know how you're feeling," I say. "My dad lied to me my whole life. It sucks. I know."

Zane nods and turns away, resuming his search of the closet on the other side of the room. I carefully replace the chips back in the protective sleeve and insert it into the back slat of the desk. The drawer slides easily into place this time. I'm about to turn and begin searching the cabinet to my left when Zane calls out, "Found it."

I hurry over to the walk-in closet that's filled with various sports jackets, a couple of extra pairs of dress shoes, as well as a safe and a chest of drawers. Zane holds up a device with a white screen and handles on either side. "This is Genex, the latest advancement in x-ray technology."

"You're going to use that to see if I have something in the back of my head?"

"Exactly." Zane waves me over to the desk. "Go ahead and have a seat, and I'll take a look."

I'm about to take a seat at the desk when the door to Mr. Ryder's office springs open. Steele stands in the doorway, his arms crossed over his large chest.

"You should have told me you were coming, Zane," Steele says, looking down his nose at us.

I notice Zane hide the Genex behind his back as he squares his shoulders.

"I have just as much right to be here as you, Steele," Zane says evenly.

"In our father's office?"

A muscle in Zane's jaw twitches. "This will be my office someday."

Steele's eyes narrow as they swing to mine. "This is a family matter. So if you'll excuse us—"

"Anything you have to say to me," Zane interrupts, "you can say in front of her."

Steele and Zane stare each other down for a full minute before Steele finally speaks. "Lock the door on your way out." A moment later, he's gone.

After making sure Mr. Ryder's office is exactly as we found it, we sneak the Genex out of the building. Solan is still standing guard at the entrance, and he gives us a polite nod as we leave.

"Have a good afternoon, Mr. Ryder," he calls.

"You too, Solan," Zane says, and then, once we're a few feet away, he mutters under his breath, "you traitor."

I stifle a giggle.

Zane's chauffeur is still waiting at the curb for us. Once Zane and I are settled in the back and the driver has eased into the city traffic, Zane pulls the Genex from his waistband. His hands are gentle as he eases my neck forward. "Let's have a look," he says. He brushes my hair to the side, his fingers sweeping across my skin and sending a shiver through me. "Sorry," he apologizes. "My fingers must be cold."

I'm about to tell him that *no, his fingers aren't cold at all,* but then I hear the whirring of the machine and decide to press my face into my knees instead. Just as he's about to touch the device to my neck, I sit up.

"Is it safe?"

"The x-ray machine?"

"Yeah. Is it safe? I'm not going to end up with radiation poisoning or anything, right?"

Zane chuckles. "In small doses, it's perfectly harmless, just like our food warmers. I wouldn't recommend using it over and over again, but one time is fine." He pauses. "Okay?"

I nod and resume the position of hugging my knees.

"This will only take a moment," Zane says. "Hold perfectly still… Got it." His body shifts beside me. "You can sit up now."

I sit up too fast and the blood immediately rushes to my brain. "Well?" I say, peering at the device in his hands.

Zane's face scrunches up as he studies the screen. "There's definitely something there. Like a chip or something? See?" He points to the screen where there's an x-ray of the back of my head. I see the bones of my spine and the base of my skull, and then a tiny, square-shaped dark spot.

"That's the chip?" I ask.

"I think so."

I swallow hard. I don't like the idea of something foreign inside my body, messing with my brain and all my memories. "Can you get it out?"

"Me?" Zane shakes his head quickly. "No. I'd rather not try." At the disappointed look on my face, he continues, "But I think I know someone who can."

"Who?" I know Zane has lots of connections, so this doesn't really surprise me.

"It's the guy I told you about before. The one who helped me get into the AIG facility."

"No way. I'm not going back to that lab." I cross my arms over my chest. "For all I know, he's my dad look-alike who did this to me. Hell no."

"I promise, he's not your dad look-alike. He's young, about my age. We went to University together."

I chew on my lower lip, contemplating. The thought of going willingly back into that lab scares the hell out of me. Just thinking about it brings a lump to my throat and a tightening in my chest.

"Hey," Zane says, cupping my chin in his hand. "I promise I won't let anything happen to you." His eyes are warm and soft. "Do you think I'd take you back there if I thought they could hurt you?"

As I stare into his eyes, those genetically modified eyes that remind me of chocolate and warmth and goodness, I get swept away. I'm swirling, down this dizzying hole where every fear I've ever had melts. I want to curse him for making me weak, for making me care. But more so, I want to curse the person who put this thing inside of me. If I ever see my dad look-alike again, he will pay.

"Okay," I say. "Call him. The sooner I get this thing out, the better."

"Come, I want to show you something," Zane says later that night as we're lounging around the motel room—well, as much as one can lounge around a room where you don't want your feet to touch the floor or your body to touch the bed or couch.

He waits for me as I slip on my shoes, and then grabs my hand, leading me to the door. His chauffeur is waiting for us outside in the parking lot. There are only a couple of other cars in the lot, indicating that there are only a few other people crazy enough to stay here.

Zane lifts open the door for me, and I slide into the back of the car. As we're driving, I try to tease the information of where we're going out of him, but he only smiles and squeezes my hand. We leave the rotting part of the city behind, headed toward the beaches. When Geoff stops the car near the boardwalk, I'm not incredibly surprised. I've only mentioned to Zane how much I love the ocean like fifty times in the past two days.

As soon as we're out of the car, Zane slips his fingers through mine. I glance down nervously at our interlocked fingers. Arian is sleeping at a friend's house tonight on the other side of Rubex, but still. What if someone sees us? Everyone in Pacifica knows Zane's betrothed to the perfect girl for him.

"It's okay," he says, almost as if he's reading my mind.

I smile and squeeze his hand as he leads me down the sidewalk.

The night air is cool, the sun long since gone to sleep. Now the three-quarter moon shines down in all her splendor. The streets aren't very crowded, only a few other people are walking in the dark. Instinctively, I pull closer to Zane, so close that we're almost walking as one.

We walk parallel to the ocean until we've passed the boardwalk and reached a stretch of sandy beach. Zane kicks off his shoes, stooping down to pick them up with one hand, and I follow suit. The sand is a little cool. When I squish my toes further in, I remember doing this as a child. I remember the feel of the sand beneath my toes, the salty ocean water on my skin, and begging my dad to bury me until all that was left was my head sticking out. My favorite was when Dad made me a mermaid tail, and I pretended I was princess over all the mermaids.

Zane's thumb traces circles on the back of my hand as we walk along the water's edge. The water is cool—that's how the ocean is in Pacifica, even in the summer. The smell of salt and seaweed hangs thick in the air, and a slight breeze ruffles the hair off my neck.

"What did you want to show me?" I murmur once we've walked in silence for a while.

"Almost there."

When we reach a spot further down the beach, Zane instructs me to sit before settling next to me on the sand, our shoulders and knees touching. "Now," he says. "Look up."

When I look up, there are a million stars winking and blinking above. For some reason, it reminds me of another night, another star-filled sky. The dark water of the ocean dances, the moonlight reflecting off its surface. It's so beautiful that I pause to catch my breath.

When I glance back down, my arm is glowing. "What the hell?" I raise my arm and skim my fingers over the intricate purple design that looks like looping and twirling butterflies. Another glowing flower-shaped pattern is on my upper arm. "What is this?"

Zane touches the pattern. "This… is the Fringe tattoo." His fingers run down my arm, causing me to shiver. "And this is something you got because you thought it was pretty."

The words *scenery tattoo* pop into my mind. *This is my scenery tattoo.* An image of a majestic tree floats into my mind. "Trey has one too," I say.

Zane nods. "That's right. His is a tree; it represents leadership or something."

"When you tell me about the Fringe, I start to remember things," I say. "Maybe if you take me to their hideout—"

"You mean the Compound?"

"Right. The Compound. Maybe if you take me there, I'll remember more."

Zane hesitates before replying, "We can't, Sienna."

"Why not? It's only about an hour by bullet train to Legas. That's not long at all—"

Zane places a gentle hand on my thigh. "We can't go there because it doesn't exist anymore. There was an explosion… bombs. You and other Fringe members barely escaped. You thought Trey was dead."

My stomach clenches like I've been kicked in the gut. Flashes of images run through my mind. The sounds of screaming, the intense heat as flames lick the back of my legs, smoke… smoke everywhere, so thick it's hard to see, and then Trey—a rebar protruding from his chest and the feeling of loss, so much loss that it makes my heart ache. Tears threaten to fill my eyes, but I blink quickly, willing them away. These images are faded, blurry around the edges, like they didn't really happen, aren't really memories, but more like… like dreams.

"You remember something, don't you?" Zane asks, breaking the silence.

I nod. "But I think I liked it better when I didn't."

Zane takes my hands in his. "I know how awful that night was for you. I still dream about it, how close I came to losing you."

"You were there?" I ask, trying to sort through the memories of Zane with me at the SGF, rescuing my mother, and those of the Compound with Trey.

"Not in the Compound. After you escaped, you contacted me. Wanted me to help get your mom out of the SGF. That's when we realized Trey was still alive. We rescued him too."

"I wish I could remember," I say, staring out at the dark sea, almost hypnotized by the rhythmic lull of the tides washing against the shore.

"Good news," Zane says. "I talked to Granger, the guy I

know. He says he can see us tomorrow night." His fingers trail through the sand between us.

"So by tomorrow night…" My words die away.

"By tomorrow night, you should have your memories back."

I study his face as he says it, the way he won't meet my eyes, the way he stays intently focused on the sand between his fingers.

"Hey," I say, placing my hand on his arm, his biceps flexing in response. He turns to look at me. "Whatever I remember isn't going to change how I feel. About you, I mean."

"You don't know that," Zane says, his voice pained.

"All I know is that you've been by my side this whole time."

"Like a friend," Zane says, looking away.

I touch his face, forcing him to look at me. My voice is soft when I speak again. "You're more than a friend to me, and I think you know that."

As his eyes stare into mine, I have this insane desire to kiss him again, like we did in the rain. I can practically taste his lips and smell his skin. I'm suddenly aware of every part of us that's touching. Our knees, our hips, our shoulders. But still, I'm not close enough.

Zane leans in, as if he's reading my mind, and I meet him halfway. When his lips touch mine, there are sparks—okay, maybe not literal sparks—but every inch of me is tingly and warm. It's just Zane and me, our lips touching, our hearts hammering, our hands exploring. And when he lays me back on the sand, all I can think about is how much I need him. And then, immediately, I feel guilty. Did I feel this way about Trey? This desire, this need to be close to him, to feel his hands on my hips, his breath touching my skin, his lips against mine?

I don't know. And because I don't know, I feel awful.

I try to push the thoughts aside and just enjoy the feel of Zane's body heavy against mine, his arms around my back, the smell of saltwater and dried seaweed, the rhythmic hum of the ocean pulling back and surging forth.

But then an image of Trey pops into my mind, and I know it's more than a thought. It's a memory. A memory of the two of us, swimming in a lagoon, laughing, his hands on my waist, my arms around his neck. It feels so real that it takes my breath away.

As soon as I stop kissing Zane, he knows something is wrong. He sits up on his elbow and stares at me.

"You remembered something, didn't you?" he asks hesitantly. I think I understand his hesitation now. If I have these strong feelings and memories of Trey, where does that leave him?

I sit up and nod, pulling my knees to my chest. I'm sure he doesn't want to know that while I was kissing him, I was thinking about Trey.

"I keep getting bits and pieces…" I trail off, drawing circles in the sand with my finger.

"Of Trey?" Zane's voice comes out tight.

I glance up in time to see a muscle in his jaw twitch. "Yeah," I say lamely.

"That's to be expected." He's staring out at the ocean, his face impassive.

An awkward silence follows. I want to know—no, I need to know—where the two of us stand. With or without Trey, what are we? What will we ever be? Zane is engaged to marry someone else, someone who's pretty and perfect and everything I'm not. I clear my throat.

"Earlier when I asked why you were marrying Arian, you said it was complicated." My eyes find his. "Do you love her?"

He contemplates my question a moment before answering. "I *want* to love her."

"But?"

"But I'm in love with someone else."

My pulse quickens. "You are?"

"Yes, Sienna, I am," he says, his voice thick. "You don't remember, but I already told you how I feel."

An ache builds in my throat. I've hurt him before—it's clear in the way he draws in on himself, as if he's trying to protect his heart from being crushed again.

"I hurt you," I whisper.

"No, you told me the truth, which is what I needed to hear."

"But now?"

He sighs. "Now what?"

I struggle to convey what I'm thinking, how I'm feeling. "I feel like there's this great divide between us, keeping us apart. Arian is pulling from one side, and Trey is pulling from the other." I inch closer to him. "But what I don't understand is why not us? Why can't we be together?"

Zane sits up and faces me, placing his hands on my shoulders and staring into my eyes. I can see the moon reflected in them, a silver orb rotating around his iris. "Listen, tomorrow night, we'll go to the lab, Granger will fix your memories, and everything will be different. *You* will be different. What you feel for me, will be different."

"You don't know that—" I start to protest, but Zane places a finger in front of my lips.

"I do, because I know you. And I know that you love Trey. And I know that you won't rest until you have him back. All you need to do is remember."

Even though I don't want them, even though I curse them, tears fill my eyes. "But what if I don't want to remember?" I whisper.

Zane's thumb strokes each cheek, wiping away the tears that slide down my face. "That wouldn't be fair to you. Or to Trey."

"But tonight?"

Zane's mouth turns up into a half-smile, and all I can think about is kissing him. Kissing him until the sun rises and the moon sleeps. Kissing him for so long that I never have to say good-bye.

"Tonight is ours."

20

Sienna

The tube is an underwater, cylindrical runway made almost entirely of crystal clear Plexiglas. It reminds me of the old aquarium back home. Each year, the school took us to view the sharks, manta rays, and puffer fish, and the only thing separating us from those creatures was the thin, clear Plexiglas of the underwater walkway.

It's the next night, but before we can get to the tube, we have to get past the night guard. It's too dangerous to use a boat at night. Something about underwater spikes that are positioned every few feet starting one hundred yards from the facility. They are extremely hard to see during the day, but impossible to see at night. They use them to ward off people like us who want to try to break in.

Thankfully, we already have a plan in place, but the trick will be pulling it off. Granger warned us that in order to access the tube, we would have a retina and fingerprint scan. To bypass those safety precautions, he sent us a microchip that, if inserted into the back of the device, will override the contents. If it doesn't work, though, Zane and I could be arrested for attempting to break into a government facility.

The guard on duty is a young man, probably mid-twenties, with scruffy facial hair. He stands erect in front of the covered entry to the tube, one hand lightly resting on his M-16. He eyes us as we move toward him. It's time to set the plan in motion.

"Do you have your keycard?" Zane asks me, a bit loud so the guard can hear.

"I'm sure I do, somewhere in this mess." I pull the oversized purse off my shoulder and start to rummage around. As I do, I let the purse slip from my fingers, the contents of it scattering all over the ground. A strawberry-shaped lip balm rolls right to the guard's feet.

"I'm such a klutz," I mutter, bending to pick up the contents and place them back in my bag. Pens, pieces of chewing gum, another lip balm, coins, and a hair clip.

The guard takes the bait. Shouldering his gun, he kneels and starts gathering the items that are closest to him. "I found your card," he says, holding up the rectangular white card Granger provided for us.

"Thanks," I say, taking it from him. I don't bother to look at Zane, but I know what he's doing. Now that the guard is distracted, he's inserting the chip into the back of the scanner.

"I think that's everything," the guard says, rising to his feet and holding out the contents in his hands. I take the items and thank him again before dumping everything back into my gigantic purse.

"Sorry about that," I murmur. I stare up at him and try to look demure. "That was so nice of you to help me."

He smiles at me. "It's okay. My pleasure." He then glances over to where Zane is waiting by the mechanized glass doors.

I look at Zane with narrowed eyes. "Thanks for *your* help," I say, my tone haughty.

Zane shrugs. "It looked like you didn't *need* my help." His eyes flicker to the guard, making his displeasure clear.

I prop my hand on my hip. "He was being *nice*, which is more than I can say about you."

Looking annoyed—and very convincing—Zane shakes

his head. "How many times do I have to tell you that I don't like it when you flirt with other guys?"

"I wasn't flirting," I protest.

The guard clears his throat, looking very uncomfortable.

"You're always flirting, Magda." *Magda? I didn't realize we were changing our names too.* "A touch here, a laugh there—you don't know how to stop yourself."

My back goes rigid. "I wasn't flirting," I say, my voice low and threatening.

The guard breaks in. "Look, buddy, I was only being nice. I wasn't hitting on your girlfriend or anything. If you're here to get inside the lab, then go. If not, let's move along."

I smirk at Zane before giving the guard a big smile. "Of course. I have my keycard here." I hold up the card and move toward the gray machine that sits to the left of the glass doors. Frosted swirls are etched onto the glass.

"See, there you go flirting again," Zane mutters. He removes his keycard from his pocket and swipes. The machine beeps, indicating that it's ready for the retina scan. Leaning in, Zane opens his eyes wide as the thin laser of light scans his eyes. It beeps again, and then a green check mark appears on the screen. Next is the fingerprint scan. Zane places his finger on the holder, and the base glows bright red before going dark. Another beep, another green check mark, and the glass doors whoosh open.

My heart is thumping in my chest when it's my turn. The keycard works, but when I bend down to scan my retinas, I accidentally bump the small machine. There's a funny buzzer sound as a red "X" appears on the screen. Beads of sweat form on the back of my neck as I try to exhale slowly. Maybe it was a glitch. I decide to try again.

I let the light scan my retina, but again, there's the same buzzer sound and giant red "X."

"Everything okay?" The guard asks, coming to stand beside

me.

"I—I think it must be my contacts." I pretend to move something around in my eye. "They're new."

The guard nods. "This happens all the time. Allow me."

He punches a few numbers on the keypad, most likely to delete my entry card, and then scans his own keycard that he pulls from inside his black jacket. When he bends down to allow the retina scan, I quickly move my hand to the back of the machine, searching for the microchip. My hand passes over smooth metal surfaces until my fingers connect with the tiny adapter that the chip is plugged into. And now I know the problem. When I bumped the machine, the chip became dislodged, unable to connect with the internal system.

I slip the chip into my bag as the guard straightens up and places his finger on the pad. "Access is granted," a computer-generated voice speaks.

"Thank you," I say, flashing him a grateful smile as the glass doors whoosh open.

"Any time," he says. "Hope I didn't get you in too much trouble with him." He jerks his head in the direction of where Zane waits on the other side of the doors.

"Don't mind him," I say. "He's just the jealous type." Shouldering my bag, I hurry through the doors before they have a chance to close on me. Once I'm through and I see Zane, my heart resumes its normal palpitation.

"What took so long?" he hisses, watching the doors close behind me. Because of the frosted swirls on the glass, it's fairly difficult to see anything on the other side.

"It wouldn't work for me. The chip became dislodged. Thankfully, the guard used his to allow me access."

Zane nods approvingly. "So buttering him up did work."

"I think so."

Zane glances at his Lynk. "We need to hurry. We're already ten minutes late to meet Granger. We don't want to miss him."

Turning to the tube, Zane says, "Why don't you go first? That way, in case something happens, you'll at least make it through."

We're now standing in front of what looks to be a wall of elevators. Zane presses a button for the first one, and when it opens, it looks nothing like an elevator at all. Inside is a person-sized round Plexiglas ball with tiny holes for air. In the center are two seats, including seat restraints.

"Looks like we can go together," I say.

Zane guides me in, takes the seat beside me, and closes the hatch over us. I feel like a hamster inside one of those hollowed-out balls. And though I would expect it to smell like sweat and feet, it actually smells very clinical. Like a doctor's office.

The tube is fast, and when it begins to move, I grip the seat of my chair as we descend under the ocean. There's pressure on my ears, and as I yawn, I hear a distinct pop. We pick up speed once we're traveling straight, and it's the strangest feeling to see the blackness of the ocean all around. To know that there are animals and creatures only an arm's length away and all that's separating us from them is this ball and the tube. I'm kind of grateful for the darkness, which keeps me from seeing the deep end of the ocean, along with all those who call it their home.

The ball begins to slow as it nears the terminal on the other side.

"By the way, good acting back there," Zane says suddenly.

"You weren't too bad yourself," I say.

Zane smiles at me. "All I did was follow your lead."

Once inside the elevator-like terminal, we hear a click as the sphere locks into place. The hatch lifts open, and Zane and I climb out. We're immediately greeted by a guy dressed conservatively in a gray button-down shirt, slacks, and a lab coat. It's apparent Zane knows him. Oddly, there's something very familiar about him to me. As I stare at his nondescript features and chestnut-brown hair, I get the distinct feeling I've seen him before—recently.

Then it hits me. The guy who tried to sit next to me on the train.

He recognizes me immediately; I can see it in his eyes, the way they flit down in embarrassment. Thankfully, as Zane does the introductions, he pretends like we've never met, so I do the same.

Once we've shaken hands, and I've made a mental note of how soft his are from spending so many hours in a lab, Granger leads us down a hallway, past closed doors and darkened labs. We stop outside one with the name *Brian Phillips* and *Lead Geneticist* etched on the plaque.

"This is my mentor's lab," he explains. "As long as we return everything to its proper place when we leave, he should never know we were here."

I step into the room and look around. There are several computers on a table on the far wall, a couple more tables filled with charts and lab equipment, but the thing that really catches my eye is the examination table. Next to it is a dentist chair with one of those rotating image projector things my mother was hooked up to in the SGF.

Striding over to it, I say, "Why do you have one of these?"

"It's Dr. Phillips' latest invention."

I swivel to face him. "What is it?"

Granger shifts awkwardly. "I'm really not at liberty to say."

I cross my arms over my chest. "Well, what does it do?"

He hesitates. "I—I'm not really supposed to tell you that either."

I take a few steps toward him. "It alters memories, doesn't it? It makes people believe they're someone else, doesn't it?"

Granger's mouth opens and closes like a fish out of water. "Yes, but—how do you know that? This machine is still in the experimental stage. Only a few people know about it."

"Because my mother was experimented on. In a government facility in Legas."

"But that's impossible," Granger says, shaking his head. "We only use volunteers who have been through an incredibly traumatic event who may want to alter some of their memories to help them cope."

I think of my mother. *Volunteer?* She was the furthest thing from a volunteer. Granted, she had been through an incredibly traumatic event in the last year, but that didn't qualify her for a memory wipe.

"Well, someone is using this on people without their permission. You might want to look into that." I examine the smooth underside of the rotating arm. "Don't you ever feel like you're playing God?"

His mouth turns up in a half-smile. "God? Well, no, not really. I see it as a chance to give people a better life."

"Is that why your mentor changed my memories? To give me a better life?" My voice rises a few decibels at the end.

"Look," he says. "I'm sorry Dr. Phillips did this to you, but he was under the impression that you willingly volunteered. He would never intentionally hurt you. He's not that kind of man."

I turn away and pace around the room. The three computer screens are dark, but I notice something beside one of them. I stop and pick up a picture in a frame, a picture of a man with salt-and-pepper hair and a beautiful woman with a dazzling smile. My throat closes.

"Who's this?" I croak.

"That's Dr. Phillips and his girlfriend."

As I stare at the picture, I'm sure I must be mistaken. I search for some indication that I'm wrong, again, but the evidence is clear as day. There are no drugs running through my system, no fuzziness, no cloudy images, only clarity and disbelief.

Because, without a doubt, the man in the picture is my father.

21

Sienna

When I was five years old, my parents took me to a fair. I remember the day clearly because, while we were there, amid the food stands and twirly rides, I got separated from them. I can still taste the fear, feel the anxiety. Everyone was so tall, and all I could see was an endless sea of legs. After a frantic, tear-filled search, I finally found who I thought was my father. From the back, he looked exactly like him—same dark hair, same pants, even the same shoes. But when I latched onto his legs, the man turned, frowning down at me. It wasn't my father. There I was, this five-year-old girl, so confused. How could someone who looked so much like my dad not be my dad? And on the flip side, if *he* wasn't my dad, then where was *my* dad?

As I stare at this picture of my father, I feel like that little girl at the fair again—small, lost, confused. This man looks exactly like my dad, but it's impossible. My father has been dead for over a year now.

"Sienna? Are you okay?" It's Zane. He's now standing beside me, removing the picture from my hands.

"Huh?" I stare at him, mind blank.

Zane glances down at the picture. "Do you know him?"

"I was right. He's—" My voice cracks and I stop to look at Granger, but he's too far away to hear me, too intent on gathering up the supplies for this chip extraction.

"He's my father," I whisper.

Zane's eyes flit from my face to the picture in his hand. "That can't be possible."

"It is. It's him."

Zane shakes his head in disbelief. "So the other day..."

"Yeah."

"He's the one who did this to you?"

I nod.

Granger clears his throat. "Is everything okay?"

Turning to face him, I say, "How long has my—I mean, Dr. Phillips been working here?"

Granger scratches the side of his forehead. "I'm not sure. He recruited me from University almost two years ago. I always assumed he'd been here forever, just because he's so knowledgeable. Why?"

That was before my father's death. How is that possible?

"It's nothing," I lie. "I thought I knew him, but it turns out I don't."

Zane shoots me a concerned look, but I ignore it.

Hopping up on the examination table, I say, "Is this where you want me?"

"That's perfect. Let me finish getting everything set up and we'll get started." I watch as Granger moves around the room, opening drawers, gathering equipment, rolling over a metal tray table.

Zane asks Granger if there's a restroom he can use. Once he's gone, Granger turns to me.

"Was Zane the one with you on the train?"

"So you do remember me?" I say, my cheeks flushing.

He nods. "But I don't understand. I thought Zane was engaged to Arian Stratford, that GM girl."

"He is," I say. "But... it's complicated."

Granger's eyebrows rise.

"And no, Zane wasn't with me on the train. No one was." A flash of hurt runs through Granger's eyes. "Look," I say. "I'm sorry for lying to you. Truth is, I just wanted to be alone."

He focuses on the tubing in his hands. "I guess I can understand that. Sorry for coming off so strong. You—reminded me of someone, that's all."

"Who?"

He hesitates. "My sister."

Before he can say anything else, Zane returns. Granger gives me a silent nod, like our former meeting will remain our little secret, and then he continues to get everything ready for the procedure.

"What exactly will you be doing to Sienna?" Zane asks when Granger pulls out a long needle.

"I'm putting her to sleep so I can go in and remove the chip. Once the chip is removed, her memories should return."

"So that's it? A simple chip removal and I'll be back to normal?"

"Essentially, yes," Granger responds, his fingers untangling the IV tubing.

Zane steps in. "You're familiar with removing a blocking chip?"

Granger shrugs. "More or less."

"I don't like the sound of that," Zane mutters.

"Look," Granger says. "I've assisted with plenty of the insertions and even done a few myself."

"But?" Zane says.

"But... I've never removed one. I watched Dr. Phillips remove one. Once." His hands lift helplessly. "Not that many people who have their memories erased want to get them back."

My throat goes dry. I'm about to go under a knife, a procedure performed by an intern, not a doctor, who will remove something from my brain that may or may not give me my memories back. *What am I thinking?*

Zane glances at me, the muscle in his jaw twitching—a sign he's distressed. "What guarantee can you give me that Sienna will be okay?"

Granger tilts his head to the side and contemplates Zane's question. "I'm ninety percent sure that she'll come out of this perfectly fine, memories intact, with normal functioning brain activity."

The muscle twitches again. "And the other ten percent?"

"Well…" Granger pauses, pursing his lips together. "There's always a risk of brain damage."

The room spins a little, and I grip the sides of the examining table. *Brain damage?* I'm about to tell Zane it isn't worth it, that I'd rather live a life of not knowing than not live a life at all, when Zane looks at me and says, "I think you should do it."

"Are you *serious*?" My voice comes out high-pitched at the end.

Zane crosses the room and rests his hand on my back. Leaning down, he speaks low in my ear, his breath tickling my cheek. "It'll be fine. It's a small risk. And I'll be here the whole time."

I look at him and nod. For some reason, just knowing Zane will be here helps relieve some of my fears, like if something goes wrong, he can magically fix it, which, of course, is ridiculous.

Taking a deep breath, I lay back on the examination table. "Let's do this."

Zane takes my hand and squeezes it as Granger rolls the metal tray table over. And as he inserts an IV into my hand, Zane pushes the hair off my forehead and whispers, "It'll be okay."

Whatever is in the IV and the mask Granger places over my face makes me sleepy, oh so sleepy. I tip my head to look at Zane through half-closed lids. They are so heavy, too heavy; I don't know how much longer I can keep them open.

"You're really pretty, did you know that?" I say, smiling up at him.

Someone snickers, and Zane smiles back. "Thank you. So are you."

I'm about to say something else, the words on the tip of my tongue, sliding around, but then I lose them. The words, I mean, not my tongue. My tongue is still there, I think.

But will it still be there when I wake up?

A dull ache travels up the back of my neck and spreads through my brain. I never knew a brain could be sore, but sure enough, there's a persistent pain that edges along my nerves, rattles against the base of my head. My tongue runs over the inside of my mouth. Yep, still there.

Zane's face is the first I see. Then again, I don't know why I'd expect any different. There's a slight *beep, beep*—a heart monitor, maybe?—and the air is tinged with the sweet smell of blood. Zane hovers anxiously over me.

"Hey," I croak.

He smiles, and some of the worry dissipates from his eyes. "Hey yourself."

"Is it over?" I ask.

"Yes. And you did great."

"So my—my memories are fixed?"

Granger's voice pipes up, and I turn my head to look at him, despite the ache that returns when I do so. "It may take a few hours for all the synapses of your brain to reconnect. But, yes, I did remove the chip. Everything went well. I see no reason why all your memories should not return by the morning."

"Success," Zane whispers.

"Are you feeling any pain?" Granger asks.

I nod, and then wince. Lifting my IV-laden hand, I feel along the base of my head. There's a bandage there and some of the hair has been shaved away.

"Sorry," Granger apologizes, coming to stand next to the bed. "I had to shave a little to access the site—not sure how Dr. Phillips inserted it without doing it before—but it's underneath the rest of your hair and should grow back fairly quickly. As for the pain, it will lessen in a few hours, but your head may be sore for a few days. Any kind of over-the-counter pain meds should help." He looks at Zane when he says the last part, and Zane nods.

"How long does she need to recover?" Zane asks.

Granger glances at a clock across the room. "I'd say she should be able to move around in a few hours."

According to the clock, it's already one o'clock in the morning. I reach my hand out and search for Granger's. "Thank you," I murmur. "Thank you." My eyes feel too heavy to keep open. "Can I go back to sleep now?" I close my eyes.

When Granger speaks, it's like he's talking from a distance the way his voice is all muffled and blurry around the edges. "She's still feeling the after effects of the anesthesia," he explains in his long-distance voice.

"How long until it wears off?" That's Zane asking the question, but why does it sound like he's on the other side of the wall instead of standing right beside me?

"Maybe a couple of hours? Everyone reacts differently to it. She may be more sensitive."

There's silence, and I think maybe Zane has gone to sleep too. Then he says in his smothered voice, "What time will people start arriving in the morning?"

People? What people?

"As long as you're gone by seven, you should be fine," Granger says, his voice an underwater muffle, the words barely recognizable.

I'm not sure where they're going, but I know exactly where I'm going—back to sleep. My mind drifts, the pain dulls, and the steady hum of their words is as lulling as the rhythmic tides of the ocean. Back and forth, loud and soft, heavy and light.

"Sienna, wake up," a voice says urgently, followed by a gentle shaking. "You need to wake up now."

My eyelids are made of lead, yet I struggle to open them. In a desperate attempt to appear wide awake, I prop them open with my fingers. Zane is staring at me, a wild expression on his face.

"We have to leave. Now." He glances behind him, and his words come out in a rush. "I'm sorry, but I fell asleep. Workers are already arriving. If Dr. Phillips sees you—" He breaks off and places his hand on my back, forcing me to a sitting position.

My head feels clearer, and thankfully, the pain has lessened. My eyelids are now working on their own. I allow Zane to help me off the bed, and then I slip my feet into my shoes. Once they're laced up, thanks to Zane, I carefully twist my head a few inches, stretching out my stiff neck.

"Careful," Zane warns. "You don't want to pop your stitches." Grabbing my hand, he leads the way out of the lab. Granger is standing in the hallway, looking peeved.

"I told you to be gone by seven," he hisses.

"I fell asleep," Zane retorts. "You could have come and checked on us."

"I was neck-deep in research," Granger huffs. "Now hurry. Once I get you on the tube, you're on your own."

With one arm slung across my back, his fingers firmly pressing into my waist, Zane helps me hobble down the maze of hallways that will lead us to the wall of tubes. I keep my head down, partly because it's too heavy to keep up, and partly because I don't want to be recognized. There's a steady stream of people dressed in business suits and lab coats who are now filling the hall.

We've almost made it to the tube when a voice stops me cold. "Sienna?"

It's a voice so familiar that it produces an ache, stronger and deeper than any pain in my head. I look up, and my eyes connect with the ocean-blue eyes of Trey. He's dressed in a business suit and carrying a briefcase. His shoulders are broad, his hair as dark as I remember, and the dimple in his chin so prominent I think if I stuck my finger in there, it might get lost forever. Straightening up and trying not to look like I'm on the other side of normal, I give him a small smile. I only hope he doesn't notice the tiny drops of blood spattered on the shoulder of my shirt. "Hello, Trey. How are you?"

I can tell he's working through something. "What are you—what are you doing here?" His expression changes from surprise to confusion to... pleasure? Is he pleased to see me?

"She's—um—interviewing for a position in the lab," Granger jumps in. "As an intern. For Dr. Phillips." I smile and nod when Trey looks at me for confirmation, immediately grateful Granger is so quick on his feet.

Trey's eyes flit to Zane and his arm slung around my back. "Are you interviewing as well, Zane?"

"No," Zane answers. "I'm only here for support." I almost laugh outright at the truthfulness of that statement, because he literally is holding me up right now.

Trey looks uncomfortable for a moment. He clears his throat. "I see my advice worked." He's talking to Zane, not me.

A smile spreads across Zane's face, one so wide he reminds me of a cat that's swallowed a canary. "You have no idea."

My face heats up as I realize they're talking about *me*.

Trey nods, ducking his head. "That's great." He forces a smile, his eyes turning to me. Just being under his gaze makes my heart pause in its normal beating pattern, before resuming at a frightening speed. "Take care, Sienna. Maybe I'll see you around, especially if you get the job."

"Yeah, maybe." And even though it hurts to say the words, I force myself to spit them out. "Tell Rayne I said *hi*." I squeeze closer to Zane as if it doesn't bother me in the least to acknowledge that my former boyfriend is now engaged to another girl.

His eyes shift. "Sure." He gives all three of us a polite nod before continuing down the hall. It isn't until he's out of sight that I realize I'm shaking. Even though I know I shouldn't, even though I tell myself not to, I glance behind me. Trey's dark head is moving away from us, surrounded by several other people in the hall, and just as I'm about to face forward, he glances over his shoulder, his eyes connecting with mine. I feel like I've been seared with a hot iron as my entire body heats up, from the tip of my head all the way down to my toes. I turn abruptly, knocking into Zane, who still has his arm around me.

"You okay?" he asks.

"I'm fine. Let's just get out of here."

Granger uses his keycard, retina, and fingerprint to get us access to the tube. Once Zane and I are settled inside, Granger gives us a soldier salute.

"Thank you, Grange. I owe you, man," Zane says.

"Yes, thank you," I echo. I've stayed quiet these past few minutes, because seeing Trey has awakened a slumbering beast. All those thoughts, feelings, and memories are now surging forth, reminding me of the loss and heartache I've experienced these past few weeks. Images of the lagoon, a Phoenix spread across Trey's back, the white scar on his stomach—a gift from the Devil's men—lying next to him in his bed the night the Compound was bombed. And while it's great to not feel like I'm missing part of my life anymore, I wish I didn't remember. That I didn't know. Because with the memories comes a never-ending ache—a longing for what was and what will never be again. Maybe ignorance truly is bliss.

And the only thing I can hold on to, that keeps me grounded—steady—that keeps me from spinning off into the sky, never to be seen again, are these words: *I love him. I love him. I love him.*

22
Zane

When we reach the motel, Sienna is too weak to stand on her own, so I lift her in my arms and carry her. She buries her head in my neck, her nose pressed against my skin. I'm almost to the door when I hear the squeal of tires, a car door slam, and a voice so familiar that it makes my blood run cold. "Zane? What's going on?"

I turn slowly with Sienna in my arms, only to find Arian standing in the parking lot of the motel, her arms crossed over her chest and a suspicious look on her face.

"Arian, what are you doing here?"

Sienna's head lifts at the mention of Arian's name. Her eyes take in the woman standing in front of us.

"I saw you," Arian says, her voice flat. "I was eating breakfast at a cafe with a friend, and I saw you and Sienna exit the launch to the AIG facility. You were practically carrying her, and you've been so secretive lately. So I followed you." She glances at the motel door behind us, the one with the crooked numbering. "Why are you here?"

"Remember? I told you that they're putting in new floors in the condo this week, so we had to leave. You said you would stay at your friend Wendy's house, and I said that Sienna and I would get a hotel."

"But why are you *here*?" she asks again. "I thought you'd

be at the Windsor Hotel or Westin Valley Inn. I never pictured you *here*."

Sienna shifts uncomfortably in my arms.

"Listen, Arian, let me get Sienna inside, and then I'll explain everything. Okay?"

Arian looks suspicious at first, but then she nods.

I carry Sienna to the door, unlock it using the prehistoric brass key, and ever so gently set her on the stained couch in our tiny sitting area. She winces.

The smell when we first walk in is overpowering, so it isn't surprising that when Arian follows us through the door, she wrinkles her nose. Her eyes travel around the unpleasant room before resting on the double bed in the middle.

"Well, this is an interesting setup," she says slowly, like she's working through something in her mind.

"We use pillows between us," Sienna pipes up.

"Must be a family thing," Arian mutters.

Sienna's cheeks turn red in response.

Arian props a hand on her hip. "So why were you in the AIG? What happened there?"

"It's my fault," Sienna says, raising her hand. "I'm doing a story about—"

I can't handle it anymore. I'm tired of hiding, and I'm tired of lying.

"No," I interrupt in a tired voice. "No more lies."

Sienna opens her mouth as if she's about to protest, but then she closes it.

I turn to Arian, who is standing next to the drooping dresser.

"Arian, there's something you need to know." I pause. "Sienna isn't my cousin. And she isn't a freelance reporter on assignment in the Capital." Arian's eyes go wide, and I stop because I'm not sure how far I want to take this.

She needs to know. I can't hide it anymore.

I continue. "And despite everything—our differences, that I'm engaged to you, that she loves someone else—I'm in love with her."

Arian's hand flies to her mouth as tears fill her eyes and slide down her cheeks. "You lied to me?" Her voice is small, like a child's.

"I'm really sorry," I say. "I never meant to hurt you. Everything just spiraled out of control, and one lie led to another."

"How could you?" she says, her voice rising. "How could you let me think she's your cousin? How could you be with her right in front of me, without feeling an ounce of remorse? And how could you bring her here, doing God-only-knows-what with her?" Her fists clench in anger. "You have a lot of nerve, Zane Ryder." She takes a step toward Sienna. "And you—" she spits. "You are nothing more than a common whore weaseling her way between the best match in history."

Turning her anger back on me, she says, "You do realize you're throwing everything away for her, right? She's a nobody. She's probably not even genetically modified, is she? Do you really think your father would ever approve of a relationship with a *normal* girl? You were made for better, Zane." She sniffs. "You were made for me."

My back stiffens. She may be upset, but she has no right to talk about Sienna that way. My voice is hard when I speak. "I've made my choice. I refuse to marry someone I don't love. And if my father doesn't like it, he can go to hell."

The color drains from Arian's face. She strides to the door. "I've had it, Zane. I refuse to be treated this way. The moment I walk out this door, I'm never coming back. And all of your father's efforts will be wasted. Is that what you want?"

I hesitate. Is this really what I want? My entire life has been molded and shaped with Arian chosen for me at birth. Am I willing to give up everything?

My eyes shift to Sienna, but she won't look at me. She's too busy staring at her hands, avoiding eye contact.

"Good-bye, Arian," I say finally, and there's no mistaking the regret that creeps into those words.

Her hate-filled eyes zero in on Sienna. "I hope you're happy." With that, she throws the door open, marches out, and slams it closed behind her.

Arian is gone.

I sink onto the couch next to Sienna, my entire body sagging into the filthy fabric.

She immediately turns to me. "I'm sorry," she says.

In a tired voice, I reply, "Why are you sorry?"

She gestures to the place Arian stood only moments before. "This is all my fault."

Even though it's not, I decide to play along. "Yes," I say. "Yes, it is. If you hadn't tried to jump off the Megasphere that night or the cliff after the Extravaganza, I would not have rescued you, and therefore, I might never have met you. So, yes, it is your fault."

I expect her to frown, because she never likes it when I tease about rescuing her. But she smiles instead. "How many times do I have to tell you that I didn't need you to rescue me?"

She doesn't know. She doesn't even realize how she's changed my world. Changed it from duties and expectations, to excitement and unpredictability.

My eyes bore into hers. "No? Maybe not. Maybe I needed *you* to rescue *me*."

She stares at me, her green eyes searching my face, and it takes all my willpower not to kiss each freckle on her nose.

Something loosens inside of me, and I begin to speak, telling her about my life growing up without my mother. The expectations of who I was and what I would become ingrained in me from infancy. What it was like working in the lab with my father, and the first time I learned I was genetically matched to a girl named Arian Stratford.

"I was eight at the time, well, the first time I heard her name. From the moment I could form words, I was told I would grow up to marry a girl who was the perfect match for me. But it wasn't until I was twelve that my father arranged a meeting." I pause, remembering that day so vividly. I'd been impressed with Arian from the first moment I saw her. "We met for ice cream, after school. Her parents and my father were there, sitting in a booth across from us. It was awkward, to say the least. Arian was pretty, even at that age, but I remember being at a loss for words. I struggled to find something to talk about, so I tried to make her laugh instead." I make a face. "It didn't go well. My jokes were stupid, immature, as boys' jokes at that age typically are. And she was so mature, especially for a twelve-year-old. I was beginning to wonder if my father had made a mistake when Arian laid her hand over mine and said, 'It's okay. I'm nervous too.' It was the first time a girl had ever touched me, and I think my mind went blank." I laugh.

"My father wanted to keep her identity a secret from the public, so he kept us apart. After that meeting, I just kept remembering how nice she was. And that carried me through it all. Through the years of not seeing her. Through the years of wondering what she looked like, how she'd changed. Then, at the Extravaganza, I saw her for the first time in almost ten years. She was beautiful, of course—I knew she would be—but she was also everything I'd ever pictured my wife to be: strong, capable, intelligent, caring."

My eyes search Sienna's face. "But then, I met you. Well, for the second time at the lake. And you were everything I never knew I wanted. Independent, sassy, daring, carefree. You got under my skin that first night I saw you on top of the

Megasphere, and I haven't been able to stop thinking about you since." My fingers move to her cheek.

"Zane, I—" She stops and looks down.

I lift her chin, forcing her to look at me. "You remember, don't you?"

She nods. "And I'm not sure I can give you what you want—"

"Sienna, all I want is for you to be happy."

She slips her fingers through mine and kisses the back of my hand. "I am happy."

"You are? But I thought—"

"You thought that the moment I remembered Trey, I would forget about you?"

Of course that's what I thought. How could I imagine anything different?

"Sure, things are more complicated now," she continues, "but I care about you, Zane. I really do. And no memory of Trey is going to change that."

Unconsciously, I stroke the back of her hand with my thumb. "I don't expect anything from you right now, but as long as I know that I'm in the running, that's sufficient for me."

"Good," she says, "because that's all I can offer right now."

I wish it were more. I wish I was enough for her, but as long as Trey is in the picture, it will never be the case. I stare at our entwined hands. What would it be like if Trey and I were never switched at birth? Would she love me instead?

Then I remember the picture of her father, and the pain it must have caused her to find out he's alive.

"Sienna—" I exhale slowly. "I'm sorry about your dad."

Her face hardens, and she slides her hand away from mine. "I don't want to talk about him."

"Why not? Aren't you wondering how he's still alive and why he's working in the AIG facility?"

"I know why he's alive. He's a coward," she says through

clenched teeth.

I stare at her. "You don't honestly believe that he planned this, do you?"

"Of course I do. He faked his own death once—what's to say he wouldn't fake it again?" She sits up straight. "You have no idea how much I've learned about him this past year. How much I never knew and still so much that I don't know." She pauses, licking her lips. "Zane, my father recruited Granger *before* his death. I don't understand why. But one thing is certain—he left us. He left Mom, Emily, and me to fend for ourselves, to scrape bottom. He left me to sell my soul, to become someone else, someone I didn't like very much, but had to be. If he's really that much of a selfish coward, I want nothing to do with him."

"It's possible he faked his death," I say. "But what if he didn't? What if he's a victim? Just like you."

Her mouth moves into a grim line. "The evidence points otherwise."

We're both quiet for a moment. "I can't believe your father was the lead geneticist for my father's lab," I say.

"According to Greta, your mother is the one who helped him get a job working for your father."

To think that her dad and my mom knew each other. A grin spreads over my face.

"What?" she asks.

"Don't you find it ironic that my mom and your dad were friends all those years ago, and now here we are?"

She shakes her head at me. "Focus, Zane."

I slap my hand on my knee. "Okay, let's think. Your father was a genetic genius, not unlike Harlow. But he faked his own death after my mother died during childbirth—"

"I'm thinking…" she interrupts. "That he felt guilty about implanting two genetically modified embryos in Penelope, which in a way, led to her death. Maybe that's why he decided to leave the life of a geneticist and start fresh."

"But why fake his own death and change his name a second time?"

"Good question. Maybe he was scared of something?"

"Or someone," I add.

Sienna goes quiet for a moment. "Radcliffe told me he was the one who killed my father. Which means he's probably the one who faked my father's death a year ago. Maybe with a poison that stops the heart or something."

"And that's how he was able to convince everyone that your father was dead," I finish.

"But that doesn't make sense because my father's coffin would have been empty," she says. "Which means that several people were in on the ruse."

"Or they were bribed."

It would have to be a bribe. That's the only way to keep so many people quiet. If her dad was valuable to Radcliffe, the moment he learned her father was still alive, Radcliffe could have faked her dad's death, erased his memories, and hired him as the lead geneticist for the AIG. I'm sure if we opened up the back of Brian Phillips' brain, we'd find a chip hidden there too.

Sienna's fists clench. "Radcliffe did this," she breathes. "How much can that man take away from me? How much more will I let him?"

I wish I could remove all the hurt and pain she's felt. I would take it on myself if I knew it would ease some of her burden. "I know this has been hard, but the good news is that we now know how to restore Trey and your father's memories."

She throws her hands up in defeat. "And how would we ever convince them? The last time I tried to tell Trey his memories were altered, he ran away with some girl he claimed was his fiancée. If I try to do that again, he might actually marry her." She pauses. "And as for my dad, I'm nothing more than a stranger to him—a stranger he's already experimented on. He would have no reason to ever believe me. Or trust me."

I think for a moment. "Then we give them a reason."

"How?"

Thankfully, I know exactly what to do. "You leave the planning to me. But I will say this—you're going to need a fancy dress."

23

Sienna

Zane's plan is simple really.

Two months ago, his father received an invitation to attend the AIG's annual gala. It's a big event, a fundraising opportunity, and anyone who's anyone has been invited. When his father received the invitation, Zane didn't think much of it, and of course assumed his father would be the one to attend. But now, if Zane can convince his father to let him take his place, I will accompany him, posing as his assistant.

We are working under the assumption that my father and Trey will be there too, but just to be certain, I put in a call to the AIG facility to confirm their attendance. When the receptionist answers, I say in my most polished, professional voice, "Good morning, I'm calling from Senator Raoul's office. We never received confirmation from Trey Winchester or Brian Phillips for the gala in a few days. Will the two of them be attending this event?"

The receptionist stalls a moment, probably looking up an old document that will show she did, in fact, send confirmation for the two of them. "I'm sorry you didn't receive it, but I sent the confirmation on July twenty-fourth. They will both be attending the gala and bringing a guest."

"I'm sorry to trouble you. Must be a mistake on our end.

I'll be sure to update the system so there are no problems that night. Have a good day." I hang up and smile at Zane. "They're going." Tilting my head in his direction, I say, "Your turn."

Zane hasn't spoken to his father since he left over a week ago. And he certainly hasn't told him about his called-off engagement. But with emotions still running high, and unresolved feelings of betrayal at the forefront of Zane's mind, this conversation will be a difficult one. I stay beside him on the couch to offer moral support, just like he did for me.

With the Lynk against his ear, Zane stands and begins pacing the floor of the motel room. "Hello, Father," he says when his dad answers. He listens for a few seconds and says, "Yes, I've been meaning to call you. Remember that gala you were invited to a few weeks back? Were you planning to go?" He listens, his eyebrows drawn together. "How would you feel if I wanted to take your place? It might be a good experience for me, you know? As the future owner of the company."

Zane is hitting his father right in his soft spot. Mr. Ryder is probably thrilled that Zane is contemplating taking over the company, despite everything he's learned the past few weeks.

"That's wonderful, Dad," Zane is saying. He gives me a big grin and a thumbs-up. "I appreciate it." Then there's a pause. "Arian? No, she's not here. She decided to stay at a friend's house." Another pause. "Sienna will be my plus one, Dad." Zane glances at me before turning his back and speaking in a low voice. "I understand. But you don't have to worry. We're only friends."

When Zane hangs up, I say, "You've got your dad worried now, huh?"

He makes a face. "He won't admit it, but yeah."

"So when are you gonna tell him? You know, about you and Arian."

"When he asks?" He laughs. "I guess once I figure out what to say."

"You do realize that once Arian tells her parents and they tell their friends, it's only a matter of time before all of Pacifica knows. Including your father."

"I do," he says, leaning against the wall and crossing his arms over his chest. "But I'm banking on the fact that Arian won't tell anyone."

"Why would you think that? She's a *girl*. And she was *angry*. Don't you know that a girl's anger is never a pretty thing?"

Zane chuckles. "Yes, but Arian is a well-bred genetically modified girl. I have a feeling that, deep down, she doesn't want it to be over. And she certainly doesn't want the shame that will come from our disunion."

My mouth drops open. "So that's why you let her leave so readily? You think she'll come crawling back, begging you to still marry her, is that it?" I shake my head. "Wow, you have quite the ego."

Zane walks over and slips onto the couch next to me. "That's not why I let her leave, and you know it."

"But you aren't denying that she'll come crawling back," I retort.

He lifts his hands, shrugging. "Honestly? I don't know what she'll do. But for now, if she thinks there's any chance of us getting back together, then that would work as an advantage for me, at least until I can get everything settled here. Then I can return home and deal with the aftermath of our broken betrothal. You understand?"

I nod. It does make sense. The moment people find out about his and Arian's breakup, there will need to be a lot of smoothing over. There will be press conferences, interviews, not to mention the wrath of his father, and Zane would need to be in Legas to deal with all of it. Now is not the right time, and knowing this, I really do hope Arian believes she and Zane only hit a rough patch and will end up back together.

"Good," Zane says. "With that taken care of, we can move

on to phase two of the plan."

"Phase two?" I echo.

"Right." He gives me a big grin. "Finding you the perfect dress."

A groan escapes before I can stop it. "Did I mention that I hate shopping?"

Chuckling, Zane stands and pulls me up from the couch. "Good thing you'll have me to keep you entertained."

The shops in Rubex are trendy and expensive, and I swear I see at least two famous people from some of Chaz's favorite shows. I've never been a fan of shopping, so I'm treating this like a mission. Go in, find the dress, and then retreat. ASAP.

As fancy as the dresses are in this one particular shop Zane takes me to called *Serutica*, the decor is even more so. Crystal chandeliers hang from the ceiling, and mirrored walls give the impression that the store itself is endless, existing forever. Even the armchairs in the sitting area where unlucky mothers and husbands wait are embossed in gold. Bouquets of fresh cut flowers create a lingering smell of a florist rather than a dress shop.

Zane waits patiently as I try on dress after dress, although I don't come out and prance around to show off the dress, like some of the other women. I'm not a model, and this is by no means a fashion show. I'm doing this because I have to, not because I want to.

The silky material of the various gowns feels soft against my skin, but one cuts low in the front, revealing far too much cleavage, and another has fabric cut out on the sides so my pale bare skin shows through. No thanks.

After trying on at a least a dozen, and feeling certain that my body simply isn't made to wear a fancy gown, one of the stylists—that's what they call them here—brings me the most exquisite dress. It's turquoise with tiny silver, white, and turquoise jewels sewn into the bodice. The skirt is long and flowing, and it reminds me of the ocean. I glance at the price tag and try to shove it back in her hands, but she insists that I try it on.

When I'm alone in my dressing room, I ever so gently ease my head through the narrow opening. The dress is a little heavier than the others, probably because of all the jewels on the chest, but as it slides into place and my fingers search the back and zip it up, I realize that it was made for me. I stare at myself in the mirror, my hands running down the sides of my waist, smoothing invisible wrinkles. I sway back and forth a little, watching the skirts ebb and flow like the ocean current.

As a strapless gown, it leaves the pale skin of my shoulders and upper chest exposed, and even though I don't really like showing off my knobby shoulders and freckly chest, I'm in love with the dress. I poke my head out of the dressing room, careful not to let the dress show. Zane is seated in one of the armchairs, one leg crossed in a ninety-degree angle at the knee, staring at his Lynk.

"Hey," I whisper.

Zane glances up, and when he sees me, he smiles. "Any luck?"

"Yeah, I think so."

He motions for me to come out. "Let me see it."

"No, I want it to be a surprise."

Laughing, he says, "So, you mostly came out to tease me, is that right?"

His laugh and his smile are so infectious that I find myself smiling too. "I wanted to share the good news, that's all." I slip back into the dressing room and stare at myself in the mirror one more time before reluctantly removing the dress.

I know now why the princesses in those ancient fairy tales

I heard about as a child always wore a beautiful ball gown that transformed them into something more, something pretty, something perfect even. It's because when wearing it and standing in front of the mirror, it feels like there's a world of possibilities at one's fingertips. You can be anyone you want to be, go anywhere you want to go—for an hour or a day or a small moment, you can be someone other than yourself. Who wouldn't want to experience the splendor of that?

As I fold the dress over my arm, the one thought that keeps running through my mind is…

What will Trey think when he sees me?

At GIGA, some of our required reading included poems from poets long ago. Poets from another time, another place, a place that existed before Pacifica. I always had a hard time understanding some of the poetry. Most of them were about love or loss, longing or desperation. Things I'd never experienced until I left school.

Later that night, while Zane and I are curled up on opposite ends of the couch, facing each other, I decide to give poetry another try.

"Where's that poetry book you brought?" I ask him.

Zane gets up, crosses the room, and pulls it from his duffle bag. "This one?"

I nod and take the book from his outstretched hand. Zane settles next to me with his own book. I'm skimming through the poems when one catches my eye. It's called *Forget Thee?* by John Moultrie, a poet from the 17th Century. I read through the whole poem, but it's the last stanza that really speaks to me.

> Keep, if thou wilt, thy maiden peace,
> still calm and fancy-free,

Kristin Smith

For God forbid thy gladsome heart
should grow less glad for me;
Yet, while that heart is still unwon,
O, bid not mine to rove,
But let it nurse its humble faith and uncomplaining love;
If these, preserved for patient years,
at last avail me not,
Forget me then;
—but ne'er believe that thou canst be forgot!

I read through it twice, both times pausing after each line, contemplating the words, the lyrical phrases, and the poetic meaning. I read the last stanza over and over. As much as I would love to believe that I could forget about Trey and move on, he's left an imprint on me. Maybe that's what a first love does. It changes you, molds you into someone different, and you can never go back to being the person you were before. I can't go back to a time before I loved Trey. Nor to who I was before I met him. I can't bury those feelings or pretend they don't exist. Sure, they may fade with time, but like the poem says, "Thou canst be forgot!"

When I look up from the book, Zane is staring at me. "What?" I say.

"Nothing. You look so serious over there, like you're contemplating adaptive mutation or something."

"Just thinking," I say.

He holds out his hand. "May I?"

Before I hand the book to him, I dog-ear the page with the *Forget Thee?* poem.

"Do you want to read my favorite?" he asks, flipping through the pages. "I think I finally understand what the author was referring to." He gives me a mischievous grin before passing the book back, this time open to page 232. He points to the poem on the right titled *Love's Philosophy* by Percy Bysshe Shelley.

As I start to skim over the poem, he calls out, "Read it out loud, please."

Rolling my eyes, I give him an exasperated sigh. Then I begin.

> "The fountains mingle with the river
> And the rivers with the ocean,
> The winds of heaven mix for ever
> With a sweet emotion;
> Nothing in the world is single;
> All things by a law divine
> In one spirit meet and mingle.
> Why not I with thine?—
>
> "See the mountains kiss high heaven
> And the waves clasp one another;
> No sister-flower would be forgiven
> If it disdained its brother;
> And the sunlight clasps the earth
> And the moonbeams kiss the sea:
> What is all this sweet work worth
> If thou kiss not me?"

When I'm finished reading, Zane is grinning at me, his perfect white teeth and his perfect smile on display.

"Are you hinting at something?" I say.

Zane scoots closer and repeats the last line of the poem. "'What is all this sweet work worth, if thou kiss not me?'"

"Seriously? You're reciting me love poems to entice me to kiss you?"

"Yes. But only if it's working." His eyes search my face for a sign.

When I don't refuse, he leans in, and every nerve in my body hums with anticipation. He hasn't kissed me since the procedure, and I wonder if it will feel different. Will I still like it?

But as his lips meet mine, I feel the same thrilling rush, the same dizzying effect, and the same glowing warmth.

Then an image of Trey creeps to my brain—all broad-shouldered and smiles, and I quickly pull away from Zane.

"What's wrong?" he asks. I can see the hurt on his face, and it kills me. It really does.

My fingers cover my lips, lips that are still tingling from the kiss. Lips that still want more. But words of a different poem seep into my mind: *Ne'er believe that thou canst be forgot!*

"I don't think we should do that anymore," I say hesitantly. A part of me wants to say *to hell with it all* and kiss Zane like he's never been kissed before, but the part of me with a conscience—the little angel sitting on my shoulder—is telling me to simmer down. I haven't forgotten Trey, so why am I pretending that I have? How can I with one mouth pronounce that I love Trey and with that same mouth kiss Zane like the world is about to implode? Am I really that fickle?

Shaking my head, I rise from the couch. "I'm sorry. I think I should go to bed." My eyes refuse to meet Zane's as I place the book on the chipped coffee table and climb into my side of the bed, facing the wall. The light clicks off, and I feel the mattress shift with Zane's weight as he gets in on his side. A moment later, his hand touches my arm.

"Sienna—"

I roll over to face him, but I still can't look at him.

"I'm sorry," he says. "I know I've placed you in an awful position, and I'm sorry. It won't happen again. I promise." His fingers gently guide my chin, tilting it until I'm forced to look at him. "Okay?" he murmurs.

"Okay," I repeat. I want to tell him how I'm feeling, how torn I am between the two of them, how if there wasn't a Trey, there would be no question, but instead, I whisper goodnight and turn away from him.

24
Sienna

The turquoise dress glides over my skin as it settles into place. It's as beautiful as it was that day in the shop, and nervousness sets in when I think of wearing it out in public. It's one thing to stare at myself in a mirror wearing the dress, but it's another thing entirely for other people to see me in it, namely Trey.

When I exit the bathroom, Zane is already waiting for me. He's pacing the floor, wearing a tux. His outfit reminds me of the night I saw him at the celebratory ball at his house—the night I tried to poison his father. And here, in this pitiful excuse for a motel room, we both look tremendously out of place.

He stops mid-stride when he sees me, and his mouth drops open a little. His eyes start at my face and work their way down my body, leaving a heated trail behind. I'm so flushed by the time his eyes make their way back to my face that I feel like I need to be doused with a firehose.

Once he's recovered, he stammers, "Wow, Sienna, you look… incredible."

Ducking my head because I'm too embarrassed to meet his eyes, I say, "Thanks. You clean up nicely too."

An awkward silence follows, and I'm keenly aware of Zane's lingering eyes. After a moment, he clears his throat. "I got you something," he says quickly, holding up a plastic grocery bag.

"What is it?" I ask.

His fingers find my elbow, leading me to the bathroom. "I was thinking you need a disguise for the gala tonight. What if Radcliffe is there?"

"You already called his office and confirmed that he won't be there, remember?"

"Still. I think we should be safe." Zane sets the bag on the pedestal sink and pulls out a wig. A platinum blonde wig, to be exact.

"You bought me a wig?" I ask him incredulously.

Zane's mouth lifts into a grin. "Your red hair does stand out."

"But why blonde? Why in the world did you get blonde?"

He shrugs. "I thought most girls like blonde."

Huffing, I snatch the wig from his hands. I expect the "hair" to be coarse and totally fake feeling, but it's surprisingly lustrous and soft. "Is this real hair?"

"Of course."

Frowning, I pull the wig over my short hair, tuck in the few strands that slip out, and look at myself in the mirror. The wig is long, wavy, and curls around my face. It feels like forever since I've had long hair, but it does make me look more feminine. As for the blonde? Well, that's an analyzation for another day. All I know is that blonde makes me think of Rayne, which produces a ball of fire in my chest.

"It's perfect," Zane says, watching my reflection in the mirror. "I miss the red, but it's a great disguise."

I turn to him, making a face. "I don't know why you had to get blonde," I grumble.

Chuckling, Zane says, "Do you have your Lynk?"

As part of our plan tonight, I need old pictures of my father, which I still have embedded on my Lynk. Yesterday, as I scrolled through photos I haven't looked at in years, it made me miss all the things that made Mom, Dad, Emily, and me a family. There's one of my father and me at a middle grade Daddy/Daughter dance, and one of my dad swinging Emily around by her armpits, their mouths frozen in laughter, and another one of my mother and father dancing in our living room. I think that one is my favorite.

I pat the matching clutch I picked out, that Zane bought for me, to go with the dress he also bought. "Yep, I have it."

Offering his arm, Zane says, "Then your chariot awaits."

I slide my arm through his. Outside the motel, Zane's car and driver are waiting to take us to the Marmet, the Museum of Fine Art, where the gala will be held tonight. As Zane lifts open the door for me, I slip inside the black vehicle, carefully arranging my skirts as I do. Once he's settled next to me on the oversized seat, the door closes automatically. The nervousness that I'd managed to squash so far surges up. Tonight, I will see both Trey and my father. And this time when I see my father, I won't be drugged. I'll be fully awake, aware, and ready for answers.

Once we're on the road, I can feel Zane's eyes on me. Without turning to look at him, I say, "If you keep staring at me like that, I'm telling Geoff to take me back to the Restful 8 Motel so I can change into ratty jeans and a T-shirt."

Zane gives a low chuckle. "I'm sorry. I'm having a hard time tearing my eyes away from you. I promise I'll behave." But even as he says it, he leans over and kisses my forehead.

I turn to him, my eyes wide. "What was that for?"

"In case I forget to tell you later."

"Tell me what?"

"That I think you're the most beautiful girl I've ever laid eyes on."

"It's because of the blonde hair," I mumble.

"No," he says. "It's because of you."

Heat rises from my chest and up my neck before settling in my cheeks. I'm sure I'm all splotchy now, thanks to Zane and his flattery. Do I like what he's saying? Of course. But he's making this so much harder for me.

"Zane—" I murmur.

Zane holds up a hand to stop me. "No more, I promise. That's the last nice thing I'll say to you for the rest of the night. From now on, I'll only comment on how messy your hair is, how much you're perspiring—those kinds of things."

A giggle slips out. "And I'll be sure to eat with my hands, and wipe my nose on the hem of my dress, anything to turn you off."

Zane nods as if he's seriously contemplating this. "My own little cavewoman. I have to say, I kind of like it."

Tipping my head back, I laugh. A few of the nervous knots that have taken up residence in my stomach loosen ever so slightly.

I turn my attention to the window, keeping my eyes focused on the passing scenery. The sun is lazily setting behind mirrored buildings, causing the rest of the sky to turn from burnt orange to the color of autumn leaves. Waves of pink, like cotton candy, are smeared across the sky as though they were glossed with a paintbrush. I crane my neck to watch the colors swirl and fade as if they're being sucked into a vacuum. Soon, all that's left of the sun are tiny tendrils of light, reflected in the mirrored buildings, and then they too are gone.

By the time we reach the Marmet, the sky has darkened and tiny stars now dot the sky. I like watching the transformation of day to night. The ending of one day, the residual rise and fall of the sun, the promise of a new one to come. It reminds me of rebirth.

The Marmet is a large, ostentatious building that looks mostly like a fortress. The exterior has enough detailed carving and even a decorative parapet to give it that castle look. Depictions of coats of arms are cut into the stone and lit up with a spotlight. A line of sleek black vehicles has already started to form in front of the steps that lead up to the entrance. I watch as couple after couple exit their vehicles, women wearing expensive gowns, their chests and ears bedecked in sparkling jewels, their fingers gripping tiny clutches, the men in perfectly pressed suits and polished black shoes. Instinctively, my fingers touch the delicate locket at my neck. Zane wanted to buy me fancy jewelry for tonight, but I insisted this was enough. It will always be more than enough.

When it's almost our turn, Zane hands me the tiny earbud that will keep us connected throughout the night. I insert it into my ear and pull my shawl tighter around me. The last thing I need is for my Fringe tattoo to glow up in front of everyone. Zane looks at me and says, "You ready?"

Swallowing hard, I nod. We wait for the driver to lift open the door, and then Zane steps out and offers me his hand. But as I'm trying to step out, my foot gets caught in the skirt's layers. I'm about to face plant on the pavement when Zane grabs my elbow, steadying me. I give him a grateful look.

Chuckling, he slides my hand through his arm and leads me up the stairs. When we reach the threshold of the building, two guards are there checking invitations and guest lists. Zane pulls his invitation from inside his suit jacket and flashes it at the guard.

"Zane Ryder. My father RSVP'ed, so it may be under his name."

The guard raises his bushy eyebrows when he hears Zane's name. His eyes flit to me—and I stiffen—then back to Zane, before settling on me. "And you are?"

"This is Shauna Tate, my assistant," Zane smoothly says, repeating the lie we concocted earlier.

A small line of people has started to form behind us, and I can feel sweat beading up under my armpits. Thankfully, Zane appears calm and collected beside me.

The guard consults his list one more time before saying,

"Welcome, Mr. Ryder. It's a pleasure to have you with us tonight."

Zane nods. Placing his hand on the small of my back, he guides me into the museum. When we first enter, all I want to do is stop and stare, but Zane continues to propel me forward until we're out of the way of the people behind us.

"It's beautiful," I murmur, my head tipping back to stare at the columned arch openings, the grand staircase leading to the second level, and the high ceilings and skylights that allow a view of the stars. There's even a fountain in the middle of the atrium, complete with multiple tiers of trickling water, adding a peaceful, calming effect.

"You've never been?" Zane asks, keeping his voice low.

"Is it that obvious?" I whisper back.

Zane chuckles. "Only a little." He glances around. "Should we split up or stay together?"

"Let's split up. Once you have eyes on either my father or Trey, let me know."

"Okay." He looks at me. "Be careful."

"I will."

I'm about to walk away, but Zane grabs my arm and pulls me back. When he speaks, his voice is low, urgent. "If Radcliffe is here, we abort. Remember?"

"I know." Running into Radcliffe has been our biggest concern since we first started planning this. But he's not supposed to be here. Zane called Radcliffe's secretary a few days ago and confirmed this. It seems odd that Radcliffe, as the head of the AIG, would choose to miss this event, though.

I slip my shawl off and drape it across my arm, giving Zane an encouraging smile. "I'll be fine," I whisper, but as I turn away, I can feel his concerned eyes boring into my back.

As I walk through the large hall, I pretend to scan the paintings, but instead, I'm surveying people. When a caterer offers me a sparkling glass of champagne from the tray he's holding, I shake my head. I try to blend in, to pretend I belong, but I suddenly wish Zane were with me. It would be so much easier to fit in with Zane and his overabundance of confidence beside me. I'm about to ask him where he is when a voice behind me says, "You know, they have coat closets where you can hang your shawl."

I know that voice. I know it so well that I could pick it out in a crowd of a thousand people, and as I turn to face him, a tremor runs through me.

Trey is staring at me, his head cocked to the side. His eyes run over my face and travel down the length of my body, and I suddenly feel as if every part of me has gone up in flames. His hair is slicked back, and his muscled body is enveloped in a tux that fits him snug in the shoulders and drapes the rest of his frame like it was made for him. And when I see him standing there, a cocky grin on his face, his hands large and familiar, all I want to do is wrap my arms around his neck and kiss him.

I shake my head a little. "I'm sorry. What did you say?"

Trey nods to the shawl in my hands. "Your shawl. There's a place to hang it." Before I can protest, he grabs the shawl from my arm. "Come. I'll show you where it is."

I follow him across the room, my eyes sweeping the space, searching for Zane. When we reach the coatroom, an attendant is in there, taking coats and giving stubs. Trey hands it to the girl who's working, a girl with mousy brown hair and light eyes.

"Sienna Pr—" Trey starts to say before I interrupt him.

"Shauna Tate," I say quickly, flashing the girl a smile.

"Yes," Trey says slowly. "Shauna Tate."

Wordlessly, the girl hands me the stub, which I put into my clutch. As we're walking away from the coat check, Trey's fingers latch onto my elbow and pull me to the side, to the base of one of the columns. "I almost didn't recognize you. What's with the blonde?"

"Well…" I shrug. "I've always heard that blondes have more fun." I'm keenly aware of his hand still touching my elbow, burning a hole through my bare skin.

He smirks. "Is that why you're here? To have fun?"

"Maybe."

Trey's eyes narrow, analyzing me. "Why are you *really* here, Sienna?"

"It's not because of you, if that's what you're thinking," I retort.

His hand drops. "No—I mean, I wasn't thinking that."

"You sure? Because you act like my whole life revolves around you. And it doesn't." Okay, so maybe I'm stretching the truth, but I can't stand his smug look.

His eyes soften. "I'm sorry. Truth is, I haven't been able to stop thinking about what you said to me at Zane's house. Before I left with Rayne."

The rhythm of my heart changes. "What do you mean?"

"I keep thinking about what you told me. You know…" He looks uncomfortable. "About how you feel about me."

Ah, so he feels guilty. Guilty that he pushed me aside so easily without a thought or care for my feelings.

His eyes find mine. "I've also—" He stops and glances around before leaning in. "I've been having these dreams."

My breath catches. "What about?"

"Weird things. The desert, underground rooms." He pauses for a second before he says softly. "You."

My heart pounds like it's about to come right out of my chest. "Me?"

Trey nods. "And I don't know if these are dreams or if they're…" He lets the idea hang.

"Memories," I whisper.

"Right."

The hired orchestra plays in the background, a low, soulful tune. I notice that a few couples are already slow dancing to the music in the open space of the main hall.

Trey glances around. "Care to dance?" he asks, holding out

his hand.

For a long moment, I stare at it, not sure what this invitation entails. "Where's Rayne?" I ask.

With his hand still outstretched, he replies, "She wasn't feeling well. Decided to stay home."

I place my clutch on a nearby table and fit my hand in his.

He leads me to the dance floor, turning me until I'm facing him. With gentle fingers, he lifts my hand, placing it on his shoulder while his other hand finds mine, fitting our hands perfectly together. When he wraps an arm around my waist and pulls me to him, we're chest to chest. He's so close that I'm scared to breathe. It's all so familiar, yet it's foreign at the same time.

I would never have guessed that Trey could dance, but surprisingly, he's really good. I'm probably awkward and stiff, but I try to follow his lead as we step and twirl around the room. I'm not sure what dance we're doing—or if it even has a name—but I do like being in his arms, the solidness of them around me.

As we move around the room, my fingers inch toward the base of his neck, wanting to confirm what I already know to be true. He raises an eyebrow as I pretend to play with the hair curling against his neck. "I've always liked the way your hair curls back here," I murmur, running my fingers along his hairline. And that's when I feel it—the puckered skin so similar to my own. Trey's mouth moves into a half-smile before he dips me low.

The orchestra plays an even slower song and then we're moving ever so slightly, more like a sway than a dance. I'm staring at a fixed spot across the room—a painting of a bowl of fruit—but when I feel Trey's eyes on me, I look up. Big mistake.

He clears his throat and says, "You look beautiful tonight."

My cheeks flame, and I'm suddenly self-conscious of my exposed skin. My pale skin with the million freckles. I wish I still had my shawl.

"How are things with you and Zane?"

"Complicated."

Right then, static buzzes in my ear and Zane's voice comes through. "Sienna, I have eyes on your father."

Trey and I are standing so close that I panic. *Could he hear that?* I step out of his arms, and Trey gives me a puzzled look.

"Everything okay?" he asks.

"Of course." I smile. "Do you want to get some air? I heard there's a garden in the back."

"Sure," Trey says.

I grab my clutch from the table, turn my ticket stub in at the coat check, and retrieve my shawl, draping it around my shoulders. As we're walking through the hall to the door that will lead to the gardens, my mind is racing. I can feel myself drawing closer to Trey, and now might be the time to give him some proof about his memory loss.

Twilight has turned to night, and as we step outside, I peer into the darkness. There are a few hanging lanterns that light the path through the gardens, but instead of taking that path, I motion for Trey to follow me to the darkest corner of the garden. He seems hesitant at first, but when I say, "Come on, I want to show you something," he relents.

We walk through a vine-draped trellis and take a seat on a wooden bench. I turn to face him, my heart pounding so hard in my chest I'm sure he can hear it. *Now is the time.*

"Trey, have you noticed the tattoos on your arm? A tree? A flower of life?"

He eyes me. "You know about those?"

I let my shawl slip off my shoulders, showing him my internal tattoos that glow in the darkness. The purple light seeps through my skin, creating an intricate web of butterflies. I run my hand up my arm and point to the Fringe tattoo.

"See. I have one too."

Trey leans closer, his eyes narrowing. His fingers reach out, but stop when they're only inches from my skin. He glances up at me, like he's asking permission. When I nod, his fingers trace the outline of the Fringe tattoo and the interconnecting circles creating a geometric flower-like pattern.

"What is it?" he whispers.

"It's my Fringe tattoo," I say. "All members have one. It distinguishes us. Sets us apart."

Even in the darkness, I can see his body go rigid. "Why do I have it?"

"I told you before, Trey. You're the leader of the Fringe."

"This can't be right," he mutters. He's quiet for a moment, thinking, before his fingers trail down my arm, sweeping over the glowing skin and sending a volt of electricity through me. "I like your butterflies."

Tears well in my eyes when I think of the last time he said those exact words, the night the Compound was bombed. "I know," I whisper.

Surprised, Trey glances up. "How?"

"Because you've told me before."

Trey stares at me for so long that I almost forget what we're talking about. And then in a voice that sounds like an apology, he says, "I don't understand any of this."

"It's okay," I say in a rush. "I'll explain everything. All you have to do is come with me—"

"No," Trey says firmly. For the first time, I see something in his eyes I don't quite understand. It looks like fear.

"No," he repeats. "You have to go."

"Trey," I plead. "Please. Give me a chance to explain what happened to you—"

Trey grips my arms, hard. "Go. Now."

"I'm not leaving," I say stubbornly.

"Dammit, Sienna," Trey says, his voice fierce. "They're here. They're coming for you, for Zane. You need to run. Now."

My body turns to ice. "What?"

Trey shakes his head. I've never seen him look so angry, and I'm not sure if it's directed at himself or me. "It's a setup. Can't you see that? I lured you in."

The sound of a heavy door flinging open reverberates through the night. There's shouting, and my mind becomes a dizzy blur of emotion. *He tricked me. He pretended to care, and he tricked me.*

"Sienna," he says, fear clouding his voice. "Run!"

Adrenaline kicks in. I gather my skirts and take off running through the dark garden, hoping and praying there's another way out. Pressing my finger against my ear, I say in a choked voice, "Abort, Zane. Abort. Get out of there now!"

I only hear static on his side of the line. I'm on my own.

I weave through bushes and fruit trees, rose bushes and flowerbeds. This part of the garden is darker and more overgrown—like someone became too tired to walk all the way out here to care for it. I hear the pounding of footsteps behind me, still a little ways back, but ever gaining on me, and the shouts of the Enforcers. I'm waiting for one of their laser bullets to whiz past.

My breathing is hard and shallow, and my lungs feel like they're about a second from exploding. My hair clings to my forehead, a tangled, sweaty mess. I kick off my heels, and now I'm running blindly over rocks and acorns and tiny sticks that litter the overgrown path. My feet scrape against the concrete pavers. Each step I take, one rock or another becomes embedded in the soles of my feet.

Tears and sweat mingle and run down my cheeks, the saltiness of both stinging my face. Just when I think I'm about to collapse because I can't run one more step in this dress that drags me down, I see it. A seven-foot brick wall lines the property, but there's an iron gate at the far left corner. Hurrying over, I try to open it with trembling hands, only to discover that it's padlocked shut.

No.

The Enforcers are gaining on me. I can hear their labored breathing, their guns slapping against their thighs. As soon as they round that last tree, they'll see me and all it will take is one shot to the chest to lay me flat.

I curse my dress and hike the skirts up to my waist before placing my foot on the first foothold I can find on the gate. My foot slides off. I try again. This time, I get a good grip and continue to climb, the curved ironwork digging into my feet. I'm halfway up when I see the Enforcers. They're shouting and raising their guns in warning. Without stopping to think, I scramble up the rest of the way, my dress getting caught at the top. I pull hard and tumble backward as a laser bullet narrowly misses my head. I land on the other side of the fence on my back, the breath knocked from me like a sledgehammer to the chest. It takes a few seconds to recover, laser bullets whizzing through the decorative ironwork, before I limp to my feet, crouch low, and take off running again. I'm in the middle of the city, though. And running through the city in a dirt-stained dress, twigs in my wig, and barefoot, not to mention my internal Fringe tattoo that glimmers on my skin, is like asking for the Enforcers to pick me up.

As I'm running, I rip off the wig and drop it on the ground, leaving it behind. I'm in an alley when I'm certain I'm caught. An Enforcer vehicle pulls up, blocking the entrance and the exit, and two black-clad men hurry out with their guns drawn. I think they've found me but I still try to hide, hunkering down behind a large trash incinerator. But it isn't me they're after.

"Enforcers! On your feet and in the vehicle!" Their guns are pointed at a figure huddled on the ground, one I hadn't noticed. It's a man, and he's rocking back and forth, holding something in his hands. One Enforcer shines a light on the man and the item in his hand.

A toy truck.

"Sir, we need you to get up and come with us. You can't sleep out here. It's illegal." An Enforcer with a gentler voice tries to reason with him, but the man continues to sit on the ground, rocking back and forth, holding his truck. He then begins to hum softly.

The Enforcer grips the man under his arm, producing a wail unlike any I've ever heard. "My truck! My truck," the man screams.

"Shut this guy up," the other Enforcer says, putting his laser gun to the man's head.

The man stops screaming and whimpers like a confused puppy.

"We need to take him in and put him with the others. Those are our instructions," the nicer Enforcer says firmly.

"This guy? He's a nut. There's no way he'll be beneficial. I think we should just put him out of his misery." But even as he says it, he lowers the gun.

"We've been told to round people up from the streets, including the mental cases. Do you want to disobey orders?"

The man babbles again. "My truck, my truck, my truck."

In one swift movement, the Enforcer raises his gun and shoots the man in the head. The truck falls to the ground and rolls a few feet.

I cover my mouth to stifle a cry.

"What the hell did you do that for?" the nicer Enforcer hisses.

"He wasn't any good to us. In order for the procedure to work, a body still needs working brain cells."

"That wasn't your call to make."

The Enforcer shrugs. "Maybe not. But who's gonna miss him?"

The two men get back in their vehicle and drive away, without a second glance at the innocent man they killed.

Once I'm assured they're gone, I come out of my hiding place. Creeping along the wall of the alley, I make my way over to the man. My stomach heaves when I see him, the smell of burnt flesh penetrating the air. I don't need to check his pulse to know he's dead.

Picking up the truck, I place it in his hands and whisper, "I'm sorry."

I stick to the alleys, cutting a path toward the ocean. The steady hum of Enforcers' vehicles and the continuous whirring of their alarms grow louder and softer as they search the streets of Rubex. And as I move, never stopping to think about the dead man, the blood on my feet and pain shooting up my back, or Trey's betrayal, I tell myself, *The ocean. I only need to make it to the ocean.*

When we lived in the suburbs and owned a pool, I'd swim laps every day until my arms ached. It was my exercise of choice, and I loved the way my body skimmed the surface of the water, making me feel unburdened and weightless.

When I crest the top of a hill and see the pier and ocean in the distance, I only hope my arms will remember the strokes and my body won't give out. By the time I reach the bottom of the hill, I'm limping so badly I can barely walk.

Twenty feet.

Ten feet.

The sand is cool, but it digs into the cuts on my skin, grinding and rubbing against the tender wounds. It also slows me down as I now have to hobble, fully dressed, in a ball gown.

Five feet.

At the water's edge, I find the zipper in the back of my dress. With shaking hands, I unzip it all the way. Glancing around to be sure no one is on the beach, I slide out of my dress and fling it into the ocean. *Let them think I drowned.*

The air is cool, and when it hits my bare skin, I shiver. But it's nothing compared to the water I'm about to immerse myself in. I breathe deeply a few times, psyching myself out for the swim that will get me to safety. This was Zane's plan, his emergency exit strategy should anything go wrong. At the time, I'd thought it was ridiculous to moor a boat one hundred yards off shore, but now, I'm incredibly glad he did. I can barely make out the beacon of light in the ocean, a tiny speck of red against an otherwise black backdrop.

I wade into the water, wincing as the saltwater touches my feet and then laps up my bare legs. Each step takes me further into the ocean, the sixty-degree water stinging my skin, numbing my toes. The water laps against my underwear, and then my belly button. I step on something sharp, a rock perhaps, and that's when I decide to swim. Letting my legs float up behind me, I keep my gaze focused on the red light in front of me. If I lose sight of that and get turned around in the ocean at night, I'm as good as dead. I decide on breaststroke because it allows me to keep my head above water. As I swim, my heart beats fast, pumping blood through my veins, and warming me enough to keep swimming despite the numbness creeping up my legs. I try not to think about what else is in the ocean, what else might be swimming right below me.

When I'm halfway to the boat, something brushes against my leg. I go completely still, floating in the water. I bite my lip to stifle the scream that surges up from my chest. *It's a shark, it's a shark, it's a shark.*

Something bumps against me again, testing me, and this time, the scream fights its way out. Putting my head in the water, I begin to kick and swim as fast as my arms and legs will go. I glance up every few seconds to be sure I'm on the right track. I keep waiting to feel sharp teeth and strong jaws latch on my arm or leg, but I continue swimming, praying I will make it to the boat. But when I glance up again, I don't see the light. Frantic, I turn, scanning the blackness, searching the horizon. But there's nothing. I turn to look back toward the shore, but in the dark, everything looks the same. There is no end and no beginning to the sea, only a never-ending backdrop of water and blackness.

"Please, God, help me," I sob. I turn again, my eyes searching. I'm frantic, desperate. I don't know how long I can continue to swim before the cold gets to me, an ocean creature takes me down, or I sink from pure exhaustion. My legs kick out, keeping me afloat, and I can only hope that whatever was testing me before is long gone now.

Then, when I'm on the brink of despair, I see the light, glimmering like a beacon off to my right. The current has steered me in the opposite direction, and I've actually overshot the boat. I'm further from shore than I should be. I now swim parallel to the shore, keeping my head above water, never taking my eyes off that red beacon of light.

When I reach the boat, my arms are like jelly and can barely latch onto the ladder. I pull myself up, my entire body shaking from fear and cold, and collapse on the floor of the vessel. My teeth chatter as I search for the bag Zane said he stashed here. To my immense relief, I find it tucked under the passenger seat. I pull out a fluffy towel that I wrap around myself and sink down into. Sitting on the floor of the boat, cocooned in the towel, I wrap my arms around my knees and rock back and forth, trying to get warm.

My hand reaches up, searching for the locket he gave me, needing the comfort of it. But it's not there. I glance down to confirm what I already know.

The locket is gone.

Probably swept away during my swim to the boat.

A small part of me mourns the beautiful locket and lost connection to Zane. I have no idea if he made it out safely.

Hopefully, he did, and at any moment, I'll see him slicing through the water, swimming toward me.

I focus my anger on Trey and the red-hot fury that boils up, warming my insides. He betrayed me. He told me I looked beautiful, that he remembered us together. He lured me in. I wouldn't be here, hiding out in this boat, if it wasn't for him. I left my mom and my sister to "rescue him" when he couldn't care less about me. I've been drugged, cut open, shot at, and now almost attacked by a shark, all to save him. I've allowed myself to care too deeply, to become weak, incapable. Well, that ends now. Because I realize something—love makes me weak. Love makes me do stupid things.

Never again will I allow myself to be hurt like this.

Love is for the weak. And I, Sienna Preston, am anything but weak.

25
Zane

Once I have Dr. Phillips, Sienna's father, in my sights, I send her a message over the receiver. She doesn't respond, so I assume it's because she's busy. My part of the plan is to keep him occupied until Sienna can get here. I take a few steps forward, intent on striking up a conversation with the man, but then I see three guards making their way toward me. I turn quickly and try to duck into the crowd, but it's not soon enough.

Two of the guards latch onto my arms, firmly. "Come with us, please."

"Is there a reason—" I start to say until I feel the butt of the third's gun resting between my shoulder blades.

"Now," he says, sneering.

They lead me to a room down the hall from the main atrium. This room must be the break room for employees as it houses a few tables, chairs, and vending machines. Once they've forced me inside, they push me into a chair and tie my hands behind my back.

"What is this?" I ask, irritation settling in. "Is there a reason you're treating me like a common criminal?"

"We have our orders," the skinny guard with the pocked face says.

"Release him," an authoritative female voice demands.

Heels click against the tile, and I'm shocked when Assistant President Neiman enters the room. Her bright red lips enhance the scowl on her face.

Pressure releases from my arms as the guards untie me. I flex my tight muscles and glare at the men who held me captive.

"Please forgive the misunderstanding, Mr. Ryder. My boys didn't realize who was in their possession."

"Why was I dragged in here to begin with?" I ask, rising to my feet. My mind flits to Sienna. *Is she okay?* "I've done nothing wrong."

Madame Neiman walks a tight circle around me, like a predator stalking her prey. "You've only been aiding and abetting a fugitive. An attempted murderer. A member of the Fringe." She comes full circle, standing right in front of me. "Is this correct, Mr. Ryder?"

My shoulders stiffen. "I don't know what you're talking about."

She props a hand on her hip. "Do you or do you not know a young woman by the name of Sienna Preston?"

I clear my throat, not sure where this line of questioning is headed. "She's a friend."

"And has she or has she not been staying with you in your condo in Rubex?"

Technically, no. We're staying in the dirtiest, scummiest motel money can buy.

"I'll be straight with you, Mr. Ryder," she continues. "The government doesn't look kindly on those who help the Fringe. You may think you're protecting her by denying that she's here in the Capital, but you're only hurting yourself." One long fingernail taps her blood-red lips. "Or more so, her family."

"What do you mean by that?" I demand, my blood pressure rising.

Her pale gray eyes bore into mine, like smoke rising, choking. "You have a safe house in the mountains, don't you,

Zane?"

Every muscle in my body tenses. "How do you know?"

She smiles and leans close, pressing a sharp fingernail against my chin. "I know everything," she whispers.

"What do you want?" I say through clenched teeth.

She straightens up and smiles. "I want your little girlfriend."

"She's not my girlfriend."

"Whatever you call her."

My fists clench, and it takes all my willpower not to deck this woman in front of me. "What makes you think I would ever give up her location?"

Madame Neiman smiles at me, a cruel, crooked smile. Her two canine teeth are pointier than they should be. *Like a predator.*

"She was here tonight, wasn't she? My men had her in their sights but lost her on the streets of Rubex."

I try to remain impassive, even though I'm immensely relieved. If she followed the plan, she's now headed to the boat where she'll be safe until I can get there.

"You'll make a mistake at some point, and you'll lead us right to her," Madame Neiman continues. "You can't bear to be separated from her, can you? Your little heart wants to protect her and make sure she's safe."

"You know nothing about me," I snap. "And I've had it with this line of questioning." I start to move toward the door, but the guards block my way, their hands resting on the butts of their guns.

"I know this," Madame Neiman says cruelly. "You're pining after a woman who will never love you, who will never see you the way you want her to." She rests her hand on a table, leaning into it. "How does it feel to be second best?"

Anger wells inside. "That's enough."

"You were made for more, Zane Ryder. You were made to lead, to show the world what a perfect society looks like." Her expression turns frank. "She'll only hold you back, Zane. Hold our society back."

"I don't care," I seethe, "about this stupid society. I've seen what it makes people do, what it makes them become. I don't know if I *want* to be a part of it."

Madame Neiman's eyes turn hard and a low guttural sound escapes her throat, similar to a growl. "Watch your tongue, boy. I'd hate for you to lose it." She spins around and walks to the door. With a flick of her hand, she says, "You know what to do, boys."

When the two men grab my arms, forcing them behind my back, I holler, "Hey! What is this?"

Madame Neiman stops and turns. "A warning." Then she strides out of the room.

As soon as the door clicks into place, the third guard moves toward me, a sick grin on his face.

"I'm gonna enjoy this one," he says, cracking his knuckles.

Instinct kicks in. I've never been much of a fighter—never had a reason to be—but my body knows exactly what to do. Sure, I've sparred a little, but it's always been done in fun, never as a means for saving my own neck.

I kick the knees of the men holding me and they crumble, cursing in pain. The third guard advances toward me with his meaty hands, but I'm ready for him. I duck his first punch and hit him hard with a left hook. My hand connects with skin that feels like overcooked steak.

By now, the other guards are up, encircling me, their fists ready.

"We have a tough guy on our hands," one of them says, and then he laughs cruelly.

"Yeah, a tough guy," the other mimics.

I eye the three of them, mentally calculating how much force it would take to render them unconscious.

When the meaty guard moves behind me and wraps his

arms around my body, pinning my arms to my sides, I use my own weight to propel us backward, causing the guard to lose his balance. We fall on the ground, the guard's head hitting the floor with a sickening crack. I jump to my feet and stare down at him. He's out cold.

The other two guards rush me. One pulls out a gun and shoves it in my face, but I knock it from his hands before he has a chance to realize what's happening. The other guard manages to punch me in the gut, knocking the air from me. I straighten quickly, elbowing the gun guard in the nose, and kneeing the pockmarked guard in the face.

They're injured, but not ready to quit. As they advance on me again, I grab one of the folding metal chairs and hold it in front of me threateningly.

"This isn't going to end well for either of you," I warn. I'm still not sure what I'll do with the chair, but they don't need to know that.

They both laugh. "I was about to say the same for you," the gun guard sneers.

They rush me at the same time, and I swing the metal chair as hard as I can. It connects with the gun guard's skull, and the sound is enough to make my stomach churn. As he's falling to the ground, something hits me in the jaw, snapping my head back. I hear the one remaining guard laugh. With pain shooting from my chin to my ear, I open my mouth to pop my jaw back into place. I can see Pockmark in the corner of my eye, his foot flicking out toward my ribs. In one swift movement, I drop the chair and grab his foot, twisting until he lands flat on his back in pain. I straddle him, punching him in the face until his eyes close and I know he's out.

When I stand, my body groans. I flex and unflex my hands a few times, stretching the tight, sore muscles. One thing is for sure—I may know how to fight, but I don't enjoy doing it.

With three guards littering the floor, I have to get out of

here before someone sees me. I slip out the door and try to walk normally down the hallway, but my body is still pumped up on adrenaline.

Once my car has been pulled around by my driver and I'm seated inside, my breathing finally returns to normal.

My first thought is that I have to know if Sienna is okay. I'm about to tell Geoff, my chauffeur, to drop me off at the beach, but then I remember. They're watching me. If I go to our emergency escape place, I could lead them right to her.

I pull out my Lynk and dial hers instead. When she doesn't answer, but goes straight to a message screen, I try to remain calm. I decide to leave her a message.

"Sienna, I'm okay. I made it out of Marmet. Please call and let me know you're safe."

In case they're bugging my phone and tracing my phone calls, I leave it short and sweet, with no indication of where I'm going.

When I hang up, I place my head against the smooth glass of the tinted windows. Something nags at me. Something Madame Neiman said…

I sit up straight.

The safe house. They know where it is, and they know who's hiding there. Vivian and Emily aren't safe. And right now, neither is Sienna with me here in Rubex. She'll reach out to me, and when she does, they'll find her.

I don't want to. Every sane thought is telling me not to. But I know what I have to do.

I must leave Rubex.

26

Sienna

I wait for Zane until my eyelids are too heavy to keep open. The gentle rocking of the boat and the complete darkness around me doesn't help my campaign to stay awake. Fortunately, Zane was smart enough to pack a pair of sweatpants and sweatshirt he found at some discount store, so I slip those on once I'm dry.

The bow of the boat has a padded seat that's perfect for curling up on. Using my damp towel as a pillow, I lay back and stare up at the stars. Millions of stars and hundreds of constellations look down on me. I can see Orion, Ursa Major, Ursa Minor, and even Canis Major. And for a moment, I picture lying next to my father on a blanket in our backyard as his steady hand points out various constellations. I don't think we could ever see them as clearly as I can tonight though.

Thinking of my father sends a pang through my chest. Because of Trey, I never had a chance to see or talk to him tonight. The coals of my anger burn a little hotter. Just one more reason to hate Trey.

As my eyelids grow heavy, I jerk myself awake, intent on waiting for Zane. But when hours have passed, or so it feels like, and there's still no sign of him, I pray he's safe and drift to sleep.

When the first rays of sunlight peek over the horizon,

bathing the sky in hues of pink and red and pumpkin orange, I'm awake and starving. I rummage around in the bag Zane packed and find half a dozen granola bars. I tear into two of them.

Now that it's daylight, the ocean doesn't seem quite so frightening, but since Zane never came, my imagination is running wild. Either he's safe, or he's locked away somewhere. I try to pretend it's not the latter.

Not for the first time do I wish I could call him or send him a message, but just like my locket, my Lynk is gone, carried away by the ocean currents. There's no way to get in touch with him until I can find a burner Lynk.

I've never driven a boat before, but I imagine it can't be that hard. The keys are already in the ignition, so I give the key a good crank, and the boat roars to life. I search for a pedal or something to make the vessel move forward, but there's nothing. Then I remember Zane saying something about a throttle. There's a gearshift thing next to the steering wheel, and I see the word *Neutral*. I must be in neutral, which is why I'm not moving. I'm about to push this throttle forward when I remember the anchor. Keeping the boat on, I lean over the bow and pull up the frayed rope until the anchor lifts with it. I set the anchor on the floor and move back to the captain's chair.

Just a touch of the throttle and the boat surges forth. I ease back, bobbing over the waves, and then try again. It is then, as I'm struggling to maintain control, that I realize how hard and potentially dangerous this could be. Images of the boat, capsized, float into my brain.

"Come on," I say. I push the throttle again and the boat responds, leaving a trail of exhaust fumes in its wake. As I run the boat parallel to the shore, I'm on the lookout for any large rocks or sandbars. The wind stings my cheeks and whips through my hair, and I breathe deeply, inhaling the salty air. I follow the shoreline until I find a good place to come ashore,

but now I have to go over the break, the place where the waves swell, and the very thought scares me. These are six, seven-foot waves, large enough to capsize a small vessel like this one. I'm right at the place where the waves swell, and the small boat can't handle the constant battering of the thousands of pounds of water against its side. *Think, Sienna, think.*

I picture a surfer on a surfboard, gliding on top of the water, riding the swell, taking it all the way in until the wave dumps him out and drags him down. And amazingly enough, I know what to do. I'll turn the boat into a giant surfboard, one with a motor and half a ton of aluminum.

I carefully maneuver the boat until I'm perpendicular with the waves, then when I see the swell forming, I push the throttle hard and ride the top of it. I can feel it break beneath me, and I'm so thrilled that I managed to make it past the breaking waves that it isn't until I look up and see land looming ahead that I pull back on the throttle and put the boat in neutral, allowing the wave to carry me the rest of the way.

The boat hits sand and rocks, the motor grinding into the ground. *Oops. Probably not the best idea.* With Zane's bag on my back, I cut the engine, grab the rope with the anchor, and jump out of the boat, splashing through the water as I do. I set the anchor as far up on shore as I can and take off running, wincing at each step. The grainy sand cuts into the sores on my feet.

"Hey," someone hollers, a man out for his early morning walk on the beach. "You can't park there!"

"Sorry," I call back, hobbling away. Moving on sand is like having dumbbells attached to your legs, but I manage to make it to the boardwalk and then the street. I decide it might be best to try to blend in, so I slow down and walk at a brisk pace instead.

Thankfully, Zane was smart enough to put a micro card in the backpack, for emergencies. And this definitely counts as an emergency.

I hail an air taxi, a vehicle that hovers only a few inches from the ground. They are the latest craze in the Capital because they help preserve the roads with less wear and tear.

Once inside, I direct the driver to take me to the Restful 8 Motel. He weaves into traffic, ranting about city drivers. I insert the micro card in the slot and watch as the numbers on the digital device steadily climb.

It's a good thing Zane has money.

When I reach the motel, the door is unlocked. At first, fear claws its way to my throat. I picture his ransacked condo, and I'm fairly certain that when I open the door to our motel room, it will look much the same. But then I remember. Zane left it unlocked last night for this very reason. If we were to get separated, since we only had one key, he wanted to make sure I'd still be able to get into the room.

I go inside, and everything is right where we left it. Duffle bags on the dresser, Zane's athletic shoes next to the door, and the clothes I was wearing yesterday draped across a chair.

Closing the door behind me, I call softly, "Zane?" I guess I'm going off a small prayer that he somehow made it out of the Marmet and returned here last night instead of going to the boat. But there's no sign that he's been here. Even the book he was reading yesterday while he waited for me to finish getting ready still rests on the arm of the couch.

Where is he?

After I take a quick shower to wash off the seawater, and then dress in clean clothes, I empty the bag Zane packed for the boat. I restock it with a couple of changes of clothes, a handful of granola bars, a few water bottles, the micro card Zane gave me, and the wire cutters I find in his duffle bag—not sure why he had them, but they might come in handy. Then, I grab one of the guns I'd hidden under the mattress. Tucking it in the back of my pants, I do a quick sweep of the motel room.

One thing catches my eye. Striding to the coffee table, I pick up the poetry book, flip to the *Forget Me?* poem, and rip the page out. I shred it into tiny pieces and watch as they fall like confetti to the floor.

Never again.

I place the book on the table and walk out the door without looking back.

The first thing I do is buy a burner Lynk from a man off the street. I'm only a few blocks from the motel, and the area hasn't changed much—it's still as sketchy as the place we've been staying. There are more people here, though, and litter clutters the streets. The constant smell of sewer permeates the air, not to mention the dark-haired women who sit on the curb with crying babies in their laps, and tanks full of eels, fish, and crabs on display on the sidewalk.

Moving out of the way of the people on the streets, I try Zane's Lynk. Disappointment fills me when I only get his voice message. I try not to think about all the bad things that could have happened to him, but it's hard not to.

The next person I call is Chaz. I explain to him all that's happened since I arrived in Rubex. He listens patiently, his expression serious, his eyes widening at certain parts. When I finish, the first words out of his mouth are, "What can I do?"

"You're not gonna like this, but I need to know where Radcliffe lives."

Chaz closes his eyes for a second. "Christ, Sienna, are you trying to get yourself killed?"

"No, I'm trying to get Zane back." When he remains quiet, I say, "Do I need to ask someone else? You know, you're not the only hacker the Fringe uses." Of course I'm lying.

"Fine, I'll help you. But you have to promise me that you'll be careful."

"Aren't I always?" I say lightly.

Chaz gives me a disapproving look and moves to his computer. "What's this guy's name?"

"Colonel George Radcliffe. I believe his permanent residence is somewhere in Rubex." I hear the clack of computer keys as Chaz begins his search.

"Got it," he says after only a minute.

"That was fast," I say, not sure if I should believe him.

"Yeah, well, it's a lot easier to pull up someone's home address than it is to hack into a complex security system."

"Makes sense. What's his address?"

"Hang on. I'm sending it to your Lynk now."

"Wait. Send it to this one. This is my burner. Only use this number from now on. Got it?"

"Okay, sending the address now." He pauses and looks at his computer screen. "And based on where you are now, I'd say he lives about five miles away."

Damn. I could really use my Harley right about now.

I thank Chaz and hang up. Glancing around, I notice a weathered man sweeping the sidewalk outside a shop that sells martial arts equipment.

"Excuse me, sir?"

He stops and looks up, his eyes squinting beneath wired frames.

"Are there any air taxis around here? Any that might take me to Ridgepoint?" Ridgepoint is the area of Rubex where wealthy Citizens live, those who aren't in condos by the ocean, that is.

"You rent bike?" he asks in broken English.

"Um, sure. I could rent a bike instead."

"I got bike," he says. Pausing in his sweeping, he leans into his shop and calls out a name. A teenage boy with olive skin comes out of the shop.

"Ren, girl needs bike. Help her." The man turns away and resumes his sweeping.

The boy named Ren gives me a once over. "Let me just grab the key," he mutters before disappearing in the shop.

When he emerges with a key dangling from his hand, he motions for me to follow him around the side of the building, into the alley. I hesitate, because these streets are so different from the other parts of Rubex. The alley is dark and doesn't look like a place I'd like to go. Plus, I stick out here with my fair skin and freckles.

I decide to follow him anyway.

"Your hair is very… red," he says, glancing over his shoulder as we walk.

"And yours is very black," I reply.

The boy chuckles, stopping beside half a dozen rusted bikes, chained together.

"I only meant—" He exhales, and my eyes are drawn to his high cheekbones and the way they stand out when he breathes deeply. "You don't see that color much."

I shrug. "I get it from my mom. She's a redhead."

I watch as this boy, Ren, unlocks the bikes and rolls out a blue one that doesn't look quite as old as the rest.

"Sorry, this is all we have," he says.

"No, it's okay—" I start to reassure him, but I'm interrupted by the blare of an air horn. The boy's eyes go wide.

"Hide," he hisses.

He shoves the bike in my hand and takes off running down the alley in the opposite direction of the shop.

"Hey! Where are you going?" I call after him.

When he reaches the end, he collides with two Enforcers who are entering the alley. They grab him and twist his arms behind his back, his screams rolling through the alley. Heart racing, I crouch down behind the row of bikes, praying they don't come down here.

"This looks like a good one," the Enforcer with shoulders the size of a tank says.

"Let's put him with the others," his companion agrees.

The boy kicks and screams in protest as the Enforcers drag him away. Once they are out of sight, I shoulder my backpack, hop on the blue bike, and pedal out of the alley. When I get to the street, I pause. The street is crawling with Enforcers. Men and women are running down the middle of the road, dragging their children between them. Others are crying and begging the Enforcers to leave their families alone.

"Please, don't! He's only fourteen! He's still a child," one woman cries, tears streaming down her cheeks. The Enforcer has a well-built boy in his grasp and pushes the mother out of the way. She falls to the ground, sobbing.

As they throw the boy into the covered back of a military truck, I catch a glimpse of several other boys, even girls, who can't be much younger than I am.

I want to stay and help the woman, but I can't afford to be caught. I pedal hard, weaving past the surging crowd of brave people who are shouting and throwing things at the Enforcers, trying to fight back. There's gunfire, and I glance over my shoulder in time to see a few of the rioters fall to the ground. An Enforcer at the edge of the crowd with his gun raised sees me pedaling away.

"Hey! Stop! *Enforcers*," he shouts.

Ignoring him, I turn down a side road to get away. I pedal faster, my calf muscles flaming, my heart hammering an uncontrollable rhythm.

What happened back there? Why were the Enforcers capturing those boys and girls?

My head is spinning as quickly as the spokes of the wheel.

I ride past shopkeepers with their colorful silks and knock-off purses, past men selling comscreens from makeshift tables, and stray dogs that stop and pee on things like light poles and fire hydrants. After a mile, the smell of sewer and urine dissipates, and once again, I'm staring at a sea of tall skyscrapers and mirrored condos. I slow down and pull my Lynk from my pocket, consulting the data map. As I near the city, it has me turn and head away from the ocean.

I try to put aside the image of the boy being captured by the Enforcers and the fear in his eyes when he heard the air horn—almost like he knew what that meant. He expected the Enforcers to come with force.

Hide, he'd said to me.

He knew they were coming for him. For the others.

Where did they take him?

It's slow moving on a bike, especially compared to my Harley with its roaring motor and neck-breaking speeds. Right now, I miss her more than I ever have before.

A couple of times, I hear the whine of Enforcers' vehicles in the distance. The sound makes my heart pound harder than normal, but it also makes me pedal faster. The address Chaz gave me leads to a wealthy community called The Gates. I'm not sure why it's called that considering there isn't a gate at the entrance.

Radcliffe lives a few streets into this affluent community. As I ride the bike slowly past his house and stop on the opposite side of the street a few houses up—doing recon surveillance— it feels kind of surreal that a man like Radcliffe would live in a neighborhood. A neighborhood that looks so *normal*.

His house sprawls across an immaculate green lawn with flowerbeds and a sprinkler system currently watering his yard. The stucco tiles on the roof of his home are similar to those you might find in Legas. And as I stare at his house, I think how it could be anyone's house. It could be the home of a doctor or lawyer who kisses his family before going to work, but instead, it belongs to one of the cruelest, most ruthless men I've ever known.

A shadow moves behind the window, forcing me to duck behind the bushes. *Is he here? Or is that the help?*

I picture Radcliffe's leering face, his cold tone as his goons water tortured me in the basement of the SGF. I remember my mother, bound, gagged, and stuffed in the back of Radcliffe's SUV like an animal. Then, I picture the SGF and Radcliffe's contemptuous declaration that he's the one who killed my father. I can still feel the gun in my hand as I pulled the trigger. Twice. And shot out his kneecaps. I should have killed him that day.

That's okay, because tonight, I will remedy that.

When the sun is but a distant memory in the sky and the moon is now white and full, I arrive back at Radcliffe's house. I've spent the day riding around town, always moving, never staying in one spot for too long. My legs are tired from pedaling, and I have no idea where I'll sleep tonight—it's probably not safe to return to the motel—but I'm not too worried about it. Right now, I'm focused. Right now, I have a job to do. And I won't leave until it's done.

I already have Chaz on the line to help me with whatever security system I might face when I get inside. I park the bike behind some bushes several homes up, and crouching low, creep to the back of Radcliffe's house where I find an enclosed porch made completely of glass. From here, I can see the keypad on the other side of the glass, beside the door. Pulling out my Lynk, I show Chaz. "What do you think?" I ask him.

"Hang on. I'm taking a picture now." There's a click, and then he says, "Now I'm superimposing it on my computer, so I can see it better." After a minute, he says, "I think he has a TREXUS."

"What's that?"

"A high-tech security system that detects any abnormal movement and will immediately alert the Enforcers as well as his own Lynk."

"Is there any way to get around it?"

"Let me think for a sec."

I stay quiet, staring at the blinking red light on the other side of the glass.

"Okay, I think I got it. If you cut the power source, then the TREXUS will go temporarily offline, which should give you enough time to get in."

"And what about getting out?"

"Well, that's when you run. The moment TREXUS comes back online, the Enforcers will be alerted."

Crap. "Okay, how do I cut the power source?"

"We have to fake a blackout. Because if you cut power only to Radcliffe's home, then TREXUS will know and alert the authorities."

"Where's the main power source?"

"Underground." His keyboard keys click out a rhythm. "I'm looking up the electrical grid now." After a few seconds, he says, "You're in luck. There's a main transistor above ground on the street corner, only a few houses up."

I take off running in that direction. There's also a streetlamp on the corner, humming, with dozens of insects flitting around the flickering light like moths drawn to a flame. The transistor is a metal box with a padlock.

"It's locked," I huff.

"Well, break it open," Chaz says.

"Okay." I search the ground for a large rock. When I find one, I grasp it in my hand and strike the dangling padlock. The clashing noise is so loud I fear it may wake every person in the neighborhood. I crouch low, glancing up and down the street, waiting for lights to appear in bedroom windows. But the street remains still and quiet.

I try again, striking the padlock with such force that it causes my fingers to bleed and the lock to spring open. I wipe the blood on my pants and hurry to lift open the lid of the metal container. Once inside, I see wires that criss-cross every which way. Holding up the Lynk, I show Chaz. "Now what?"

Chaz is quiet as he studies the complex system. "Okay, I need you to clip the three blue wires and the one red wire, but don't touch the two yellow, three green, or one black. Got it?"

I nod, but then remember he can't see me. "Got it."

Pulling the wire cutters from my bag, and glad I thought to bring them, I carefully cut the three blue wires. The lamppost above me goes dark, the only sound the hiss of insects getting electrocuted as the light dies out. Using my Lynk as a light source, I search for the one red wire. When I see it, I grasp it with the wire cutters and slice through. Immediately, the entire street goes dark. There are no entryway lights, no streetlights, nor the soft glow of light from a comscreen in a living room. There are only the outdoor solar lights that still highlight the landscaping or particular architectural feature of a house.

"You have two minutes before TREXUS is back online. Now go!" Chaz says, his voice urgent.

I run harder than I've ever run before, cutting across lawns and hurdling over bushes. When I reach Radcliffe's glass-enclosed porch, I don't hesitate. I wrap a towel around my arm and break through the glass of the sun porch. Reaching through, I unlock the door and open it from the inside. There's no alarm, only the beautiful, sweet sound of silence.

Once I'm inside, my steps make no noise as I wind my way through his home that smells of fresh baked cookies and household cleaner. It smells so oddly familiar that I hesitate at the base of the stairs. *What if I have the wrong house? What if Chaz made a mistake?*

I shake off the feeling and start up the stairs, pausing to listen when I make it to the top of the landing. I hear heavy footsteps and move toward the sound. It's coming from a bathroom inside an oversized bedroom with draping curtains and a king-sized bed. The room is completely dark, of course. Only a faint glow comes from beneath the closed bathroom door. I imagine Radcliffe with his own Lynk light. I flip my light on and shine it around the room. One side of the bed has been turned down, like only one person is about to sleep in it. A military uniform is perfectly pressed and laid out across a chair. I recognize the uniform as the same one Radcliffe wore when I met him in the SGF under the pretense that he would release my mother in exchange for Zane's Re0Gene serum. *Another one of Radcliffe's lies.*

A toilet flushes, so I know it will only be a few moments before I come face to face with the man who has caused me too much grief. I move over to the window where there's another armchair hidden in the shadows. I remove the gun from the back of my pants and take a seat on the edge of the chair, placing the weapon in my lap but leaving the backpack on.

My hands are shaking, but my insides are ice. I am hard, I am cold, I am a murderer, and I don't have to convince myself this time. I just am.

I could do it now, catch him completely off guard, in his most vulnerable state, but no, I decide to wait. Besides, I'd like to have a little chat with him before I put a bullet in his brain.

The sound of a faucet turning on is what I hear next, and then the sound of someone spitting. *Is he brushing his teeth?* Well, at least he has good hygiene. And he'll have clean teeth when he dies.

The door to the bedroom opens. My eyes are now adjusted to the dark, so I see him clearly, but I know he can't see me. Dressed in a bathrobe, he fumbles around for a moment, his Lynk light illuminating the hardwood floor in front of him. I can see the glint of steel from his prosthetic limbs as he walks.

"Damn power," he mutters, feeling his way to the bed.

Once he's there, he clicks off his Lynk light and sinks down onto his bed, his bathrobe flapping open. Disgusted, I look away, but when I look back, I realize that, thankfully, he's wearing boxers and a T-shirt beneath. I watch as he twists one leg off and then another before placing them on the floor beside him. He removes the brace that keeps his titanium legs in place and drops that on the floor too. As he's struggling to push himself back on the bed, his legs mere stumps, I feel a pang of sympathy for him. He wriggles and moves, grunting from the effort. I hear him curse before he's properly positioned, his back resting against the headboard, his breath coming in spurts.

And all I can think is *I did this to him. This is my fault.*

Before I can feel enough sympathy to make me change my mind, I rise from the chair and raise the gun. "Hello, Radcliffe."

27

Sienna

"Just do it," he says, like he isn't the least bit surprised to see me. "I've been waiting for you to come back and finish me." He gives a harsh laugh. "It's the least you can do after making me a cripple."

"Oh, I'll definitely put you out of your misery," I say. "But I want some answers first." I inch closer, keeping the gun trained on him. But I don't know why I bother. This man is helpless. He's a shell of the man I knew in Legas.

Radcliffe heaves a heavy sigh. "What do you want to know?"

"First of all, where's Zane Ryder?"

"How should I know?" Radcliffe holds up a finger. "Wait, don't tell me—the saga of Sienna Preston continues and you lost another boyfriend. What's the matter, Sienna, can't keep your boy toys on a leash?"

"Don't play dumb with me," I threaten. "Last night, Zane and I went to the gala at the Marmet. We were ambushed. He didn't make it out." I move a step closer. "I want to know where he is."

"It's out of my hands. He's not my problem anymore. You're not my problem anymore." Radcliffe's face turns harsh. "Don't you get it, Sienna? I'm no good to them. I'm a cripple. I'm only bait."

"What? Wait... Are you saying you had no idea they were going to ambush us last night? That you weren't the one behind it?"

Radcliffe leans forward, his eyes hard. "My career is over. They don't include me in any plans, and they certainly don't need my permission for any ambushes."

"What about the AIG lab?" I ask. "Did you order them to erase my memories?"

"I was called in for one last assignment, yes. And I am the one who drugged you to get you there. But other than that, I haven't been to the AIG lab since you gave me those," he says, looking disgustedly at his prosthetic legs lying on the floor.

"Why did you drug me?"

"Because I was ordered to."

My mind is spinning. *If Radcliffe isn't the one behind this, then who is?*

"My father is still alive," I accuse. "And you knew, didn't you? This whole time you let me—you let us—believe he was dead. Why?"

Radcliffe sighs again. "Because that's what he wanted."

All the air in my body is sucked out of me. I lower the gun. "What did you say?"

"I gave him the poison that slows the heartbeat until it's undetectable, hired emergency services to take him away, helped plan his funeral minus the body, got him relocated to the Capital, and erased his memories."

"Why?" I choke out. "Why would you do that?"

His voice is harsh when he says, "Because I was told to do it. Because it was my job."

And then it hits me. *Radcliffe is a pawn. He's nothing more than a pawn.*

Then I hear something that makes my heart stop and my blood run colder than ice.

"Daddy?" a small voice calls from the hallway. "Daddy?"

I watch as Radcliffe closes his eyes. "What is it, pumpkin?"

Tiny footsteps approach, and I dart behind the door as a small girl, no more than seven, appears in the doorway. "Daddy, I'm scared. The light went out in my room."

Radcliffe opens his eyes and smiles at his daughter. "It's okay, sweetie. I think the power's out. It should come back on soon."

The little girl goes up to Radcliffe's bed and leans in for a hug. My chest squeezes as Radcliffe's arms wrap around his daughter. When she pulls back, she says, "Daddy, will you tuck me in?"

"Not tonight, sweetie. See?" He points to the floor. "I already took my legs off."

The girl pouts. "I don't like your new legs."

Radcliffe chuckles. "Me neither. Now hurry back to bed."

"G'night," she says, already retreating into the hallway.

"Goodnight, pumpkin."

I listen as the footsteps recede down the hall, and then I come out of my hiding place. "You have a daughter?" I hiss.

Radcliffe nods.

"Where's her mother?" I'm suddenly desperate for information. If I kill this man, that little girl will be fatherless.

Radcliffe pinches the bridge of his nose. "She died in a car accident two years ago."

"But your daughter—I mean—when you go away for work—"

Radcliffe seems to understand what I'm trying to convey. "She has a nanny."

The room spins like I'm upside down on an old-fashioned roller coaster. One hand still holds the gun, but I rest my free hand on the nightstand to brace myself. Nothing is what it seemed, and now I'm not sure what to believe.

"Who's behind this?" I whisper. "If it's not you, then who?" As I'm straightening up, I accidentally knock a picture frame to the floor. I'm bending over to retrieve it when there's the sound of glass breaking and a soft thunk, like the breath is knocked out of someone. There's glass from the window on the floor, and when I look at Radcliffe, all I see is red. Red blood seeping from the hole in his chest, and red drool coming out of his open mouth.

"Oh no. No, no, no," I say. I try to cover the wound with my one free hand, but it's gushing, blood seeping through my fingers, staining them red. It's too late.

"Daddy?" a small voice says. Then it rises hysterically. "Daddy!"

I try to comfort the girl, to shield her from the sight of her father, but she shrieks and runs to the far corner of the room. Her accusing eyes flit from me to her father. From the blood on my arms to the gun in my hand to her father's open mouth.

"No," I say, shaking my head. "I didn't do this. I promise, I'm innocent."

It doesn't matter that ten minutes ago I had plans to do this exact thing. It doesn't matter that I'm the one who broke into Radcliffe's house and put a gun to his head. Because in the end, I'm not the one who pulled the trigger. I wasn't going to do it. The moment I saw the little girl, everything shifted. But it doesn't matter, because now Radcliffe is dead, and his blood is on *my* hands.

My eyes fill with tears for this little girl who will live the rest of her life without her father. "I'm sorry," I whisper to her. "I'm so, so sorry." Then I turn and run. Down the hall, down the stairs, and through the house. As I reach the back porch, the automated voice of TREXUS kicks in.

"Unauthorized visitor. Please remain calm. Enforcers are on their way." I can already hear the whine of the Enforcers' vehicles drawing closer.

I burst through the door and take off running. Once I reach the hidden bike, I shove the gun into the pack and hop on the bike. I pedal as hard as I can. I've never longed for my Harley as much as I do at that moment. This bike is slow and awkward, not exactly what you want when you're trying to make a quick escape.

My arms are coated in Radcliffe's blood, and the sound of the sniper shot coming through the window replays in my mind. Someone was watching him. Someone knew I was there, questioning him. And someone wanted to make sure Radcliffe kept his mouth shut.

An air horn blares in the distance, and the hum of Enforcer's vehicles is like the sound of an active, buzzing hive. I pedal faster, my chest heaving, my breath coming in short, stuttered spurts. I stick to back streets and people's yards.

As I hurry away from Radcliffe's neighborhood, the sky is as black as the wings of a crow. In the distance, light flickers from the giant netscreens, leering at me from the sky. As I get closer to the city, I let my eyes wander only briefly up to them. I recoil in horror when right after a picture of a scantily clad woman—an ad for undergarments—my picture from GIGA flashes up on the screen with the following headline beneath:

Sienna Preston: 17-year-old female
Height: 5 feet 2 inches
Weight: 115 lbs.
Wanted for the murder of Colonel George Radcliffe. A reward of one million pacs for any information leading to her capture.

Swallowing hard, I duck my head and hurry faster. Air taxis rush past, hovering only a few inches from the ground. I keep moving because the moment I stop, I risk someone recognizing my face. Thankfully, my hair is much longer in the picture, and I look so much younger, more innocent even.

That photo was taken before my life was shot to hell. Before everything turned upside down. Back when my only worry was getting good grades on exams. And agonizing over whether I might one day fill out my gym clothes like the rest of the GM girls. How things have changed…

A few minutes later, I venture another glance above at a different screen lighting up the sky. This one also displays my picture and the same headline beneath. It plays over and over like a song on repeat—my picture, followed by the headline. My picture, followed by the headline.

They're framing me. Trying to make it look like I'm the one responsible for Radcliffe's murder.

The air is tinged with the smell of briny seawater, lifting up off the bay. I breathe deeply and fill my lungs with the smell. To me, the ocean is freedom. It has no boundaries, no borders, and it makes me feel like I'm the teeniest, tiniest person in a too-big world. Like I'm someone who can hide and never be spotted.

Keeping my head down, and hoping no one notices the blood coating my arms and clothes, I make a series of turns, pedaling away from the city and straight toward the beach, constantly looking over my shoulder to see if I'm being followed. I have to maneuver around joggers out for a run and businessmen walking home from a late night at the office. Once I hit the sand, I tumble off the bike and stumble to the water. This part of the beach is empty, although the tinkling sounds of laughter and the blaring of an air taxi's horn drift on the wind. All I can think about is getting Radcliffe's blood off me. Maybe if I can remove it from my skin, I can remove it from my mind.

But as I rip my shirt off and scrub my arms in the ocean, so vigorously that my skin stings, I keep picturing Radcliffe's daughter asking him to tuck her in bed. Tears wet my eyes and drip down my chin as I think of that little girl who will never see her father again, who will never shake the image of his blood seeping from his chest, who will be haunted by his death for the rest of her life. She'll never have peace as long as her father's killer is roaming free. And she thinks his killer is *me*. And that is probably the saddest part of all. I don't want to be the one responsible for taking a girl's father away from her.

And yet, I am.

If I hadn't sought him out, if I hadn't questioned him, he might still be alive.

So, no, I might not have pulled that trigger, but I did kill him.

28
Sienna

Not surprisingly, the boat is not where I left it this morning. The beach patrol must have taken it back to the marina Zane rented it from. Not to worry, though, because the marina is only a short walk from here.

I pull a tank top from my bag and slip it on, tossing the bloodied shirt in a trash incinerator. Heading back to the boardwalk, I walk the short distance to the marina. When I reach the boat-stocked area, I try to pretend like I belong here, walking with short, purposeful strides. I hurry down the narrow docks, surrounded on both sides by all kinds of boats—large yachts, striking sailboats, fast speedboats. I pass boat after boat, looking for the one I left behind on the beach. Then I see her, the white-and-maroon sleek speedboat with the words *Lady Mist* etched in swooping gold letters on the back.

Before I climb aboard, I glance around. It's late, so thankfully, the marina is completely empty. Once on board, I fumble around, trying to find my way in the dark. Unfortunately, the keys aren't in the ignition where I left them, but a quick search of the cabin reveals them in the glovebox. The small brass key dangles from a miniature buoy keychain. I grab the key and insert it into the ignition, hoping the boat will start immediately.

When I turn the key, the engine purrs like a tabby cat. I

quickly untie the ropes holding us to the dock, and back the boat out of the marina space.

The moon is hidden behind clouds, making it darker than a starless sky. I obviously don't have much experience commandeering a boat at night, so my pulse behaves erratically as I maneuver past the no-wake zone and into the bay. Even though I can't see the waves, I can sense them. They heave against the boat, pulsing their own oceanic rhythm. I push the throttle forward and the bow of the boat rises up so far, I fear we may flip end over end. Then she rights herself and keeps going, bouncing over the waves. Since I can't see very well, I drive the boat slowly, searching the water for signs of the AIG.

Then I see it, its U-shaped body lit up like a giant horseshoe suspended in the air. When I'm at least one hundred yards away, because I don't dare go any closer due to the underwater spikes, I anchor the boat and dial Chaz. His face is worried when he answers.

"Sienna, where have you been? You were supposed to call me an hour ago."

"I'm sorry—" I start to say before he interrupts.

"It's all over the news," Chaz rushes on. "How you killed Radcliffe—"

"I'm being set up. A sniper took him out right in front of me."

"They found your fingerprints everywhere—"

"I'm sure they did. I didn't have time to wipe things down."

Chaz frowns. "You didn't think to use gloves?"

"I didn't exactly have a plethora of items at my disposal," I retort. "I am, after all, hiding out on a boat."

Chaz goes quiet. "On the news they're saying there was girl there. His daughter. Did you… did you see her?"

Daddy, will you tuck me in?

A lump climbs up my throat, and I nod. "She saw it, Chaz. She saw everything."

Chaz closes his eyes, and he looks like he's about to be sick. "Oh God, Sienna."

"I swear, Chaz, if I'd known he had a daughter, I never would have gone to his house." A sob escapes from the back of my throat, and then I'm crying—hot, fat, ugly tears that spill down my face, run into my mouth, and blur my vision. Whenever I think of that little girl, I picture myself, finding my father dead on our kitchen floor, and I know how that will haunt her, will keep her awake at night, will eat at her during the day, and I'd give anything to take that away.

But I can't. And it's that hopelessness that brings me to my knees and causes an ache so deep that it hollows out a place for the pain, pain that burrows down past the point of feeling to the place where only the worst kind of pain can exist. A place that traps the pain, gives it life and a place to grow, but never a way out.

Chaz is speaking to me, but the Lynk is upside down on the floor of the boat. I pick it up and hear his voice. "You need to come home, Sienna. Hop on the next bullet train and get your ass back to Legas."

"I can't, Chaz. I won't leave Zane. And my father—" My words sputter off. "I just can't."

"Sienna, they think you killed a government official. There will be no leniency—"

The sound of a drone fills the night sky, its red light like a laser beam cutting through the darkness, its infrared heat element tuned to find warm-blooded animals.

"I'm sorry, Chaz. I gotta go." Before he can say another word, I click the Lynk off and toss it on the boat seat. Climbing on top of the bow of the boat, I take a deep breath, trying to prepare myself for what the cold water will feel like as it hits my skin. I tell myself that there are no creatures in the ocean—it's just the water and me. Then I dive in.

The water is a shock to my system, and I come up gasping

and sputtering, swallowing a mouthful of seawater as I do. I gag a little, and once I can breathe normally again, I duck under the water, kicking like a frog, my hands outstretched so I don't accidentally impale myself on the underwater spikes. My hands hit rusted metal, sliding along the sides until I'm past it. I swim like this, moving mechanically. Not like a girl with a broken heart, not like a girl with a crushed soul, and certainly not like a girl who is now a fugitive.

When I can't hold my breath any longer, my head breaks the surface, gulping deep breaths.

The drone is closer now, almost directly overhead. Filling my lungs with precious air, I plunge under the water, and continue my frog kick, my hands searching for the metal spikes the width of my waist. Every time I surface, I search out the U-shaped building and pray I'm able to reach the AIG before the drone senses the heat I'm emitting.

The cold seeps into my bones, numbing my fingers and toes. I'm shivering when I surface again. As I tread water, gulping air, my leg grazes a spike I missed with my hands. Pain sears through my leg, and I cry out. The last thing I need is fresh blood oozing from me while I'm swimming in the ocean. My heart hammers as I submerge myself again and search for the hidden spikes in the black water.

When I reemerge the next time, I'm only feet away from the platform. With trembling hands, I haul myself up, my body slipping and sliding over the smooth surface like a seal out of water. I almost end up back in the ocean, but I claw at the lip of the platform and pull myself to a sitting position.

The drone hovers directly above, sensing my heat. I look right at it, daring it to do something. What would it do? Drop a bomb on its own facility? Shoot me dead right here?

On my hands and knees, I quickly move to the door labeled Authorized Personnel Only. As I stand, I briefly inspect my leg. It's not too bad, more of a deep scrape than a gash.

There's a trickle of blood down my leg, but I don't have time to worry about that.

I give three hard knocks and stand to the side of the door, hoping someone will come. After a few seconds, I repeat. This time, I bang as hard as I can for as long as my fist can stand it. The whole time, my eyes never leave the drone. It still hasn't moved, almost as if it's daring me to try to get into its facility.

A moment later, a man wearing a janitor's uniform opens the door slightly. I push my way through, half-expecting the drone to put a bullet through me as I shoulder my way in.

"Hey!" the man hollers. "You can't be in here!"

My knee hits him square in the jaw and he stumbles backward, falling to the ground. As his hands fly to his face, I grab his transmitter and tuck it in the waistband of my shorts. I yank his key card from around his neck and slip it onto my own. He seems harmless so I leave him there and sprint down the stairs, taking them two at a time. Despite being soaking wet and shivering from the cold, I've never felt more alive.

When I reach the lower level, the part of the facility built underwater, I choose the first door I see on the right. I'm glad I thought to grab the key card, because it's locked. I scan the card, and when the lock clicks, I ease through the door, hoping it's a place I can hide out until the drone leaves.

It's a lab, very similar to my father's, minus the rotating image projector. Thankfully, the transmitter in my hand doubles as a flashlight. I click it on and study the various test tubes and labeled beakers behind the glass refrigerated doors. I read labels with words like: *Strength, Courage, Intelligence, Athleticism, Discipline.*

I pass upright comscreens with the flashing AIG logo and government motto: *Progress is our future.*

Along one wall, dark curtains hang from floor to ceiling. I assume they block windows, perhaps ones that look out at the vast underwater ocean. I pull the curtain back on one side and peer out, but it's not the ocean I see or even lights from the city. There's a window, but it doesn't look to the outside. It overlooks another room. I press the light up to the glass and inhale sharply.

The room is the size of an arena. Inside it are wall-to-wall beds. Occupying those beds are people.

29

Sienna

What the hell?

I stare at the sight before me, too stunned to move. The light from the borrowed transmitter sweeps over the still bodies of men and women, boys and girls too close to my own age to bring anything but fear.

My light rests on the face of a boy I recognize, a boy whose olive skin and high cheekbones stand out too much to be ignored.

Ren. The boy who gave me a bike and told me to hide. The boy who was taken away.

They brought him here. Why? Who are all these people? What are they doing to them?

I back slowly away from the curtain. There must be at least three hundred people in there. Hundreds of people who are drugged or brainwashed or something. Do they have families who miss them? Are they delinquents? Drug addicts? Is that where I would have ended up if Zane hadn't found me?

And then an even worse thought hits me. *Is Zane in there?*

I hurry out of the room, making sure to close the door behind me, and take the stairs to the upper level two at a time. When I reach the second floor, I scan the key card, then burst through the door and eye my surroundings. It sure looks like the level Granger brought us to before, the one where my father's lab is located. I hurry down the hall, leaving a wet trail as I go. The air cooling units are kicked up in here, and I find myself crossing my arms over my chest to conduct a little bit of heat. I pass door after door, lab after lab, until I see it. Brian Phillips.

Brian Phillips. Ben Preston. Mitch Hoover.

How many names will my father have before he's content with the life he has?

The door is closed, so I ease it open and find Granger hunched over a computer keypad. He jumps when he sees me. "Sienna, what are you doing here? And why are you dripping wet?" His eyes shift to my leg. "You're bleeding."

"Zane. Where's Zane?" I say, moving toward him. If he doesn't want to cooperate, I have no problem making him talk.

Granger must see the wild look in my eyes because he rises from his stool and lifts his hands in surrender. "I haven't seen him, Sienna. I swear to you. The last time I saw him he was with you."

"Check the system. I need to know if he was brought in." I hesitate, wondering if I should trust him. "I saw those people."

Granger's eyebrows knit together. "What people?"

"The ones in the lab down below. There are hundreds of them."

Granger shakes his head slowly. "I don't know what you're talking about."

The door of the lab opens. "Granger, I couldn't sleep. I think I've had a major breakthrough—" It's my father. He stops short when he sees me. "Oh, I didn't realize you had... company." He looks at Granger. "Who's this?"

My mouth goes dry because it's as if I'm seeing a ghost. Here is the man I buried, the man whose body I shed countless tears over, the man I longed to have hold me again. And now he stands only feet from me, but we might as well have an ocean between us.

Granger looks from me to him. "This is… Sienna."

My father smiles and holds out his hand, but I can see he's wary by the way his eyes take in my wet hair and drenched clothes. "Sienna, forgive me for asking, but why are you all wet?"

For some reason, I don't feel like lying to him. "Because I swam here."

He nods as if that's the most natural answer in the world. "Have we met before? You look oddly familiar."

"You don't recognize me?" I say. How can he not remember I'm the girl who "volunteered" to have her memories erased? "You don't remember inserting a chip in the back of my brain?"

He blinks a few times before he nods slowly. "That's right. I do remember you." His eyes swing from Granger to me. "But you disappeared before the procedure was complete."

"I didn't *disappear,*" I say. "I was *rescued*. I was brought here against my will."

My father's face goes slack. "I was told you volunteered. If I'd known—"

"You mean like the hundreds of people in the arena down below? Did they volunteer as well? Or were they dragged here against their will?"

His eyes flit to the corner of the room, right below the ceiling. I follow his gaze. There's a security camera there. I wonder how long I have before the Enforcers show.

He clears his throat. "Why are you here?"

"I'm looking for a friend of mine. His name is Zane Ryder. I need to know if he was brought in."

My father rubs his chin. "No, I'd know if he was here. I'm very familiar with the Ryders, especially his older brother Steele."

"You know Steele?"

"I work for him."

My throat constricts. Suddenly, I'm finding it difficult

to breathe. If he works for Steele now, maybe he remembers working for Harlow. And if he remembers working for Harlow, maybe he remembers parts of his old life. With us. When I had my computer chip, I still remembered certain things, images that would pop in my mind. Maybe…

I take a couple of steps toward him. "Do you know who I am?"

He tilts his head, studying me. "I believe we just discussed this. You're Sienna."

"Yes. But my real name is Sienna Preston." I grasp the wet hem of my tank top. "Does that sound familiar?"

"No, it doesn't. Should it?"

I close my eyes, struggling to know what to do. Do I tell him the truth and risk scaring him off? *I have to try.*

When I open my eyes, I say, "Yes. Because I'm your daughter."

My father moves swiftly to a button on the wall. "I'm calling security," he says through gritted teeth.

Granger stares at me, as if he's trying to unravel some mystery. I'm slipping. I've already lost my father once, and I can feel myself losing him again.

"Wait!" I cry out in desperation. "Let me at least try to explain!"

He stops, his hand hovering over the call button. I take it as my invitation to speak quickly.

"You have a scar too. Have you not noticed it? They gave you a chip to alter your memories. In Legas, you have a wife and two daughters, Emily and me. Emily's five and has these adorable blonde curls. You used to make us chocolate oatmeal and dance around the house with Mom." Tears are streaming down my cheeks now. "We used to go stargazing, don't you remember? You taught me all the constellations and the stories behind each one. Please," I sob. "I need you to remember."

The pictures on my Lynk. But it's too late. That Lynk is long gone, and now, I have no proof.

My dad stares at me as I wipe the tears from my face and try to compose myself, my eyes never leaving his hand that hovers only inches from the button. When he sighs and turns away from me, I know it's too late.

"You need help," he says. He presses the button and an alarm immediately sounds.

I jump to my feet and run out the door, Granger calling after me.

"Sienna!"

When I'm halfway down the hall, Granger catches up to me.

"Sienna, wait."

I stop and face him, my eyes trained on the hallway behind him.

"I believe you," Granger says. "I mean, I can see it. The facial resemblance, mostly the nose and mouth, but I see it. And it all makes sense now."

"What makes sense?" Footsteps pound down a corridor near us.

"There's something you should know." He shifts uncomfortably. "You aren't the only one who lied about the bullet train."

The alarm whines around us. My voice is even when I speak. "Granger, what are you saying?"

"I lied about why I was staring at you." His head shakes in frustration. "I don't even have a sister. When your father came to visit me at University and recruited my help, he only had one request. Well, two actually. He wanted me to keep tabs on you, your mom, and your sister, but he made me promise I would never tell him about you or mention your names again. He said you were a relative, that your mom was recently widowed, but he'd had a falling out with his extended family years before. Even though he'd changed his name and no one knew he was still alive, he wanted to make sure your family was watched over and protected."

I take a step away from him, trying to sort out what he's telling me.

"I was in Legas," he continues, "to check on you. I staked out your house for a couple of days, but you never showed. Then I saw you at the train station. I guess I was a little surprised to see you."

"You've—you've been to my house?"

He nods. "Only three times. I try to come every few months, but sometimes things get busy here and I can't leave."

"So my father knew he was going to fake his death and change his name, but he asked you to check up on us?"

"I believe so."

My mind spins, trying to make sense of it all. All this time, Granger's been like an older brother I never had. He's been watching, maybe even protecting, us.

But if my father made a deal with Radcliffe to fake his death, change his name, and come work for the AIG, why did Radcliffe try to destroy our family a few weeks ago? After he found me with the stolen computer chip, why was he so intent on ruining me?

He wanted Trey. I was merely a means to an end.

The footsteps are closer now, the shouting only around the corner.

"Listen, Granger, I need you to know something. Something very important."

"What?"

"I didn't do it." I start to back away from him. "Just remember that. I didn't do it," I repeat. Then I turn and run down the hall. I've almost made it to the stairwell when I swing around the corner and collide with something solid. A chest.

I look up into blue eyes the color of the ocean and stumble backward. Trey's hands steady me.

His voice is rough when he speaks. "It's you, isn't it? The alarm is for you."

I try to shove past him, but he grabs my arm. "What are you doing here? Don't you know that every Enforcer in all of Rubex is looking for you?"

"And do you realize that there are hundreds of bodies in the basement?" I retort.

"What the hell are you talking about?" Based on the blank look he's giving me, he clearly has no idea.

Instead of answering him, I hold my arms out wide. "I'm right here. Why don't you call the Enforcers and tell them where I am since you're so good at being a snitch? Perhaps I should wait for them to come and cuff me."

Trey's eyes go hard. "You're the one who decided to kill George Radcliffe."

"I didn't kill him," I spit. "A sniper took him out."

"While you were standing right beside him? How convenient."

My throat constricts, even though I thought I buried the pain down deep. "No, it wasn't convenient. It was awful. And that little girl will be scarred for life." I turn away from him and shove my way through the stairwell door.

"Sienna, wait." But I ignore him. I can hear him coming down the stairs after me, which only causes me to pick up the pace.

On the next landing, he grabs my arm and spins me around to face him, but I jerk my arm from his grasp.

"Don't touch me," I snap. "You don't have that right. Not anymore."

He looks like he's been slapped, but at least his hands drop. "You're not safe," he says.

"Why should you care?"

"I—I don't know. Where will you go?"

"It doesn't really matter, does it?" My eyes burn with hatred

as I stare at him, my lips curling in contempt. "Zane is missing, so it doesn't really matter."

"Missing?"

"That night at Marmet. I escaped, but he…" I bite my lip. "I don't know where he is. And it's your fault." I strike him hard on the chest. "It's all your fault." I pound my fist again on his chest. When he just stands there and takes it, I hit him with the other one. Suddenly, I'm flailing on him, tears running down my face. He grabs my arms and spins me around, pinning my arms to my sides, with my back pressed against his chest.

"Shh," he says, low in my ear. "It's okay."

"Let go of me!" I try to fight him, but he tightens his grip.

"Not until you've calmed down," he says. And that only infuriates me more. The alarm continues to wail all around us.

I stamp down hard on his foot. He howls in pain, but lets me go. I'm not thinking clearly. My mind is a jumble of hurt, confusion, and emotions, and Trey is the only outlet for my anger.

I kick him hard in the knee, and he curses.

"Dammit, Sienna, what's wrong with you?"

I move to knee him in the stomach but he grabs my leg and twists, knocking me off-balance. I land hard on my back on the concrete floor. Pain shoots down my spine and lodges in my tailbone.

Grunting, I roll over and jump to my feet. Trey's face is a mixture of shock, confusion, and irritation. This is much different from when I fought him in the Compound. My movements are quicker, my kicks stronger, my punches more accurate. I try to punch him in the jaw, but he blocks it. His large hand wraps around my fist, and he squeezes. "Stop acting like a child," he hisses.

I rip my hand from his grasp, the tendons in my fingers aching. I just want him to leave me alone. I want to forget he ever existed, that I ever cared for him. So I do the only thing I can think of.

I kiss him.

At first, shock makes Trey's lips freeze, but then it's as if a light switch turns on. His hands tangle themselves in my hair and he's kissing me back. Kissing me so hard I'm sure my lips will be bruised by the time we pull apart. When I think he's had enough, I shove him away. I try to ignore the hurt in his eyes, the confusion I see. Instead, I turn away and sprint down the rest of the stairs.

"Sienna! Wait!" His tone is desperate.

I kick open the Authorized Personnel Only door and then I'm on the platform, the cool August breeze raising the hair on my arms. By some small miracle, the drone is gone.

"Sienna, please!" Trey bursts through the door and stops short. "Where are you going?"

I back toward the edge. "Good-bye, Trey."

I dive into the water, the churning black ocean swallowing me up. And I don't look back.

30
Zane

The safe house is a rustic cabin in the mountains a few hours northeast of Legas. When I was a boy, my father would bring me here in the winter to go skiing. The chairlifts had long since shut down, but Father jerry-rigged a device that carried us up to the top of the mountain. I'll never forget my first run—the exhilaration I felt, the icy cold air on my skin, the clinging smell of spruce trees. The white blanket of snow that covered the ground and the trees made everything so quiet, so peaceful. It was always one of my favorite places.

Father referred to the safe house as a cabin, but to most people, it would be considered a chalet.

I park my car in the gravel drive and make my way up the front steps. Mentally, I'm preparing myself for what I'll tell Sienna's mother. I need to convince her to come back to Legas, without worrying her about her daughter's safety.

As soon as the door opens and Emily sees me, she flings her arms around my legs. I lift her up and ruffle her hair as she squeals in delight. As fond as I am of Sienna, Emily comes in a close second.

After spinning Emily around a few times until I'm dizzy myself, I set her on her feet, making sure she's steady before letting go completely. She wobbles a little, and then runs to her mother's outstretched arms.

"Well, Zane, I didn't expect to see you so soon," Vivian Preston remarks, her eyes searching my face. "I thought you were in Rubex with Sienna."

"Yes, ma'am, I was." I brace myself for her reaction. "I'm here to bring you back to Legas. Sienna and I feel it would be safer for both of you."

Vivian's eyebrows crease in concern. "Is everything alright?"

"Of course. We've received some new intel, and we believe you'll be safer staying with my family and me in Legas. Besides…" I wink at Emily. "I bet you've missed the swimming pool."

Her little face breaks out into a huge grin. "Yes, I want to go! Can we, Mommy? Can we?"

Vivian studies me, probably trying to determine if I'm telling her the truth. I flash a wide grin, and her face softens, her lips parting into a smile. "Of course, sweetheart. Let's pack up our things and we can be on our way." As Emily goes running from the room, giggling, Vivian turns to me. "Will Sienna be joining us?"

Swallowing hard, I plaster an encouraging smile on my face. "Unfortunately, not yet. She still has some business to attend to in Rubex. But not to worry," I reassure her. "She'll be back soon enough."

Vivian wrings her hands together. "I'll never stop worrying about that girl." She sighs and leaves the room to begin packing.

"Neither will I," I whisper to an empty room.

The next morning, I'm lying in bed, my hands behind my head, second-guessing my decision to leave Rubex. I've yet to hear from Sienna, so I've no idea if she's safe or if she's wondering where I am. The not knowing is torture.

I've tried to locate the tracking signal in the necklace, but unless Sienna is at the bottom of the ocean, I'd say she lost her necklace at some point during her swim to the boat. At least, I hope that's the answer.

I roll over and grab my comscreen from the nightstand, clicking it on. The news is the only thing that distracts me.

As soon as the screen flares to life, an important bulletin scrolls along the bottom.

> Seventeen-year-old Sienna Preston is wanted for the murder of Colonel George Radcliffe. A reward of one million pacs will be given to anyone with information leading to her arrest.

Oh crap.
She did it. She really did it.
I don't know whether to be angry with her for putting her own life in danger or proud that she got rid of the man who has terrorized her and her family.

But now she's a wanted criminal. And the government will not stop until they find her.

Frustration builds inside. *She needs me.* Screw Madame Neiman and her threats.

Jumping up from the bed, I grab my Lynk and dial Chaz's number. "Hey," I say as soon as he picks up. "Have you talked to Sienna?"

"Man, she's looking for you. Are you okay?"

"I'm fine. But I'm worried about her. I just saw the news about Radcliffe."

"She didn't do it. It was a setup."

I sink down on the bed, ingesting this information. I'm not sure if I'm relieved or disappointed. "But she's okay?"

"For now. But those government pricks are on her ass like

flies on doo-doo." Chaz pauses. "Man, where are you?"

I can't tell him, not when it makes me look like a coward who ran away with his tail tucked between his legs.

"Listen, Chaz, can you connect me with Trina and Jeb? I think they may be able to help Sienna."

Chaz gives me a ten-four salute. "I'm on it." Then under his breath, he mumbles, "But don't say I never did anything for you."

Trina is breathless when she answers her Lynk, her face flushed. "Zane," she says. "I heard about Sienna."

"She's in trouble," I say. "I had to leave Rubex, but I'm worried about her. Can you help?"

She grins. "Hell, yeah. I've been waiting for this call. Although, I thought it would come from Sienna, not you."

"Sienna isn't the best at seeking help, so I took it upon myself to involve you. I hope that's okay."

"Of course! We'll be on the road in half an hour," she promises before hanging up.

I set the Lynk on my bed and pace the floor of my bedroom. *I should be there. I should be helping her hide. I should be with her.*

I'm about to look up the bullet train schedule when my Lynk buzzes. Certain it must be Trina calling back to go over more details, I snatch it up and mutter a cursory hello.

"Zane?"

I tighten my grip on the Lynk when I hear Sienna's voice.

Her face pops up on the screen and her words rush out before I can get one in. "Are you okay? Where are you? Why haven't you contacted me?"

"I'm fine," I reassure her.

"I thought you'd been captured—"

"I was. But they let me go once they realized who I was. Didn't you get my message?"

She shakes her head. "I lost my Lynk the night I escaped from the Marmet."

My heart sinks. "So this whole time you thought I was…?"

Tears fill her eyes. "I thought they had you. That's why I went to see Radcliffe, but they killed him. Right in front of me."

"Oh, Sienna, I'm so sorry. I thought you'd gotten my message—"

She interrupts me. "Where are you now?"

I long to tell her the truth. But if she knew that her family was threatened, she'd probably go after Assistant President Neiman. "I'm in Legas, actually."

It pains me to see her face fall, her expression changing from happiness to confusion. "I—I don't understand," she says.

"I needed to return to Legas—there was business to attend to. I didn't want to leave, but it was necessary." My eyes meet hers for the first time, and hers are so sad that they make my heart split wide open. "I'm sorry."

She gives me a curt nod. "And my mom? Emily? How are they?"

"Doing well. I, uh—" I struggle to know what to tell her. She's so perceptive that if I told her they were now at the house with me, she would glean the truth from it. Or, at least, tear it from my throat simply by giving me a Sienna-look. "I visited with them upon returning to Legas."

"And they're okay? You'd tell me if they weren't, right?" She's suspicious.

"Of course. They're fine."

I see her hesitate, glancing at something off screen. By the caw of gulls and the sound of the ocean in the background, I can only assume she's on the boat I rented.

When she turns back, her eyes are urgent, maybe even a little wild. "Zane," she says. "You have to promise me something."

"Anything."

"Promise that if something happens to me, you'll take care of my mom and sister."

I can't bear to hear her talk like this. I close my eyes and tighten my fists. "Sienna, please come home." My eyes open, pleading with her.

"I can't. You know that." She leans closer to the screen. "Promise me."

"Yes, of course. I promise." She starts to look away. "Hey," I say, drawing her attention back to me. "I contacted Trina, and she and Jeb should be there in a few hours."

Her face lights up. "They're coming?"

"Yes. So please, don't do anything stupid before they get there."

"I won't."

"And stay hidden. Are you on the boat? Stay on the boat until they come."

"I will."

"And if something goes wrong, go to the Match 360 Headquarters. I'll alert Steele and let him know to be on the lookout for you."

Her lips purse. "You want me to hide out in the Match 360 Headquarters?"

"Only if you need to." I want to beg her to come home, to give up this quest to bring Trey back. But instead, all I say is, "Please be careful."

And despite her promises, when we hang up, I have a feeling that something's about to go terribly wrong.

31

Sienna

When the Lynk clicks off, it takes me a moment to breathe normally. The waves beat against the small vessel and the sun glares down from a cloudless sky, warming my skin and causing pink splotches on my arms. But the only thing I can think about are the three little words seared in my brain.

Zane left me.

32

Sienna

On the boat, there is no shade, no respite from the heat. The sun bakes my skin and dries my lips until they're cracked in multiple places. I'm now out of water, and my throat aches from being so parched. What I wouldn't give for a sip, for something, anything that can wet my lips and quench my thirst. Here I am surrounded by millions of gallons of water and yet, there's not a drop that's drinkable. It's torturous.

When almost six hours have passed, it's time to meet Trina at the agreed-upon location. I spoke with her shortly after talking with Zane. She and Curly were already on their way.

The trip back to the beach is a little easier this time, maybe because the swells aren't quite so high. I moor the boat at the same marina that has a sign saying they charge by the hour. I'm not too concerned because I don't plan to come back for it. The Enforcers will soon be hot on my trail, which will only lead them to this vessel. I have to abandon it now before it's too late.

Ever since I spoke with Zane, my mind has replayed scenes from last night's encounter with Trey, when I kissed him. It wasn't meant to signify anything; it was merely meant to be a distraction. But I can't tear from my mind the feel of his lips on mine, the familiarity of his hands and his skin. And every time I try to forget, memories surge forth, refusing to let my mind still and my heart heal.

Dressed in Zane's hoodie, his backpack slung across my back, I make my way down the streets of Rubex, pausing at each corner. With the hood pulled over my head and a pair of cheap sunglasses I managed to steal from a street vendor covering my eyes, I try to blend into the crowd of people on the streets. There's a bald man with a graying goatee selling switchblades. I slide one off the table and hide it under my sweatshirt as I walk past.

My heart swells when I see Trina leaning casually against a building, her long legs clad in tight pants and a sleeveless top showing off her toned arms. Her face breaks into a grin when she sees me. I fling my arms around her. It isn't until we pull away that I notice Curly standing beside her. He wraps me in a hug, his curls tickling the side of my face.

"I can't believe you guys are here," I say.

"The barn was getting a little old." Trina rubs her hands together. "I'm ready for some excitement."

"Me too," Curly pipes in.

"So what are we doing first?" Trina asks. She pushes up on the balls of her feet as if she's just itching to get into trouble.

All morning, I've been thinking about how I might get close to Trey, maybe even convince him about the computer chip stashed in his brain. I don't want anything from him. He's rejected me too many times for me to ever see a future with him, but he deserves to at least remember the Fringe. Curly, Nash, Trina—they're all counting on him. Whether or not I'll ever play a role in his life really doesn't matter. I'm not doing this for myself—I'm doing this for them.

And I think there's really only one way to do it.

"I need you to create a distraction."

"Done," Curly says, making a check mark in the air.

I laugh. "I haven't even told you who you'll be distracting."

"Anything will be easier than breaking into a highly secure

underground bunker," Curly says, referring to the last time they helped me when I was trying to rescue my mother.

He has a point. "Follow me, then," I say, starting toward the center of the city where the high-rise apartments overlook the ocean and the Four Corners—the main intersection of Rubex where giant statues rest on each corner of the intersecting streets. Erected shortly after the last war, each statue is a different color horse, representing the Four Horseman of the Apocalypse. The white, red, black, and bronze horses depict Conquest, War, Famine, and Death, reminding the citizens of Pacifica of the horrors and trials that come when our nation is at war.

Using the coordinates Chaz sent me earlier, I find Rayne Williams' apartment, a high-rise made completely of pink glass. It shimmers in the sun, reminiscent of a beautiful painted sunset. Just as I suspect, there are two Enforcers stationed right outside her building, their hands resting on the butts of their guns tucked into the holster around their waists. Their eyes scan the crowd, looking for something. No, looking for someone.

Me.

My pulse spikes, and I pull Curly and Trina to the side of the building before the Enforcers can spot us.

"I need to get into that building," I say. "Do you think you can create a distraction?"

Trina gives Curly a flirtatious smile. "How would you like to pretend to be married?"

Curly slings his arm around Trina's shoulders. "I thought you'd never ask."

Trina shrugs his arm off and says, "Just follow my lead. Got it?"

I watch as the two of them hurry over to the Enforcers, who immediately grip their guns but don't remove them from the holster.

"Please, sir, help me. I can't find my baby! She was right

here, but now—" Trina lets out a sob.

Curly gestures frantically with his hands. The Enforcers take a few steps away from the entrance to the high-rise. One has pulled out a handheld comscreen and appears to be taking notes. The other glances behind him before leaning in to hear Trina and Curly better. Now is my chance.

I stride past the four of them and slip into the building. Chaz is pulled up on my Lynk before I've made it halfway to the elevators. Once inside, I have no control over the buttons because residents must insert a keycard to gain access to the controls.

"Overriding system," Chaz says, low in my ear. I'm grateful he thought to speak soft because I'm now sharing the elevator with two others—a man and a woman, who both eye me curiously. With my sweat clothes and hood pulled over my head, I'm sure I don't look like the typical occupants of this building.

"Get off on floor twenty-six," he says.

When the elevator dings on floor twenty-six, I maneuver past the others and step out.

"Which way?" I whisper.

"Apartment twenty-six twelve."

One wall of the hallway is lined with stone and water trickles down over it creating a waterfall effect. It's so pretty I almost stop to admire it.

Stay focused, Sienna. You have a job to do.

Rayne must have been paid off. This is an expensive apartment building. Her parents may be wealthy, but I find it hard to believe they'd be willing to support this lifestyle, especially for an eighteen-year-old girl.

When I find the apartment, I knock softly on the door and wait for her to answer. After a minute passes, I hear the unmistakable sounds of someone inside, unlocking the latch. When Rayne pulls the door open, she stops, her face a mixture of surprise and annoyance.

"What are you doing here, Sienna?" she asks, her voice even.

I push my way past her, ignoring her protests. "I thought we should have a little chat."

She crosses her arms over her chest. "I have nothing to say to you."

As I pull the knife from the pocket of my sweatshirt and flip open the blade, her arms drop and her expression changes.

"Maybe not," I say, "but I have plenty to say to you."

She takes a couple of steps back. "None of this was my idea."

"Then whose was it?"

"I—I can't say."

I take a menacing step toward her. "You will tell me."

She swallows hard and glances around the room like someone might be listening. "It was Assistant President Neiman. She sought me out. Forced me to go along with this. Said they'd give me money and a condo in the city if I'd pretend to be this guy's fiancée." Her expression turns fearful. "How could I say no?"

The muscles in my neck tighten. "Were you expected to marry him?"

"I don't think so. I told them I wasn't willing to take things that far."

"But you were okay making out with him, is that right?" I retort, my blood pressure rising, despite my best efforts to stay in control. "Trey had a life. He had people who cared about him, who loved him, even. And you took all that away."

She shrugs, and I want to smack her. "If it wasn't me, it would have been someone else. You know that as well as I do."

I take a couple more steps toward her until we're practically nose to nose. Her eyes widen.

"Well, now you can do something for me. Without

anything in return."

She smirks and tosses her long, blonde hair. "And why would I do that?"

I press the knife to her jugular, watching as she swallows hard. "Because I think you'd prefer not to have blood all over your pretty cream carpet. Am I right?"

She nods quickly, causing the knife to press further into her skin. I remove some of the pressure and nod to her Lynk, which is sitting on the table by the couch. "Call Trey and ask him to meet you at your favorite restaurant tonight."

As she reaches for her Lynk, she asks, "What are you going to do?"

"Don't worry about that. Just make the call. And put it on speaker but not view."

I take a step back as Rayne dials Trey. She blows her bangs off her forehead as she waits for him to answer. When he does, her voice is sickly sweet, a false smile plastered on her perfect face. It takes all my willpower not to heave all over her floor. *So disgusting.*

Trey agrees to meet her at a restaurant called Timber tonight at eight o'clock, which is only two hours from now. My stomach rumbles at the thought of real food.

Once they've hung up, I grab a kitchen chair and drag it to the bedroom, one hand latched on Rayne's arm. I plop the chair in the middle of the floor and force Rayne into it before searching for some rope or something I can use to tie her up.

"Come on, Sienna. Is this really necessary?" she asks, her eyes pleading with me.

I don't answer her. I find a long, turquoise scarf in a bottom drawer that turns out to be a great restraint. After the scarf is looped and tightened around her hands, which are pulled behind her back, I stand up and eye my handiwork. There's no way she's getting out of that.

Then I start toward her closet. I can't possibly show up

to this Timber restaurant wearing sweats. Sure, Rayne may be taller and more endowed, but surely, I can find something that fits me. I flip through shimmery skirts, cybergoth corset tops, rave bras, and dozens of other articles of clothing that leave little to the imagination.

"Don't you have anything that actually covers your body?" I scoff.

She shrugs and turns up her nose. "Why should I cover a body that looks like mine?"

Rolling my eyes, I turn back to my search. The last half of her closet appears more fruitful. My hands run over a silky, off-the-shoulder top that ties at the waist with an oversized diamond belt. A super short skirt accompanies the ensemble.

I hold the skirt up to my waist. The hemline falls midway between my hip and knee, which means on Rayne, it probably barely covers her rear.

"Seriously?" I say.

She shrugs again and turns to stare out the window.

Grabbing the clothing, I head for the bathroom where I slip out of the old sweats and into Rayne's clothes. The shirt is a little baggy in the chest area but once the belt is cinched around my waist, you really can't tell. The skirt turns out to be a good length, even though my pale legs are on display. Once I'm dressed, I search the bottom of her closet for shoes. Despite her height, she wears a size seven, just like I do. I slide my feet into a pair of rhinestone-studded sandals, take a quick look in the mirror, and then I'm ready.

As I'm walking out of her closet, Rayne says to me, "Can you untie me now? I think I've been helpful."

I laugh at her stupidity. "You think a little insider information is enough to get you a pass? I don't think so."

As I stride out of her room and to the front door, she screams after me, "Get back here, Sienna Preston! I mean it. If you walk out that door—"

She's way too loud.

I hurry back to her room and grab a scarf from her drawer. She watches me with wide eyes.

"Now, Sienna, I really don't think that's necessary—"

Before she can say anything else, I shove the scarf in her mouth. She shakes her head, her eyes pleading with me. I hesitate only a moment before turning to leave. Her angry yells are nothing more than muffled cries now. And when the door slams shut behind me, it drowns out her muted moans.

As I exit the building, Trina and Curly are nowhere in sight, but the Enforcers are once again standing guard outside. My palms begin to sweat, but I hold my head high and pretend like I belong here—not hard to do considering the clothing I'm wearing. The Enforcers don't even give me a second glance.

Once I'm a few blocks away, Trina and Curly appear from nowhere and fall into step beside me.

"How did it go?" I ask under my breath. I don't turn to them, trying to pretend as if we are strangers on the street.

"Good," Trina mutters. "I think I could have been an actress in another life."

Curly snorts beside me.

"I'm sure you were very convincing," I say, staring straight ahead and barely moving my lips.

"Where to now, boss?" Curly asks a little too loudly.

I shoot him a scathing look. As we pass a deserted alley, I pull him and Trina into it. "I'm meeting Trey for dinner. You guys are my backup."

"Backup," Curly echoes.

For the next few minutes, pausing occasionally to glance over my shoulder, I go over the plan with them. I can see in Curly's eyes that he's doubtful we can pull it off.

"The most important thing is securing the chloroform," I say. "Do you think you can handle that?"

Trina nods without hesitation.

"Good. Meet me at Timber at eight-thirty, and whatever you do, don't be late."

Timber is fancier than I anticipated. Located in the historic district of Rubex, where many of the buildings are crafted of old brick, dozens of twinkle lights wrap around the few trees leading up to the entrance. Before walking into the restaurant at eight, I take a deep breath and steel myself. I refuse to feel anything for him.

When I enter the building, a hostess greets me. I tell her I'm there to meet Trey Winchester, and she ushers me right in. As I follow her through the restaurant, I try to absorb it all. The white tablecloths, the glass votives in the center of the tables that emit a single flame, the soft music that reminds me of birds singing and waves crashing. The lights are dim, but when I spot Trey across the room, dressed in slacks and a sports coat, my pulse still behaves erratically. I curse my heart as I slide onto the seat across from him. He's looking down, counting the tines of his fork, but as soon as I sit, he glances up. His fixed smile quickly disappears.

He curses as I lean toward him, resting my elbows on the table.

"Where's Rayne?"

I give him my sweetest smile. "She's a little *tied up* at the moment."

"Did you hurt her?"

"Of course not. What kind of person do you think I am?"

Trey stares at me, hard. "You shouldn't be here."

"You're right," I say. "You're absolutely right, but thanks to you—wait…" I pause like I'm thinking, "Should that be *no thanks to you*, instead? Anyway, doesn't matter. Point is, because of your little tip off, I got chased through the streets of Rubex, had to hide out in a boat for two days, and Zane left me." I lean forward, my eyes narrowed. "So, you're right, I shouldn't be here, but I am. And I'm pissed." I pick up the steak knife and twirl it between my fingers.

Trey's eyes zero in on the knife. "What do you want, Sienna?"

"Why did you do it?"

"Do what?"

"Why did you tip them off? Do you hate me that much?"

His face softens, but before he can answer, a waiter comes by to take our order. Even though my stomach growls at the thought of eating something other than granola bars, I don't plan to be here long, so I only order water.

"I don't hate you at all," he says once the waiter has left the table.

The way he says it and the way he's looking at me produce emotions I don't want. I shove them down deep. "Then why?"

"Because I was scared."

"Scared?" I scoff. "Of what? The Trey I knew wasn't scared of anything."

"But I'm not him." He sighs, glancing down at the table. "Truth is, I've been having dreams, just like I told you." His eyes meet mine. "Dreams about you. About us. At first, I thought it was just stress, that you'd somehow managed to get into my head, made me believe things that weren't true." He pauses, and I wait for him to continue. "But then things weren't adding up. The cafe that was bombed is still there. Rayne never wants me to meet her parents or her friends. There's a blank spot in my mind where all these memories should be." He gestures to his arm. "And now these tattoos. Nothing makes sense."

My breath catches. A part of me longs for him to remember, but the other part—the part that doesn't want to be hurt again—decides to act indifferent. I have to stick to the plan.

"Well, that sucks. I tried to help you, but you turned me

down. Twice." I tap the knife on the table. "In my mind, you're a lost cause. You and Rayne can get married, have adorable babies, and live a lie. I don't care." Even as I say the last words, my chest squeezes, but I ignore it.

Trey stares at me. "You don't mean that."

"Sure, I do." I lean forward. "You know the difference between you and me, Trey? I never gave up on us. Did you know I had my memories wiped? But I fought to gain back what was mine. I didn't roll over and die, like you." Even though I promised myself I'd never cry over him again, I can feel tears filling my eyes. "I will not waste one more minute on you. I refuse to let you hurt me again." I swipe at the tears and rise quickly from the table. "That's all I came to say."

"Sienna, wait."

With tears blurring my vision, I weave in and out of tables. I hadn't planned to become so emotional, but this may work to my benefit.

"Sienna, wait!"

I push past the people who are standing at the front of the restaurant, waiting for a table. When I burst through the door, the cool night air dries my face, leaving a trail of tears and mascara. Trey's hand latches onto my arm and swings me around to face him. With his hair disheveled and the distinct fury in his eyes, he looks so much like the man I used to love that it makes my heart ache in so many places. And for a moment, I forget all about the plan. It's just Trey and me.

"I said wait," he growls.

I rip my arm from his grasp. "Why should I listen to you?"

"Because I have something to say."

"I don't care what you have to say," I retort.

Trey's hand encircles my neck and brings me closer. "Sienna, please, just shut up and listen."

My heart is pounding so hard I'm not sure I'll be able to hear his words over its steady thrum.

His face softens. "I'm sorry. I'm sorry I let you down. I'm sorry I didn't live up to your expectations. But mostly, I'm sorry I didn't believe you."

I swallow hard, my voice catching in my throat. *Where are Trina and Curly?* "What are you saying?"

Trey's other hand slides to my waist and draws me closer, so close that we're touching. "I don't want you to give up on me."

Before I can respond, a hand presses a handkerchief over Trey's nose and mouth, and he crumples.

33
Sienna

Ignoring the stares of passersby, we shove Trey into the nearest air taxi. Trina and I climb in the back of the taxi with Trey between us, and Curly sits in the front.

"Where to?" the driver with dark bushy eyebrows and a heavy mustache asks.

I rattle off the address as he gives Trey the once-over.

"He's had too much to drink," I explain as Trey's head lops onto my shoulder.

The man shrugs and pulls out into traffic, without checking to see if it's clear. A few horns blare, and the man reaches out his window and flips off the person behind us. "Crazy drivers," he mutters.

Trina looks at me and presses her lips together, suppressing a giggle.

When the driver pulls up in front of Rayne's high-rise, we have a problem. At least a dozen Enforcers are milling around outside the building, guns in hand. I curse under my breath.

"What is it?" Trina asks, eyeing the black-clad men with the thick white stripe running down the shoulders of their uniforms.

"It's Rayne," I say through clenched teeth. "She must have escaped and called the Enforcers."

There's no way we can get into her building now.

"Uh, Sienna," Curly says. "I don't think she escaped." He points out the window where emergency services are wheeling a stretcher through the pink glass doors of Rayne's apartment building. And on that stretcher is a body zipped up inside a body bag. A lock of blonde hair has escaped from the bag and hangs limp, its owner an unknown face.

But I know who it is.

Drawing a shaky breath, I place my hand on my chest.

Rayne is dead. And I'm probably the last person to see her alive.

"Keep driving," I tell the man, turning my face away from the window as one Enforcer keenly watches our vehicle.

The driver's eyes flit from the crowd of Enforcers to the passed-out Trey, and then to my face. "I know you!" he cries out. "You're that girl they're looking for!"

The Enforcer watching us slowly approaches our vehicle. The driver leans out his window and hollers, "She's here! She's right here!"

It all happens too fast. Curly punches the man, then reaches over and opens his door, pushing him out. The man rolls out onto the concrete, and the Enforcer raises his wrist to his mouth and shouts something before pulling out his laser gun. He runs toward the air taxi as Curly scoots over into the driver seat and presses the gas pedal all the way to the floor. We shoot out into traffic, the vehicle swaying side to side as Curly tries to regain control.

"This is harder than it looks," he mutters, sweat beading his forehead. I hear the sound of bullets hitting the sides and back of the vehicle, more like a hiss than a ping. I can only imagine the tiny holes left in the side of the frame from the heat of the lasers.

Curly curses, glancing down at the dashboard. "They hit the fuel pump." His eyes go wide as he looks in the rearview mirror. "Crikey. They're behind us."

I twist in my seat and spot two Enforcers on jet bikes gaining on us. They weave in and out of the traffic, their thighs practically touching the pavement as they maneuver around cars.

The air taxi shudders a bit, and my heart leaps into my throat. "Come on, Curly," I urge him. "You have to outrun them."

Curly licks his lips, crosses himself as he says a quick Hail Mary, and turns the steering wheel hard until we're cruising along the sidewalk instead of the road. A small potted tree looms in front of us and I grip the seat, bracing for impact. At the last moment, Curly muscles his way back into the lanes of traffic. My fingers relax as I exhale in relief. I turn around, keeping my eyes trained on the Enforcers behind us. Just when I think we've lost them, they pop back up again.

"I can't drive forever," Curly says through gritted teeth.

"I know, I know. Let me think." We can't go to Zane's condo or the Restful 8 Motel because both will surely be overrun with Enforcers by now. We can't get on a bullet train and go back to Legas because the netscreens are sure to show my picture everywhere, including the train station.

I think back to what Zane said after I found out he was in Legas.

If something goes wrong, go to the Match 360 Headquarters.

Looks like there's only one option.

"Take a right up here," I say. "Then a hard left. And another right. We need to lose them before we get there."

Curly looks at me in the rearview mirror. "Where are we going?"

"The Match 360 Headquarters."

Curly frowns but doesn't object. Trina, however, turns to me and says, "I hope you know what you're doing."

I'm not sure if I do. But we have no other choice.

The Match 360 Headquarters is just as impressive as the last time I saw it, but I don't take the time to admire it—my eyes are trained behind us. We lost the Enforcers barely ten minutes ago, but I'm still on edge that they'll find us.

When we pull up to the guard gate, I lean over the seat to speak to the black-clad guard. The air taxi shakes a little as it touches ground.

"We're here to see Steele Ryder," I say.

The guard bends down to peer into the back of the car. When he straightens, he says, "Is he expecting you?"

"Yes," I lie.

The guard's eyes narrow, but he radios to someone in the building. "What did you say your name is?" he asks, looking directly at me.

"Sienna. Sienna Preston."

The guard repeats my name into the transmitter. My hands grip the vinyl seat back, sweat sliding through my fingertips. The next thing I know, he's waving us through.

A whoosh of air rushes out as I exhale and lean back against the seat. As we lift off the ground again and drive past, I glance in Curly's rearview mirror and see the guard making a note of our license plate on a handheld comscreen. Soon, he'll realize this is a stolen vehicle.

Curly parks the air taxi in a parking space, and we wait until we've touched down before we exit. Curly and Trina drag Trey from the car and carry him toward the building, with me following close on their heels.

"I hope you know what you're doing," Trina says again through clenched teeth, but I can't tell if it's because she's mad or because of the effort she's exerting from carrying Trey.

When we enter the building, we're greeted with stark white walls and clean lines. Yet, despite the minimal furniture, the facility oozes wealth. A sleek receptionist desk with an interior lighting system, glowing a geometric pattern on the frosted glass, sits in the middle of the high-ceilinged room. Two pendant lamps dangle above the desk, and several streamlined chairs rest in the waiting area—clearly bought for appearance, not for comfort.

The receptionist is a dark-haired woman with a kind smile that falters when she sees Trey propped between Trina and Curly.

"I'm sorry, miss," she begins, "but this isn't a hospital."

"We're here to see Steele Ryder," I say.

The woman nods and presses a button on an intercom. Her voice comes through a little shrill as she pages Steele to the waiting room.

"Why don't you have a seat?" she suggests. "It may be a few minutes."

"We're fine," I say.

Curly grunts in response, his shoulders taking the brunt of Trey's weight. "Why is this starting to feel like a common thing between Trey and me?" He gives me a wry smile, no doubt thinking of when the Compound was bombed and it was him alone who carried Trey to safety. If Curly hadn't been there—I don't want to think what would have happened. I never could have gotten Trey out of the bombed-out Compound by myself. I could barely get my own self out before the drones returned and lit the place up. I shudder, remembering that night.

When Steele does show up a few minutes later, he's dressed in a business suit, indicating he's probably in charge of the business side of things, and not so much the lab work. His mouth turns down into a sour frown when he sees me.

"Sienna Preston." He says my name as if he's trying to work around a mouthful of dirt. "You've made quite the impression on the Citizens of Rubex." He clicks on a wall comscreen, and the news is the first station that pops up. Not surprisingly, my

picture fills the screen with a similar headline as the one found on the Bulletin scrolling beneath.

> Sienna Preston—wanted for the murders of Colonel George Radcliffe and eighteen-year-old Rayne Williams. Any person with information that leads to her capture will be heavily rewarded.

Of course they would blame Rayne's death on me. Squaring my shoulders, I say, "It wasn't me."

Steele scowls. "And to think that you're dragging my brother down with you. It doesn't seem quite fair, does it?"

"I didn't kill Radcliffe," I say through clenched teeth. "Or Rayne."

Steele nods to Trey. "Who is this?"

"Your brother," I say. I wait for the shock to register on Steele's face, but it never comes. He remains cool and collected.

"Why did you bring him here?"

"Zane told me to come. We need your help." I see Trina wince under the pressure of holding Trey upright. "Now."

Steele's eyes are cold, hollow almost, like whatever emotion he had in them left years ago. "Mina," he barks, his eyes never leaving my face. "Show them to an examination room."

Mina hurries around her desk, her heels clicking against the smooth stone floor. She motions for us to follow her, and Trina and Curly immediately stumble after her. I, however, hang back.

"I need your best geneticist," I say to Steele.

He stares down at me. "Why do you think I'd ever do anything to help you?"

"Because he's your brother, whether you like it or not. He has a chip at the base of his skull that needs to be removed."

"Why? So he can become a rebel again? No, thank you. We don't need scourges like him running around creating havoc. Our society can be better than that."

I take a few steps closer and narrow my eyes. "Your company is all about helping people. It's time to step up and act. Trey needs your help." And then, because I like to hit below the belt, I say, "Zane would do it if he were here."

Steele's jaw clenches and unclenches. "One thing you need to learn, Miss Preston—I'm nothing like my brother." With that, he turns on his heel and strides away, down a different hall. I'm tempted to follow him, but I decide it's best if I stay with Trina, Curly, and Trey. Grunts and groans come from a room down the hall, so I move toward that one.

Trina and Curly have managed to get Trey on an examination table, but he's still passed out. Mina excuses herself when she sees me and shuts the door behind her.

"How long until that stuff wears off?" I ask.

Curly shrugs. "Depends on how much we gave him."

"And how much did you give him?"

"Don't know. Something about you multiply weight by height to figure out dosage and frequency." He shrugs again. "Never was good at math."

I groan. "Are you telling me you have no idea how much you gave him? He could be knocked out until next week."

"Exactly." He grins and gives a little bow. "No need to thank me."

Trina is staring at Trey. She reaches out and touches his forehead. "He looks so... different."

"I know." I move to her side. "Remember, underneath the clothes and the hairstyle is the same Trey. We just have to find him."

Trina nods, letting her hand drop. "How do you know you can trust this Steele guy?"

"I don't," I reply. "I'm hoping I can, that's all. We're out of options and barring a miracle, we're screwed."

A low moan comes from Trey's slightly open mouth. I move to his side, and Trina goes to the other. We stand there, waiting for him to open his eyes. When he does, he tries to lick his lips, and then he says, his voice hoarse, "Water."

Trina hurries across the room to the small sink, fills a paper cup, and brings it back to him. She helps him sip the water, holding the back of his head and gently pouring the cool liquid into his mouth.

"Thanks," he says, once he can speak. His eyes rove over her face. "Do I know you?"

Trina smiles. "I'm Trina."

Trey smiles back, but when his head turns and he sees me, it fades. He only utters one word. "Why?"

Leaning over, I kiss him lightly on the cheek, and then whisper in his ear. "Because I'm just as good at lying as you are."

Trey's eyes darken. "I wasn't lying, Sienna."

"What about in the garden at Marmet? You weren't lying then?"

"Yes, but—"

"So you expect me to believe that you had a sudden change of heart, a moment of clarity, and now you remember everything?"

A muscle in his jaw jumps. "I never said that—"

"Then what did you say?"

Trey shakes his head. "Just forget it." He glances around. "Where the hell are we? I want to go home."

I cross my arms over my chest. "I'm afraid that's not possible."

Trey's eyes shift to Curly, who's standing erect in the corner like an armed guard. "Who are you?"

Curly clears his throat and takes a step forward. "I'm Jeb. But Sienna calls me Curly. Sir."

"And I know you?" Trey asks, his eyes narrowing.

"Um, yes, sir. You did." Curly appears very uncomfortable with this line of questioning. Maybe it bothers him to see Trey like this? I'm used to it by now, but I try to remember what it was like when I first realized Trey had no memories of his past.

It hurt like hell.

I'm about to cross the room and reassure Curly when the door to the room bursts open, an army of black enters, and then shouts and gunfire rain down on us. No, wait. The gunfire isn't raining down on us, but all around us. The Enforcers are firing up at the ceiling, and bits of the tiles fall down, covering us in white and gray confetti. Rough hands force me to the ground, my face pressed into the cold concrete floor. A sharp pain shoots up my arm to my shoulder as my arms are twisted behind my back and rubber-and-metal cuffs clicked on.

Heels click and I see a sideways version of a woman with short, blonde hair. She's dressed in a navy business suit with the Pacifica crest—the three running legs symbol—embossed on her left shoulder. I know her immediately. Assistant President Neiman.

"Leave the Winchester boy to me," she says in an authoritative tone. "The others are yours."

I'm dragged to my feet. Trey is sitting up on the exam table, a dazed expression on his face, but no one has dared to touch him. Trina and Curly's hands are both bound behind their backs. At least half a dozen black-clad Enforcers take up the room, their laser guns held steady in their hands, aimed at the three of us. Madame Neiman gazes at me, her eyes cold, her mouth severe. She turns to the man standing in the doorway. Steele Ryder.

"Thanks again for the tip, Mr. Ryder."

Steele nods. "Always a pleasure to work with you, Madame." He gives me a contemptuous look.

He ratted us out. The growing knot in my stomach turns into a fireball of shame. Then realization dawns. The computer chips in the back of the desk. Mr. Ryder's denial of his involvement… *Always a pleasure to work with you.* This isn't the first time they've worked together.

I think back to the words Steele spoke in the hallway about Trey and the Fringe. *We don't need scourges like him running around creating havoc. Our society can be better than that.*

I turn and glare at Steele. "You're the one, aren't you?"

"Pardon?" His tone is more of a sneer than an actual question.

"You're the one," I repeat. "The one who's been experimenting on juvenile inmates."

Steele's eyes turn as hard as his name. "Stop sticking your nose where it doesn't belong, Miss Preston." He turns to go, but stops himself. "And leave my brother alone. You'll only ruin him." Before I can say anything, he strides out of the room.

With Steele gone, Madame Neiman's cold eyes focus on me. "Miss Preston," she says. "You've caused me nothing but trouble. And yet, I don't believe we've had the pleasure of making each other's acquaintance." Her lips curl into a sneer.

"Allow me to introduce myself," she says. "Assistant President Andrea Neiman."

She looks different from her broadcasts on comscreens. Her skin is paler, her lips redder, and her scowl ages her by at least ten years.

"Are you the one who ordered the hit on Radcliffe? And Rayne?" I growl.

She taps a finger on her lips as she pretends to be concerned. That's when I notice her excessively long fingernails, like mini daggers.

"How can you say such a thing? Colonel Radcliffe was a fearless leader of the Commonwealth of Pacifica. His death was a great tragedy to us all."

I snort. "Yeah, I'm sure."

"And that Williams girl?" Neiman shrugs. "It appears you

broke into her apartment and took care of her yourself."

My eyes are full of hate for this woman who disposes of life without a second thought. And blames me for it. "You murdered them!"

In a few short strides, Madame Neiman is in front of me, one knife-like fingernail lifting my chin until I'm looking directly in her eyes. Her fingernail burrows into my skin, but I don't cry out, not even when I feel droplets of warm blood running down my neck. Her cold, gray eyes scrutinize mine like she's trying to read my thoughts. "Have you ever stopped to think that perhaps Radcliffe wasn't the target?"

My breath catches and my mind spins, remembering that night. When I was in Radcliffe's house, I bent down to retrieve the picture frame at the exact moment the bullet pierced his chest.

It was me. The sniper shot was meant for me.

"You have a lot to learn, Miss Preston," Madame Neiman continues. She draws her hand away and looks at the blood trickling down her finger. My stomach heaves as she brings her index finger up to her lips and then presses it to her tongue, tasting it. Bile rises in the back of my throat as I get a whiff of the metallic scent of my own blood. Her eyes never leave my face, watching me for a reaction. I give her none.

"A handkerchief, please," Madame Neiman barks. A hankie is placed in her outstretched hand, and the purity of the white linen is immediately stained with the bright red of my blood. After wiping her hands, Madame Neiman carefully tucks the handkerchief into her suit pocket. "Blindfold and gag them. We don't need them causing trouble on the way to Maximum Confinement."

At her words, my heart trips over itself. Maximum Confinement? *No.* I can't let them take us there. With its steel walls and heavily armed guards, we'll never escape. The security in real Confinement is quadruple what it is in the

Juvenile Division, which is where Kaylee and the other juvenile delinquents were held in Legas.

Because I'm shot up on fear and desperation, I do the only thing I can think to do—which turns out to be the stupidest thing I could do. As the Enforcer with white-blond hair tries to gag me with a scarf, I bite down as hard as I can, until I taste blood. He lets out a string of curses. Something hard, like the butt of a gun, knocks me across the back of the head. A lightning burst of pain explodes through my brain.

And I slump to the floor.

34
Sienna

The bouncing and jostling only exacerbates the pain in my head. Moaning, I try to open my eyes, but all I see is blackness. When I blink, my eyelashes catch on the rough material of a blindfold. When I try to swallow, I gag on the cloth stuffed in my mouth. It's worse than the tongue depressors the medics use to swab your throat.

"She's awake," I hear a gravelly voice say.

Someone slides closer to me, a sweaty hand presses against the back of my neck, and then hot breath grazes my cheek as a voice whispers in my ear, "I liked watching you sleep."

Shuddering, I shift away from him, which is difficult since I have no access to my hands or sight. He laughs harshly. "I love it when they put up a fight."

"Simon!" someone barks. "That's enough."

I'm racked with a coughing fit, which turns into gags and dry heaves since I can't breathe past the cloth in my mouth. Every time I inhale, I taste sweat and dirty socks. Clearly, this rag wasn't a clean one, which causes another round of dry heaves.

"Um, she's gagging back here," the pervert who whispered in my ear only moments ago says.

"Ignore her. It's just a ploy."

I suddenly can't breathe. I try to inhale through my nose,

but it's plugged with snot from so much gagging. And when I try to breathe past the sweaty socks, my gag reflex kicks in. I try to tell myself that it's mental, but after a few moments where I'm only able to take in tiny bits of stale air, I start to panic. I throw my head back and try to cry through the cloth.

"Hey, man, I don't think she can breathe."

Yes, idiot, that's correct.

Tears are streaming down my cheeks now, and even though my mind screams at me to get a grip, I can't manage to get a hold of myself. Just when I start to see twirling stars behind my closed lids, someone says, "Be careful, soldier. She has one hell of a bite."

The pressure in my mouth lifts and I spit out the cloth, gulping large amounts of air.

"See, told you," the pervert says.

Once I've recovered, I croak, "Where are my friends?"

I can feel his breath on my cheek as he says, "Not to worry, sweetheart. They're right behind us."

A few minutes later, the vehicle comes to a stop, and doors open. Rough hands grab my arm and yank me out, causing me to hit my knee against something hard. Stumbling, I wince as I hobble across a rocky surface that feels like gravel underfoot. The sandals I borrowed from Rayne are gone. *They must have taken them while I was knocked out.* There's the sound of other footsteps shuffling through the gravel.

"We can remove the blindfold now," the one in charge says. "Once inside that building, they ain't ever leaving, so it doesn't really matter what they see."

The blindfold falls from my eyes, and I blink rapidly against the morning sun. Trina and Curly are doing the same thing only feet away. And when I see the bruise on Trina's face and Curly's swollen eye, I know they tried to fight too. And lost.

I'm not sure where we are or how long I've been

unconscious, but one thing is certain, it was night when we were captured, and now it's daytime. With our hands still cuffed behind our backs, we're forced into a boat. There are the three of us Fringe members and four guards—one for each of us plus the leader. My pervert guard keeps a hand on me at all times, like he thinks I might try to hurl myself over the side of the boat or something.

As the boat moves, the wind picks up, gliding over my skin and dragging through my hair. The sun heats my back and warms my face. Tilting my head back, I drink it in. Who knows how long it will be until I feel the sun again?

It's a short ride to the fortress they're taking us to. I can see it, rising out of the ocean like a sentinel. Rocky cliffs, concrete walls, barbed-wire fencing. It is said to be impenetrable. No one has ever escaped in the hundred years it has been in existence. Convicts go there to die.

The closer we get, the harder my heart hammers. I glance over at Trina and see the fear in her eyes. As tough as she is with her combat boots and fierce attitude, even she knows we're riding toward our death sentence. When I look over at Curly and he flashes me a wild grin, tears fill my eyes. Even now, amid the danger of our imminent imprisonment, Curly remains upbeat. I wish I had a piece of his optimism inside of me. Because all I feel now is despair.

The guards dock the boat and help the three of us prisoners climb out onto the rocky soil. A long row of steps has been built into the side of the cliff, and we climb them steadily. The next few minutes are a blur of gray concrete, harsh hands, and the slamming of metal cell doors.

I try to get a feel for the guards as we pass through cell block after cell block. *Which ones are nicer than others? Which ones might show a little compassion?* It leads me to wonder…

Can any of them be bribed?

As much as I'm hoping they'll put Curly, Trina, and me

together, they separate us, of course. Pervert guard shoves me into a concrete room with no windows and only a thin mat on a sagging cot. A crude bucket in the corner of the room is where I'm supposed to defecate.

"Home sweet home," the guard sneers. His hand lingers a little longer on my shoulder than necessary before moving behind me to undo my handcuffs.

Once my wrists are free, I feel a snap at my waist. Rayne's diamond-studded belt falls to the ground. I spin around, my throat closing.

"Relax," the guard says. He bends over to pick up the belt. "This," he says, holding it up, "is considered a weapon. Can't have you choking one of our guards with it."

Rubbing my sore wrists, I take a few steps back to put some distance between us.

"However, if you get lonely—" he starts to offer with a patronizing smile.

I glare at him. "I won't."

He tips his head back and laughs before sauntering to the door, the belt swinging from his hand. "Well, if you change your mind…"

"Get out," I hiss.

He chuckles and slams the metal door behind him.

As soon as he leaves, I sink down on the cot, my head dropping into my hands. All this time I thought Mr. Ryder was the one feeding those inmates into the experimentation system. I thought he was the evil one who didn't care about anything but making money. That may still be true, but now I have someone else to hate, someone else to blame.

Steele Ryder.

This is it. There's no escaping this time. Of all the decisions I've made this past year, this is by far the stupidest one. What was I thinking going to Steele for help? Why did I ever think he would come to the aid of me and my renegade friends?

Because Zane told me he would. I trusted him and look where it got us.

How did Zane turn out so good when the family members surrounding him are so bad?

Just thinking of Zane causes a pain in my chest like slivers of glass piercing my heart. He left me in Rubex all alone. When I needed him most.

I want to believe he had a good reason, but the truth is, he's committed to Arian, not me. Which means that he probably went back to smooth things over with her.

Did you expect anything less?

No. No, I didn't. But I guess I hoped for something more.

35
Zane

The news of Sienna's arrest is broadcast over all the news stations and on every comscreen.

"Sienna Preston, the seventeen-year-old girl wanted for the murder of Colonel George Radcliffe, was captured last night at the Match 360 Headquarters in Rubex. It is believed that Miss Preston is also responsible for the death of eighteen-year-old Rayne Williams, who was found in her apartment earlier this evening. Authorities say that at the time of her arrest, Miss Preston was traveling with two Fringe companions and another young man they'd kidnapped. The three Fringe members are currently being held in maximum-security Confinement as they await the results of their trial. If found guilty, young Miss Preston and her cohorts will be executed."

I click the screen off and sink down onto the couch, so shocked that I can't think clearly. *They have Sienna... this is my fault... I told her to go to the Match 360 Headquarters... if I'd been there...*

Executed.

No. No way. I will not allow Sienna to die for crimes she didn't commit. There must be someone I can speak to, someone I can reason with. Perhaps even bribe.

Swallowing my pride, I stride to my father's office, swinging the mahogany door open without knocking.

"Zane." He looks surprised to see me.

"You've heard, haven't you? About Sienna?" I demand.

My father takes his reading glasses off and sets them down on his desk. "Why yes. How unfortunate. I suppose she thought she wouldn't get caught."

My fists clench. "She didn't do it. She may have hated Colonel Radcliffe, but she didn't kill him. And Rayne? She would never."

"And you have proof of this?"

"I have her word. And that's enough for me."

My father clasps his hands together and rests them on the desk. "Then what is it you want?"

"For you to secure her release. You know the President. I'm sure you've had dealings with Madame Neiman as well. Your reach is far greater than mine." I take a deep breath. "And you owe me this much."

He stares at his hands, not speaking for a moment. "This girl is no good for you, Zane. I know you think you care about her, but she isn't your match—"

"This has nothing to do with my feelings. This is about an innocent girl who, if found guilty, will die."

Peering at me, he says, "And you are still fully committed to Arian? Ready to be married and start a family in only a few short weeks?"

Every muscle in my body goes rigid. Can I make that kind of promise? Can I force myself into a life I don't want? *Yes, if it means saving Sienna.*

Steeling myself, I reply, "Absolutely. Nothing has changed."

My father heaves a deep sigh and says, "All right then, I will do my best." He slips his glasses back on, focusing on his desk-screen, signaling the end of our conversation.

As I leave the room, I hope his *best* is enough.

36

Sienna

The hours turn into days, and then weeks, or possibly months. I'm not sure of the passing of time, just that it does pass.

The air in the cell is warm, stale, and reeks of feces. After a few days of holding in my bowel movements, because I refused to use the metal bucket in the corner, I couldn't hold it in a moment longer. The pain in my side had become too unbearable. Hovered over the tin like a common dog, I finally relieved myself, and ever since, the stench has been a constant reminder of my weakness.

Every day, twice a day, through a small opening in the bottom of the door, my tiny rations are slid through on a crude metal bowl. A piece of bread, two slices of beef jerky, and a cup of water. Enough to keep you from starving, but not enough to give you the energy to try to escape.

The nights are cold and leave me shivering, and the days are hot and long and leave me sweating. There is no escaping the cold or the heat, so I've resigned myself. This is my life. This is my punishment.

Hour after hour, day after day, I sit and wait. I'm not sure what I'm waiting for. To see a familiar face? For someone to come clean my poop pail? For interaction with someone other than myself?

When I do use my voice, mostly to talk to myself, it sounds foreign to my own ears. Perhaps it's the way it echoes off the concrete walls or maybe that it sounds hollow without Curly's witty banter or Trina's cute remarks coming back at me. I've taken to humming instead, a lullaby my mother used to sing to me when I was a child. I try not to dwell on thoughts of my mother or Emily, because when I do, the sobs bring me to my knees and expend any energy I have.

I've grown accustomed to the constant groaning ache in my back and the dryness in my mouth. The lumpy cot has springs that poke into my side when I lay flat, which is why I try to sleep sitting up.

The days are a constant reminder of all I've done wrong in my life and the many mistakes I've made that have put others' lives in danger. Over and over, I dream about going back in time, erasing all that's happened and all that has yet to happen.

When the door to my cell finally does open, and two guards enter and move to the sides, standing at attention, I barely care enough to lift my head.

Heels click against the concrete floor, and the freshly scrubbed image of Madame Neiman enters the room. Once again, she's wearing a navy business suit with the emblem of Pacifica on her left shoulder.

"The convict will rise," she orders, her voice cold and authoritative.

I just stare at her, too weak to stand. She snaps her fingers and the guards move to my side, dragging me to my feet.

"Convict one-four-zero-two, also known as Sienna Preston," she says, her voice ringing through the small cell, "has been found guilty for the deaths of Colonel George Radcliffe and Rayne Williams. Her execution is set for the day after tomorrow." Her eyes never meet mine, but I sense the satisfaction in her words.

"What about my friends?" I cry out. "What will happen

to them?"

But the woman doesn't answer me. Instead, she turns on her heel, waits for the guards to open the door, and leaves without ever looking back.

When the door chinks closed behind them, I crumble onto the cold stone floor and weep for everything I've lost and everything I'm about to lose.

37

Sienna

The day of my execution, I feel a calmness I don't expect. I've spent the past two days reflecting on my life thus far, beating myself up over my decisions, and wondering how my mother and sister will handle my death. But today, I push all of that out of my mind. I will go down with dignity. Well, somewhat.

Holding my breath, I scoop out some of the feces from the metal chamber pot and smear it over my arms and legs, even up my neck. When I do inhale, I end up gagging from the stench. After a few minutes, and a few tepid breaths, I'm somewhat used to it and can breathe again through my nose. When I'm significantly covered, and the poop is nice and crusty on my arms, I sit on my bed and wait for them to come get me. I want to make this as painful as possible for them.

As I wait, my mind wanders. I wish I knew what was happening with Curly and Trina. Did they receive a reprieve? A lighter sentence? Will they rot their life away in this prison hell? I think I'd almost prefer death to staying in this never-ending repeat of concrete, stench, and loneliness.

When they come for me, I hold my head high. I have to suppress a grin when they enter the room and begin gagging.

"What the hell? Is that shit?" the pervert guard asks, eyeing me with a hand over his nose and mouth.

"It sure smells like it," his greasy companion says.

Without saying a word, I rise from the bed and walk toward them. They want to treat me like a rabid animal, I can tell, yet they unwillingly latch onto my arms and cuff them.

"Ugh, this is disgusting," the perv says, wrinkling his nose.

I shrug and wait for them to lead me out of my cell.

The pervert guard gingerly grips my arm and then turns away, dry heaving. "I can't do it, man. It's too gross."

The other guard steps up and snatches my arm out of his grasp. "Let me handle this." His hands are rough, digging into my arm until I wince in pain. "I'll be glad when we're rid of her."

I bite my lip to keep tears from welling as he leads me out of the cell and down the long corridor. We pass through several cell blocks before we reach the threshold to the outside.

"Madame Neiman wanted you to come out early so you could watch the execution of your friends."

My heart stops in my chest. "Execution?"

Before he can answer, the doors are pushed open, and there's a blinding light. I squint into the sun, my eyeballs searing in pain after being locked up in that room for who knows how long. As my eyes adjust, I see Curly and Trina, already outside, their hands bound behind their backs. Curly is standing on a raised platform, and he gives me a half-smile when he sees me. A thick noose hangs above his head.

Hanging. Death by hanging. The very thought sends a shiver through me.

Madame Neiman stands off to the side, monitoring the executions. *Does she do this for all the convicts or only the high-profile ones?* Seems like she would have better things to do with her time than watch people die.

This. It all comes down to this moment. Curly pretending not to care about his imminent death, Trina sobbing quietly on her platform, and me, head high as I death march to my own center platform and climb the steps.

The two guards begin adjusting the noose.

"Any final requests?" Madame Neiman calls out.

"Yes," I say. "Let me say good-bye."

Neiman hesitates before nodding her assent.

The guards lead me down the steps and over to Trina's platform first. "Can I give her a hug?" I ask the pervert guard.

The guard looks over at Madame Neiman. "Prisoner one-four-oh-two requests physical contact with prisoner nine-eight-one-seven."

Neiman nods. "Permission granted. But be aware."

I hear the click of guns as one of the guards removes my cuffs. As soon as my arms are free, I fling them around Trina. She winces and takes a step back.

"What the hell is that smell?"

When I pull away, I say, "My crap."

Tears seep from Trina's eyes as she looks at me and smiles. "There's no one else I'd rather die beside."

I begin to openly sob now. For all my pretenses at being brave, seeing Trina and Curly has gouged out a deep hole in my chest. "I'm so sorry," I say through my tears. "This is my fault."

"It's okay," Trina says, her tears collecting on her chin and falling onto her chest. "I chose this."

"Time's up," Neiman calls out.

Rough hands pull me away from Trina, and all I can think is that I'll never see her again. My mind flashes through our time together in the Compound—when she showed me the hidden entrance to the outside and trusted me not to tell anyone, when she helped break into the underground government bunker using only her "assets" and the triumphant look on her face, when she taught me how to can tomatoes and we shared secrets and swapped stories. Our days in the Compound seem like a lifetime away.

They drag me to Curly next, passing Madame Neiman,

who watches us with eager eyes. Her expression says it all. *This is as much for her entertainment as it is for me to say good-bye.* Anger batters my insides, and all I want to do is get a hold of her face and smash it into the dirt until she can't breathe.

I don't ask if I can embrace Curly, I just do. When I pull away, Curly is grinning at me. "I like the poop. Definitely makes a statement. The whole, *I don't give a crap what you do to me.* Very badass of you."

I smile at him through my tears. "I'm sorry, Curly."

"Don't be sorry. You let me ride your Harley, remember? Totally worth it." His smile falters a little. "It was one helluva ride, wasn't it?"

I know instantly that he's not talking about my bike anymore. "Yeah," I say, my voice catching in my throat. "It was."

"Time's up," the she-devil calls.

I shake my head and reach for him. "No. Not yet."

The guard's hands pull me away, and even though I try to struggle, I'm too weak to fight.

As two guards fit the noose around his neck and tighten it, Curly says to me, "See you on the other side."

The guards drag me down the steps and back toward my own platform. Tears stream down my face as I twist my head, trying to see Curly in his last moments. His eyes follow me, sending me a million words with one look.

This can't be happening. Please, God, let me wake from this nightmare.

Curly closes his eyes as a single tear slips down his cheek. Madame Neiman raises her arm above her head, and then quickly lowers it. It's over before I realize what's happening.

The platform drops from beneath Curly's bare feet and then he's dangling there, his body twitching, his face expressionless, all except for that single tear, leaving a silver trail down his cheek. Even in death, with his dark curls flopping around his face, he's beautiful.

I fall to my knees as sobs rack my body. "No," I scream. "No!" My fingers claw at the dirt until my nails bleed.

The guards drag me to my feet, back to my platform where my same fate awaits. I stumble, not caring. I can't watch my best friends die. Their blood is on my hands. That thought alone produces a guilt that burrows deep beneath my ribs, making it painful to breathe.

Kill me now, please.

But they're not done with Curly. Madame Neiman crosses the expanse of the prison yard, kicking up dust as she goes. In her hand is a knife. My stomach turns over on itself when she slits Curly's throat and then cuts him down, his body flopping to the platform with a thud. Two guards rush over and lift his body between them. The platform is already stained red.

"No," I murmur. "No, no, no." I watch as two guards walk past the barbed-wire fence and to the edge of the cliff. With a heave, they throw Curly's body over to the churning, angry ocean below. It tumbles away like a beautiful, broken doll.

I can't look at Trina. I hear her sobbing, but I can't look at her. I try to remove myself from this horror by pretending this is all a dream. When I wake, I'll be at home in my trailer and Emily will be crawling into bed beside me, asking me to make her chocolate oatmeal. I squeeze my eyes closed, willing it to be true, wishing there was a way out of this nightmare.

When I open my eyes, I see Trina with her head bowed, saying a silent prayer. The noose is tight around her neck. I watch as Madame Neiman raises her arm—

"No!" I scream.

And then a gunshot rings out.

38

Sienna

It all happens so fast. One minute, Trina is gearing up for her own death, and the next, she's jumping off her platform, her hands still bound behind her back. Smoke engulfs the prison yard as more bullets whiz past.

"Get down," she shouts at me.

The two guards who were tying the noose around my neck are now on the ground, blood oozing from their gunshot wounds.

I'm frantically trying to work my neck free—it's hard with no hands—when the entire rope crumbles around me. It still encircles my neck, but it's not attached to the wooden beam above me anymore. I see the frayed edges where a bullet sliced clean through.

"Come on," Trina yells.

I see her hovering behind her platform and I run, bent over at the waist, toward her. I dive behind the platform as a bullet whizzes by my head. The dirt and dust I kicked up settles in my lungs as I breathe deeply, my chest heaving. Trina's eyes scan the smoky yard like she's mentally calculating our best chance for escape.

"Stay low and follow me," she says, speaking close to my ear.

And then we're up and running, heads bent, legs slicing

through the air. There's so much smoke and dust it's hard to know where we're going or if we're headed straight toward a crowd of guards. I hear shouts and more gunfire, and I'm waiting for my body to be pelted with bullets, for my fight to be over. But still we run until I realize that she's leading me straight toward the edge of the cliff. I try to dig my heels in, but Trina won't let me stop.

"This is suicide!" I scream, an image of Curly's body being tossed into the sea seared into my mind. By now, the sharks have surely come.

"It's the only way," she hollers back.

I hesitate for only a second before I nod. If my body ends up broken and battered on the rocks under this cliff, or if I'm consumed by the waiting sharks, at least I won't be alone.

But then, there's a sound that makes my heart stop.

"Don't move or I'll shoot!" Somehow, miraculously, Madame Neiman is still alive and pointing a gun at us. She's at least ten feet away, but by the look on her face, I can tell she's itching to pull the trigger.

Trina looks at me and I at her, and without saying anything, our eyes communicating everything, we heave ourselves over the cliff.

39
Sienna

There's that moment when you're first in the air that you feel like you're flying. But then you quickly realize you're not flying at all, but falling. Down, down, down to a sea that will swallow you up, toward rocks that will break you, toward your own end.

Right after we've propelled ourselves over the cliff, a gunshot rings out and a sharp pain shoots through my shoulder.

I've been hit.

Before I can contemplate what that means, my body slams into the water, my legs scraping against submerged rocks. I start to sink like a concrete brick, the water pulling and tugging me down to its depths.

I try to kick to the surface, but without the use of my arms and a noose still tied around my neck, it seems fruitless. The further I sink, the more desperate I become.

You can do this, Sienna.

My lungs burn, but I refuse to die at the hands of this wild, untamed ocean, this living, breathing thing that has consumed every prisoner who has tried to escape. I try to tell myself that I am different. I am stronger than all of those others combined.

With determination that comes from beyond me, I kick toward the surface, a frog-like kick. With my chin tilted up, my eyes open wide and focused on that spot where life-giving air waits, I move toward it. My lungs ache and burn, the raging fire causing black spots to swim in front of my vision.

No, not yet. I can't pass out yet.

Still, I kick upward until that moment when I can't hold my breath a second longer, and my head bursts through the surface. I gulp huge amounts of air, coughing and sputtering as a wave hits me in the face. The briny smell of seaweed fills my nostrils and the salty taste of the seawater burns my raw throat.

I search the water for Trina. Somewhere between flying and falling, I lost her. And now, she's nowhere in sight.

A sharp pain shoots through my shoulder, and it's then I remember I was shot. When I glance down, there's dark red blood pooling around my body. My stomach goes weak.

Kicking as hard as I can, I move away from that spot, searching the horizon for some indication that help is on the way. Someone stayed our execution. Someone came to our rescue, but where are they now?

"Sienna!"

It's Trina. As I turn, searching for her among the gray ocean waves, I spot her, bobbing twenty feet away. I'm not sure how she got so far from me, but she's a beautiful sight.

I kick toward her as she does the same to me, her eyes widening in horror when she sees the trail of blood following me.

"You're bleeding," she says.

The pain has turned into an aching throb, and I'm suddenly weak, my legs screaming at me from trying to stay afloat. It takes all my effort to keep my head above water.

Trina turns and scans the horizon, just like I did only moments before. "Oh, Christ," she says, fear making her voice tremble.

"What?" But she doesn't have to say anything else. I see it—a large dorsal fin slicing through the water about fifty yards away.

"Swim!" Trina hollers.

But I can't. I'm too weak. The loss of blood is slowing my thoughts, my reflexes.

And then I hear a sound that is sweeter than any other. The whining sound of a boat's engine, coming closer, moving toward us. It could be the guards, but at this point, I don't care.

My legs have stopped kicking. I mentally scream at them to keep at it, but they won't. They can't. My body is disjointed, unconnected. My brain is unable to send signals to the rest of my body. I close my eyes as a wave rolls over me, dragging me down, down, down…

Strong arms encircle my waist and pull me to a solid chest, propelling us upward until my head breaks the surface. There's shouting and the whining sound of a boat engine. Trina is screaming something about a shark, but none of it makes sense.

Inch by inch, my body is lifted out of the water and plopped down onto a hard surface on my side. The cuffs are clipped from my raw wrists and the noose removed from my neck. When I shiver from the cold, a blanket or towel or something equally soft is placed over me.

Seawater surges from my lungs, and I cough it up, gagging on the saltiness of it.

A large hand rubs my back as I hunch to the side, spewing on the floor of the boat. "That's right. Get it all out." I recognize that voice, that deep melodic voice. When I finally do open my eyes, I'm staring into the warm brown ones of Zane Ryder.

"What are you—?" I start to say before he hushes me.

"Is she okay?" I hear another familiar voice and glance up to see Trey hovered over me, his hair and clothes dripping wet, his eyes full of concern. Zane moves to the side as Trey kneels beside him. "Hey," Trey says to me. "That was a close call."

I nod, trying to swallow the lump that's rising in my throat. For the first time since this whole ordeal started, he's looking at me like he did before his memories were erased. Before he forgot everything.

"Trina," I whisper.

"She's right here," Zane says.

I whimper out the next name. "Curly."

Zane's eyes fill with sadness. "I know. I'm so sorry. We were too late."

A heart-wrenching sob escapes from the back of my throat as I picture his body, hanging limp as the life drained from him.

"It's my fault," I say. "It's my fault." The words are drowned out by my tears and sobs. Zane helps me sit up and draws me to his chest.

"It's okay. It's over now."

Trey looks away, but not before I see tears well in his eyes. *Why should he care? He doesn't even remember him.*

I close my eyes.

All of a sudden, Trey says, "There's a lot of blood. Did you scrape your arm?"

I open my eyes, wincing as he pulls my shirt away from the wound.

"Oh God, Sienna, you've been shot." He calls out for Nash, which doesn't make any sense because Nash is still in Legas. Isn't he?

The shirt is torn from my shoulder, and I'm too weak to care that part of my bra is showing. I just want the pain to end, and the tiny colorful dots to stop spinning around in my vision.

Zane gently lays me back down.

"Trey, we've got trouble." It's Nash, but his voice sounds so out of place here. Nash and the ocean... Those two aren't meant to go together. Nash and the desert... Now that one makes sense.

Trey rises to his feet and curses. "Get us outta here, Nash."

The boat engine roars to life, like an animal coming out of hibernation. As we bump over the waves, I hear the scream of someone in pain. It takes a moment for me to realize that the person screaming is me.

A warm hand encircles mine. "It's okay, Sienna. I'm right here." Zane's voice is soothing, but it can't stop the tears that stream down my cheeks.

A cloth presses against my wound, and then there's that ear-splitting scream again. I clamp my mouth shut and bite down on my tongue, my body shaking from the flames that lick my shoulder and spread out, engulfing my arm and torso. Before long, my entire body will be consumed by the raging fire.

"We need to remove the bullet," Trey says, but it sounds like he's very far away.

"I can do it," Zane says.

There's silence, and I picture Trey staring him down. "No, I'll do it."

I'm waiting for Zane to argue with him, to say something about how he doesn't trust him—hell, I don't know if I trust him—but there's only silence. Trey kneels beside me again.

"Hey," he says before the boat lurches to the side and his arms flail out, grabbing hold of something. He curses, and then leans back over me. "We're gonna get you all fixed up. I promise."

Gunshots fill the air around me.

"What's going on?" I whisper. My teeth are chattering now, so hard I can barely speak.

Trey leans closer so he can hear me, his body swaying as Nash makes another tight turn. "A little incoming fire. That's all. Nothing to worry about." He gives me a wobbly smile.

"Where's our backup?" he calls to Nash. "Where is Paige and the rest of her crew?"

Who's Paige?

"I don't know," Nash hollers back. "After the sniper shots, they went quiet."

Sniper shots?

Flaming pain sears through my shoulder as Trey removes the cloth and prods with his fingers. "Yeah, the bullet is still in there." He turns to speak to someone. "Zane, hand me that knife over there."

I see a flash of a blue-handled pocketknife that looks surprisingly similar to the one Trey's dad gave him. But that can't be right. Why would the new Trey have the old Trey's pocketknife?

Trey leans close and begins talking. "Remember when I removed your tracker at the top of the Megasphere?" He doesn't wait for me to respond. "Remember how brave you were then? I need you to be just as brave now. Think you can do that?"

I'm confused why he's mentioning my tracker. How does he know? Did someone tell him about that?

At my confused look, he says, "We have a lot to talk about—"

A bullet ricochets off the bulkhead right by my head, and Trey curses. "Dammit, Nash, can't you drive this thing any better? We need to lose them!"

"I'm trying, Trey," Nash replies, but it sounds like he's saying it through clenched teeth.

The boat lurches again, seawater spraying over the sides and raining down on me. With a trembling hand, I wipe the water from my eyes.

"Zane," Trey says, looking up. "She's gonna need you."

My eyes are closed again, but I feel a body settle beside me, and someone take my hand. My body feels blurry—like if I were looking at an image of myself, the edges would be faded away.

"Here," Zane says. "Bite down on this." When I open my eyes, Zane is holding out a brown leather belt. "It might help with the pain."

Nodding, I let him place the belt between my teeth, clamping down as Trey begins to inspect the wound. Trey is kneeling on one side, his forehead furrowed in concentration, his eyebrows pulling together, and Zane is on the other, his hand tight in mine, his voice soothing.

When the knife digs into the wound, I scream, but it's muffled by the leather strap in my mouth. I bite down as hard as I can, until my teeth sink almost through the belt and I swallow the metallic taste of blood.

I squeeze my eyes closed.

"I think we've lost them," Nash calls out, his voice breaking in the wind.

The knife digs deeper and I abandon the leather strap, opting instead for a good old-fashioned scream. Trey murmurs something about being sorry, and Zane says something about holding me down—or maybe it's the other way around and Trey wants me held down and Zane is sorry. I'm not really sure anymore. Everyone is starting to sound the same.

But it doesn't really matter. Right now, all I want is to remove myself from the pain. My body drifts away across endless gray oceans and frothy tides, and I am gone.

40

Zane

I'm helpless as I watch Trey remove the bullet from Sienna's shoulder. All I can do is hold her hand and check to make sure she's still breathing. The rise and fall of her chest gives me some comfort, but we're not in the clear. She's lost a lot of blood. Her eyes are sunken in and her skin is a sallow, sickly color.

Now that we've lost our tail, Nash drives the boat to the AIG facility. As we get closer, Trey sends Dr. Phillips a message.

"We're coming in. Lower the spikes."

When I look up and see Trina, huddled by herself in a corner of the boat, I feel guilty. Trey and I have both been so consumed with caring for Sienna that we haven't devoted any attention to Trina.

I move toward her, one hand holding on to whatever it can find to keep me steady, and collapse on the seat beside her.

"Hey," I say. "How are you holding up?"

Her teeth chatter as she wraps the towel tighter around her shoulders. "I've been better."

There's blood on her legs. Upon closer inspection, it looks like a deep gash on her thigh.

"Are you all right? That looks like it hurts."

She glances down. "Yeah, I think I hit a rock when we jumped."

"Let me help you with it." Reaching behind her, I grab an extra towel and shred it up to make a bandage. I try to clean the wound as best I can. She winces when I tie one strip of cloth around the wound.

"Just keep pressure on it," I murmur.

Her fingers automatically move to press down on her leg, but her face remains impassive like her body is numb.

"Is she going to be okay?" Trina asks, eyeing Sienna's pale face.

"She'll be fine." I smile. "And so will you."

Her shoulders shake as tears slide down her cheeks. "I miss him. He was the biggest pain in the ass, but I miss him."

I wrap my arm around her shoulder, bringing her close. "I know you do. I'm sorry we didn't get there in time."

She pulls back, sniffling. "Thank you. For rescuing us." When she turns away, cradling her knees to her chest, it's clear she wants to be alone.

I move back to my spot beside Sienna and take her hand in mine again. She hasn't had a chance to come to terms with Curly's death. And I'm not sure how she's going to handle it.

41

Sienna

When I inhale, I expect to smell the saltiness of the ocean and dried-up seaweed, but instead, there's a very clinical smell—the smell of rubbing alcohol, cotton balls, and tongue depressors—like I'm waking in a doctor's office.

The rocking of the boat is gone, so is the roar of the engine. The surface I'm lying on feels solid, but soft. My eyes move behind closed lids, trying to find the strength to open. I do a quick assessment of all my body parts. My shoulder throbs, but it's not the shooting, fiery pain it was before. My knee aches from slamming into a rock when Trina and I jumped off the cliff. My wrists are sore from being cuffed for so long. Other than that, I'm alive, and that's enough to celebrate right there.

But then my thoughts drift to Curly. In all the horror, I haven't had time to mourn him. When I think of his teasing grin, I just want to curl into a ball and lose myself in my guilt. His death will forever be etched in my memory. No matter how hard I try to wipe it, scrub it even, there will be no erasing it. It's one thing to lose your friend—it's another completely to watch them die. And know you're the one responsible for their death.

Tears flood my closed eyes and stream down my cheeks. I force my eyes open and bite my lip to keep a sob from escaping.

I'm in a room that looks oddly similar to ones in the AIG lab. Trina is resting on a bed next to mine, and Zane, Nash, and Trey are seated a few feet away, hovered over a comscreen.

"Where am I?" I ask, my voice hoarse.

The three men exchange looks before Trey rises from his chair and comes to stand next to me. "We're in the AIG facility."

Before he can say anything else, the door opens and in walks Dr. Phillips, my father.

As soon as I see him, I whimper. *He will turn us in.* He will turn his back on me, his daughter, and he will hand me over to the people who just tried to kill me.

But to my shock, his eyes are soft when they meet mine, and when he speaks, it's as if he knows everyone in the room. He looks at Trey. "The lower levels are clear so far," he says.

To which Trey replies, "I'm still waiting to hear from Paige. As soon as I do, it's a go. We'll need to get moving soon. Sienna and Trina's faces are all over the news—the story of the escaped convicts who were slated for execution today."

Trey sounds so much like his old self, so in charge, that it makes my stomach throb.

My dad looks at me and smiles before turning back to Trey and the others. "Can you give us a minute?"

Trey nods, and all three boys leave the room.

When the door has closed behind everyone except Trina, who's asleep in the bed beside me, the slight whoosh of her breathing a comforting sound, my dad slowly approaches.

"Hi, sweetie," he says. "May I?" He looks down at my hand.

When I nod, he takes my hand in his and offers me a hesitant smile. "I'm sorry I didn't believe you the other day. I was... in shock. If I had known—" He stops himself as his eyes become watery. "I'm so sorry, Sienna. For everything I've put you and your mother through."

An ache fills my chest, cracking it wide open and exposing the raw pieces inside. "You know?"

His fingers move to the base of his skull. "It was Granger. He convinced me. It wasn't too hard after you left that day. I felt the puckered skin and knew they'd done something. Granger removed it for me."

I swallow hard. *I have to know the truth. I have to.* "Is it what you wanted? Did you ask to have your memories erased?"

My father's face falls. "You have to understand. It wasn't what I wanted. But it was necessary. To protect you, your mother, and Emily. They promised that if I went along with their plan, you would be safe. Protected."

I snort when I think of all Radcliffe did—using me to get to Trey, abducting my mother, erasing my memories. There was no protection. He tried to destroy our family.

"They lied," I say, my voice flat.

"Yes," my father confirms. "It would appear so."

A sharp pain plunges through my shoulder. I exhale slowly until the stinging subsides. "Why did they want you? Why did they want to fake your death?"

"Steele and Radcliffe have been working together for years. Steele's been selling Chromo 120 secrets to the government for a profit. He claims that after the death of Mitch Hoover, Harlow's lab was never able to recreate my genetic codex. They came close, but never reached perfection. When Steele learned I was still alive after all these years, he and Radcliffe approached me. Said they needed me. That the future of Pacifica rested in my hands. I turned them down, of course." His face grows grim. "They threatened you and your mother if I wouldn't cooperate. I didn't have a choice."

"You always have a choice," I say, my tone harsher than I mean it to be.

"Sienna, I know you're angry with me. But please understand that I was only trying to protect you."

"But you lied to us—to me and Mom—for years. You were never Ben Preston. You're Mitch Hoover, lead geneticist for

Harlow Ryder. Do you know what it was like to find that out after you died? Why didn't you tell us?"

My father's eyes are full of pain. "To protect you. That's all I've ever wanted to do."

I close my eyes, trying to dispel the anger and hurt I feel from my father choosing to leave us. I sold my soul while my father was gone—all for the sake of my family. I'll carry that guilt and burden forever.

"But, Dad, I've done horrible things—" My voice breaks, and I pause. "You have no idea what it was like without you. Mom got really sick, and I—" Heat fills the back of my eyes. "I did terrible things."

Dad pulls me to his chest, his arms tight around me, my head nestled beneath his chin. He may have spent the past year in a lab, but he still smells the same. A mixture of shoe polish and old books.

"It's okay," he murmurs. "I should have never put you in that position. You kept your mother and sister safe, which is more than I could have hoped for. You're a strong woman, Sienna, and I couldn't be more proud that you're my daughter."

I can't hold them in anymore. Great sobs rack my body and my shoulders shake. "Daddy."

His hand strokes my hair. "It's okay, sweetie. I'm right here. I'll never leave you again."

His words are exactly what I need to hear. They melt away my anger and hurt until the only things left are love and hope. But the thrill of being in my father's arms is quickly replaced with the anxiety of what I'll tell my mother. How will I ever explain to her that the husband she thought was dead is, in fact, alive?

I pull back and wipe the tears from my cheeks. "Does Zane know about Steele? That he's selling Chromo 120 secrets to the AIG? Steele is also the one who turned us in to Madame Neiman at the Match 360 Headquarters. He's responsible for

Curly's death."

Just saying Curly's name sends a knife-like stab through my heart.

My father nods. "Yes, he knows."

The door opens and the three boys file inside, Trey first, followed by Nash, with Zane bringing up the rear.

Dad smiles at me before addressing the group. "I need some coffee. Would anyone else like some?"

Nash raises his hand. "I'll help you," he grunts.

"We should probably get moving soon," Trey warns him as he and my dad head for the door.

"Not before coffee," Nash says.

"Moving?" I echo. "Where?"

"We have to get out of the city," Trey says. "Paige and her crew will be waiting for us outside the AIG launch and will take us to their hideout."

There's that name again. I lick my lips. "Who's Paige?"

"Paige is the leader of a group called Zenith. They live in the mountains a few hundred miles east of here. Since they're off the radar, they can help the rest of the Fringe get back on their feet. And their camp will be a great place to hide out until the dust settles."

"Zenith?" I repeat. *How does he know so much?*

Before Trey can answer, Zane moves to my side and takes my hand in his. "I'm sorry about Steele," he says. "If I'd known he was a traitor, I'd never have sent you to him for protection—"

"It's okay," I interrupt him. "It's over."

Zane shakes his head. "Not for Steele, it's not. At least, not yet. I can't believe he was working against my father and me this whole time. Selling our company's secrets." A muscle in his jaw twitches. "When my father finds out, there will be a reckoning."

"I take it you and Harlow worked things out?"

Zane's smile doesn't quite reach his eyes. "I guess you

could say that."

"I don't understand," I say to Zane. "You left me. You went back to Legas. How did you end up at the prison?"

Zane takes a deep breath. "I think I need to explain."

"Please do," I say. The pain of him leaving me is like a scabbed-over wound. It may be healing, but underneath, it's still raw.

"They threatened your mom and your sister."

"What? Who did?"

"That night at the Marmet, I was captured and taken in for questioning. When they discovered who I was, they let me go, but not before Madame Neiman showed up and issued a warning. Said they knew where our safe house was. Said they were watching me and knew I would eventually lead them to you. I had to get to your mom and sister before they did."

I sit up straighter. "Are they okay?"

"Yes, they're fine. Trey helped me get them to a more secure location."

"Where are they?"

"They're at the Zenith camp now. You'll meet up with them in a couple of days."

I close my eyes, trying to take it all in. He didn't leave because he didn't care. It's because he cared that he left. He left to protect my mom and sister, which is exactly what I would have done in the same circumstances.

Opening my eyes, I say, "Why couldn't you just tell me this when I called?"

"I didn't want to worry you."

I turn to Trey. "And you—I don't understand. You helped get my mom and sister to safety?"

Trey and Zane exchange a look. With the two of them side by side for the first time, I can see what makes them brothers. Same nose, same mouth, same broad shoulders, but that's where the similarities end. Trey is as dark as Zane is light, and

Zane's chocolate eyes are a big contrast to Trey's sky-blue ones.

"A lot happened while you were in prison," Zane says.

"Yeah, a lot," Trey echoes.

"How long were we there?" I ask.

"A month," Zane answers.

One month? That's it? Then why did it feel like my life was slowly slipping away, that my body was rotting in that cell?

My mind shifts to Curly and his infectious grin. "Curly's gone," I say, like I'm still trying to convince myself. Or maybe I'm hoping it isn't true and that he'll miraculously walk through that door and crack a joke about Trina's assets or my Harley. I glance over at Trey. His whole body sags, and he leans against a lab table to steady himself. He blinks several times.

"I know," he says.

"Why should you care?" I say, tears springing to my eyes. "He probably means nothing to you since you can't remember him."

"But, Sienna, that's what I've wanted to tell you." Trey's voice is urgent now. "Granger removed the chip. See?" He turns and lifts the hair off the base of his skull, showing off the tiny scar where Granger cut into his scalp.

I stare at the scar, then my eyes go to Zane's, and he nods in confirmation.

"It's true," he says.

Trey turns back to face me.

"But how?" I say. "How did you know about the chip?"

"When you were taken away to Confinement, I contacted Zane. I knew he would want to know. That's when he told me everything and convinced me to remove the chip."

I focus on Zane again. "Is this true?"

Zane rubs his chin. "In order to rescue you guys, we needed the help of the Fringe. But I knew they wouldn't listen to me. I had to get the old Trey back."

"So you convinced him to remove the tracker, and then

what?" I'm really asking if Zane told Trey the truth about who he is.

"We went to the Fringe," Trey says, stepping in.

Zane must recognize the earnest question in my eyes because he nods. "I told Trey that he's my brother."

"And?"

"And that he's genetically modified."

"And?"

Zane hesitates. "And that he's the rightful heir to the company since he's my father's real son."

"What was his response?"

Trey scowls. "Guys, I'm right here. You don't have to talk about me like I'm in another room."

I turn my attention to Trey. "You're okay with all of this?"

"Do I really have a choice?" Trey says. "Besides, after the ordeal I've been through, being the son of Harlow Ryder and a GM seems like the easiest thing ever."

"That's one way to look at it," I mutter. My eyes find his. "So you... you remember *everything*?"

"Yeah, I do." Trey winks and gives me a crooked grin before turning to Zane. "Can we have a sec?"

Zane's eyes flit from me to Trey before he hesitantly nods. Once Zane has moved over to the next bed to check on Trina, Trey takes a deep breath and pins me with his gaze.

"I'm sorry, Sienna." His blue eyes are achingly sincere, and I suddenly find it hard to turn away. "I never meant to hurt you."

"I know," I say. "But you did."

"This—I—I don't know what to say to make things right between us."

I give him a sad smile. "I don't know if you can."

"Don't say that. Please," he pleads. His hands are smooth as he takes mine in his. They are such a contrast to that rough, callused hand I clasped when we first met after he rescued me from the Satellite Government Facility. And so different from Zane's.

"I thought you were dead, Trey," I say, my lower lip trembling. "I mourned you. And then when I found you in the SGF still alive, I couldn't believe I could be so lucky. I sat by your bedside for a week, waiting for you to wake up, to see me. And when you did—" A tear slips down my cheek. "You didn't remember me. And that was hard, really hard. But it wasn't as bad as when Rayne came to Zane's house, claiming she was your fiancée. Do you have any idea how much that hurt? To see you with her? Kissing her, holding hands, doing God-only-knows what else?" I swipe at the tears that keep falling. "You didn't know what was going on, I understand that. But it hurt. It still does."

Trey's eyes are full of pain. "I know," he says, "and I'm sorry. So, so sorry." He rests his forehead against mine. "Is there anything I can do to make it better? To make things right?"

I shake my head a little, and Trey pulls back, staring at me.

"Please, Sienna. I don't want to lose you." His voice goes soft. "I love you."

How long have I waited to hear those words from him? To know that he feels the same? But now, with all that's happened, instead of feeling elated at his words, I only feel a hollowness inside.

Trey leans close, his eyes fixated on my mouth. My heart hammers beneath my ribs, so loud I'm sure he can hear it, but before I can say anything, his lips touch mine. They are warm and familiar and soft. A hundred memories surge forth, some of Trey and me together, but more of me with Zane. Guilt fills me.

I gently push Trey away, but not before Zane sees us.

I don't want to look at Zane's face. I can't bear to see his expression. When I do venture a peek, the hurt is written there, but he tries to hide it by straightening his shoulders and turning away.

"Zane," I call out.

He refuses to meet my eyes, too busy tucking the blanket around Trina's legs.

"Sorry," Trey mutters. "Bad timing?"

Nash and my dad enter the room, two steaming disposable cups in hand. They appear to be deep in conversation, and I'm both shocked and relieved that my father and the man who once tried to kill me are on such good terms.

Trey's Lynk buzzes. As he glances down at it, he says, "That's Paige. They're ready for us. Time to move."

I start to slide off the bed, wincing in pain as I do, but stop when I realize that while I'm now dressed in clean clothes, I have no shoes.

Trey glances down at my bare feet.

"Ah, yes. Shoes." He reaches under the bed and produces a pair of ankle boots. "They might be a little big..."

I grab them from his hand. "They're fine. Thanks."

My shoulder pulls, sending a shooting pain down my arm as I tug the boots on.

"Let me help you," Trey says.

"I'm okay," I say. "Why don't you help Trina instead?"

Trey hesitates, staring at me before nodding. "Okay, if that's what you want."

"Let's move," Nash calls out.

"Where are we going?" I ask.

My father takes my arm, and we follow Nash and Zane to the door. Trina groans behind us. "Why do I have to wake up?"

"Let's go, sleepyhead," Trey says, lifting her into his arms. "I'm thinking I gave you one too many painkillers."

"Is there such a thing?" Trina mumbles, her head lopping onto Trey's chest.

"Let me take the lead," my father says. "I know these hallways." The five of us file in line behind him, moving toward the emergency stairs. I try to catch Zane's eye, but he's focused straight ahead, his jaw clenched unnaturally.

"Hey," I say, my fingers sliding down his arm and grasping his hand.

"Hey." He barely looks at me.

I lean close and whisper in his ear. "It wasn't what it looked like."

He's quiet for a moment, and at first, I'm not sure he heard me. "It doesn't matter," he says finally. He slides his hand from mine and lengthens his stride until he's several feet in front of me and directly behind Nash. I try not to let his indifference bother me, focusing instead on Trey's soothing voice as he tries to get Trina to wake up.

Our footsteps echo in the hallway. I assume we'll take the back exit, the one that will lead us to the boat, but instead, we follow my father to the tube.

"What about the night guards?" I ask as my father swipes his card, records his fingerprint, and scans his retina.

"Paige and her crew took care of them," Trey says. He barks orders. "Nash, you go in the first launch and make sure everything is clear. Zane, you take Trina in the second, Sienna and I will take the third, and Mr. Preston can bring up the rear. Sound good?"

I don't like the idea of leaving my father behind, and I tell Trey this.

"He has to be last," Trey says. "He's the only one with access to the launch."

Once Nash disappears in the tube, Trey carefully lowers Trina onto the seat and buckles her in. Her eyes open briefly. "You're going for a little ride, Trina. Okay?" She nods, her head then lolling to the side.

Zane eases his body onto the seat and wraps an arm around her, her head now falling onto his chest. Before Trey closes the hatch, he says, "See you in a minute." When he presses the button, the elevator-like doors close. We hear a small whoosh as the Plexiglas ball is launched through the tube.

"Our turn," Trey says, offering me his hand.

I'm still a little peeved that he thought it was okay to kiss me, especially in front of Zane, so I ignore it. Instead, I turn to my dad, who is standing by the scanner. "Thanks, Dad."

He gives me a tired smile, and I realize right then how much I've missed it. I throw my arms around his neck and breathe him in. "I'm so glad to have you back," I murmur.

With Dad alive, we can be a normal family again. Emily will know her father, and my mother will have someone to hold her again. Granted, we'll be like fugitives on the run, but at least we'll be together.

"Sienna, we've got to go," Trey warns, glancing at his Lynk.

Rising up on tiptoes, I kiss Dad on his scratchy cheek. "See you in a minute," I say.

"Fifty-three-point-eight seconds, to be exact," he clarifies with a smile.

I climb into the ball, Trey settling beside me. With a hiss, the hatch begins closing over us. It's almost shut when there's the most terrifying sound: footsteps pounding down the hall, men shouting, and the angry click of guns. A throng of Enforcers surrounds my father, their laser guns pointed at his chest. The hatch closes with a whoosh… and then it's like we're watching a silent movie. Through the clear Plexiglas, Dad looks at me, and I stare back at him.

"No!" I scream, pounding my fist against the glass, the sound nothing more than a dull, muffled thud. My fingers search for the latch, trying to force it open, but it won't budge. We're already sealed in. "Let me out!" I pound so hard that my hands ache. "Please, Trey, help me!"

Trey tries to kick open the hatch while I scream at my father. Several of the Enforcers turn their guns on us.

One Enforcer waves his gun in warning, probably telling

my father not to move. But I can see it in his eyes. He isn't going to listen. He knows I won't press the button inside our compartment and leave him to face the Enforcers alone. To manually override the system, he has to press the button to the right of the tube.

The next few moments happen in slow motion. Dad lunges for the button at the same time that the Enforcer pulls the trigger. The laser bullet gets him straight in the shoulder. My father's mouth opens, but his screams of pain are muffled by the glass. He doesn't stop moving though. His fingers are only inches from the button.

"No!" I scream again. "Please, no!"

Blood seeps from the wound on his shoulder, and I can see it so clearly as he dives for the button. At the exact moment he presses it, the Enforcers open fire.

My fists pound, trying to break through the glass.

Dad's body jerks in response, the laser bullets raining down on his chest. Trey forces my head down as the bullets pelt the sides of the Plexiglas ball.

I'm sobbing openly now.

He's down, his face turned toward the tube, his body riddled with laser wounds. His eyes are open, unmoving, unfeeling.

No, this can't happen. Not again.

There's a whoosh as the doors close and the ball begins to move, dropping swiftly beneath the ocean.

I can't breathe. I can't breathe.

"Take me back," I sob. "Stop this thing right now!"

But Trey's helpless. We both are. We can do nothing but sit and wait. Wait for the pressure to stop, the darkness to lessen, the ride to end.

It's the longest fifty-three-point-eight seconds of my life.

When we reach the other side, and the doors open with a swish, I stumble out, headed for the outgoing tube.

The other three who went ahead of us—Zane, Trina, and Nash—are surrounded by a group of people I don't recognize. For a second, I think they've been captured by Enforcers too, but then I realize they are part of the Zenith group Trey told me about. The dark clothing and guns strung across their shoulders make that evident.

Hurrying after me, Trey grabs my arm, forcing me to a stop.

"We can't leave him there," I say, tears streaming down my cheeks. "We have to go back!"

Trey shakes his head sadly. "He's gone, Sienna. There's nothing we can do."

"No," I stammer. "No, I refuse to believe that. He conquered death once. He can do it again."

Trey's hand is warm against my shoulder. "I'm sorry."

It hits me then. I sink down to my knees and curl into myself like doing so can protect me from the pain. Maybe if I hide from it, it won't find me. Losing him once was unbearable. I can't even begin to embrace the idea of losing him a second time.

42

Sienna

Everything is a blur. Trey's hand on my arm, pulling me to my feet. Zane beside me, asking what happened. The thud of our shoes on the pavement as we run like thieves in the night through the darkened park. The steady beat of my heart, pulsing pain from one part of my body to the other until I feel like I might collapse from grief.

And yet, there's no time to mourn. No time to feel the pain. We have to keep moving. Keep moving or else the Enforcers will find us, will end us, just like they did my father.

My father. My chest cracks open, and then I'm bleeding everywhere. My hands are stained with my blood, his blood, and I can't wipe them clean.

"Keep moving," the girl in the front calls. I assume she's Paige, not that I care that much. "We're almost there."

Trey continues to pull me along, past trees and park benches, but there's a never-ending whine in my brain like a toy fire truck with dying batteries. Even when Trey speaks to me, it's hard to understand what he's saying.

His mouth is moving, and he's looking at me.

"Huh?"

"Are you okay?" He says it slowly, like he's enunciating each precious syllable.

I shake my head a little, but not before I notice the concern in his eyes.

Then we're at a truck. A dark vehicle parked next to the curb on the other side of the park. The three Zenith members climb in the front while the rest of us struggle to get into the back. The bed of the truck groans under our weight, and Trey helps me settle with my back resting against the cab.

"What happened?" Zane demands, scooting over to sit next to us.

"He's dead," I say. I surprise even myself with the lack of emotion in my voice.

"Your father?"

I nod.

Zane bows his head and curses. His eyes are moist when he looks up. "What happened back there?"

Trey steps in so that, thankfully, I don't have to speak. "Enforcers showed up as Sienna and I were about to launch." He pauses, clearing his throat. I want to plug my ears so I don't hear the rest. Remove myself from this nightmare.

"They shot him," Trey finally says. "And we had to watch."

Zane takes my hand in his, and it feels like a lifeline. Like I've been treading water, hardly able to keep my head above, and someone has finally thrown me a buoy. "I'm sorry," he whispers.

The dam bursts. I cry for everything I've lost. For the truth I'll have to carry, never able to share with my mother. It would kill her to know that she was so close to having her husband back. No mother, no daughter, should have to experience the death of the same loved one twice.

Zane pulls me to his chest, and I cling to him, my face pressed against his neck, my tears bathing his skin.

"It's okay," he murmurs, stroking my hair. "It's okay."

But it's not. It's not okay. It will never be okay. I'm a wanted criminal for crimes I didn't commit. My father is dead. And I'm a fugitive.

We bounce along in the back of the truck, my tailbone pressing against the cab, for who knows how long. Zane's arms are tight around me, and I keep my head buried under his chin. I refuse to look up. I don't want to see Trina or Nash's faces. I don't want to see anyone's pity or fear. And for some reason, I can't bear to look at Trey right now. He was there. He was there with me, and he did nothing to stop them.

I close my eyes and focus on the last hug I gave my dad. The last hug I'll ever give him. His warm body, the scent of shoe polish, his salt-and-pepper hair.

It hurts. Why does it hurt worse than when I first discovered him on the floor of our kitchen? Is it because I watched him die this time? Felt the bullets like they were hitting my own skin?

Is it because he sacrificed his own life for mine?

We're out of the city now. The sound of horns and the smell of exhaust have been replaced with the earthy smell of rocks and dirt and the sound of coyotes howling in the night. The truck slows to a stop, and Trey calls, "We're here. Everybody out."

Zane shifts beneath me, and I pull back to look at him. In his eyes is all the sorrow I feel.

"Are you okay?" he whispers.

I rake my palms across my face, drying the last of my tears. "I will be."

Trey leans down and offers me his hand, and this time, I take it, wincing as the skin pulls around my shoulder.

"How's the shoulder?" he asks.

"Still there," I reply in a tired voice.

Trina is wide awake now, and as I jump down from the bed of the truck, she flings her arms around me. She doesn't say anything, but it's okay. Her hug tells it all.

"What are we doing?" I ask whoever will listen.

That Paige girl is striding toward us with her crew. When she hears me, she says, "Time to catch a train." She grins. "And

I don't believe we've met. I'm Paige."

"Sienna." Trying not to study her but wanting to at the same time, I take note of her olive skin, her dark hair that's plastered to her head in cornrows, her cocky stance, and her cool gaze. "You're the leader of Zenith?"

"I'm the leader of this division of Zenith. We all have our jobs, and mine is to protect people." She shrugs. "What can I say? I'm good with guns." She leans forward with a teasing grin. "You're welcome, by the way."

I stare at her, confused. Trey steps in. "Paige is the one who stayed your execution by taking out the guards."

I remember the rope snapping from the beam like a bullet had severed it clean through.

"That was you?" I ask.

She nods, looking embarrassed and proud at the same time, if that's possible. But then she says, "Well, I can't take *all* the credit. Grey and Asher helped too." She nods toward the two boys standing next to her with their arms crossed over their chests, showing off an insane amount of muscles. One is tall with smooth skin the color of coffee and the other is just as tall but with shockingly white-blond hair that stands on end.

"They're snipers," Trey explains. "They were on the mainland while Nash, Zane, and I came by boat."

Nash is standing off to the side, scowling. "Can we get this party started?" he asks, his tone sarcastic.

Paige purses her lips and claps her hands together. "Right, well, now we wait for the big engine." Pulling a Lynk from her back pocket, she glances at it and says, "Shouldn't be long now."

"I didn't think normal trains still ran," I say.

"They don't," Paige answers. "We commandeered an old steam engine, got it working again." A grin spreads across her face. "Now, there's no better way to travel. Sure beats waiting for the bullet train, and the crowds—well, nothing like having a train all to yourself."

I glance around. We're parked on the side of an empty desert road. Even though we're far from the city now, the lights of Rubex illuminate the sky above so that it glows like a storm in the clouds. "I don't see any tracks," I say.

"This way." Paige motions for us to follow her, and the seven of us do.

My footsteps are hesitant at first because the more I take, the further I get from my father. I know he's gone, but there's still a cord tethering me to him. Leading me back to Rubex. I turn and look back, one last time, and whisper good-bye.

43

Sienna

We've only walked about two hundred yards when we hear it. The faint *chug, chug* of an oncoming train. The metal track, only a few yards away, glints in the moonlight.

"He won't be able to stop," Paige calls out, her voice getting lost in the rising wind.

"What? Why?" Trina asks.

"Too much momentum. And it takes too much steam to stop and start. He'll slow down a bit, but we'll have to hop on."

"While it's still moving?" I say, my voice incredulous.

"Right."

Zane gives me a reassuring look, but when Trey tells him to be in charge of making sure Trina gets on, I can see the disappointment in his eyes.

Why does it feel like Trey is doing his best to keep us apart?

The rumbling sound of the train can be heard cutting through the night. For some reason, that sound alone gets my heart rate going faster than normal. My palms sweat as I think about jumping onto that thing. *Do they not remember my short legs?*

The train screeches as it begins to slow, its headlight shining down the track and illuminating the endless expanse in front of us. For a second, I'm blinded by the light. Blinking quickly,

I look away until the white spots have faded from my vision.

There's a low whistle like a soulful cry for help, and then it's closing the gap.

As soon as the engine and first two cars pass, Paige hollers, "Let's go!" She starts to run, looking over her shoulder to make sure we're coming. The other two Zenith members take off running, followed by Nash and then Trina. Zane hesitates for only a second before he starts moving too.

"Come on, Sienna," Trey says, his voice urgent. "We have to go."

I shake my head. "I can't do it."

Trey's eyes are fierce. "Don't you give up now. I won't let you. Come on!" His fingers wrap around my hand, pulling me alongside him as he begins to run. I trip, almost falling over myself as my feet try to remember how to work again. My shoulder throbs a pulsing beat of pain, similar to what I feel in my heart.

My heart may be fragile, cut from glass and breakable, but I'm strong, immovable, and I can rise up into the sky like a beacon in the night. Like a skyscraper.

I can do this.

Or at least, that's what I try to tell myself.

Up ahead, Paige and her crew have swung their bodies into a boxcar. I watch as Nash and Zane do the same, holding their hand out for Trina to grasp. She runs like a gazelle, lean and beautiful and effortless, and all I can do is watch her in awe. Medication must work differently on GMs, because none of the usual lingering effects of painkillers are obvious in her actions. She grasps Zane's hand, and he pulls her easily into the car.

My breathing is hard and labored, my chest heaving. My arms pump, trying to propel me faster.

"We'll never catch them," I gasp.

"It's okay. Let's try for this one." He glances behind him at an approaching boxcar, its door swung wide open.

"Ready?" he asks, his muscles tensing.

I nod. The moment the car is only a few feet behind us, we pick up speed, his hand clutching mine, pulling me along, holding me up.

He lets go only long enough to swing himself onto the train. He makes it look so easy. "Give me your hand!" he shouts, holding out his.

Without him pulling me along, I can feel myself slowing down. The train is moving ahead. Without me. I curse my legs and force them to move faster. My lungs are exploding, my legs trembling, my heart bursting.

"Hurry," Trey hollers. And for the first time, I see doubt in his eyes. *He doesn't think I can do it.*

And for some reason, that's all I need to know.

With a burst of speed, I reach out and grasp his hand. In one swift movement, he pulls me up into the train, the momentum making me crash into him. He stumbles and loses his balance. I end up sprawled on top of him, my shoulder throbbing in pain. When he looks up and smiles, my heart flutters.

"Hey," he says, his voice low.

I roll off and sit up shakily, my hands swiping through the dust on the floor. My breathing is still heavy, and I try to slow my heart rate by taking deep breaths. Trey sits up and looks around.

"This isn't so bad," he says. Then, giving me a mischievous grin, he adds, "I kind of like having a car all to ourselves."

Gulping, I turn away from him and rise to my feet. I ease to the edge. With one hand on the door opening, I stare out at the darkness. The stars are a million times brighter than I've ever seen them. Tears fill my eyes as I think of my father, his finger pointed toward the sky, his voice low as he named one constellation after another.

Trey comes up beside me and gently rests his hands on my shoulders, careful to avoid my wound. I suddenly feel grounded, like maybe I won't go spinning off into the sky after all. He leans close and whispers in my ear, "I'm sorry, Sienna."

I turn and face him. "For what?"

"For everything. For all I put you through. For your father. For not being able to do anything." He sighs. "I felt helpless. Watching him…"

"I know," I say, wiping my eyes. "It was awful."

His hands slide down my arms until they're grasping my waist. "What can I do to make it up to you?"

This conversation sounds oddly familiar. I believe those were the same words he said to me in the Compound after he kissed me and then ignored me for days. Feels like an eternity ago.

I look away. "I don't know."

Trey's hands drop. He moves to the other side of the car and slides to the floor, his back resting against the wall. After a few moments, he says, "What happened between you and Zane?"

I turn and stare at him.

"I mean, I know he's in love with you. That I remember, but—" He exhales. "I don't know how you feel about him."

I close my eyes and rest my head on the wall.

"It's just that—I need to know, Sienna."

When I open my eyes, Trey is looking at me with such earnestness that it sends a pang to my chest. I walk over and sink down next to him, facing him.

"I don't know," I say, my voice barely above a whisper. My fingers trail through the dust around me. "How did you feel about Rayne?"

Trey makes a face. "She's not my type. I would never choose her."

"But you did," I say softly.

His eyes turn sad. "That wasn't me and you know it."

An image of Trey and Rayne, lips locked, bodies pressed together, heat practically steaming off their skin, sears into my mind. My stomach clenches as I look away.

"Maybe not," I say, "but it sure looked real."

Trey heaves a sigh and scoots closer. "It was supposed to. That's what they wanted."

"But you liked it, right? I mean, you liked kissing her?" I don't know why I can't leave this alone, forget it ever happened. Rayne's dead. Why can't I just let it go?

I guess because a part of me needs to know the truth, even if I'm terrified of it.

He frowns. "No. When I kissed her, I thought of you. Every time. Which didn't make sense because there wasn't an *us*. There wasn't supposed to be an *us*. At least, not in my mind." He clears his throat and runs a hand through his hair. "What about you and Zane? Did you kiss him?"

Guilt fills me like marbles filling a glass jar. A part of me wants to lie to him, but the other part wants him to know the truth.

"Yes," I whisper.

A muscle in Trey's jaw clenches and he looks down, fiddling with his shoelace. "I suspected as much." When his eyes lift, there's pain inside.

"I'm sorry," I say.

Trey laughs, but it's a harsh sound. "Why should you be sorry? After all I put you through?" He claps his hands on his knees and gives me a wry smile. "Technically, I gave you permission."

He's referring to the day Rayne showed up at Zane's house and Trey told me he wasn't the one for me. And then hinted that Zane was.

"You practically threw Zane on me," I remind him.

When he chuckles, it sounds real. "I know. What an idiot

I was."

"But a very well-dressed idiot," I say, biting my lip to keep from smiling.

"A clown suit."

We both chuckle at that.

"So do you remember everything from when you had the chip?" I ask.

"Yeah."

I think back to what I saw in the basement of the AIG facility. "When I snuck in the AIG, I discovered hundreds of people, lined up in rows on beds, in the basement. Do you know anything about that?"

Trey's forehead wrinkles. "No, I never saw them. They mostly had me doing research. Sometimes, they studied my DNA."

"Studied your DNA?"

"Yes, said they were trying to recreate a perfect genome."

"So you were—" I pause. "A test subject?"

Trey cocks his head to the side and grins. "Well, I never thought about it like that before, but yes, I suppose so." His smile fades. "And you were experimented on also, right?"

I nod. "They removed any memories I had of you." I look away, folding my hands in my lap. "I didn't remember what I'd lost, so in a way, it was kind of nice."

"And that's when you and Zane became close?"

I turn to look at him. "Yeah. But he's the one who insisted that we figure out what they did and how to get those memories back."

"So I should thank him?" he teases.

"You can."

Trey grows serious and opens up his arms. "Come here."

Scooting closer, I lean into him, resting my head on his chest. I can hear the steady rhythm of his heart through his thin T-shirt and feel the hard muscles of his chest. It's all so...

familiar.

"I've missed you," he whispers.

I swallow hard. "I've missed you too."

Breathing deep, Trey pulls me closer. The steady rocking of the train and the low rumble of the wheels beneath us combines to create a soothing sound. I close my eyes and relax my mind, removing myself from every bad thing that's happened in the past year and a half. It's just Trey and me on a runaway train. Going everywhere. Going nowhere.

44

Zane

The surrounding darkness and the rhythmic movement of the train along the track should be conducive to sleep, and yet, I cannot. When I close my eyes, I see her. With him. And I can't bear it.

The inside of the train car is a mixture of light snores and heavy breathing. I rest my head against the metal wall of the train, willing the morning to come. I'm not sure if I've slept since Sienna was captured a few weeks ago. I've been on edge, blaming myself for leaving her in Rubex, leaving her vulnerable. And ever since she was imprisoned, I've been trying to find a way to secure her release.

In the end, there was no amount of connections, no amount of money, and no amount of power that could save her. We were seconds away from seeing her die. *Too close. Much too close.*

And we couldn't save Curly. If we had gotten there a minute early…

Sixty seconds was all we needed.

I bow my head and thank God that Sienna is alive.

But now I must make a decision. Do I return to Legas? Do I take my place as heir of Harlow Ryder's company and the fiancé of Arian Stratford? Do I marry a woman I don't love but could maybe grow to love in time?

Forgotten

It all hinges on one thing. One person.

And if she can't give me the answer I need, then I know what I have to do.

45

Sienna

A grinding noise shocks me awake. Sunlight streams in from the open doorway as the train squeals to a halt. Trey and I are curled up next to each other on the floor, my head resting on his chest, his arm around my waist. We slept like this all night.

Someone jumps into our car. I blink quickly, trying to focus on the person.

It's Paige.

I sit up too fast, and the blood rushes to my head.

"This is our stop. We walk from here," she says. She jumps down from the train.

I shake Trey awake. He groans and rolls over onto his back. "What's going on?" he mutters.

"We have to get off the train."

He rises slowly to his feet. "That sucks. I was having the best dream…" His eyes find mine. "You were in it."

My cheeks flush, and I stand and turn away. Everyone else has exited the train and is waiting next to the track. I hop down, my knees taking most of the impact.

We're still in the desert, with orange cliffs rising in the background. Paige is handing out backpacks that she says are filled with food, water, a flashlight, and an emergency blanket.

"Should we become separated for any reason, these packs

have everything you need to sustain you in the desert for three days. But..." She looks directly at me when she says this. "I don't anticipate this happening. This is only a precaution."

Trey jumps down from the train and saunters over to stand next to me. Paige hands me my pack and I put it on, wincing when it hits my shoulder.

"Here, let me carry that for you," Trey offers, one hand already reaching for the pack.

I readjust the pack so it's not rubbing against my wound. "No. If I'm part of this group, I have to carry my own weight."

"But Sienna, you were just shot. Everyone understands—"

"I don't care," I say stubbornly.

Trey sighs. "You better let me know when it becomes unbearable. Got it?"

"Sure."

I look around for Zane, but I don't spot him immediately because he's standing a few feet from the rest of the group. I'm starting toward him when I hear the low gunning sound of a vehicle approaching. *Enforcers.* My pulse kicks into overdrive, and I shout, "Everybody down!"

Before I can slam myself on the ground, Zane raises his hands. "It's okay, everyone. They're here for me."

Sure enough, a black sedan is off-roading over the desert terrain. I turn to him, surprised. "What? I don't understand. You're not coming with us?"

He shakes his head, his jaw clenching. "It's not my fight, Sienna." He turns and strides toward the vehicle.

I hurry to catch up to him, putting distance between us and the rest of the group. "But, Zane—"

Pivoting around, he interrupts me. "Do you love me?"

I'm so surprised that I take a step back, not sure how to respond. "What?"

"Do. You. Love. Me." His face has a fire in it I haven't seen before.

"I can't—"

"After everything we've been through?" His voice grows fierce. "Just say that you don't love me. Say you don't love me, and I'll leave you alone forever."

I bite my lip as tears fill my eyes. "I can't—"

"Why?" he asks, his voice rising a few decibels.

When I stand there, saying nothing, doing nothing, he throws his hands up in the air. "Forget it. I'm done. I have a fiancée waiting for me. And you clearly have Trey now, so what more could you ever want?"

I want to run after him and tell him the truth. I want to throw my arms around him and never let go, but my legs won't move and my mouth won't open. Instead, I stand there and watch him walk away. Watch until his car is only a speck on the horizon.

Because, Zane, I do.

Acknowledgements

Much gratitude and many thanks go to the following people for guiding me and helping me bring this book to publication:

All of the Clean Teen Publishing Team for making me feel like I won the lottery when they offered me a contract to publish Catalyst. You gals are seriously the best! Cynthia Shepp, my amazing editor who helps whip my book into shape. Rebecca Gober, for her sound marketing advice and general awesomeness. Marya Heidel, CTP's talented graphic designer, for creating brilliant covers that truly reflect my work. Courtney Knight, who makes the inside of the book just as beautiful as the outside. Melanie Newton, our social media guru, who is always available to answer a question or steer me in the right direction. My proofers, Lauren Dootson and Kelly Risser, for combing through my book and finding those odd word choices and little mistakes. Thanks to you all!

My wonderful critique partner, Leandra Wallace, who is quick to answer emails with the subject line of "Help!" Thank you for cheering me on throughout this journey. You're next!

My awesome friend, Beth Ellyn Summer, who gives such good advice when it comes to writing. I'm so excited we get to be Pitch Wars mentors together!

My super-fast beta readers Tasha Stoddard and Jamie

Dalton, for diving into Forgotten at the twelfth hour when I needed fresh eyes and another opinion. Thank you!

These incredibly talented authors: Kimberley Griffiths Little, Jessie Humphries, Ilima Todd, Sherry Ficklin, Stephanie Faris, and Mark Noce, for reading and providing an awesome blurb for Catalyst.

My Charlotte writer friends: Monica Hoffman, Holly Hughes, and Jacy Merrill, who inspire and uplift me every time we get together to chat about writing and books.

My dear parents for their continued love and support. I'm proud to be your daughter.

My sons: Corbin, Hayden, Ethan, Liam, and Declan, for being patient and understanding and oh-so-excited about Mom becoming an author.

My sweet husband, Adam, who is always my first reader and full of ideas to make the book better. I hope you'll be reading my work for many, many years to come.

God. You had me worried there when I couldn't finish this book, but thankfully, You came through for me—as You always do.

My awesome readers, for loving the first book enough to read the second.

About the Author

Kristin Smith is the author of the best-selling young adult novel *Catalyst* and its sequel, *Forgotten*. When she's not writing, you can find her dreaming about the beach, beating her boys at Just Dance, or belting out karaoke (from the comfort of her own home). Kristin currently resides in the middle-of-nowhere North Carolina with her husband and five sons. To read more about her obsession with YA novels or her addiction to chocolate, you can visit her at kristinsmithbooks.com.

CPSIA information can be obtained
at www.ICGtesting.com
Printed in the USA
LVOW03s2238060717
540518LV00003B/4/P